The Windhaven Saga

Windhaven Plantation symbolizes both a proud heritage and a manifest destiny. And as the plantation passes from one generation of the Bouchard family to the next, as it survives the onslaught of the Civil War and the Reconstruction period, as it plays host to great passions and torn loyalties—always, the plantation, the land, and its legacy endure. . . .

"A soaring, magnificent series of books . . . I was caught up in every volume."
—Leigh Franklin James
Saga of the Southwest Series

"History comes to life in this engaging series about a family with noble aspirations . . . the Bouchards are an inspiration!"
—William Stuart Long
The Australians Series

"Early America means a lot to me, and I was captivated by this imaginative account of one family's close association over several generations with the rich and beautiful country along the Alabama River and in South Texas. The Bouchards are a memorable clan, larger than life."
—Donald Clayton Porter
The White Indian Series

OVER 7 MILLION COPIES SOLD

The Windhaven Saga:

WINDHAVEN'S FURY

Marie de Jourlet

Created by the producers of Wagons West, White Indian, The Australians, Rakehell Dynasty, and The Kent Family Chronicles Series.

Executive Producer: Lyle Kenyon Engel

PINNACLE BOOKS **NEW YORK**

WINDHAVEN'S FURY

An original Pinnacle Books edition, published for the first time anywhere.

Produced by Book Creations, Inc.; Lyle Kenyon Engel, Executive Producer.

First printing, December 1982

ISBN: 0-523-41112-X

Cover Illustration by Bruce Minney

Printed in the United States of America

PINNACLE BOOKS, INC.
1430 Broadway
New York, New York 10018

Gratefully dedicated to Marla and Lyle Engel, whose inspiration and confidence in me made it all happen.

Acknowledgments

The author wishes to express her indebtedness to Helen and William Deer, lifelong friends, whose special interest in and research of the Baby Doe legend contributed many colorful and authentic touches to this novel.

In addition, she wishes to pay tribute to the loyalty, conscientiousness, and tireless work of her transcriber, Fay Jeanne Bergstrom, without whose aid these past six years the Windhaven novels could not have turned out as they did.

Finally, to the entire hardworking and dedicated Book Creations, Inc. team, the heartiest plaudits for providing research data on the most obscure points, without which the author's deficiencies would be even more glaring.

Marie de Jourlet

THE BOUCHARD FAMILY AT WINDHAVEN PLANTATION

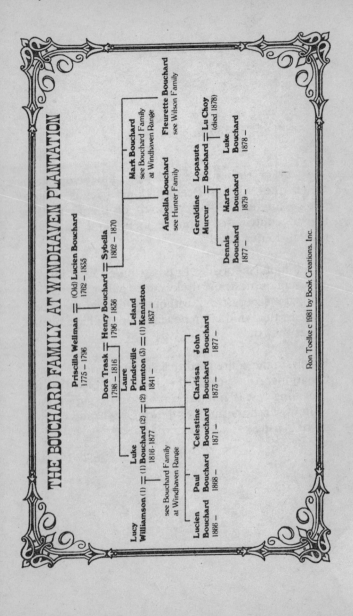

Priscilla Wellman = (Old) Lucien Bouchard
1775 – 1796   1762 – 1855

Dora Trask = Henry Bouchard = Sybella
1798 – 1816   1796 – 1836   1802 – 1870

Laure
Prindeville   Leland
Luke   = (2) Bouchard (3) = (1) Kenniston
Bouchard (2)   1841 –   1857 –
1816 – 1877

Lucy
Williamson (1) = (1) Bouchard (2)

see Bouchard Family
at Windhaven Range

Lucien   Paul   Celestine   Clarissa   John
Bouchard   Bouchard   Bouchard   Bouchard   Bouchard
1866 –   1868 –   1871 –   1873 –   1877 –

Mark Bouchard   Fleurette Bouchard
see Bouchard Family   see Wilson Family
at Windhaven Range

Arabella Bouchard
see Hunter Family

Geraldine   Lopasuta
Murcur   = Bouchard = Lu Choy
                       (died 1878)

Dennis   Marta   Luke
Bouchard   Bouchard   Bouchard
1877 –   1879 –   1878 –

Ron Toelke c 1981 by Book Creations, Inc.

THE BOUCHARD FAMILY AT WINDHAVEN RANGE

Dora Trask = Henry Bouchard = Sybella

Luke Bouchard = Laure Prindeville Brunton
1816-1877   1841 –

Lucy W.
1817 – 18...

...son = ...

...en Edmond
...chard

Maxine
Kendall
1840 –

see Bouchard Family
at Windhaven Plantation

Arabella
see Hunter Family

Fleurette
see Wilson Family

Maybelle
Williamson (1) = (2)
1820 – 1879

Mark
(1) Bouchard
1819 – 1864

Henry
Landry (1) = (1) Belcher (2)
1821 – 1879

Conchita
Valdegroso

Charles = Laurette
Douglas   Bouchard

see Douglas Family

Millie
Landry (1)
1834 – 1865

Timny
Belcher
1853 –

Luisa
Belcher
1879 –

Walter
Catlin = Connie
        Belcher
        1856 –

Henry
Catlin
1878 –

Gloria
Bouchard
1872 –

Ruth
Bouchard
1878 –

Diane
Bouchard
1870 –

Edwina
Bouchard
1868 –

Hugo
Bouchard
1861 –

Carla
Bouchard
1860 –

Ramón
Hernandez = Mara
1840 –   Bouchard
             1837 –

Luke
Hernandez
1868 –

Dolores
Hernandez
1871 –

Mar...
Hernandez
1877 –

Jaime
Hernandez
1869 –

Edward
Hernandez
1872 –

Ron Toelke c 1981 by Book Creations, Inc.

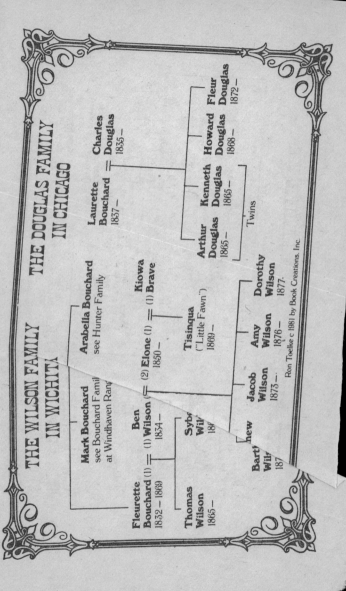

THE WILSON FAMILY
IN WICHITA

THE DOUGLAS FAMILY
IN CHICAGO

Mark Bouchard
see Bouchard Famil[y]
at Windhaven Rang[e]

Arabella Bouchard
see Hunter Family

Laurette
Bouchard = Charles
1837 – Douglas
1855 –

Ben
Fleurette Bouchard (1) = (1) Wilson (= (2) Elone (1) = Kiowa
1832 – 1869 1834 – 1850 – (1) Brave

Tisinqua
("Little Fawn")
1869 –

Thomas
Wilson
1865 –

Syb[il]
Wil[son]
18[ ]

Bart[hew]
Wil[son]
187[ ]

Jacob
Wilson
1873 –

Amy
Wilson
1876 –

Dorothy
Wilson
1877.

Arthur
Douglas
1865 –

Kenneth
Douglas
1865 –

Howard
Douglas
1868 –

Fleur
Douglas
1872 –

Twins

Ron Toelke c 1981 by Book Creations, Inc.

THE HUNTER FAMILY IN GALVESTON

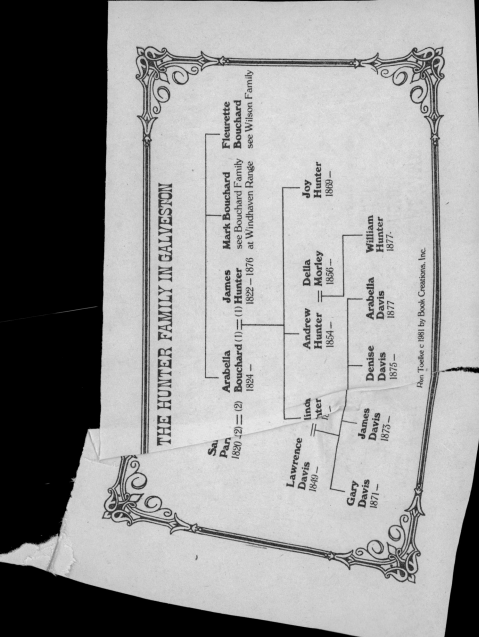

Sa... Par...
1820 (2) == (2)

Arabella
Bouchard (1) == (1)
1824 –

James
Hunter
1822 – 1876

Mark Bouchard
see Bouchard Family
at Windhaven Range

Fleurette
Bouchard
see Wilson Family

...linda
...ter
...

Andrew
Hunter
1854 –

Della
Morley
1856 –

Joy
Hunter
1869 –

Lawrence
Davis
1849 –

Denise
Davis
1875 –

Arabella
Davis
1877

William
Hunter
1877–

James
Davis
1873 –

Gary
Davis
1871 –

Ron Toelke c 1981 by Book Creations, Inc.

WINDHAVEN'S FURY

Prologue

The year of 1880 had dawned, and it was a time of prodigious development. The population of the United States had reached 50,155,783, compared to 39,818,449 in 1870. This year would mark the beginning of a decade of unprecedented railroad construction, so great that by 1890, a total of more than 70,000 miles of track would be laid between the Mississippi River and the Pacific Ocean for five separate transcontinental rail links.

In this new decade, the Western states would become a font of opportunity for women, with nearly four times as many woman lawyers and twice the number of doctors and journalists per capita as their Eastern counterparts.

This year would see the placement of the Egyptian obelisk called Cleopatra's Needle in New York City's Central Park. The creation of this urban retreat, with its lawns, lakes, foot paths, drives, and woods, had been begun more than twenty years earlier by Frederick Law Olmsted, but it was just now realizing the finishing touches. However, if this monument served to focus attention on the bustling, growing metropolis of New York, it also underlined the contrasts of its citizens' lives. For at the opposite end of the economic spectrum, the city was ripe with poverty. The effects of the East European immigrant invasion, the direct result of the harsh anti-Semitic pogroms in Russia, were beginning to be felt. The majority of immigrant families arrived in New York with less than twenty dollars in their pockets, and most of these arrivals were obliged to settle in the squalid tenements of the Lower East Side. By the end of this decade, the twenty-year-period figure of immigrants landing at Castle Garden would number well over five million, and the population density of the tenement areas would swell to over five hundred people per acre. In 1880 in New York City, the average dwelling housed more than sixteen people—compared to fewer than six in Philadelphia and eight in Boston—and the death rate was higher in New York than in any other American or European city. Perhaps not coincidentally, this was the year that the Salvation Army began its humanitarian work in the United States.

This new year would be memorable also because it was to be an election year. Four years earlier, following the corruption of the last year of Grant's second term, public sentiment had demanded a change. Unfortunately, another Republican—Rutherford B. Hayes—had replaced Lincoln's favorite general after a bitterly fought campaign. The election results actually had the Democrat—Samuel J. Tilden of New York—winning the nation's popular vote, yet he lost to Hayes after the dispute of the electoral vote had been resolved by a congressional commission rating along strict party lines: eight Republicans against seven Democrats. . . . The result had damned Hayes's victory with the charge of "stolen election" and himself with the caluminous epithet of "Old Eight-by-Seven." There was talk in this new year of 1880 that Ulysses Simpson Grant, now more popular out of office than he had been when in, would make a strong bid to regain the presidency. Even in the South, where the wounds of the Civil War had slowly been healing, there was a resurgent admiration for the man who had forced Lee's surrender at Appomattox.

It was a raw, blustery mid-January day in Dodge City. Five inches of snow the night before had blanketed the streets and had, like a capricious painter, given the drab rows of framework saloons, dance halls, and stores a semblance of bright cleanliness—a semblance that would disappear long before spring. There was little activity in Dodge City this time of year. At the Comique, most of the gaming tables were idle, and a green baize curtain hid the raised stage that, when times were flourishing, served as a theater. There were only three

2

patrons standing at the long, wide, polished walnut bar, behind which a huge mirror ran the entire length. Glumly, silently, they drank their whiskey without even glancing upwards at the oil painting in its gilt frame, an opulent Rubenesque blond, naked on a chaise longue, one of her knees enticingly raised. This evening, her provocative smile seemed singularly out of place. There was only one bartender on duty, wearing a bored expression as he industriously polished glasses and set them back into neat rows behind him.

There were four men seated at a table at the far wall of this spacious saloon. A bottle of Maryland rye whiskey and a brand-new deck of playing cards, together with four neatly polished glasses, rested on a tray at the edge of the table, but this array had thus far been ignored by the quartet. One of them glanced over at the bar and then nodded to himself, satisfied that what he had to say could not be overheard. He was a man in his early fifties, with a huge paunch, a double-chinned, flaccid face, and squinty, watery blue eyes. His dirty gray Stetson was pulled down to one side. With ostentatious ceremony, he took out of his vest pocket a gold-plated watch with ornamental fob and squinted thoughtfully at it before putting it back with a satisfied pat. "Like I told you boys already," he declared, "cattle days are comin' to an end. You can see it now with all the railroads they're buildin'. There won't be any need to drive cattle from Texas on up here, or even to Colorado, to feed what damn Injuns we got left. No, sir, they'll drive them a coupla miles, put them into a pen right by a railroad feeder line, and when the cars come by, pack them inside and ship them off. Anyhow, ever since that fellow Glidden invented barbed wire, open ranges are becomin' a thing of the past. All of which means, boys, if we want to make some real cash, we've gotta shift our attention somewheres else. Besides, it'll be a helluva lot safer. If we operate outside of Kansas in other territories, chances are it won't be easy to track us back here to Dodge."

"Makes sense to me," the man at Jeb Cornish's left declared with a nod. This man—Jack Hayes—was stocky, in his mid-forties, his thick, black beard flecked with gray. His nose was bulbous, and his mouth was thin and cruel. He wore a black patch over his left eye, and there was an ugly, purplish scar running from the edge of the patch down almost to his

3

jaw, the mark of a hunting knife used on him by a man whom he had cheated at cards. The other man had ordered two of his friends to hold Hayes down while he wielded the knife, but Jack Hayes had taken his revenge a few weeks later. Catching his enemy in an Abilene alley without his friends to aid him, Hayes had knocked his assailant unconscious, dragged him into an abandoned shed, gagged him, and worked him over with his own knife.

"Makes a lot of sense," the man at Cornish's right put in. He was Reuben Huntley, a burly man in his late thirties who sported a bright red beard. He had been recruited last year by Jack Hayes for a bushwhacking gang whose marauding tactics included cattle rustling, raids on isolated farm settlements, and, occasionally, bank robberies staged in unprotected small towns.

The black-haired man seated opposite Cornish was twenty-five-year-old Gabe Penrock. Slim and wiry, his boyish good looks were emphasized by his clean-shaven face. Like Hayes and Huntley, he was one of the few survivors of the band that had tried to ambush Ramón Hernandez the previous summer when the Windhaven Range men were driving breeding stock to a Colorado rendezvous with a Wyoming rancher.

Jeb Cornish, a government Indian agent by appointment, was also the sole owner of the Comique. Two years ago, his partner, Frank Thompson, had tried to fleece Ramón Hernandez, and Thompson had been killed by Ramón after he had tried to shoot the Mexican in cold blood. Cornish now eyed his youngest gang member, who had been an outlaw since the age of fourteen, and impatiently demanded, "Well, Gabe, what's your view on the matter?"

"If what you say is right, Mr. Cornish"—Gabe Penrock chose his words carefully—"this scheme you've got in mind could sure make up for that damn bushwhacking fiasco we had last year. That is, if you're sure of the facts."

Cornish chuckled, then leaned back and shoved his Stetson upward. He took a cigar from his coat pocket and lit it, puffing at it to make sure that it was drawing well. Once again, he glanced sharply over at the bartender, who was still busy polishing glasses and setting them up. The three patrons were finishing their whiskey, and one of them beckoned to the bartender for a refill. Expansively, the Indian agent chuckled

4

again, then leaned forward and finally responded, "It's a sure thing, Gabe. Even though you just joined up with us last year, you know that I sometimes operate outside of Kansas. 'Course, you found that out when you went along with Jack and Reuben here to wipe out that damned greaser"—momentarily, a scowl replaced the fat Indian agent's oily smile—"and I'm not done with him yet, not by a long shot. But to get back to those facts you just asked me about, lemme tell you, they're going all out for silver in the mines over at Leadville, Colorado. Now, there's a telegraph agent in Pueblo, fella by the name of Len Harstens. I've got him in my pocket. He swears his information is a hundred percent keerect: Once a month a train loaded with eighty thousand dollars in miners' pay comes down from Denver and is shunted onto the sidin' at Pueblo before heading west to Cañon City to connect with the Leadville stage. Somewhere along the line, it'll be easy pickins', for sure." He leaned back and gleefully rubbed his hands.

"It's like this," he went on, certain that he had his listeners' full attention. "The Denver & Rio Grande Railroad runs south to Pueblo. Now, the Atchison, Topeka & Santa Fe runs over to Pueblo from here in Kansas—and one of these days, when the time's right, you boys will be on it. You'll change trains in Pueblo. Do you begin to git my drift?"

"Yeah, boss, that's real smart." Hayes grinned wickedly. The other two men eagerly nodded their understanding.

"Yep, I can see you all do," Jeb Cornish acknowledged. Then, with an extravagant gesture, he cleared his throat and ordered, "I've been doin' a lot of palaverin' these last coupla minutes, while you poor fellas are sittin' there all attention and dry gullets. It's time to break out that whiskey and drink a toast to what I've got in mind. It'll make us all rich—and it'll be a damn sight easier than bushwhackin' a cattle drive with ornery bastid vaqueros that carry Spencer repeaters!"

"Yeah," Hayes growled as he reached for the bottle, drew his Colt from its holster, then expertly cracked off the neck of the bottle with a swift, glancing blow. He poured generous portions in each of the four glasses, passing the first to the Indian agent.

"Jeez, Jack, can't say as I like the way you open a fresh

5

bottle." Cornish lifted his glass and anxiously squinted into it. "What the hell—s'posin' there's pieces of glass in my drink?"

"No need to worry, boss," the black-bearded outlaw assured him. "It comes off clean as a whistle 'cause I know how to do it. 'Sides, think I'd want to try to kill the goose that's layin' all these golden eggs for us poor boys? Not that way, that's for damn sure."

"Well, thanks." Cornish gave him a dubious half-smile and cautiously took a sip from his glass. Reassured that no shards had fallen into the drink, he took a more generous swig this time, then set the glass down and smacked his lips. "Best whiskey there is. Anyway, let's get back to the golden eggs—though I can't say I much appreciate being called a goose, Jack."

"I had me a smatterin' o' school back when I was a tadpole," Hayes sniggered, "and there was a real cute l'il schoolmarm teachin'. . . . Jist so happens some of what she taught me still sticks in my mind."

"Yeah, I'll bet," Reuben Huntley jeered at his crony, and got a dirty look for his pains. "Anyhow, go on, Jeb, how does this plan work?"

"Well, like I said, these two trains run into Pueblo, and the Denver'll be put onto a sidin'. Len tells me that the train sits there a coupla hours takin' on more wood, water, and supplies. Well, while it's waitin', any passengers from the Santa Fe line have all the time they need to transfer with their baggage onto the Denver. So you men will be joinin' the other passengers boardin' the train headin' for Cañon City. We'll have another dozen men—they'll be travelin' with you as far as Pueblo—ride ahead on horseback to a point just east of Cañon City. While the two trains are bein' stalled waitin' for transfers, these dozen riders will have plenty of time to get into position. You three on board the Denver are to get into the engine cab just before it reaches the town."

"Hey, that's a doozie!" Huntley tugged at his red beard and energetically nodded, then reached for his glass and downed half of it in one gulp.

"Yeah—I sorta think the engineer is gonna listen to reason and stop his train when he's told to, once he looks down the

6

barrel of a Colt—don't you, boys?" Cornish added with a harsh laugh.

His three hirelings joined in the laughter and nodded. But Hayes suddenly scowled and shook his head. He then asked, "Hey, boss, what about Bat Masterson? Seems like I heard he was in Pueblo—went there with a posse to help out those Santa Fe workers who were havin' trouble from the Denver & Rio Grande men lookin' to capture the pass through Royal Gorge."

"You heard right about that, but take it from me, there's nothin' to worry about," Cornish assured him. "You see, Bat Masterson's job finished there when the battle ended with a truce between the Sante Fe and the Denver. Seems like the Denver's been awarded the Leadville line by the courts—but they was almost wiped out from all the men they had hired to try to block the Santa Fe. Hell, they was burnin' bridges, movin' survey stakes, buryin' roadbeds under avalanches and whatnot. But now the little Denver's got the rights, and old Bat's back to chasin' horse thieves right here in Kansas. So you see, boys, we got nothin' to worry about, nothin' at all!"

"When do you think we'll pull it off, Mr. Cornish?" Gabe Penrock had ingratiated himself into the Indian agent's favor by his respectful demeanor toward the older man—and, oddly enough, it was sincere.

"No hurry. From the looks of things—and from what Len tells me—those silver mines in Leadville are going to be turnin' out ore for a long time. And that means lotsa miners workin' the ore, and a payroll sent on the train like clockwork to pay them off." Cornish gave Penrock a broad wink. "We won't move till this damn snow 'n winter's done with—early spring's the way I see it. That'll give you plenty of time to catch up on your honeymoonin' with that cute wife of yours."

The two other men guffawed, and Gabe Penrock's affable, eager look suddenly turned into a sullen, brooding one, which quickly vanished when Cornish, with an obsequious gesture, shoved the bottle toward him. "Fill your glass, Gabe, boy." Suiting action to word, he declared, "I take my hat off to a smart young fella who can handle a gun the way you do and take orders—and still have time to go sparkin' a pretty gal.

Wish to hell I could myself. Anyway, now that our serious business is over, let's see if any of you fellas kin beat the old master at poker. Table stakes, draw, but no deuces wild, understood?" As they nodded, he reached out to the tray and took the deck of cards. He broke it open and began to deal with his pudgy fingers, grinning in anticipation of the coup he was planning.

One

On the afternoon of this same mid-January day, nearly a thousand miles away, two tall, almost motionless figures stood reverently watching as the vaqueros of Windhaven Range put the finishing touches on a new church. It was a replacement for the one that had been leveled during a devastating tornado that had struck Windhaven Range the previous September . . . a tornado that had ended the lives of Maybelle and Henry Belcher, several vaqueros, and also Friar Bartoloméo Alicante, who had been praying at the very moment the tornado struck down the church he had helped dedicate years before.

Catayuna, now forty-one, yet as beautiful as the day Sangrodo, chief of the Comanche, had captured her, sighed deeply and turned to the gaunt, black-robed woman beside her. "It will be blessed, Sister Martha. His spirit dwells within it, just as it did when he was alive."

The mother superior made the sign of the cross and nodded. "Yes, my daughter, you are right; he was a saintly man. I will always praise God for His kindness in leading Friar Bartoloméo, as well as your stepson, Kitante, to meet us near the Rio Grande when I was seeking a new refuge for my flock. I am sure that He ordained it that this kind, good priest should entreat Señor Bouchard to take us in and end our wanderings. We have been allowed to live here in peace and harmony; we have had a school for the young children of the vaqueros and the adjoining community. And you, Catayuna, you have helped us in our loving work, and I know that it has eased your bereavement. There are those who would call your late husband a savage, but from what Friar Bartoloméo told us about Sangrodo, he had as much nobility of spirit and ethos in him as any Christian. This is all that God asks of man, and He does not question in which house of prayer a man may go to worship, so long as he lives a life of kindness and understanding."

"This is what I've always felt, Sister Martha." Catayuna

9

lowered her eyes for a moment, then looked back at the old woman. "I've heard that Señor Bouchard has proposed that you and the sisters start a new school in Colorado."

"That is true, dear Catayuna." The old nun's face was bright with her sudden smile. "He explained how this new place we should go to—when the time is right—is far to the north. There are many families with children who have followed their men to the mines. These children work equally as hard as their fathers and have no opportunity for education—or for the salvation that comes from within. If we can help do this good work, we shall more than justify the vows we took when we entered the order. In a sense, it will be like the work of missionaries, Catayuna, for I have heard these places are rife with sin and corruption, peopled with rough men and women who care little for anything except the immediate gratification of the flesh." Then, warmly, turning to the handsome Mexican widow, she took Catayuna's hand and said softly, "It was good to see your stepson again when he and his lovely young wife, Carmencita, came to visit last week. He is of the faith, so although he is young, he will be a great chief for his people, for he leads them in the ways of peace. And you have such wonderful grandchildren, Catayuna. Your grandson is already so handsome, and their daughter—that was a lovely gesture to name her after the true mother of Carmencita. She told me how her father had become a bandit and abandoned her mother for a reprehensible young woman. Do you see, my daughter, how the hand of God manifests itself in many ways? If her blasphemous father had not decided to become chief of the *bandidos* and establish his village near the stronghold of Sangrodo, Kitante might never have met Carmencita, might never have saved her from the shameful life her father proposed for her to lead with one of his scurrilous men."

The two women fell silent. They turned toward the setting sun; its fiery, red glow descended quickly, the sky darkened, and the twilight spurred the twittering of the birds. There was a peace and stillness all over Windhaven Range, and this peace was a just reward for those who had fled from the tyranny and bigotry of the Civil War to find a new home in southeastern Texas. They had, through their faith and their love for one another and their fervent loyalty, withstood the

10

adversities of wind and storm, just as they had the man-made storms of hatred and greed and evil. . . .

Ramón Hernandez and his beloved wife, Mara, stood on the porch of their house. His left arm was around her waist and their fingers were intertwined as they watched the sunset together. At forty, Lucien Edmond Bouchard's Mexican-born brother-in-law was as slim and wiry as he had been at twenty. Only a smudge of gray hair near his temples marked the passage of time since he had come to warn the new occupants of Windhaven Range against the impending attack by a ruthless bandit horde. He had stayed on, fallen in love with Mara, Luke's sister, and married her. As they stood beside each other, there was unspoken devotion and love between them, conveyed by the mutual pressure of their fingers.

Mara Hernandez was now forty-three, but in Ramón's eyes she was as beautiful as the day he had first beheld her. She wore her black hair in a single thick plait that fell nearly to her waist, and there were only a few strands of gray to reveal her age. The sun had darkened her skin to the color of Ramón's, as if they had been born of the same race; and their amalgamation had strengthened and proved the Bouchard belief that neither race nor creed could pose any harmful barrier to those who believed in loyalty, devotion, and truth.

Ramón glanced back up at their house, which had miraculously withstood the ravages of the tornado. *"Querida,"* he murmured, his arm around her waist drawing her still closer to him, "God has been very good to us. He spared our children as He spared our house. But this evening I meet with Lucien Edmond—and Lucien Edmond thinks that the time has come for me to consider moving to Leadville."

The previous July, on the way back from a long cattle drive to Colorado, Ramón and his men had happened upon an old man who had been left to die by bushwhackers. Frank Scolby was a prospector who had recently made a large strike just outside Leadville, Colorado, and he had been so grateful to Ramón for saving his life and caring for him that he had pledged one half of his share in the mine proceeds to the partners of Windhaven Range—Ramón, Lucien Edmond, Joe Duvray, and more recently, Lucas Forsden.

"I know what you want to ask me, Ramón, and you must know what the answer will be—always yes. Like Ruth in the

Bible, where you go, I will go. You are *mi esposo*, the father of my children, my lover; I love you as I love life itself, for the happiness you've given me and the children I've borne for you."

"I am so grateful, *querida*. But this is something you must think about very seriously. You came from a rich plantation in Alabama, where life was serene before the war. Here in Texas, we've been happy, and for the most part, we've had no real hardships. But a mining town may not be a place for a mother and children, *querida*."

But Mara shook her head and squeezed his fingers more tightly as she answered, "You seem to forget, Ramón Hernandez, that I'm no longer the spoiled, pampered girl I was when you first met me. I've stood beside you and fought against the bandits and the bushwhackers."

"My darling one," he murmured, and bent to kiss her. "Well now, let's have a leisurely dinner together and talk about our future in Colorado—and reminisce about our past. Then, I'm going to meet with Lucien Edmond, Joe, Eddie, Lucas, and Señor Scolby to make plans for working the mine. Oh, yes, it will be a while before you join me, but I want to make certain that everything is in readiness for you when you do."

"You know I don't care about wealth or comfort, Ramón. Even if we have only a meager cabin up there in Colorado near the mine, I'll be happy. I'm not a woman who needs to be important in an artificial society. My life is with you and the children." She suddenly laughed as she watched the antics of her oldest son. "Just look at Luke," she said to Ramón. "He's appointed himself a sort of second father to the others. I'm so glad we named him after my wonderful father, and every day I see in him more and more the qualities that his namesake had. And even though Jaime is almost two years younger, he's bidding fair to be the third head of the house. You know, between the two of those boys, they look after the others."

"Yes I've noticed that, too." Ramón smiled as he led Mara into the house. "Incidentally, in case you've been concerned about them at the mine in Colorado, you can be sure that at least they'll get a good education. Lucien Edmond plans to build a school there, which the sisters will operate— not just for our children, but for any of the children in

12

Leadville.'' He reverently crossed himself and added softly, ''I pray that Friar Bartoloméo will look down upon us and bless us in our new venture.''

''Amen to that.'' Mara turned back a last time to look at the darkening sky. And then, as if trying to hide her emotions, she blithely declared, ''I hope you're as hungry as I am, *querido,* for I made a big kettle of beef stew this afternoon.''

''*¡Bueno!* I *am* famished, and we have plenty of time before I meet with Lucien Edmond, so that I can enjoy what you set before me.''

As they went in, he stealthily kissed the back of her neck, and Mara sent him a look of utter contentment.

A young, weatherbeaten man stood shielding his eyes from the last rays of the sun. Robert Markey had just come out of the stable after feeding his mare, Jenny. Sitting at his feet glancing up at him, its tongue lolling out of its mouth, was the long-muzzled mongrel, Tramp.

The young man had found this dog last year on his agonizing journey from his wretched Kansas farm, where the winter blizzard had taken the life of his young wife and baby daughter. His desperate grief had instilled in him a single obsessive thought that held him to sanity: Somehow, he had to find Ramón Hernandez, the sympathetic trail boss who had given him this very mare and provisions almost two years before. Ramón's vaqueros had been ready to lynch him when he tried to feed his starving family by cutting the Bouchard herd.

Jenny was thriving now, healthier by far than she had ever been before, and Robert Markey still rode her out of choice. By now he had learned to wrangle horses and to break tough, wild mustangs, winning the approval of Eddie Gentry and Ramón himself.

He let his eyes slowly survey the ranch laid out before him in the peaceful moments before twilight. Robert drew in a deep breath and sighed, then squatted down and took the mongrel's head between his hands and spoke to it, as he had been wont to do all during that seemingly endless solitary ride from Kansas down to Carrizo Springs. ''We've found a home, Tramp, boy—and Jenny, too. I mustn't think about what I once had—although I sometimes pray to Marcy, and I hope that she hears me and forgives me. I tried my best, I truly

13

did. And since I came here to Windhaven Range, Tramp, they've treated me like a real man. I've got my pride back, and it's made me want to do things to make up for all the mistakes I made in the past. And I hope one day, Tramp boy, Marcy'll be proud of me—and she'll have forgiven me. I'll keep her memory alive by making a good life and helping others, just as Ramón Hernandez helped me, Tramp.''

He straightened, rubbed his knuckles over the dog's long muzzle, and sighed again. ''I've still got a lot to learn, but I'm more a ranch hand now than I ever was a farmer, that's for certain. I just hope I'll get a chance to pay my debt off to Mr. Hernandez. It's not paid yet, not by a long sight. But when it's paid, then maybe I can start to make plans for myself—maybe think about having a family I can keep this time. I think I'll have better luck because I won't be so stupid and helpless as I once was.'' The sun was now nearly below the horizon, and the soft patina of darkness had begun to touch the rich, fertile grazing land of Windhaven Range. ''Anyway, Tramp, I've sure made lots of friends here.'' He laughed suddenly. ''I've heard Mr. Bouchard and his nice wife calling me, Walter, Eddie, and Nacio Lorcas the four musketeers.'' His expression grew wistful. ''Yep, I've got a lot to be thankful for.''

He lifted his face to the sky now, and his eyes were moist. His parents had been God-fearing Methodists, but they had never talked to him about hellfire and damnation; instead they had let him feel that God was the sort of person you could talk to—tell Him your troubles and explain where you'd gone wrong and ask for help. He said in a soft voice, ''Thank You, God, I'm much beholden. I've got a long ways to go, but with Your help, I'll make it. Thanks an awful lot for bringing me here safely, me 'n Jenny 'n Tramp.''

The Belchers' house on Windhaven Range had been destroyed by the tornado, and Henry and his wife, Maybelle, had died in each other's arms. The rubble had long since been removed, and the Windhaven Range vaqueros had recently finished building a stronger house on the old foundation. Henry's children by his first wife now shared the house with their spouses and their children. Connie and Walter Catlin had a son named Henry, who was now thirteen months old, while Timmy and his Mexican wife, Conchita, had a nine-

14

month-old daughter they had named Luisa, after Conchita's long-dead mother.

Like everyone else on Windhaven Range, Timmy and Connie knew of the Colorado silver mine, and both of them had told their spouses that remaining at Windhaven Range would only serve to continue their grief over the loss of their beloved parents. This feeling had prompted Connie and Timmy to ask Lucien Edmond if they and their families might not go on to Colorado and start a new life at the site of the mining operation.

Walter and Connie were sitting on the front porch, watching the sunset. Connie cradled Henry in her arms while Walter, his face serene with happiness, rested his arm around her shoulder. The haunted look that he had worn during all the years he had spent tracking down the man who had been responsible for the death of his first wife and their child was now completely gone. He turned and smiled at his wife, his eyes warm and tender. "I wish I could paint some, Connie, honey," he vouchsafed. "You and the child, the darkness falling over the land—it's a picture I won't ever forget. I've sort of come home, Connie, and yet I know what you've been telling me the last few days, and I understand it. I'll go wherever you will be happy; you don't have to ask me twice."

"Thank you, dearest Walter." She leaned over to kiss him, and then continued, "Pa was such a wonderful man, and I'm so glad that Mother Maybelle made him happy during his last years here. But now they're gone, and I just don't feel right about staying on here. You know how it is—"

"I admire you and respect your feelings, Connie. It shows how much you thought of your pa and your step-ma," Walter softly answered. "I liked them a lot, too. And I think they'd want you to live where you'll be happy. From what Ramon tells me, a number of the men and their families are planning on moving to Colorado, so we won't really be saying goodbye to Windhaven Range. Why, even some of the nuns are going."

"I know, and I'm so glad. They've been awfully kind," Connie declared as she moved closer to her rangy husband. "When Sister Martha said the service for Pa and Ma, it comforted me a lot. It did for Timmy, too. Well, I'd best go in and feed Henry now. Conchita and I will fix dinner in a jiffy, Walter.''

"No hurry, honey. I'd like to sit out here a bit longer, just breathing in the air and watching the night settle in. I sure do like how quiet it is here. And, Connie—''

"Yes, Walter?'' she asked, as she stood on the threshold and turned to look at him.

"I love you very much. I could never find the proper words to express it, but I think you know what you mean to me. I thank God you said yes to me, Connie. I'll work hard all the rest of my life to make you happy—I just want you to know that.''

She bit her lip and blinked her eyes rapidly to clear them of her sudden tears. Then, jauntily, she called back, "Land sakes, Walter Catlin, you don't have to spark me any more. We're married now—and here's Henry to prove it!'' Then, noting the expression on his face, she added, "Oh, Walter, I hope I haven't hurt you! You can spark me all you want— even when I'm an old, white-haired lady, I'll still love it, darling!''

She vanished before he could tell her that he intended to do just that. Turning back to the vista, he said softly to himself, "I've been real lucky. Heck, I even feel a lot younger than I am, and it's all because of Connie—and settling past accounts that I no longer have to think about. Yes, I'm real glad to be alive.''

He bowed his head, lost in thought. How different his life was now, after the years of suffering he had endured. For many long years, he had wandered across the country, searching for the dissolute gambler who had stolen his first wife— his pretty Sarah—while Walter had been away fighting during the Civil War. The man had been responsible, at least morally, for both her death and that of their child. Then, nearly two years ago, Walter had run into the gambler in Dodge City, where the Windhaven men had gone on a cattle drive. After killing the man in a gunfight, Walter's old ghosts had been exorcised. . . .

"Sarah, girl,'' he whispered softly, "I don't know if there's a hereafter, or if you can hear me, or if you'll ever know how I paid that no-good Brainard back for what he did to you and our child. Maybe if there hadn't been a war, we'd still be together—but I'll never forget what you meant to me. Maybe

16

God has given me a second chance with Connie, the chance to find happiness with her like you and I might have had together, Sarah."

He turned abruptly and rubbed the back of his hand over his eyes, then walked down the steps and out to the gate of Windhaven Range, staring to the west. Darkness was quickly enveloping the rich grazing grass of the vast land, which stretched as far as the eye could see. As he started back to the house, he saw Timmy coming out the door and, shaking off his pensive mood, greeted the young man. "Hi there, Timmy. How are you?"

Timmy Belcher smiled affably as he came down to face Walter. "Just fine, couldn't be better, thanks. Conchita and Connie have dinner just about ready for us. Connie sent me out to fetch you."

"I was just coming in," Walter said, and smiled back at his young brother-in-law. "Connie said you want to move to Leadville, too. Is that right?"

"Yes, Conchita and I would like to move away. She took on awful bad about my folks, even though she didn't know them too long. And you know how I felt about them both, of course. When Connie and I came here with Pa, years ago, after Ma died, I was really worried about him. Then he met Maybelle, and from then on we felt like a family again. She was a wonderful woman—I'm glad they went together and didn't suffer any."

"Yes, I know just what you're thinking. Well, I suggest we all go talk to Mr. Bouchard first thing in the morning, and remind him that we'd like to pitch our tents up there in Colorado—you know, start things up and help him out." He paused and cocked his head. "Well, our ladies are calling us, Timmy. We'd best get ourselves inside."

"We'd better make some more, Juanita," Felicidad Forsden said with a laugh to the younger of her two assistant cooks. "The men seem to be even hungrier today than they usually are. It's as if all the effort they have been making these past months to rebuild after the terrible wind has reached a peak today. And when a man is well fed, he is at peace—and, if he has a wife, he is more loving toward her."

"*Es verdad*, Señora Felicidad." Juanita, a comely twenty-two-year-old from the province of Chihuahua, giggled and

17

blushed. "I have already learned that secret. When Pancho and I had our first quarrel—I do not even remember what it was about now—I cooked him some *carne asada* and some *flan*, and he was like a crooning dove."

"I know how that is." Felicidad laughed again, thinking that she, too, had worked this magic on Lucas. Turning to the other assistant, a taller, more reticent young woman of twenty-five, she added, "Juanita has just given me a very good idea, Maria. It would be a treat for the vaqueros to enjoy some *flan*. There is time to make it, if we all work very hard. Come now, I will help you."

Felicidad Forsden was now twenty-nine. Years before, when newly orphaned, she had been brought to Windhaven Range by a kindly vaquero, and she had later married sturdy, handsome Lucas and borne him three children. Felicidad was now head cook for the workers, having volunteered for this service after Maybelle Belcher's death, and she had able assistants in the young Mexican wives of two of the vaqueros. Felicidad was very happy these days, for Lucas had been made a partner upon his return from the trail drive to Colorado last year. He was now constantly with her at the ranch, and both of them could enjoy watching their children grow. As she worked now, directing the two young women, her mind was on what Lucas had told her about the old prospector and the silver mine. She was wondering if perhaps she and Lucas and their children would accompany the others to Colorado.

Over in the hacienda, the Bouchard family was also preparing for their evening meal. Maxine Bouchard was now forty, yet in Lucien Edmond's eyes, she was as lovely as the day when he had first met her back on Windhaven Plantation and had fallen head over heels in love with her. As she set the elegant mahogany table, she smiled to herself, thinking about the letter she had received from Carla this noon. The letter was brimming with excitement, for Carla and Hugo were enthusiastic over their stay in Chicago with Cordelia Thornberg, the wealthy spinster who was a neighbor of Laurette and Charles Douglas. Carla had enclosed a small watercolor of the Chicago Academy of Fine Arts, where she was studying painting, and she had written in lavish detail about how many things there were to do in this booming, midwestern city. She had made many new friends, and she promised faithfully that, in her next letter, she would tell her mother all about them. She added that Hugo, who was studying very hard to become a doctor at Rush Medical College, was so busy with his lessons and lectures that she could almost scold him for being such a stick-in-the-mud. "But, of course," she had written, "by summer, both of us will have ample time to explore Chicago, which has been so remarkably rebuilt after that terrible fire nine years ago."

As she finished setting the silverware, Maxine wondered if her husband's new venture would take them permanently to Colorado. Following dinner, he had told her, he was to meet with the other men of Windhaven Range, to discuss their prospects for the coming year. Maxine had come to love Windhaven Range; now that her eldest children were off on their own, and seemed to have found what they wanted most to do in life, she felt a serenity and peace that allowed her a good deal more contemplation of the future. If Lucien Edmond would come to devote most of his energy to the development of the silver mine as their principal source of revenue, of course, it would mean fewer and fewer of these prolonged cattle drives, during which she had always felt herself to be a virtual widow, always worrying that a stampede or a storm or some ambush by rustlers might plunge him into inescapable danger. On the other hand, the rough, almost primitive life of a mining town had its own hazards. Still in all, she had perfect confidence in Lucien Edmond's judgment. Initially he planned on going to Leadville simply to oversee the construction of the mining facilities—but perhaps he would one day decide to relocate there permanently. *Well,* she mused to herself, *if it comes to that, then of course I will go with him. It is what I must do, and what I want to do.*

Two

"That was a wonderful dinner you had Rosita prepare, Maxine." Lucien Edmond watched his beautiful wife as she entered the study with a tray on which she had placed bowls of nuts and raisins and a decanter of tawny port. From the shelf over the desk she took down a box of Havana panatelas. A dozen boxes of these fine cigars had been shipped to Lucien Edmond, as had been an Irish lace shawl for Maxine. They had been Christmas gifts from Lopasuta Bouchard, for in his position in New Orleans as lawyer to Leland Kenniston—a prosperous importer—such exotic luxuries were now easy to obtain.

Maxine smiled down at her husband, then lightly touched his shoulder as she discreetly withdrew from the study, knowing he wished to be alone with his guests. She softly bade the men goodnight and noiselessly closed the door behind her.

"Well, gentlemen, I've called you together to plan for the immediate future," Lucien Edmond abruptly began. Rising, he went to the table and filled six exquisite, hand-blown Belgian wine glasses with the port. Taking one, he went over to the couch and handed it to Frank Scolby. "It's only fitting that you should have the first glass, Mr. Scolby, since this meeting couldn't have been possible without you," he declared graciously.

"Shucks, Mr. Bouchard," the white-haired old prospector chuckled deprecatingly, "you're makin' me feel awful fidgety. I guess I'm not used to being treated as if I was important."

"But you are, indeed," Lucien Edmond reassured him, as he handed the remaining glasses to Ramón Hernandez, Joe Duvray, Lucas Forsden, and Eddie Gentry, then took his own and raised it. "To the mine—and may it match the Matchless!"

"That's a tall order, Mr. Bouchard." Frank Scolby chuckled again and shook his head as he took a tentative sip of his port. "Hey now, this is mighty good stuff. Ain't never had nothin' this good in all my days, far as I can recollect." He

20

smacked his lips in appreciation. "I'm glad you fellers found out that I wasn't fibbin' any, and I'm mighty glad there seems to be a fair share of good ore in that mine I found. But hell, you'd have to go some to keep up with old Horace Tabor, from all I heard when I was around Leadville."

"Just the same," Lucien Edmond pursued, "I'm very optimistic about your strike, Mr. Scolby. And when we get up there and get ourselves a top-notch mining engineer, I'm willing to wager—though I'm not usually a betting man—that you're going to be rich beyond your wildest dreams. And you deserve it, after your long, hard life."

"That's mighty kind of you to say, Mr. Bouchard." Frank Scolby leaned back and took another sip of his port, again smacking his lips. "You know, I sort of half wish you're right, Mr. Bouchard. Then I could treat myself to fancy drink like this. What is it, anyhow?"

"It's port wine, Mr. Scolby, and the English enjoy it after a fine meal, such as we just had," Lucien Edmond amiably explained. Then turning to Joe Duvray, he went on in a more serious tone, "Since when we returned from our initial scouting mission to the mine, you made such an efficient report on what we found there, Joe, I'm putting you in charge as permanent overseer with Ramón, because I'll only be there for the start-up operation."

"Thanks, Lucien Edmond," Joe declared. "I don't mind telling you, Margaret's already told me she won't mind at all following me to Colorado. Having our lovely house destroyed by the tornado was very hard on her, and she's really never gotten over what happened to her father—I don't have to tell you how I want her to overcome that," he said, referring to what happened ten years earlier. Margaret's father, Robert Caldemare, who for years had kept his daughter in a private school and rarely visited her, had suddenly become Lucien Edmond Bouchard's neighbor. He had put up wire fencing and hired a crew of *pistoleros* to bushwhack Lucien Edmond's herd, the result of which had been a deadly duel between the two men, and Lucien Edmond had had to kill Caldemare after being seriously wounded by him.

Lucien Edmond's face was shadowed with recollection as he nodded. "I understand. But, from the outset, Joe, I think it best that all the women and children stay behind here on the ranch. That is, at least until we've gotten the mine into start-up operation. And one of the things we're going to decide this evening is how many vaqueros will be needed to help us with the new project.''

"Whatever you decide is fine with me, Lucien Edmond,'' Joe soberly declared, folding his hands and looking down at the floor.

"I appreciate your trust in me, Joe, and all I can say here and now is that I'm very glad my father hired you and your friend, Andy Haskins, off that New Orleans dock back in '65. Well now, gentlemen, help yourselves to the nuts and raisins. And these cigars—'' He turned back to the tray and broke open the box of Havanas. "These are some of the best cigars you'll find anywhere. All right, then. Now as to Windhaven Range itself, since that terrible tornado last September, our men have done a wonderful job in rebuilding. Don't by any means think that it's in my mind to give up our ranch and go lock, stock, and barrel to Colorado, however rich Mr. Scolby's mine turns out to be. Our country seems to be on the verge of an enormous expansion, and the more diversification we have, the more secure we'll be when it comes to capital and revenue and judicious investments. And speaking of judicious investments, since Eddie so ably handled the role of foreman all the time you were on the cattle drive, Ramón, I'd like to propose that he be made a partner.''

Eddie Gentry blinked, stared incredulously at Lucien Edmond, and then stammered like a school boy. "That—that's a mighty big responsibility you're handing me, Mr. Bouchard,'', he said in an unsteady voice.

"Nothing you can't handle. Since you came to us, you've more than pulled your weight in every chore we've set for you, Eddie. And you know I believe in rewarding those who work hard and prove their loyalty over the long haul. That's why Lucas, here, was made a partner last year, and why it's your turn now. Besides, you and Maria Elena and your children have roots here, and I don't propose to dislodge them. No, you're going to continue the interbreeding of our Texas steers with the Herefords and the Brahmas. And whenever I'm up in Colorado, you and Lucas will be entirely responsible for the sale of cattle to army forts and the more immediate markets of New Orleans and San Antonio. As I've said before, it won't be long before the railroads have feeder lines down here into Texas, even this far, and long drives from

22

here to Kansas will be a thing of the past. I also think we'll soon see very little open range left—all the more reason why I want to keep our acreage held fast and develop it to its fullest potential and profit. And, Eddie, this interbreeding means finer stock, the kind we sold to Maxwell Grantham last year. Good beef is going to demand a premium now that everyone wants it. Transportation of it is faster than ever before, thanks to the railroad expansion, so the market will expand accordingly."

Lucas now spoke up: "I'm sure glad this has happened, seeing as how Eddie has done so much around here. And I know I'm going to enjoy working with him here on the range, this summer."

"I've every confidence in you both," Lucien Edmond replied, "and I know you're resourceful enough to find on your own a few more markets for our quality beef. Eddie, I'll have an agreement drawn up between you and Ramón, Joe, Lucas, and myself for you to sign before we leave for Colorado. It will give you an incentive percentage of the profits you'll make from any new business you bring to Windhaven Range. I've already made the same arrangement with Lucas and the other partners."

"That's very generous of you. Thank you," Eddie softly replied.

Lucien Edmond gestured with his hand to indicate that no thanks were needed. Then, going back to the table and refilling his glass, he took a sip and reflected a moment before going on. "Sister Martha, our mother superior, has told me that she would like to come with us immediately to Colorado, with three of the sisters." He made a rueful grin before continuing. "I tried to convince her that it would be best if she waited until we had our homes built, but she's a very determined woman. She feels that since we won't have our operations completed much before fall, it would make sense for the new school to start up in September. But, in the meantime, she feels very strongly that the sisters could be of help in supporting the widows and children of men killed in mining accidents—in fact, she has proposed that some of the sisters should run a school while others of them should organize an institution for the welfare of these penniless folk. I had to admit to her that it sounds like a wonderful idea."

The other men nodded their heads in agreement, and then

Lucien Edmond put in, "Incidentally, I wrote a letter to Maxwell Grantham up in Wyoming last year after our cattle deal had been completed—just to tell him how much we liked doing business with him—and I told him about our new venture. I asked him if he could give me some further details about Leadville—you know, a bit more insight into the situation than we were able to gather in just the short time we were there—and I've just received a letter back from him. He strongly suggests that we should watch our step there. He even was kind enough to enclose a copy of the Leadville *Chronicle* sent to him by a friend who lives there." Lucien Edmond reached into his desk drawer, pulled out the creased newspaper, and handed it over to Ramón. "If you men will take a quick glance at this, I think you'll see why Mr. Grantham said what he did. There's one article in there that crows about the rapid growth of the town—as a matter of fact, I guess you might almost call it a city, since more than twenty thousand people poured into it just last year alone—but there are plenty of stories detailing the darker side of this boomtown. Apparently it's full of cheats and scoundrels ready to part a man from his hard-earned money."

He paused and took another sip of the wine before continuing. "That's nothing new, of course, since every boomtown of the West has seen the same thing. But these miners seem to be a breed apart. It's not just the usual saloons and gambling halls—which we saw plenty of when we were there, not to mention the houses of prostitution and dance halls. These people pouring into Leadville are apparently so desperate for a stake of any kind—even if it's just a plot of land on which to build yet another saloon—that they're literally shooting people and stealing their land. Why, one story in here tells how a church—the First Avenue Presbyterian, I believe it was called—finally gave up trying to protect its tract and decided to build over in a less desirable location."

Ramón interjected, "If what you say is true, Lucien Edmond, then I would say that Leadville is very much in need of a woman with the courage, dedication, and kindness of Sister Martha. I think she'll be respected, she and her followers. Still in all, it'll be up to us to give her all the support we can with our vaqueros, so that there aren't any unpleasant incidents while she and the sisters are founding their institution."

"I'd say, Mr. Bouchard," Frank Scolby spoke up, "that

rememberin' what I do about Cap'n Sutter and the gold rush in Sacramento, them miners may be an ornery lot when it comes to fightin' for what they panned, but even so they're mighty decent and respectful-like to any women around. And sure as shootin', they ain't likely to give the holy sisters any trouble.''

"I'm inclined to agree with you, Mr. Scolby," Lucien Edmond nodded, "especially since this newspaper makes mention of the fact that a lot of the miners are Irish—and, therefore, they're likely to be good Catholics. Well now, there remains the business of deciding exactly when we'll start out for Leadville. Mr. Scolby, you, Ramón, Joe, and I will go. Ramón, do you think that, say, between six and eight of our best men would be enough to accompany us?''

"I think so, Lucien Edmond," his brother-in-law agreed. "We've got a few volunteers already from what I hear—Connie mentioned to Mara that she and Timmy want to get away from here and forget what happened to their father and mother, so Timmy and Walter will no doubt want to go.''

"Yes, they've already spoken to me." Lucien Edmond sympathetically nodded.

"And our newest hand, Robert Markey, he told me he'd like to come along too, Lucien Edmond." Ramón frowned thoughtfully and pursed his lips a moment. "Yes. He's worked hard here, and he's made friends with all the vaqueros. He's very loyal, and he feels he has a debt to pay. I think with that determination he'd be a valuable man to have around in a rough-and-tumble situation, such as we're likely to encounter in Leadville.''

Lucien Edmond nodded. "By all means, take him along with us, Ramón. Now, you didn't go with us last time, of course, so you don't know what kind of journey it is. We'll board our first stagecoach in San Antonio, then a second one from El Paso will get us to Lamy, New Mexico. There, we'll finally be able to pick up the Santa Fe railroad and go by train to El Moro, Colorado." He laughed and declared, "It's too bad all these railroad companies have different pieces of the pie, because we'll have to keep changing trains along the way. At El Moro, we switch to the Denver and Rio Grande to go on to Pueblo. And, finally, after a stopover at Pueblo, we go on to Cañon City, the end of the line. There we'll catch a stagecoach through the Royal Gorge into Leadville. The entire trip will take us about three weeks, since we'll have to stop along the way and rest up at hotels. The weather will also be a factor in the length of the trip.''

"They have winter longer in Colorado than we do down here, that's for certain.'' Lucas put in with a laugh, "Down here we don't even see a single flake of snow.''

"Indeed, that's true. Up at those elevations—about eleven thousand feet, I believe—they get snows some dozens of feet deep. That will certainly make for poorer connections than usual. And since Sister Martha and her nuns will be going with us, I want to spare them as much physical discomfort as possible. We shouldn't plan on leaving before March at the earliest. If we reach Leadville in April, by then the worst of the winter should be over. But I must say, I'm sure eager to hire an engineer and get a smelter built, all of which we'll need before the mine can be put into paying operation. Well then, gentlemen, that's the long and the short of it.''

"I think we've covered everything, Lucien Edmond.'' Ramón rose to his feet and headed for the tray, where he helped himself to a handful of nuts and raisins. He put his arm around Eddie Gentry's shoulders. "Right now, we've got about two thousand head of prime stock. By spring, judging from the number of cows that will be calving, we should have at least another five hundred.''

"I'd like to keep at least five hundred of the best stock for interbreeding, and not sell them off this year.''

"I agree with you, Eddie. We'll talk about that tomorrow. And I've a few ideas about where you can go after new markets for our cattle. I'll pass them on to you, and you can make notes, if you want. Well then,'' Ramón turned back to his brother-in-law, "as I see it, we should have everything going smoothly by midsummer, by which time our families can join us.''

"I agree,'' Lucien Edmond Bouchard declared. "And I must say, I think summer will be beautiful in the mountains—not too warm, as it is so often around here.'' He went over to the couch and offered his hand to old Frank Scolby. "It was a lucky day for all of us, Mr. Scolby, when our men found you out there in the desert. And you have my pledge again that, in return for your extraordinary generosity in deeding over half of this mine to us, we'll do everything we can to make certain that the rest of what I hope will be a very long and happy life

26

will be one of luxury and comfort for you. Who knows—with all the energy and thinking that we'll be putting into this mine, maybe my original opening toast about matching the Matchless Mine will come true after all!''

Three

Laure Bouchard, mistress of Windhaven Plantation, the Bouchard family home near Lowndesboro, Alabama, was in the study, seated at the *escritoire* that had once belonged to her late husband, Luke. As she sipped a cup of breakfast coffee that Amelia Coleman had just brought to her, Laure's face reflected the emotions churning within. Just before breakfast this gloomy Friday morning of the last week of February, a courier had ridden from Montgomery to the red-brick chateau to deliver a telegram addressed to her. She had thanked the courier and tipped him, quickly retreating behind the door. She had sensed that it was from Leland Kenniston, and hurriedly tearing open the envelope, she had seen that indeed it was.

After reading the telegram once, then a second time, she had begun pacing up and down the foyer of the stately mansion. This majestic replica of the birthplace in Normandy of Luke's grandfather, old Lucien Bouchard, no longer seemed so much like home to Laure as it had when her husband was alive. She had never been able to resign herself to the solitary life of a widow living in the country, and as she read the telegram yet a third time, her heart bounded; she suddenly could almost sense the presence of the dashing Irishman to whom she had been most attracted and to whom she indeed almost—but not quite—pledged herself, after their idyllic meeting in New York City last year.

Having tucked the telegram into the pocket of her wrapper, she had gone to the kitchen to find Amelia preparing breakfast, not only for her husband, Burt, who was spending this month on Windhaven Plantation to help Marius Thornton, but also for Laure's children. ''Just a cup of coffee for me, if you please, Amelia,'' Laure had requested. And then, with a soft

27

smile on her lips, not yet willing to reveal what this telegram portended, she had gone directly to Luke's study. Sitting now at the writing table, she disciplined herself to sip her coffee so that she would be fully awake and her mind clear to relish and deal with the news that this unexpected message brought.

Only when the cup was half-empty did she draw out the telegram, take it out of its envelope and unfold it, and lay it upon the desk before her.

There was a flush to her cheeks, and she looked far younger than her thirty-nine years. There were no wrinkles to mar her forehead and cheeks, nor, for that matter, in the exquisite column of her neck. Her golden hair, pulled tightly back into a thick twisted "lover's knot" just above her nape, was lustrous and without the slightest trace of gray. The soft light in her green eyes, as she absorbed once again each word of the telegram before her, was like that of a young girl who experiences her first true love affair.

Then, aware of what room she was in and before whose desk she sat, her face suddenly shadowed with remembrance. She glanced around, almost as if the ghost of Luke were there to comfort and reassure her, to tell her that he understood that she was still in the full zenith of her womanhood. That he, of all men, would understand if now, in her loneliness, she was drawn to another man who could be worthy of her, as he himself had tried to be.

The telegram read as follows:

Just arrived back in New York last night and wanted to get this off to you, dearest Laure. I plan to go to New Orleans for the first week of March, which, as you probably know, will this year mark the beginning of Mardi Gras. It would be wonderfully romantic to have you there with me and to talk things over again.

Your devoted,
Leland Kenniston

As she read the telegram again, she traced each word with a slim forefinger, and when she reached his name, she touched her fingertip to her lips and closed her eyes. She was remembering their tryst in New York last August, when Leland was

28

preparing to accompany her oldest son, Lucien, to his new school in Ireland, the place of Leland's birth. It had been much more than a consummation of their need, each of the other; and now she was filled with a keen awareness that she had missed him more than she had ever believed possible, since they had parted in New York. She realized that, without knowing it, she had thought of him all these long months while busying herself with the affairs of the plantation, keeping in close communication with the bank at New Orleans and with her adoptive son, Lopasuta, and his wife, Geraldine, as well as with Jesse Jacklin, who managed the prospering casino that she owned in the Queen City.

Again, as deliberately as before, she forced herself to drink the rest of her coffee. She was fully awake, her mind was clear, and there were no feverish illusions about him, such as a young girl eager to meet an exciting lover might blind herself with. No, she was certain that Leland Kenniston was far more than just an illusory dream.

Moreover, Lucien, in writing to his mother of his pleasure in his new school, had unknowingly confirmed her own very favorable impression of Leland. His first letter, which she had received last October, had been devoted almost entirely to an excited description of the engrossing time he had spent with the handsome businessman on the voyage across the Atlantic. "What I like best about Mr. Kenniston, Mother," he had written in that letter, "is that he never talks down to you. I know I'm still young, but almost every night after dinner, Mr. Kenniston walked out on deck with me and talked to me about the history of Ireland, the politics, the emigration of the poor farmers to the United States. And he asked for my views, just as if I were his own age. It makes me want to learn all I can so that I can keep up with a man like that—and he's so friendly and kind. He's a wonderful friend, Mother."

A wonderful friend. Laure remembered these words as she closed her eyes for a moment. But he was much more than that to her, though Lucien could not know it—and would not know it until the proper time. How discreet Leland had been when they had had that one night of absolute ecstasy, making certain that, in no way, could Laure's son suspect that there was anything between them. He had such a sense of propriety for the obvious conventions, and that was admirable in a man, especially one who was a mature and wealthy bachelor.

At last, she folded the telegram, put it back into the pocket of her flannel wrapper, and rose. She walked slowly to one of the windows facing north, threw open the shutters, and stared out onto Pintilalla Creek. She loved this particular view, a less spectacular one, perhaps, than that from the windows that looked out over the rushing Alabama River. Here, rather, was a gentle vista, with early-blooming spring flowers beginning to show their colorful heads, carrying the eye to the babbling creek beyond. The sky was still gray, a reminder of the rain the night before, yet now she could see some sunlight breaking through with a hint of brightness for the hours ahead. That was a good omen.

She sighed, and her mind drifted back to the telegram. What Leland Kenniston had done for young Lucien proved that he was genuine and sincere. And her son's enthusiasm for the man helped influence her own decision—which, almost sheepishly now, she realized she had made in advance. In fact, perhaps she had been waiting expectantly for just such word as this—and now it had come.

Yes, she would meet Leland for Mardi Gras. And if he proposed marriage this time, as he had done last year in New York, would she accept? She was sure her other children would be as responsive as Lucien had been to this man who would become their stepfather. In no way would he be inferior to Luke. In no way, so far as she knew, would Luke himself have frowned upon her choice of another husband, a companion for the years ahead, when age and loneliness would otherwise take a dreadful toll and make her live too much in the past.

She smiled. She was still young enough to have a soupçon of coquettishness, and she glanced down at herself and, with her slim hands, stroked her hips and thighs, grateful that being just a year short of forty had not made her less desirable as a woman. What she felt with Leland was a more lasting and spiritual inspiration than the all too often used justification for a relationship, that of sexual desire. And yet . . . A wry, taunting little smile played on her lips—one that Luke himself had first observed years before and had made him fall in love with her against his will. Laure Bouchard admitted that since she could pronounce herself still in her prime of womanhood and yearning for a zestful life and love, then assuredly Leland Kenniston, a virile and yet tenderly considerate lover, would bring to this marriage—if indeed it would take place—an indescribably rewarding physical companionship.

Four

Once having made the decision to meet Leland Kenniston in New Orleans, Laure Bouchard completed her plans for the journey that very morning. Before leaving Luke's study, she wrote out two wires. One of these was to Lopasuta and Geraldine, informing them that she planned to arrive in New Orleans the following Sunday, and asking Lopasuta to reserve a suite for her, if possible, at the St. Charles Hotel. The second was to Leland, accepting his invitation, telling him that she would meet him in New Orleans. And then, out of a capricious impulse, she added: "I'll send word to your office of when and where and how we shall meet."

This done, she went back to the kitchen to ask Amelia Coleman to send one of the workers off to Montgomery at once to dispatch the wires. Then, smiling to herself and feeling the warm tingle of her pulse, she climbed the stairs to her bedroom, and she dressed. After the children had had their breakfast and the older ones were driven to the local school, she drew Clarabelle Hendry—their genial governess—into one of the guest rooms. "Clarabelle, dear," she confided, "I want to go to New Orleans for Mardi Gras, and I plan to leave on the steamboat tomorrow morning so I can arrive there in plenty of time to be settled before the festivities start. Now, I know you'll look after the children as wonderfully as you always do, but I wonder if you could set aside some time to spend privately with Paul. This will be difficult, I know, because the younger children—John especially—require most of your attention. But Paul is growing so fast now and becoming so mature in the way he thinks and talks. He might be a little put out that I didn't take him along on a trip, as I did Lucien last year, but his time will come soon enough.

31

Make him feel that he's the man of the house while I'm gone and ask him to look after his sisters and John.''

"Of course I will, Laure. I'm sure the trip will be good for you. Can I help you pack?''

"No—'' Laure's cheeks were pink with excitement, and she scarcely managed to suppress a most unwomanly giggle, "—I'll be traveling light. Oh, Clarabelle, I'm so excited! It's the most colorful and happy time of all in New Orleans, and I'll buy myself a special costume to take part in the celebration. You remember, of course, that I was born in New Orleans, and I haven't been to Mardi Gras in longer than I want to remember.'' She smiled at this faithful employee who had become, over the years, a good friend and confidante. "You see, Clarabelle, Luke always felt that Mardi Gras was a frivolous waste of time. Maybe it is—'' she laughed, "—but it's also a great deal of fun! And I'm going to try to make up for the years I've missed, this time!''

"I hope you have an absolutely wonderful time,'' the mature, pleasant-featured woman declared, "and you needn't worry—I'll see to it that Paul doesn't feel neglected.'' Her devotion to the children was maternal, and she had the knack of making all of them feel individually special without seeming to show any particular favoritism toward one or the other.

"You're a treasure, Clarabelle.'' Laure spontaneously hugged her friend, and then declared, "Well, I'd best do my packing. Fortunately, a single valise will be quite enough.''

Then suddenly she remembered the afterthought to the wire for Leland Kenniston and, clapping a hand to her forehead, gasped, "Oh, dear, I just remembered—excuse me, Clarabelle!''

She hurried back downstairs to the kitchen, and breathed a sigh of relief when, before she could say a word, Amelia Coleman volunteered, "Henry Davis just finished his chores in the garden, Miz Laure; he's saddling up a horse, and he'll be off any minute now for Montgomery.''

"Oh, good! I—well, I'll go catch him. I—I forgot something in one of the wires,'' Laure lamely explained as her cheeks colored vividly. She hurried out of the kitchen.

A lanky, affable young black worker whom Burt Coleman had hired three months ago was leading a saddled mare out to the mounting block at the front of the chateau. "Just a moment, please, Henry,'' Laure called. "I want to add something to those wires. Oh, I'm so glad I caught you in time!'' she declared, catching her breath.

"I'm mighty glad you did, too, Miz Bouchard.'' The man doffed his cap and grinned at her, then put his free hand into the pocket of his jacket and drew out the two folded sheets.

"This will only take a second—'' She unfolded both sheets, then selected the one to Lopasuta and Geraldine and added a final line to the message she had written: "Be sure not to tell Leland Kenniston where I'll be staying—but meet me at the St. Charles Sunday afternoon.''

"There! They're ready to go now, Henry. And thank you ever so much!''

"I'll get them in real fast, Miz Bouchard, you can depend on it.'' He carefully tucked away the sheets of paper, then replaced his cap squarely on his head. As he did so, he glanced up. "Nice mornin'. Seems like we'll get plenty of sun today. Well, I'll be off then, ma'am.'' He swung himself into the saddle and spurred the mare into a canter toward the trail that led to Montgomery.

Once again, Laure found a worrisome thought leaping into her mind: What if Lopasuta couldn't get her a room at the St. Charles? New Orleans was always jammed with visitors, as well as with people from the upriver homes wanting to enjoy the spectacle of Mardi Gras before the dour Lenten season. *Well,* she thought to herself, *if anyone can get me a room there, it'll be dear Lopasuta, since he's become so well known in New Orleans as a lawyer. I'm so proud of him—and Luke must be, too.*

"How good it is to see you both again, my dears!'' Laure Bouchard exclaimed, as her adoptive half-Comanche son and his lovely wife rose from their seats in the luxurious lobby of the St. Charles Hotel and came forward to greet her. A young bellman took Laure's valise and respectfully moved away from the trio to give them privacy for their reunion.

"How wonderful you look, Laure!'' Geraldine declared, as she hugged the golden-haired widow and then kissed her affectionately on the cheek.

Disengaging herself from the embrace, Laure held Geraldine at arms' length, looking her over with a merry gleam in her eyes.

"And I might say as much about you, Geraldine! In fact, I

33

can tell from the way you *both* look that there isn't a single cloud on your horizon. Oh, it is so good to see you both,'' she said with a gentle smile. Then her eyes widened with anxiety, and she asked the tall young lawyer, "You *were* able to get me a room here, weren't you? I realize it was rather short notice, and New Orleans can be dreadfully crowded for Mardi Gras.''

"The manager of the hotel owed me a favor for some legal advice I gave him a few months ago, Laure,'' Lopasuta cheerfully announced, "and so he was able to reserve a suite for you on the top floor.''

"How marvelous! I can't thank you enough. And—and you haven't told anyone?''

There was a twinkle in Lopasuta's eye as he shook his head. "Not a soul. Would I be presumptuous in thinking that your reason for insisting on staying in a hotel and not with us has something to do with Leland Kenniston?''

Color flamed in her satiny cheeks. "You are obviously the lawyer I know you to be, since you have so easily inferred that, Lopasuta,'' was Laure's saucy riposte. "By any chance, do you know if he's in town?''

"Oh, yes, he arrived yesterday. He's staying at the St. James Hotel, next to the Board of Trade Building. It's a small hotel, very charming, and there's an excellent Creole restaurant just down the street from it. Well now, let's see you up to your suite, Laure. Did you have a pleasant trip downriver?''

"Oh, yes, it was delightful. The weather was surprisingly pleasant. I do hope it continues and that we'll have a wonderful, sunny day for Mardi Gras,'' Laure exclaimed animatedly. Lopasuta excused himself, went to the hotel desk, conferred with the clerk, and returned with the room key.

"The suite is ready now. I'm sure you'll like it.''

Laure sighed happily as she entered the elevator, to be taken to the topmost floor. Already this unexpected trip to New Orleans had turned out so well. This hotel was assuredly the most luxurious in the Queen City, and Lopasuta's luck in finding her an entire suite at such a time made her feel that the gods of happiness were smiling down at her. And when the bellman opened the door of the suite and ceremoniously ushered Laure, Lopasuta, and Geraldine inside, Laure exclaimed, "Oh, my! It's beautiful! It couldn't be nicer! Thank you so much, dear Lopasuta!''

"My pleasure, Laure. Here you are, young man," Lopasuta said to the amiable bellman as he handed him a four-bit piece. The man thanked him, executed a very proper bow to the two women, and then exited.

Laure and Geraldine moved around the rooms of the suite, exclaiming over the sumptuous elegance of its furnishings. Laure paused by a small Chippendale desk and breathed deeply of the long-stemmed red roses the manager had thoughtfully provided.

"Tonight, Laure, Geraldine and I plan to take you to a wonderful restaurant we discovered on Common Street. It's called McDonnell's, and I'll warn you in advance to be prepared for a virtual banquet," Lopasuta proffered, as Laure finally seated herself on an elegantly upholstered chaise longue. "We patronize it on special occasions—and when we're really hungry."

"But it's dreadfully fattening," Geraldine laughingly broke in. "It makes me groan just to think about it, Laure. You start with soup and fish, and these are followed by an entreé— a sweetbread or a lamb chop. After that, you are served either a spring chicken or roast beef or roast mutton or veal, accompanied by one or two side dishes of vegetables. But wait! We're still not through yet. For dessert, there'll be fruit or jelly, and cheese, as well as coffee and liqueurs."

"If I were to consume all that," Laure merrily laughed, "I'm afraid I should have to pay an immediate visit to a corsetmaker in a no doubt fruitless attempt to hide the avoirdupois such a meal would bestow upon me!" The three of them joined in laughter, and then Laure turned to Geraldine. "Are you going to wear a costume for Mardi Gras?"

"Oh, yes—and so is Lopasuta. We are so looking forward to it! I haven't dressed up in costume since I was a little girl, and this will be a first for Lopasuta," Geraldine replied. "My dapper husband will go as a Spanish don, complete with baskethandle rapier and a papier-mâché morion. Honestly, it looks like real silver! The people at the costume shop are so ingenious, Laure! And I'll be a Turkish harem girl, with a veil covering my face below my eyes, very voluminous—but not too gauzy— pantaloons, and the most darling little slippers with turned-up toes, just like out of an Oriental fairy tale. I think they call the veil a yasmak—isn't that what the proprietor called it?"

"I think so, Geraldine, dear," Lopasuta replied with a

grin, regarding his wife with evident admiration, as if picturing her in this sensuous garb.

"Do you know," Laure leaned toward him, "I came a few days in advance because I very much want to go in costume, too, and I was hoping to find something in time. Geraldine, I wonder if your costume shop would be open today?"

"Oh, yes! Till nine o'clock this evening. I know, because Lopasuta and I are going to pick up our costumes there after dinner."

"I know it's terribly late, but I do hope I can find something for myself there."

"The owner is a darling old man, a Creole with the most courtly manners." Geraldine giggled at her recollection. "He has such a large shop and so many things that I'm sure, even on such short notice, he'll be bound to find you something very becoming."

"That's wonderful! Well then, let's have an early dinner—and I assure you I'm not going to eat everything on that outrageously tempting menu you've described—and then we'll see what I can wear for Mardi Gras!" Laure's eyes were sparkling.

Lopasuta and Geraldine exchanged a knowing look, which Laure, in her reflective anticipation, did not observe. Both of them understood that Laure Bouchard had come to New Orleans on a most romantic mission—one of which they both heartily approved: to be reunited, and perhaps, this time, for all time, with the one man who could replace Luke Bouchard in both her esteem and yearning.

Five

Lopasuta and Geraldine called for Laure at her hotel at six o'clock, and because the evening was fair and warm, they decided to forego a carriage and walk to the restaurant. Although the official start of Mardi Gras was still two days away, there was a sense of excitement in the air that was downright contagious. By the time the threesome reached the restaurant, they were laughing and behaving almost like children let out of school.

With some difficulty, Lopasuta composed himself as they reached Common Street. Geraldine and Laure managed to follow suit, so that by the time they were ushered into the restaurant, they were quite self-possessed—although neither dared to look at the other, for fear they would dissolve into a fit of giggling.

"Oh, Lopasuta, this is enchanting!" Laure declared as she looked around McDonnell's. Situated on the ground floor of an old brick house, the restaurant had been allowed by the management to retain the original charm and details of the former public rooms of the once-private dwelling. The soft light thrown up by the gaslights, placed at discreet intervals along the walls, accented the mellow wood moldings and finely wrought plasterwork.

They were shown to a table in a corner—large and round as were all of them, guaranteeing sufficient room for the assortment of dishes that were normally served. In the center were several lighted candles and a small vase holding a single yellow rose.

The dinner was just as lavish and delicious as Lopasuta and Geraldine had promised. Laure, however, contented herself with a small portion of broiled redfish and the white meat of a spring chicken, with appropriate vegetables, followed by fresh fruit and coffee. They all shared a bottle of claret, and by the end of the meal, they were in a most relaxed and satisfied mood.

Walking out onto Common Street, they immediately hailed a carriage and instructed the driver to take them to the costume shop just off Bourbon Street. Although it was nearly eight o'clock on this Sunday evening, the lights in the shop were still burning brightly. As Lopasuta handed Laure down from the carriage, she again became anxious and sighed. "I do so hope it won't be too late to get a costume."

"I'm sure you'll charm the proprietor, Laure," the tall Comanche smiled. "Besides," he continued, with a conspiratorial wink at Geraldine, "we both had a kind of premonition that this time you might like to take part in the revelry, and I told M'sieu Dagronard to hold some things particularly admirable for a very beautiful lady."

"Why, my dears! That was ever so kind of you!" Laure

37

cried with delight, clapping her hands, as a child might, with pleasure. Then her brow furrowed with reminiscence. "Dagronard, Dagronard—wait! Can that man possibly be any relation—I remember that Luke on several occasions mentioned that when he and his family left Windhaven Plantation for Texas—after the fire that the Union troops started—he ordered wagons to be built for the journey from a wagonmaker with the very same name—yes, I'm sure of it!"

"It is a most unusual name, so it's possible," Lopasuta agreed. "Why don't we go in and find out?"

He led the way into the shop, where a frail, stooped, white-haired man, with tremendous *joie de vivre* in his twinkling blue eyes, came forward to greet them. "*Soyez les bienvenus,* M'sieu, Madame Bouchard!" He greeted Geraldine and Lopasuta and extended his hand, which Lopasuta warmly shook. "Ah, this must be *la belle dame* of whom you apprised me. Fear not, madame," he said with a smile at Laure, all the while twirling the ends of his enormous mustache. "I purposely held back one or two costumes—"

"I fear I have given you a great deal of trouble, m'sieu." Laure enchanted the old man by giving him a curtsy. "Since it's only two days from Mardi Gras, it was very gracious of you to save something for me."

"Ah—but we Creoles believe that beautiful women come first in life. And besides—to put a practical view upon it— even if you do not like anything that I have to offer, I shall undoubtedly be completely sold out of costumes by the time Mardi Gras dawns. Come this way, if you please!"

"A moment, sir. I'm curious about something. My late husband was Luke Bouchard, and he told me that when he came to New Orleans just after the Civil War, he had magnificent wagons made for his journey to Texas by a wagonmaker whose name was the same as yours: Dagronard."

"Yes, madame." The stooped old man bowed his head for a moment. "That was my older brother, Emile. He died two years ago, of the fever. For many years I told him that he had long since earned his rest and should have retired, but he was proud of his work—as I myself am. What a coincidence, and how sad it is that poor Emile could not be here to welcome you, Madame Bouchard. I am Baptiste, *à votre service*. Yes, now it comes back to me, for my brother told me how he admired this M'sieu Luke Bouchard. He told me how he did his best and forced his 'stupid workers,' as he always called his men—though they knew it was only in jest—to exceed themselves in preparing wagons that would last and give good service.''

''My stepson tells me they are still in use at Windhaven Range, M'sieu Dagronard. So they stand as a kind of memorial to your brother,'' Laure softly said.

Overcome with emotion, the old Creole took her hand and kissed it, as he would that of a princess. In a voice hoarse with emotion, he declared, ''I can only hope that what humble costumes I have left will not be unworthy of so gracious and beautiful a lady. Come this way. As you see, we are still at work. This is the one time of year when all New Orleans forgets its miseries, the fever, all that went before, and thinks only of revelry, beauty, music, good food, and wine! It is a show, a spectacle offered by no other city in the world, and that is why I am proud to be a Creole and part of it.''

He led them past long tables, at which men and women were working, and Laure observed an incredible array of grotesque masks, hugely exaggerated, depicting animals, demons, kings, and great warriors. The old man made a sweeping gesture toward the tables and explained, ''Until recently, it was thought that these masks and costumes had to be made in France. But there are still people here of the old tradition, people who have the spirit of Mardi Gras in their very blood. And they have skills, too, as you can see. As you may know, Madame Bouchard, Mardi Gras means more to us than a celebration; it is almost connected with the founding of New Orleans itself. Because, even though our great Queen City was not founded until 1718, it was on Mardi Gras itself, in 1699, that the Sieur d' Iberville rediscovered the Mississippi River and camped for the night. In honor of the day, he named the spot Bayou du Mardi Gras. That was the first place named in *La Belle Louisianne*. Thus it was that our Mardi Gras tradition started.''

''My goodness!'' Laure declared. ''I thought I knew everything about my home city, but that I hadn't known, M'sieu Dagronard. Thank you for telling me. Oh, my! What wonderful masks these are, and what realism. Your workers are indeed very skillful.''

''Ssh! Do not say it too loud, or they will ask for more money when this is over,'' the old man whispered with a sly wink. "But now, let us go into my private office at the back of this den—which is what we call the place of costume makers, Madame Bouchard—and you will see in my closet what I have managed to keep away from the inquisitive and the greedy, especially for you."

Laure laughed with pleasure and entwined her fingers with Lopasuta's while putting her arm through Geraldine's. "How very thoughtful it was of you both to think of me. But how could you guess that I wanted to do exactly this?"

"Perhaps it is because of my background as a Comanche, dear Laure," Lopasuta solemnly responded. "I am sure that you have heard the Indians commune with the Great Spirit and often receive messages in the night, which only they hear." Try as he might, he could not suppress a broad smile.

"Well," Laure laughed, "whatever prompted you, I'm grateful for it. I can hardly wait to see what M'sieu Dagronard has held aside for me."

She went ahead of Lopasuta and Geraldine and caught up with the old man, who with a low bow and a flourish of his hand, ceremoniously ushered her into his spacious office. Lopasuta turned to Geraldine and whispered, "I hope that this time Laure and Leland decide to do something about the love they obviously have for each other, and will form a permanent relationship such as you and I have, my dearest wife."

"And so do I, Lopasuta. However, I don't think we should let her know just yet that we've guessed her secret. But you can see from the happy look on her face that, at last, she's forgetting the sorrows of losing Luke."

"Just as you have made me forget those dreadful months of being so far away from you across the ocean, Geraldine." Lopasuta took his wife in his arms and, stepping into the shadows to one side of the old man's office, kissed her warmly.

Baptiste Dagronard went directly to a large closet that completely lined one wall and threw open both doors. A lighted lantern glowed on his desk, and he walked over to the desk to fetch the lamp, then returned to the closet. Holding the lamp high, he turned to Laure for her approval.

In the closet were three costumes, but Laure's eyes went immediately to the one in the middle. It was a theatrical version of a gown worn by a high-born woman during the

Italian Renaissance. The topmost layer was a magnificent cloak, cunningly fabricated to look like ermine, but actually ingeniously made of hand-painted brushed velvet, created with such craftsmanship that, at first glance, one could scarcely distinguish it from the priceless fur. It had a high collar that framed the neck from the back, deeply slashed sleeves for the arms, and a brocade hem. Under the cloak was worn a square-necked gown in a garnet-red color. Pinned to the gown was a shiny object. Curious, Laure fingered the object and realized it was a diadem of multicolored glass stones.

Baptiste Dagronard observed Laure's enthusiasm and hastened to take the costume on its hanger out of the closet to show it to her. "It befits you, Madame Bouchard! You will look like a queen, and the diadem will set off your beautiful golden hair."

"It lacks one thing only, M'sieu Dagronard," Laure uttered in an amused voice. "A black domino mask."

"But, of course, that's the simplest of all things to obtain." He looked at her fondly and sighed. "Madame, though I am old and feeble, I have not forgotten my Creole gallantry. And what you have told me of your husband and the great compliment you paid my brother for those wagons . . . Madame, I wish to offer this costume to you with my compliments—and my hope that you will enjoy Mardi Gras as never before in this lovely city of ours."

"Why—" Laure was breathless at this generosity "—I— you're much too kind—"

"Madame, I will not hear another word. It is yours." He took Laure's hand and kissed it. "May your celebration be the happiest of your life, dear Madame Bouchard!"

Six

This March of 1880 was a tumultuous time both climatically and politically. It was the month in which the Supreme Court held unconstitutional a West Virginia law, dating from 1863, that excluded Negroes from jury duty. In this same month, the issue of the proposed Panama Canal had become a controversial one for the nation's leaders, and President Hayes declared that it was the policy of the United States for any canal constructed in the Isthmus to be strictly under American jurisdiction. In the Colorado Rockies, there was a near blizzard, which held up train service for three days. And in Texas, there was a week of unseasonably heavy rain and high winds.

On the first Monday of this unsettled month, Eddie Gentry walked over to the hacienda to say good-bye to Lucien Edmond Bouchard, who was leaving that day for Leadville. As he shook hands with his new partner and wished him Godspeed, Eddie remarked, "I'll be rounding up and branding the cattle—including those on Emory Carruthers's old land. On those head, I'll be sure to use the C & C brand, since I remember you promised the old man's attorney that the Carruthers mark would be retained. There are two prize bulls there, and I'd like to breed them with some of our Hereford heifers."

"That's excellent, Eddie. You know, I'm more than ever convinced that you will take good care of everything while I'm gone."

"Thanks, Mr. Bouchard. If any crisis comes up, I can send a telegram to you in care of the box you'll have at the Leadville Post Office."

Lucien Edmond clapped Eddie on the back. "I've already arranged with our bank in San Antonio through a power of attorney to let you sign such checks as are needed for the payroll and the expenses of running the ranch."

"That's fine, Mr. Bouchard. You know, Maria Elena is pretty good at figures. She's offered to keep the accounts for me, so that everything should be in tip-top shape when you come back.''

"Of course it will. Stop worrying." Lucien Edmond chuckled, then added by way of afterthought, "It's a hundred twenty miles to San Antonio, Eddie. Since the good sisters will be in one of the wagons, we'll probably do no better than twenty miles a day, so we'll reach there in about a week. When you send the men into San Antonio for supplies in a couple of weeks, you can have the vaqueros pick up the wagons and the horses—I'll leave them at the stable where we have an account—and bring them back.''

"Sure thing, Mr. Bouchard, I'll take care of it. Well then, have a good journey, and I'll be anxious to hear from you how that silver mine turns out.''

"You'll be one of the first to know, Eddie. After all, you're a partner in Windhaven Range now. You, Joe, Lucas, and Ramón, just as I myself, will all figure in the profits." Again he shook hands with Eddie, who then turned and walked outside.

Lucien Edmond spent a few minutes clearing up some papers on his desk, then he left the study and strode into the parlor. He called out to his wife and children that he was ready to leave, and they came rushing in to say their good-byes.

Lucien Edmond felt a lump welling in his throat as he beheld his family—the last time he would see them in many months. *My*, he thought to himself, *Edwina is really quite a young lady these days. She's going to be as much of a beauty as her mother, I'm sure. She even seems to hold herself in that same almost regal way—even though she's not yet twelve!*

He smiled at his daughters and broke his reverie as Diane, very much a tomboy at nine, and Gloria, seven years old and a bundle of energy, both flung themselves into his outstretched arms for a last kiss from their father. He hugged them to him tightly and tousled their hair, then reached for the more reserved Edwina. He kissed her gently on her forehead and gave her a hug. Then he reached for Ruth, the two-year-old, who was being held in Maxine's arms.

After kissing his youngest daughter, he smiled at the girls crowded around him and said, "Now you be sure to look after your mother while I'm gone. If all goes as we plan, I'm hoping that you can all come up to Leadville when I'm ready to return. That way, you'll all have the chance to see the mine—and to see the Rockies. There's nothing like them anywhere else in the country. Mountains so high that they poke into the clouds, and gorges so deep that you can't see — the bottom.

"Well, my dearest," he said as he turned to Maxine, "it's time for me to go. Walk out with me to the wagons, won't you?"

They walked out of the hacienda, hand in hand, and no words passed between them. When they reached the wagons, Lucien Edmond put his arms around his lovely wife and held her in a gentle embrace for a long moment. He whispered in her ear, "Don't worry about me, Maxine. Promise me that you won't. Everything will be just fine."

Holding back the tears, Maxine whispered, "I know it will, my darling. I have every confidence in you. It will be hard to be without you all these months, but I know that when you return, we'll probably never have to be parted ever again. Godspeed, my love."

After a lingering kiss, Lucien Edmond turned and waved good-bye to his daughters. He walked quickly to his horse, mounted it, and rode to the head of the little procession that was bound for San Antonio and, ultimately, Leadville, Colorado.

Eddie Gentry stared after him and blinked his eyes to rid them of the sudden, uncharacteristic tears. He was remembering how, eleven years ago, he had come to Windhaven Range. He thought to himself that he had come a long way—from an unemployed Texas cowhand, scrounging at the Corpus Christi dock in hope of earning enough for room and board till he could find another job, to a partner—a *partner!* —at one of the best spreads in all of Texas. "Funny how life can be," he said under his breath, remembering the circumstances. Ben Wilson had hired Eddie to drive his children to the ranch after the death of his wife, Fleurette, and when they had arrived, Dr. Wilson had earnestly urged Lucien Edmond Bouchard to hire Eddie. That had been the beginning of an incredible new life. He felt the weight of the responsibility Lucien Edmond had entrusted to him, and he swore to himself to use his stewardship wisely on behalf of the Bouchards.

*   *   *

Ramón Hernandez stood on the porch of his house with his family gathered around him. His sons—Luke, now twelve, and growing taller by the month; Jaime, a somewhat shorter ten-year-old; and Edward, a chubby seven-year-old—all solemnly shook their father's hand. After equally solemnly shaking their outstretched hands in return, Ramón threw back his head and laughed, and grabbed each boy in turn in a crushing bear hug. He smiled tenderly at his daughter Dolores—who was going on nine and was, like her good friend Diane Bouchard, something of a tomboy—and hugged her to him while planting a kiss on the top of her dark-haired head.

He felt a tug on his trouser leg, and looked down. Mara, his youngest child, who had celebrated her third birthday just two days earlier, was looking up at him with an earnest, tearful expression on her face.

Ramón looked down at her and asked, "Why the long face, Gatita?" He had nicknamed his daughter the Spanish for "kitten" shortly after she had been born, and he had remarked to his wife, "Her hair is as soft as a kitten's fur." The nickname had stuck, for which her family was grateful, since it served to differentiate her from her mother, after whom she had been named.

Ramón now squatted down, lifted the little girl into his arms, and kissed her resoundingly on both cheeks, then soothingly said, "Gatita, it is much more important that you stay here and look after your mother. I promise I will send you some presents, and I will write to you and send you many hugs and kisses like these!" He squeezed her tenderly, kissed her on the nose and then the cheeks again, and set her down. The child burst into tears and flung her arms around her mother's skirts, hiding her face. Ramón walked over to his wife, and they exchanged a long, passionate kiss.

Mara laughed when Ramón released her, then said, "My goodness—if we had kissed any longer, the children might have feared we were permanently glued together!"

Ramón smiled and hugged her to him again. "I had to make it last, *querida*," he whispered, "because that one kiss will have to hold me a long time."

After a last hug for each of his children, he turned and walked across the compound and over to the lead wagon in which the nuns were to be seated. "A good day to you, Sisters," he said to the four women standing by the wagon.

45

He made the sign of the cross as the mother superior, tall and gaunt, smiled amiably to him. "I have taken the liberty of appointing myself your driver. I assure you that between here and San Antonio, your journey will be as comfortable as I know how to drive the horses," he told the old woman.

"We are all of us in God's hands, Señor Hernandez," Sister Martha pleasantly replied as she crossed herself. "But," she smiled wryly, "since it's true that you're an expert horseman, it's a good augury that you will be guiding us on this first stage of our journey." She turned to the three nuns who had volunteered to go with her, all of them Mexican, two of them in their early thirties and the oldest about the same age as Sister Martha herself. "The sun is shining, and that is a good sign, too. May the blessed Lord watch over all of us and over these we leave behind, who live by His Commandments." She turned to those who remained behind and who watched, all of the vaqueros gathered in the yard outside of the new bunkhouse, and made the sign of the cross to them as they bowed their heads, reverently removing their sombreros to accept her blessing.

Ramón made sure that they were all comfortably ensconced before clambering into the driver's seat and taking up the reins. Earlier that morning, the vaqueros had furnished the wagon with pillows and thick blankets. Across the width of the wagon, they had clamped sturdy boards, against which the pillows were propped, to act as backrests so that the four women might recline in ease and comfort during the tedious journey to San Antonio.

Sister Martha, seated behind Ramón, tapped him on the shoulder. When he turned, she said, "You know, Señor Hernandez, I am very excited about this new venture of ours. I feel certain that the hand of God is upon us—that it was He who led you to Mr. Scolby. Just think! Because of the mine, the sisters and I are now able to do God's work among those who so desperately need it. We will be able to feed the hungry and shelter the homeless, aside from tending to their educational needs."

"But, Sister Martha," Ramón protested, "surely you have been doing good works here at Windhaven Range. You have done a wonderful job teaching all the children of the vaqueros and the neighboring ranchers."

"That is true, my son," she said with a smile. "But we

46

have had a very easy life here at Windhaven Range, and I think that God means for us to do more than have a life of ease. Of course, many of the sisters—and Catayuna, as well—will be continuing the schooling here, but not all of us are needed for that. We are much more needed in a place like Leadville—and it is the duty of our calling to go where we are needed most. I know it will be difficult—that we will meet many obstacles in a rough-and-tumble mining town—but," she concluded with a wry smile, "I think that God wants to keep us on our toes!"

Walter Catlin and Timmy Belcher were the drivers of a second wagon, which followed the one driven by Ramón and which contained provisions for the men and the nuns for the journey to San Antonio. Earlier that day, Walter had had to resist Connie's entreaties to go with him then and there, instead of coming to join him—as had been planned—later in the year. But Walter had told her that the winter was long and difficult in the Rockies, and that there would be no real accommodations for any family until at least the middle of summer. "By then, honey, everything will be ready for us. We'll have our own house for you and Henry, and it'll be a better way to start life in a new place, just as you want. Please don't make it hard for me—God knows I don't want to be away from you any longer then I have to. But what we're doing now, going to that silver mine, Connie, is going to mean a brand-new life for all of us. I'll be able to give you and Henry all the things I've dreamed of being able to. Please don't cry, honey, or you'll make it even harder for me—that's my girl! I'll write you, I promise."

With that, he turned away and started toward his wagon, suppressing his sorrow at parting from this young woman who had almost miraculously come into his life, a life he had thought forever blighted but now seemed so full of promise.

The old prospector, Frank Scolby, who would ride beside Ramón, ambled over to the wagon and greeted the occupants. When he had been told that he wouldn't be riding on horseback, he had indignantly protested, "Shucks, I'm still purty spry for my age, I'll have you know!" To this, Lucien Edmond had good-naturedly retorted, "That's very true, Mr. Scolby. Just the same, a week on horseback can be an ordeal even for the youngest of our vaqueros, and now that you're going to be our partner, it's to our own interest to make things easy for you. And besides," seeing the old man's face fall, he quickly added, "you'll have ample opportunity to prove how capable you are, because you'll be spelling Ramón driving his wagon." This considerably mollified the old prospector, and so he now mounted the wagon and seated himself beside Ramón in reasonably good spirits, even glancing rather proudly around to make certain that his passengers observed how erect he could be in the seat.

Manuel Olivera and Felipe Sanchez, who had accompanied Ramón to Colorado last year to convey the herd to Maxwell Grantham, had also volunteered for the Leadville journey. They were experienced men; they had been exposed to hardship, and each, in his turn, had told Ramón that since young Hugo Bouchard had helped save his life by the medical attention the young man had given, he felt he owed it to the Bouchard family to contribute to the success of this new venture. Four other vaqueros who had gone on the drive last year—including Felipe Sanchez's close friend, Narciso Duarte— had also been selected by Ramón to go on this trip, for each of them had shown courage and resourcefulness in handling the stampede and driving off Jeb Cornish's bushwhackers. All of them would be well armed, with Colts and Spencer carbines and rifles, for neither Lucien Edmond nor Ramón had illusions of there being less danger in Leadville than in driving a herd of cattle from Texas on to Kansas or Colorado. After reading the newspaper that Grantham had sent, it was obvious that Leadville was comprised of many unscrupulous characters along with the hard-working men who hoped to strike it rich.

Robert Markey exited from the barn, leading his mare, Jenny. As he stopped to tighten the saddle cinch, his mongrel, Tramp, came furiously barking from around the side of the bunkhouse. He jumped up on his master and wagged his tail, wanting to go along.

"No, Tramp, boy, not this time. You've got to stay behind and look after the people on the ranch. Besides, old boy, I don't think they'd let you on either the stagecoach or the train. No, you be good now, and you guard this ranch and all the people on it." He squatted down and, cupping the dog's long muzzle, stared into Tramp's eyes. The mongrel whined once, then quieted. Robert rose and called over to Lucas, who was crossing the dusty yard, "He likes you, Lucas, so if he tries to start running after me, would you call him back and be firm about it?"

"I sure will, Robert. Here, Tramp, you stay right beside me. That's a good dog." Lucas bent down and hugged the dog to his leg, repeatedly stroking the mongrel's head. Robert quickly climbed into the saddle of his mare and, forcing himself not to look back, rode off to catch up with the others.

Tramp whined and looked anxiously up at Lucas, who shook his head and said, "No, Tramp. You stay."

All the same, the dog's eyes did not leave Robert Markey till he and the others were almost invisible in the distance. Only then did Tramp lie down with his head between his paws and a sad look in his large brown eyes.

Seven

The first leg of this journey up to Leadville was accomplished in a leisurely fashion and took a week. Happily, the rains had stopped, but the air was unseasonably cool for March in Texas. The nuns—Sister Martha and the other three sisters—insisted on preparing the meals each day, a decision that delighted all the men. Prefacing each meal, Sister Martha said grace for the bounty that God set before them. The easy acceptance by the nuns of this primitive camping out greatly impressed their male escorts. The women never once complained of the jostling, rugged wagon ride, nor of the frigid nights that they spent huddled around the campfire bundled in blankets for warmth.

Perhaps Robert Markey was the traveler most aware of the influence of these gentle, dedicated women, who accepted without a murmur the dour hardships of riding over desolate miles of uninhabited prairie and plain. On the evening before they reached San Antonio, after bedding down his faithful mare, Jenny, for the night, he strode to the campfire, where

Sister Martha was ingeniously improvising a stew out of strips of beef jerky, potatoes, wild onions, and some wild carrots that she had found in an overgrown garden patch near an abandoned farmhouse some twenty miles south of San Antonio. "May I help you, Sister?" he politely inquired.

"That's kind of you, Mr. Markey, but you know that old saying about too many cooks spoiling the broth—or in this case, stew," was her grinning retort.

He laughed with her, somewhat surprised that this woman of the church had a worldly sense of humor.

"Let me suggest, Mr. Markey," she went on, "if you like, you may stir the stew while I make the coffee."

He took the wooden ladle and began to stir it energetically.

"Oh, no, not so fast! We're making dinner, not running a race!" Sister Martha laughed again, a rich, easy laugh.

"Excuse me—I guess I'm not very good at some things."

"But, from what I hear, you're very good at others. Don't be so hard on yourself, Mr. Markey," was Sister Martha's soft reply. "Are you, perhaps, of our faith?"

"No, Sister." Robert stook his head with a small smile. "My folks were Methodists, and my wife, Marcy—" he paused, wincing at the memory of how his young wife and baby had died the previous year, "—I guess—well, we were sort of easygoing when it came to religion. We just believed in God—tried not to hurt people and to do as much good as we could."

Sister Martha, who was ladling coffee into a battered tin pot, stopped and looked over at the young man. Cocking her head slightly to one side, she studied his face intently. "Our faith is very little different, you know. Dear Friar Bartoloméo told me about your terrible loss, and how you had come to the hacienda in search of Señor Hernandez to pay him back a debt. You are a good man, Mr. Markey. Like you, I, too, have done much wandering searching for peace. I am English-born and came with my father to Ohio after my mother's death. There I met and married a Spaniard from Madrid who had emigrated to this country, and because he was Catholic, I converted to his faith. He decided to go to Mexico City, and I followed him. He died three years later, as the result of a senseless duel—a duel that I witnessed—and I joined the convent in Mexico City. Now in my old age, as mother superior of these good sisters, we help the poor and the needy, and we seek no other reward except the work of our dear Lord upon this earth. By this, I am comforted in my loss—as by now you must surely be in yours through your unstinting efforts."

Tears welled into Robert Markey's eyes, and he bowed his head, unable to speak. The kindly words of this gentle, elderly nun had inadvertently revived all the bitter anguish, all the guilt, that he had experienced over the death of his wife and child. She saw this, and deeply moved, she put a hand to his shoulder and murmured, "Do not torture yourself. That you can still feel so strongly shows a kindness in your heart. Do not feel that you have sinned, for I am certain that our Lord and Judge—blessed be His name—looks kindly upon you. You did your best. You cannot scourge yourself eternally for what did or did not happen. You are of mortal clay, as all of us are, instruments of God, who created us. Take comfort in that."

Robert bit his lip and nodded. He brushed the backs of his hands over his eyes and then took up the large wooden spoon, and began to stir the stew slowly, as she had suggested. Finally, in a choked voice, he murmured, "God bless you, Sister."

"And you also, Mr. Markey."

The travelers planned to stay a day and a night in San Antonio, for Lucien Edmond wished to give the nuns an opportunity to rest after this most arduous part of the journey. Once refreshed, the party would board the first of two successive stagecoaches for the long journey to the Santa Fe railhead.

It was here in San Antonio that they would have to split into two groups, for each stagecoach carried a maximum of nine passengers. Lucien Edmond and the four nuns would ride with three of the men on the earlier stage, and Ramón and his group would follow on the coach due to leave six hours later. They would not all meet again until they had reached Lamy. To ensure that there would be no delays, Lucien Edmond wired ahead to El Paso and reserved the two El Paso-to-Lamy stages for his party three days hence.

The four nuns went immediately to register the party at a comfortable, clean hotel. Meanwhile, the vaqueros took the

51

two wagons and the horses to the stable, where they would be kept until Eddie Gentry had some men retrieve them in about a week. Lucien Edmond and Ramón planned to visit their bank to withdraw sufficient funds for pay, stage and rail tickets, and hotel or boardinghouse accommodations for the entourage. They would also procure a letter of credit that could be drawn on the leading Leadville bank. With it, they could engage an assayer and miners and withdraw the funds needed for building the smelter that would melt down the silver to be excavated from Frank Scolby's mine.

As Lucien Edmond and Ramón mounted the steps of the bank, they each gave a quick glance up at the impressive fluted columns, which were made of marble, as was the entire facade. Minutes after entering, they were ushered into the spacious office of the bank's president, an energetic, personable man in his early forties. His name was William McKechnie, and Lucien Edmond was impressed by him because McKechnie had taken pains to acquaint himself personally with all the customers of the bank, immersing himself in their affairs, so that he could provide sound advice for investments and the disbursement of their capital.

Lucien Edmond explained why they had come, and William McKechnie immediately began composing the letter of credit. As he drew it up, McKechnie volunteered, "You know, Mr. Bouchard, I've heard there are five banks in Leadville, and that they are overrun with deposits of people pouring into the town. From what I've been told, real estate seems to be as profitable a venture as the silver they're taking out of the mines. Why, corner lots are selling for as much as ten thousand dollars! I sincerely hope you won't have to spend all of your profits on dwellings for you and your men. Of course, I'm sure that land some distance from the town— exclusive of the mine regions needless to say—is considerably less expensive."

"Your comments interest me, Mr. McKechnie, since my partners and our men are thinking of bringing their families there in the summer, once we have our mining operation underway and things are working out smoothly." Lucien Edmond glanced at Ramón as if for confirmation.

"The impression I get of Leadville from the newspapers, Mr. Bouchard," the bank manager declared, "is that it may be an excellent place in which to make money in a hurry—but hardly the sort of place I myself would want to bring up a family and children. At least not now. It's a city that never sleeps. The theaters close at three in the morning, and all the dance houses and liquor shops never shut.''

"Hmm. I must say, you've given me food for thought," Lucien Edmond mused.

"Well, I didn't mean to influence you in any way—you should judge it for yourself. However, I'm sure *you'll* be pleased to know, Mr. Hernandez, that you won't run into any racial prejudice there. Unfortunately, that same benevolent attitude doesn't extend to the Indians and Chinese."

"That's becoming all too common," Lucien Edmond interjected. "I had heard from a relative of mine that in such areas as San Francisco and Seattle, the Chinese are looked upon as we might look upon criminals. It's such a shame." He shook his head. "I hadn't realized this attitude had spread eastward."

"That's as it is, Mr. Bouchard," William McKechnie averred. "It happens that one of our customers—a man with considerable capital to invest—spent two weeks up there recently with the idea of backing one of Leadville's magical silver mines. Well, Mr. Bouchard, this customer brought me back the latest copy of the Leadville *Chronicle*. The paper went into all-too-gruesome detail about the deaths of three Chinese laundrymen who had gone there looking for work. They were kidnapped the night of their arrival, shot to pieces, and thrown down an abandoned prospect hole. They were just found—apparently many months after their brutal murders."

"What an abomination!" Ramón muttered, and shook his head, looking over to his partner, who sat completely still in silent rage.

Lucien Edmond brought himself out of his reverie and sighed. "Well, sir, I'm indebted to you for helping us out with our transactions. And what you've told me about Leadville will make me perhaps a bit more critical than I have been until now. We'll certainly be in no hurry to move up the women and children until we ascertain for ourselves that it's safe. Incidentally, we have with us four nuns. They plan to establish a school and a shelter to help the poor and the needy in Leadville. I was told that they won't experience any annoyances by the townspeople."

"I don't think you have to worry about them, Mr. Bouchard.

53

There's a rough gallantry in towns like that, from what I've heard." He rose and stretched out his right hand, first to Ramón and then to Lucien Edmond. "At any rate, you have my warmest wishes for your good fortune there. And I'd like to say that I personally value the privilege of doing business with both of you and your other partners on Windhaven Range."

"You're very kind to say that. Well then, Mr. McKechnie, if I need any additional help from you, may I telegraph you from Leadville?"

"Of course. You may be certain I'll give you a personal and swift reply, Mr. Bouchard. A safe and pleasant journey to all of you."

With the comfort of the nuns still uppermost in his mind, Lucien Edmond Bouchard was glad that there was a scheduled stopover in El Paso before the second leg of the stagecoach trip continued on to Lamy. The first stage from San Antonio had been extraordinarily bumpy and wearisome for Sister Martha and her three companions; indeed, she remarked somewhat whimsically to Lucien Edmond that it was a pity they could not have continued their journey in the same wagon that had taken them from Windhaven Range to San Antonio, as that method of transportation had been much more restful. The road between San Antonio and El Paso was none too good at best, and it had been further impaired by the torrential rain that had unexpectedly swept Texas just before the small caravan had begun its journey.

The stopover proved to be profitable: The affable proprietor of the adobe brick hotel where they were staying told Lucien Edmond that he was anxious to obtain a source of prime beef for the two restaurants he operated, one in the hotel itself and another just off the main street of town. Before he left El Paso the next morning, Lucien Edmond signed a contract to provide one hundred prime steers at a price of twenty dollars per head, to be delivered in two shipments—one in May and the second in October. Aside from being a welcome omen for the journey on to distant Colorado, it established another market for Windhaven Range.

Lucien Edmond sent off a telegram to Eddie Gentry to apprise him of this new market. He instructed him to pick

54

fifty prime head, according to the hotel owner's specifications, and to have them delivered by the middle of May. As he settled his bill, Lucien Edmond informed his new client of his telegram to his partner. He was told in return that if, as the proprietor hoped, business continued to improve and he found it profitable to open a third restaurant, the order would be increased.

Lucien Edmond shook hands with the proprietor to seal their agreement, then picked up his valise and ambled across to the stage depot. The others had already boarded the stagecoach and were patiently waiting, tightly packed into the seats. Although the stage was large, still three of the men had to ride on top—two in a seat in the rear of the coach, while Timmy Belcher rode next to the driver.

The seats were slightly padded, but this was not enough to keep the sharp jolts and bumps from being felt. And heavy though the springs were on the overland stages, still they could not hope to smooth out the ruts and rocks in the roads.

The stagecoach journey from El Paso to the Santa Fe railhead proved to be even more taxing to the four nuns than the first parts of the journey from Windhaven Range. The road led over arid gullies and boulder- and gravel-strewn trails for many miles, and the bumpy, dusty ride was broken only by several brief stops at depot stations, where the food was barely edible and the prices outrageous. Yet the spirits of Sister Martha and her three companions remained indomitable and cheerful.

The two vaqueros who rode with the nuns were both pious Catholics, and they went out of their way to be helpful. They also made a point of asking the sisters to pray for them and their families, and for the success of the new enterprise. For all of the men, taking this trip was a welcome respite from the tedious ranching chores and of driving cattle hundreds of miles, always being on the alert for unforeseen dangers imposed upon them, not only by rustlers and thieves, but also by the unpredictable elements.

At the stagecoach stop just before Lamy, where the Windhaven party broke their journey for an unpalatable lunch, twenty-four-year-old Pablo Bensares left the depot to go for a walk. When he returned, he was clutching a bunch of sage blossoms, which he bashfully presented to Sister Martha. "I want to say *gracias* for all you have done for us, *Sor* Martha.''

The old nun's face was radiant with pleasure at this unexpected gesture. She bent to inhale the fragrance of the purple sage, smiled at the young vaquero, and graciously nodded. ''It was thoughtful of you, Pablo. I will share these with Sisters Concepción, Margarita, and Luz. I will tell them that it is from all of the *hombres* who guard us so well and look to our comfort.''

''It is my pleasure, *Sor* Martha.'' Pablo Bensares inclined his head and made the sign of the cross. Then, very gallantly, he insisted on helping each of the nuns into the stagecoach. The weatherbeaten old driver sat impatiently tapping his foot, for the stops were precisely timed, and there had been a delay of five minutes beyond the allotted schedule of this stop, the final one before the Santa Fe railroad connection.

They reached Lamy early in the afternoon. The bone-weary passengers alighted from the stage, shook the dust out of their clothes, and stretched their cramped muscles. After hauling down all of their luggage that was strapped to the top of the stagecoach, the tired travelers crossed the street to the one hotel, where they registered for rooms for the night. Lucien Edmond secured rooms as well for the men who would be coming in on the later stage—due to arrive in about six hours.

As Lucien Edmond, the four nuns, Timmy Belcher, Pablo Bensares, and Felipe Sanchez sat rocking in worn but comfortable chairs on the hotel's front porch early that evening, the stagecoach from El Paso came to a startling halt just a few feet away. Lucien Edmond leaped to his feet and ran down the wooden steps just as the door of the coach opened and Ramón Hernandez alighted. Lucien Edmond laughed as Ramón stretched his cramped muscles and groaned. ''You have my sympathy, Ramón,'' he said. ''It has taken me almost these last six hours to work out my own kinks!''

Frank Scolby's cackling laugh came welling out of the stage's interior. The sound was shortly followed by his grinning face, as he looked from Ramón to Lucien Edmond and back again. ''Don't know what's wrong with you young fellas,'' he declared. ''Hell, compared to some trips I've taken, that was like bein' rocked in a baby's buggy!''

Narciso Duarte leaped down from where he had been riding

next to the driver and called up to Santiago Dornado and Diego Martinez, who were seated up top in the rear of the stagecoach. "Hand me down the luggage a piece at a time, *amigos*. And just remember—the faster we unload the stage, the faster we'll be able to climb the stairs to our rooms and collapse for the night!" The two men answered him with shouts of appreciative laughter and quickly began handing down the battered cases.

Joe Duvray and Robert Markey joined in to help, and soon all the luggage had been transferred inside to the cramped lobby of the small hotel. The nine men then picked up their respective belongings and carried them to their rooms. They took a few minutes to wash the grime from their hands and faces, changed out of their dusty clothes, and joined the members of the Windhaven party who had traveled in on the first stage.

Reunited, the seventeen people went into the hotel's dining room, where they quickly filled it to capacity. The food in the hotel's dining room was hardly exceptional, but after the inedible fare on the journey from El Paso, it was like manna from God. Even the sisters suppressed giggles at the way they found themselves wolfing down the food, as if they had not eaten in days.

Refreshed by the food, the Windhaven party slowly made their way up the stairs to their rooms, bidding one another a good night's sleep.

Sister Martha called to Lucien Edmond and Ramón as they stood in the floral carpeted hallway outside their door. "Gentlemen," she said, "I want to thank you for everything you have done for us. I know you've been concerned about our welfare, but I assure you that we are tougher than we look— and we have gone through many harder ordeals than this one. I just want to put your minds at ease, for I know that you have been worried about us and the reception we will get in Leadville. I thank you again for your concern, but I have faith that God is directing us there. Good night, dear friends." She swiftly closed the door behind her before either Lucien Edmond or Ramón could reply.

The train was not scheduled to leave until noontime, so the band of travelers had the luxury of sleeping late and then having a long, leisurely breakfast. At the stroke of twelve on the clock in the town square, they boarded the Santa Fe line for the run north to El Moro. There, the conductor cordially informed Lucien Edmond, they would transfer to a Denver & Rio Grande train that would eventually take them to the end of the line at Cañon City. "It's about a hundred miles from there northwest to Leadville, Mr. Bouchard," the conductor went on. "Stagecoaches leave pretty regular, though—at least once a day. Folks say it won't be long before the line runs direct to Leadville. You goin' there for the silver?"

"Just to see what's left," Lucien Edmond bantered.

The conductor shook his head and chuckled, "Won't be much by now, I'll warrant, what with all the thousands of folks pouring in there. Well, we do our best to make everyone comfortable on the Atchison, Topeka & Santa Fe, Mr. Bouchard. Hope you all enjoy your trip."

For Lucien Edmond, at any rate, the scenic splendor of the landscape between Lamy and El Moro, Colorado, over the eight-thousand-foot-high Raton Pass, compensated for the physical hardships of their journey. It also confirmed his implicit belief in the convenience that would ensue with the growth of the American railroad system. Soon, the long cattle drives would be eliminated, and ranchers like himself would be able to devote more time to improving their spreads and their stock. And personally, it would ensure the apportionment of a good deal of his time to the venture that awaited them at Leadville.

At El Moro, the party changed to the Denver & Rio Grande Railroad for the next leg of the journey to Pueblo, Colorado.

As the train chugged into Pueblo, a conductor appeared in the aisles, calling out the stop. Lucien Edmond walked up to the man and exchanged a few words.

"There'll be a few hours' delay while our train takes on water, coal, and supplies, the conductor tells me," Lucien Edmond said to Ramón when he reached their seat. "I think we'll all feel better if we stretch our legs a spell. Look—there's a hawker over there at the side of the station, and it looks like his tray is piled with sandwiches and coffee and the like. I think I'll go get the nuns something to eat, then we can all get off the train and walk about to see what sort of country we're in, before the train goes on to Cañon City."

"Fine, Lucien Edmond. I think I'll join you and pick up a cheroot or two for myself. After the long trip we've had, I'm going to indulge in that minor vice."

"I think it's a very minor vice, indeed, Ramón," Lucien Edmond chuckled. "I'll go tell the sisters about the lunch." As he walked up the aisle, he stopped and clapped a passenger on the shoulder. "Well, Joe," he said to his other partner, "this is impressive scenery. Some might say that by contrast, our flat Texas ranch land is monotonous."

"I'd have to agree in part," Joe Duvray declared with a nod. "But because I'm Southern born and bred, I feel I gotta stick up for Texas. Still, I will say I've never seen so many beautiful mountains. And the fellas who laid all the track down to Lamy sure earned their keep—and my guess is it wasn't a heck of a lot."

"You're right about that. I understand the Leadville miners are unhappy about their wages, too." Lucien Edmond proffered. "Mr. McKechnie at the San Antonio bank told me that last year the miners were talking about organizing a union—there were about eight thousand of them working twelve-hour shifts and earning about three dollars a day. When you figure that everything has to be shipped into a camp town like Leadville, that three dollars doesn't go very far. It's probably filled with speculators who gouge the daylights out of people who have to work there for a living."

"That's certainly true, Lucien Edmond." Ramón had come up beside him and nodded in agreement. "And I was going to mention to you that before we start hiring a crew of miners, we agree in advance to pay them decent wages. Maybe that'll be one way that we, as newcomers, can avoid trouble."

"You're absolutely right about that—a very good idea, Ramón. Well, I'll go run my errand for the nuns. Take all the time you want to look around. That fresh, cool mountain air is certainly welcome, after being cooped up on stagecoaches and trains all these weeks." He uttered a deprecating little laugh. "If we hadn't had the good sisters with us, I'd have almost proposed that we ride all the way from Windhaven Range to Leadville—but it would have taken a lot longer, and we'd have had to leave earlier, before the weather was good." He went down the aisle and paused a few moments at the back, where the four nuns sat, and conferred with Sister Martha. She thanked him for his thoughtfulness and gratefully accepted the offer of sandwiches and coffee for herself and her companions, then he briskly walked down the steps of the railroad car.

Having overheard Lucien Edmond's conversation with Sister Martha, Pablo Bensares ran after his boss and volunteered to help Lucien Edmond bring back the sandwiches and the coffee. "Come along then, *amigo*, and breathe in this incredible mountain air. It's one thing we don't have back at the hacienda."

"That's true, *señor patrón*. When I was a little boy, my parents took me to Mexico City, and the air was much like this. I have read that these mountains are as high as those are."

"Yes, you're right, Pablo. Well then, let's go see if the food here in Pueblo is better than most of what we've been offered at those stagecoach depots along the way."

The train on which Lucien Edmond, his men, and the nuns had come had been routed onto a siding about two hundred yards north of the main station. There, too, was a westbound Santa Fe train that had come in from Kansas half an hour earlier. Lucien Edmond glanced back toward the trains and said to the young vaquero, "I guess we'll have plenty of company on the way to Cañon City, Pablo. They're starting to transfer a great deal of baggage from the Santa Fe train onto the Denver line. I guess we're not the only ones who are going to Leadville in search of silver."

"So it would seem, señor. I think there will be many who will never find it, and who will end up very poor and then very sorry that they came so far from their homes," Pablo pensively replied.

"You're quite a philosopher for your age, Pablo. And of course, you're right. A pity, too. My feeling has always been that you have to work hard to earn what you get, but far too many people these days just want to strike it rich without any work at all—just by expressing the wish of it. My father and his grandfather wouldn't have had any patience with notions like that. Well now, here's the man with the *comida*." He tapped the hawker on the shoulder. "We'd like to buy some of your wares. What sort of sandwiches do you have?"

"Ham, cheese, and sausage; best you'll find anywhere in Pueblo, mister."

"This being Friday, I think the sisters would prefer cheese," Lucien Edmond said, half to himself. "Four cheese sandwiches, if you please, and four coffees with just a bit of milk

60

and sugar. Do you have a little box I can put those things in to carry back onto the train?''

"Sure thing, mister. There you are; that'll be a buck and two bits.''

Joe Duvray and Ramón Hernandez soon wandered off the train to stretch their legs. Barely glancing up, they walked to the end of the siding along which their train was stationed, engrossed in their discussion of what was to be done when they arrived in Leadville. Ramón was concerned about where they all would stay for the first few nights, until he and his partners could arrange more permanent lodgings. "As I recall, you said the mine is just outside Leadville, Joe.'' Ramón then continued, "I suppose it would be easy to put up temporary shacks and furnish them just comfortably enough for the time being. But since it's a boomtown, it's bound to be somewhat on the seamy side, what with all kinds of people flocking there in droves. I wouldn't want the sisters to be quartered in a disreputable neighborhood, *de seguro*.''

Joe suggested, "Perhaps there's a decent boardinghouse. Maybe the conductor on the train knows something about Leadville and can make some recommendations—I'll ask him.''

"Good idea.'' Ramón yawned, flexed his arms and legs, and then breathed in deeply. "It feels good to walk about a bit.'' He yawned again.

"Well, Ramón,'' Joe observed, "this is a kind of symbolic stop here, in a way. I mean, here we are on the railroad siding, waiting to go on to something that might be bigger then even Windhaven Range. And both of us can look back and remember how hard it was at the start. You crossed the border, a penniless man who had gotten mixed up with a bandit who proclaimed himself the liberator of Mexico. Me, I came out of the war with nothing much left except my friend, Andy Haskins, and now look where he is in life, too—after being a state senator, no less. It makes a man mighty humble, Ramón.''

"That is for certain, Joe,'' Ramón softly agreed. "Now you and I are the most fortunate of men. Partners to a man we both respect and like. I'm married to his sister, and you to your Margaret. With children to make it worth our while to work all that much harder for the future, so that they can have every opportunity in this growing country. I thank *El Señor Dios* every night before I go to bed.''

''I do the same, Ramón. Let's walk back, now. I'd like to see the inside of that main station. Maybe I can pick up a paper that'll give us some more up-to-date news about Leadville.''

''Good idea. I'll go along with you.''

Joe Duvray and three of the other men had gone to the baggage car to make certain that all of their luggage was still safely secured and wouldn't erroneously be unloaded before being carried on to Cañon City. While this was being done, Robert Markey, feeling restless and wanting some solitude after the long trip, slowly stepped down the steps of the railroad car and onto the brick-paved walk that led from the siding to the station. Out of impulse, he crossed the tracks to where the westbound Santa Fe train sat waiting for the completion of the luggage transfer of those passengers who wished to switch for the run to Cañon City. He walked easily. His Stetson was tilted to the left, and his holstered Colt slapped against his thigh with each step. He walked with a wide-eyed wonder, surreptitiously watching the hundreds of different people milling about. They were much like him, but still he felt curiously out of place. Perhaps it was because he had never been so far northwest before in all his life. And yet, he felt that there was an important and impending reason for his being here with the others—why, he could not have fully explained, even if he had been compelled to do so. Part of it was that, alongside Ramón Hernandez, he felt himself more capable of repaying the debt that had become almost an obsession. He knew—and Sister Martha had come close to guessing—his real motivation in accompanying this group to Leadville: He believed that his life could not really begin again, that he would feel an ever powerful sense of omission and remission, until he fulfilled that debt. And in his mind, it was not yet fulfilled.

He thought back to the happy days he had known since arriving at Windhaven Range, of his friendship with Eddie Gentry, Walter Catlin, and the vaquero Nacio Lorcas. Deep inside, he envied them: All of them were happily married, with adoring wives and children—or the expectation of children—who would one day carry on their own hopes and dreams to fruition. What he had lost in Marcy and his daughter would forever weigh heavily on his heart. Yet for all the immediacy of the pain he felt, it seemed almost an eternity ago that he had buried them and then set a course to find the one man in the last few years who had been kind to him.

He came onto the main platform of the Pueblo station, hands in his breeches' pockets, now contemplating with almost intense absorption the passengers who were descending at sporadic intervals from the Santa Fe train and making their way across the tracks toward the siding where the Denver & Rio Grande awaited them.

An elderly gray-haired woman, her hair styled in an elaborate poof of curls topped by a flowery, wide-brimmed hat, moved alongside a corpulent man wearing a bowler and a dogged expression on his florid, heavily jowled face. He was carrying a heavy valise in one hand and, in the other, a bird cage with a goldfinch. The woman, with a shrill acerbity to her high-pitched voice, turned back to the corpulent man with a petulant scowl and scolded him. "Now mind you, Abner, don't you jostle little Dickiebird. He's got feelings."

"Yes, Agnes," the man grumbled with a hangdog expression and a stealthy moue, which fortunately for him, his embattled spouse did not perceive as she moved, almost waddling in her girth, toward the steps of one of the passenger cars. A porter attempted to help her up, but she shook off his hand, indignantly drew herself up, and shrilly chided him.

"No need for that, young man. I'm quite able to care for myself. Have the goodness to keep your hand off me. Come along, Abner! Don't dawdle, as you always do!"

Robert chuckled to himself and shook his head. He sympathized with the henpecked husband, who had little to look forward to in tenderness and compassion. He suddenly straightened, almost unconsciously, and smiled broadly: At least Marcy had never quarreled with him. They had never had a harsh word between them. Even when they were so desperately poor, at the time Ramón Hernandez had saved him from being lynched and given him provisions and the mare, Marcy had remained confident because of his love and devotion for

63

her and their baby. That was something this trio would never have. He felt his eyes blur with tears and almost impatiently blinked to clear them—yet the warm feeling persisted. In this strange, unknown place, where there was nothing to hold or attract him, he felt suddenly more at peace than he had in months.

He saw a fellow in a loud checkered suit wearing a bowler hat tilted at a rakish angle and carrying a large valise. He was talking animatedly to a tall, skinny man who wore overalls and a miner's cap. The fellow was obviously a drummer of merchandise, no doubt bound for Leadville to capitalize on the increased population, potential customers for his unidentified wares. Well, that was one way of making a living—inducing people who didn't really want to buy anything to part with their money—simply because you made the prospect so alluring they couldn't refuse. Yet to Robert, that was a shoddy business. It was no substitute for honest hard work; and it provided no opportunity for improvement of one's character. All one needed was a colossal ego. Robert chuckled to himself, this time ironically: That was one thing he would always lack, but he felt no regrets over that deficiency.

Now he saw a tall, bony woman in her early fifties, bedecked with a beaver fur around her neck and intricately draped dress, yet wearing dusty black boots. Beside her trotted a young girl, staggering under the weight of two heavy valises. He overheard the older woman caustically remark, "Now be careful, Millicent, dear; these are the latest fashions from New York, and you must be careful not to drop the valises. Once I open my shop near the Grand Hotel, I'll have all the important, wealthy people in Leadville buying my designs. Then, perhaps, I may raise your wages—if you're a very good girl!"

"Yes, thank you, Miss Elston," the drably dressed young woman humbly responded.

Behind her came two bearded men, one black-haired, the other red. Robert was repulsed by the ugly scar on the black-bearded man's face. The other man, stocky with a surly look on his face, was muttering something to his companion. A few paces behind them, a wiry, clean-shaven, black-haired younger man sauntered idly along, pausing to button up his jacket in an attempt to conceal the holster belt holding two Colts, one on each lean hip.

They moved ahead of the milliner and her meek assistant to the car just behind the locomotive, where the engineer and his fireman were working to build up steam for the remainder of the journey to Cañon City after coming down from Denver. The two bearded men hastily clambered aboard, but the younger, clean-shaven man stopped, adjusted his jacket again, looked warily around, and then prepared to climb aboard the railway car. Just as he was about to do so, a small terrier, perhaps strayed away from its owner, came running across the platform and up to the young passenger and began to bark furiously at him.

Robert took a step forward, thinking of his dog, Tramp. The terrier bounded with energy, barking loudly and repeatedly, drawing back as if to spring and then barking again. The black-haired man turned, went back down the steps, and snarled at it, "Stop it, you goddamn mutt!" And, when the dog kept up its incessant barking, the man kicked out with his right foot. Catching the terrier in the side, he sent it fleeing with an agonized yipe. Then, still glowering after it, he scrambled aboard the railroad car and disappeared from view.

Robert felt his heart pounding angrily, and his fists were clenched. He moved toward the terrier, who gave itself a hearty shake, turned, and looked back toward the train, and gave another, almost indignant yipe, then ran back whence it had come and was lost from view.

"Damn that man's soul, anyhow. What a despicable thing to do," Robert muttered to himself, and then, with a shrug, walked back to his car. All the passengers were boarding the train now, and he could see the conductor conferring with the engineer, who had come down out of the engine cab. It would soon be time to start for Cañon City.

Eight

On the morning before Mardi Gras, Laure Bouchard tipped a porter to go to the St. James Hotel and leave an envelope addressed to Leland Kenniston there. The message inside read:

Dear Leland,

I have come to share Mardi Gras with you, but you must first find me. Perhaps we shall meet as strangers.

Since it is my fondest hope that we *shall* meet, I will give you these instructions. Look for a woman in a black domino with an ermine cape. She plans to attend King Rex's ball Tuesday night at the ballroom in the Washington Artillery Hall.

However, since she does not care to be accosted by a mere plebian whom she has never before met—unless, by chance, he is gallant and interesting enough to win her fancy for this one night only—she suggests that you tell Lopasuta at once what costume you intend to don for the occasion. He, in turn, will communicate with the lady in question who is,

Your affectionate Laure

After an early breakfast, Laure, Lopasuta, and Geraldine took a carriage to the levee to welcome the arrival of King Rex in his carnival capital. This custom had begun four years ago, after an elaborate series of stories in the *Times-Picayune* described Rex's trip from his mythical kingdom.

Reaching the wharf, the threesome hurried to join the milling crowd. In the harbor, there were flag-decorated boats and ships joining in a water pageant of welcome, as everyone awaited the arrival of the *Rob't E. Lee*, the riverboat that was bringing Rex to his "kingdom." Finally, the famous vessel steamed into view, amidst the booming of cannon and the screaches of steam whistles. As Rex himself descended the gangplank, acknowledging the cheers of the crowd, he was met by a welcoming committee. Then followed a parade through the streets, in which Rex, astride a spirited bay stallion, was accompanied by a military guard of honor. He was followed by the *Boeuf Gras*—in reality the decoy bull of the New Orleans stockyards—then members of the Pack, maskers representing the fifty-two playing cards in the deck (since gambling was one of New Orleans's most popular pastimes), and finally, over five thousand maskers, either on foot or in groups on wagons and in carriages.

Laure, Lopasuta, and Geraldine stood on the sidewalk on Chartres Street, where they had had their carriage take them after the arrival of Rex, and watched the parade. There were bands of all sizes playing, each of them intoning the official Mardi Gras tune. It was a tune that had first been sung by Lydia Thompson in the burlesque "Bluebeard" back East, where the Russian Grand Duke Alexis Rominov Aleksandrovich had heard it and liked it. When the Grand Duke had visited New Orleans for the Mardi Gras of 1872, this tune had been transposed into march time and dedicated to him. Henceforth, it became the musical pièce de résistance at each carnival.

Laure laughed gaily as some of the maskers sang the choruses: "If ever I cease to love, may oysters have legs and cows lay eggs . . . May little dogs wag their tails in front, if ever I cease to love."

That evening, Laure dined with Lopasuta and Geraldine at Antoine's. The young lawyer brought with him a message he had picked up when he had stopped briefly at his office—a message for Laure from Leland Kenniston.

Her eyes shining with happiness, lovely golden-haired Laure opened the envelope, unfolded the sheet, and read:

To the *Princesse Lointaine:*

Faraway princess, New Orleans is blessed to have you journey here for Mardi Gras. At the ball, you will find every attentive cavalier ready to do homage to your beauty and your grace. But there will be one—humbler than the rest, for he is a member of no nobility except

67

the brotherhood of man—who yearns for at least one dance and one glass of champagne. . . .

You will know him because, for one evening only, he will be a French musketeer—with boots, a sword at his side, a cocked hat with a white plume, and since he wishes no other woman in the world to recognize him, a domino mask.

Till tomorrow night, and I send prayers to the demigod Comus that my dreams of Carnival will be fulfilled.

L.K.

Laure swiftly folded the sheet of paper, tucked it away in the envelope, and thrust it into her purse. She kept her head bowed for a few moments while the flush on her cheeks receded.

"Thank you so much again, dear Lopasuta," she finally said to her adoptive son. "One day, I will tell you why I've insisted on playing this little theatrical role. It—it's much like something that took place in this very city, though not at Mardi Gras. It had to do with the man who adopted you. And now," she said in a light, happy tone, "a toast to you and Geraldine, to your family, and the long, happy years ahead for all of you!"

It was Fat Tuesday, Mardi Gras in New Orleans. Laure Bouchard had spent a sleepless night, despite the luxury of a huge featherbed and pillows filled with the softest down. Although the thick rugs and carpets of the finest weaves augmented even further the silence of the suite that Lopasuta had had reserved for her, the faint noise of revelry came to her from the streets.

She turned restlessly, her mind fecund with memories of an evening in July fourteen years ago . . . an evening that seemed only yesterday. She had hired a hansom cab to drive her to the house on Greeley Street where Luke Bouchard was staying during a sojourn in New Orleans. She had given herself to him then with almost wanton eagerness—yet taunting him that their night of love in no way pledged them to a lasting commitment.

Not long after, when he had valorously confronted a mad dog running after a small boy, killing the dog with his sword cane, Laure had known that Luke Bouchard was a man of steadfast courage and, though an intellectual, capable of a deep-rooted courage that enabled him to risk his life against that which was evil. That single act had demonstrated to her how capable he was of selfless love. Nor was that love possessive or vain; he did not assume that merely because she was a widow, she would easily fall into his arms.

Now, spanning the years that had fallen away, years that had hardly seemed to touch her, she turned her thoughts to Leland Kenniston. Although he was in his forties, he still retained a boyishness, a frank, likable nature that was both romantic and yet practical. From their tryst in New York, she knew him to be a passionate, yet tenderly considerate lover. In all ways, he was assuredly the only man who could satisfy her spiritual and her physical needs.

She had chosen this little charade, not so much to test him, but as a fond reminder of how once she had been won by the man to whom she had pledged her lifelong love and devotion. A man who had been taken from her through his own heroic death while saving the life of the governor. If he had only turned that assassin's derringer an inch or two more away . . .

But such thoughts were morbid and futile, and Luke Bouchard would live always in a separate, secret compartment of her heart and soul. Because Leland Kenniston was who and what he was—so very different from Luke—there should be, there could be, no need for comparison. She smiled to herself in the darkness as again she shifted her head on the pillow, still trying to fall asleep and to dream. And certainly in no way did she regret the caprice that had seized her when she had received his telegram at Windhaven Plantation and out of impulse decided to court him, just as he would court her. Indeed, it would be a test of both of them, and how he responded to it tomorrow night would tell her for certain if they were fated to be wed and to spend the rest of their lives together.

She found it enormously flattering to be desired, knowing how close she was to the milestone of her fortieth year. Yet she sought now to halt the inexorably moving hands of the clock of time. Seeking for one last time, which would forever suffice her in this life, the ecstasy of being wooed by a man she desperately desired.

* * *

The heavens smiled down on King Rex and his "krewe" on this festive Tuesday. The elements seemed to have conspired to bring warm and serenely beautiful weather to the city of New Orleans. The sky was a dazzling blue with just a few picturesque cumulus clouds, and the air was pleasantly warm yet surprisingly dry—without the humidity that came later on in the season. The ingenious Rex had designed a special carnival flag, consisting of a diagonal bar of gold from upper left to lower right, forming an upper green triangle and a lower purple triangle with Rex's own crown in the center. He also issued a series of royal edicts, ordering a half-holiday on this Mardi Gras; all buildings were to be decorated, with the royal flag displayed, and he had set forth on a parchment (copies of which had been nailed to the doors of all public buildings) the order of marching in his parade.

Laure had breakfasted alone in her suite, and Geraldine and Lopasuta came about ten-thirty to wish her the season's greetings and to take her out to see the parade. For this occasion, she wore a periwinkle blue silk dress, and the wide-brimmed, straw hat that she wore perched above her chignon had a matching blue streamer. Pinned to the ribbon at the crown was a cluster of yellow silk flowers.

"How beautiful you are today, Laure. And I would swear that you look younger than I!" Geraldine exclaimed. They stood on the edge of the boardwalk, watching the parade of the mummers in their garish masks carrying their banner and signs, watching the splendor of the ingeniously designed floats. "Oh, what a perfect day it is for Mardi Gras!"

Laure hugged her friend's shoulders, wordlessly sharing her agreement. She then mused aloud, her green eyes warm and tender with reminiscence, "It's almost as if there had never been a war. New Orleans seems exactly as it was in the old, happy days. Oh, I feel so young, renewed, eager. . . ."

Geraldine—with a glance over at Lopasuta, whose attention was riveted to an especially attractive float—softly whispered, "And tonight you'll finally meet him, won't you, dear Laure?"

"Oh, yes! We shall meet like strangers, although we've already exchanged signs that will, I hope, lead us to each other. But perhaps he may not even find me—there are so many visitors here for this holiday!" Laure sighed.

"He'll find you, never fear," Geraldine assured her. Squeezing Laure's hand, she confided, "I'm sure Lopasuta secured an invitation to the ball for Leland, too—which probably wasn't easy, for the demand has been tremendous. But you and Luke gave my husband so much, it's little enough to give you in return. We both wish you much happiness, dear Laure."

"Thank you, Geraldine." Laure turned to the dark-haired young woman, and there were tears glistening on her long lashes. "I've really been blessed with friends like you and Lopasuta. You know," she confided, brightening, "I'm so excited that today I feel almost reborn, like a young girl again, hoping that New Orleans on Mardi Gras will bring the romantic mystery of an unknown, masked suitor who will search me out and want me and me alone—"

"He will, be very sure of that. I know he loves you—he said as much to Lopasuta. Oh, yes, Laure, my husband saw him in his office for about half an hour this morning before we met you. I probably shouldn't be telling you this—but I know it will make you happy. Leland told Lopasuta, 'In all my life, I've never met a woman I loved so much, and if the goddess Venus smiles down on this carnival and favors me, I mean to ask Laure to be my wife—however, you're not to tell her!' Lopasuta repeated it to me word for word, but don't you dare breathe a word of this to Lopasuta! He'd be furious with me! But I just had to tell you; you look so radiant, so full of anticipation and hope—and it's going to happen."

Laure could no longer control her tears, and she hugged Geraldine with a wordless sigh of blissful happiness. Then, recovering herself, she airily declared, "If we keep this up, we'll miss the parade! This year's king has really outdone himself. I've never seen such beautiful floats before, nor such wonderful masks and costumes. Incidentally, Geraldine—do you know what time the ball begins?"

"Shortly before eleven tonight. And of course, it will last until the wee hours. By the way, we'll leave your invitation at the desk for you."

"Thank you so much!" She suddenly yawned and confessed, "I barely slept last night, thinking about this evening. I hope to sleep most of the afternoon and right through to the evening. I want to look my best for—well, you know for whom."

"Yes." Geraldine quickly turned to her husband, who had

now rejoined them. "Darling, aren't these floats just too marvelous? If only we could have weather like this the year around, I'll be so happy here in New Orleans—"

"You mean you aren't, with me?" the tall Comanche teased.

Geraldine gave him a sharp pinch, which made him start. "You're just like all men, Comanche or not! You're fishing for a compliment. Well, all right, yes—I adore you, I'm happy to be here, and I can stand the heat of the city because we have the loveliest house, where we can be alone together whenever we want to be. Will that satisfy your majesty, my own king of Carnival?"

He laughed softly. Drawing her a little aside, he whispered into her ear, and Geraldine giggled suggestively. Laure observed this conspiratorial intimacy and smiled knowingly. She thought that she herself had not known such contentment and happiness since that terrible day, when the news of Luke's martyrdom had been brought to her.

The Knights of Momus, a secret society of influential Creoles organized eight years before, was not to be outdone by their illustrious predecessor, the Mystick Krewe of Comus. They had staged their own parade through the streets of New Orleans, and Laure, watching from her hotel window, was so fascinated by the colorful spectacle and the spirit of revelry that she abandoned her idea of an early afternoon nap and went back outside in order to watch it clearly. As she observed the magnificent floats of Momus, based on the theme of the gods and goddesses of mythology—with loving attention given to the goddess Venus and the god Dionysus (love and wine, appropriate themes indeed for this Mardi Gras festivity!)—she glanced here and there through the crowds of spectators, wondering if she would catch a glimpse of Leland Kenniston. She hoped she would not. For this delicious charade to be played out with its full significance, it was vital that they should first meet in their costumes and masks tonight at the ball—and then pretend to be strangers, each come from a far distance, who would meet by chance and be instantly infatuated with each other.

She was free now. Her widowhood had been dutifully and duly observed, with all the proprieties followed to the letter. If now she lacked one year of being forty, it was all the more reason, she told herself, to allow herself one final youthful caprice, if only to reassure herself that she was still desirable to the man of her choice, a man as discriminating as she was. She was sure that she had found him—and tonight she would know if what all her instincts had already told her was really true.

As the parade slowly wound out of sight, shortly after two o'clock, she finally went back to her suite for a nap. When she wakened, a little after six, she contented herself with a frugal supper of a small shrimp salad and a glass of white wine. Then, still very leisurely, she sat down and wrote a long letter to her son Lucien in Dublin, detailing the pageantry of this Mardi Gras, which more than any previous celebration in this city of her birth, meant so much to her. Nonetheless, she was careful to let no hint of her rising excitement be phrased. Surely Lucien was already sensitive and old enough to guess that she and Leland Kenniston were fond of each other, but until their anticipated union had become a *fait accompli*, there was no need to let her son believe that she had already found a stepfather for him.

Several times during the writing of the letter, she laid down her pen and let her mind drift and reflect. She dwelt, again and again, on the many kindnesses Leland had shown to both her and Lucien, and she was so very glad that her son already admired and respected this man.

By the time she had finished the letter, put it into an envelope, and addressed it, it was time to prepare for the ball.

She slowly walked to the bathroom, where she turned on the taps in the bath—a welcome luxury in this modern hotel. Slipping out of her clothes, she first sprinkled the water with an exquisite scent she had brought with her, then spent the next few minutes in languorous relaxation in the bath. Then, realizing that time was growing short, she climbed out, toweled herself off, and began to dress. After donning sheer silk stockings, she drew a risqué black garter over her right leg, giggling to herself as she did so. She went to the closet and lifted the garnet-colored gown from its hanger. She drew it over her head and reached to the side to fasten the tiny buttons that ran from the waist to the armhole. After straightening the folds, she looked into the mirror and smiled at her

73

reflection. The square-cut neckline was quite décolleté, for she chose to eschew the chemisette that would normally have filled in the gap between the bodice of the dress and her neck.

Sitting at the dressing table, she began applying her make-up. Although she usually would use little more than a touch of rice powder and rouge, tonight was special—tonight would be different. Carefully, she applied the powder and the rouge, then she drew out of the drawer some newly purchased items, as well. She squinted slightly at her face in the mirror, then applied a ring of black kohl to her lower and upper eyelids. She then reddened her lips and, as a final touch, placed a daub of perfume between the cleft of her breasts. *Oh, my! Can I really be doing this?* she thought to herself. *Yes, I certainly can be. And I'm enjoying myself immensely!*

She returned to the closet and took out the "ermine" cloak. She was just about to put it on when she remembered the diadem. Hurrying over to the dressing table again, she carefully draped it over her forehead. The golden metal caught the light, gleaming much like Laure's eyes.

As she stared one last time at her reflection in the mirror, her cheeks aflame, her eyes bright, Laure Bouchard felt a deep, warm tingle of anticipation. To be sure, she and Leland had already been lovers once, in New York, but that delicious memory only served to add fuel to the fire she now felt within her. That night alone had revealed to her more of his nature—of his wanting to give rather than to take and possess—than a dozen conventional meetings could have done.

Certainly Laure was wise enough to appreciate his intense physical desire, knowing that even in the most lofty and ennobling expressions of love, a wholesome and healthy lust is inevitably a prime ingredient, necessary for true sharing and communication. When he had wooed her that night in New York, she had thrilled not so much to his virility, which was undeniable and certainly gratifying, as to the romantic tenderness he had demonstrated toward her. And above all else, he had imparted the sense that he wished her to take command, to prescribe the terms on which she would accept him. Few men, she knew, had that intuitive gift of comprehending that a woman—even in the throes of passion—savors the knowledge that she herself may freely dictate the terms of her sexual surrender, so that by taking the initiative she binds her lover to her, and in no way denies his maleness. Luke Bouchard had been such a man, and Leland Kenniston was one also. As she felt the quickening of her heartbeat and stared at herself one last time in the mirror, she prayed that tonight would bring her the ecstasy which she hoped would be hers from this time forward.

Nine

When Laure Bouchard, covered by the ingenious imitation ermine cloak and her domino mask, swept regally down the stairs, the desk clerk beckoned to her and handed her a heavy brown envelope. Opening it, she found a garishly filigreed fan composed of five hand-painted panels. Four of the panels depicted some of the floats devised by the Comus krewe; the end panel gave the year—1880—and bore the name of Rex. This fan was the special invitation for the Mardi Gras ball at the Washington Artillery Hall.

Almost spellbound by the imaginative workmanship of this invitation—and recalling from earlier carnivals how highly prized and difficult to obtain such invitations were—Laure shook her head with bemusement. Her adoptive son had obviously performed another minor miracle. However, Lopasuta would not have taken credit for having arranged this particular pleasure for Laure. Rather, it was René Laurent, Leland Kenniston's factor, and a powerful member of the Comus krewe, who had procured the invitation and, as well, had seen to it that Geraldine, Lopasuta, and Leland would be in attendance.

With the masked ball now imminent, Laure felt herself transported into the magical realm of Carnival. The desk clerk stared at her with a frankly admiring smile, which sufficed to tell Laure that she was indeed strikingly beautiful in this costume of revelry.

She was escorted out of the hotel by the doorman, who immediately hailed a passing carriage. Helping her in, the doorman touched the brim of his hat with two fingers, then withdrew.

"Madame is going someplace special, *n'est-ce pas?*" inquired the reedy voice of the old driver. His watery blue eyes glowed with appreciation for the beautiful golden-haired woman attired in cloak, diadem, and domino mask. He sighed, remembering his own distant youth and the days when Carnival was new. For answer, Laure unfurled the invitation fan, and the driver nodded, comprehending. "The streets are crowded, but I will get you there safely and in good time to enjoy the merriment, madame," he promised.

The old driver weaved through the throng, congenially calling out to those who stood fast, reluctant to let the carriage pass by. He brought the carriage to a halt at the flag-decorated entrance of the ballroom some twenty-five minutes later, clambered down with an alacrity amazing for his age and fragile build, and opened the door of the carriage. Bowing low with a flourish of his top hat, he declared, "Allow me to escort you up the steps, beautiful lady!"

Laure laughed wholeheartedly, enchanted by this unexpected show of gallantry; indeed, it augured well for this night of nights. "I'm most grateful, and you are very gallant, m'sieu," she murmured, handsomely tipping him.

The driver stared after her as she stopped at the double doors flanked by two men dressed as Zouaves. He clapped his top hat over his heart and sighed, "If I were only twenty years younger! *Hélas!*"

The Zouaves, carrying papier-mâché rifles that looked amazingly realistic, came to attention and shouldered arms at Laure's approach. She took out the garish fan, unfurled it, and fanned herself, giving each of the handsome Creole Zouaves a roguish smile and saucy wink. She had never felt so giddy, so free and happy, so full of anticipation, so eager to plunge herself into whatever the night held—because she knew her partner would be trustworthy yet ardent, discreet yet wonderfully debonair and gallantly amorous.

She had long ago realized and understood the flair of sensuality that was within her. Together with an infallible sense of humor, these traits were ever present, even at moments of deepest despair. During the war, her father's suicide and her enforced capitulation to a Union corporal—when she had known herself to be little more than a prostitute in his eyes and those of his men—brought her to the nadir of her life. Yet her first husband, John Brunton, recognized these

76

qualities in Laure when even she had almost lost sight of them. He had saved her from the blackest anguish and restored her self-esteem. Later, after his death, these same qualities had attracted Luke Bouchard. Although he was twenty-five years older than Laure, she brought out of him a combination of romantic adoration and passion, tempered with sober and considerate wisdom. And now, she fervently hoped, Leland Kenniston would also prove to be the ideal lover-husband, because he was mature enough not to feel desperately driven to wedlock, yet young enough to feel the same reckless passion that she could feel. He had chosen her, had fallen deeply in love with her, perhaps because he sensed her hidden, smoldering needs.

She would never consign herself to the sobriety and dreariness of a token marriage with someone who did not have an imaginative bent, who lacked perception of what romance could be between man and woman, simply for the sake of security and companionship alone. She had seen too many such marriages, not only in New Orleans when she was a young girl, but also in Montgomery—dour, dreary, tasteless day-to-day regimens enforced upon loveless partners. The idea of keeping a union valid either for the sake of children or, generally in the woman's case, for financial security was totally abhorrent to her.

These thoughts vanished completely as the Zouaves opened the huge double doors of the great ballroom. Instantly the strains of a sweet antebellum tune of the old South reached her ears. It was the lovely and haunting "Lorena," played in a waltz tempo.

Laure stood at the top of a broad, carpeted stairway, listening to the song and thinking of its significance. . . . When all the dashing young Southern men had gone off to war in 1861, seeing it as a kind of glorious and heroic adventure, "Lorena" had touched upon their romantic feeling for womanhood, their longing for home and all the joys of serenity and peace that they hoped swiftly to restore to their embattled Confederacy. And yet that tune imparted also the disillusionment, the savage and punitive hurt of Reconstruction forced upon the impractical South by a stolid, unforgiving North.

She found herself softly singing the words:

77

The years creep slowly by, Lorena,
The snow is on the grass again;
The sun's low down the sky, Lorena,
The frost gleams where the flow'rs have been.
But the heart throbs on as warmly now,
As when the summer days were nigh;
Oh! the sun can never dip so low,
A-down affection's cloudless sky.

Laure sighed deeply and entered, going down the stairway and finding herself facing a huge hall at one end of which was a raised dais. Rex, in all his carnival finery, sat at one end with his consort queen. She was a stunningly handsome, red-haired, buxom actress beloved of New Orleans. Already it was being rumored that she and Rex were secretly engaged.

Laure stood, twirling her fan, conscious that the eyes of many men were on her, even those of men who escorted equally beautiful women in their own exotic costumes. It was a heady feeling, and she exulted in it without any feeling of shame or chastisement. For this one night, time stood still, and it was as if she had been transported back in the city of her birth, to her girlhood, to her very first and most important cavalier. With another twinge of bittersweet anguish, she recalled how her father had doted on her, idolized her, and how she had been pampered and brought up to believe that the world was hers on a silver platter simply because she was a Prindeville. In retrospect, perhaps she prized this evening, this night, above all others in her past exactly because of the very different turn her life had taken. She had experienced desolation, degradation, and finally the restoration of her self-esteem. A reunion with this one man, who she believed would bring the rest of her life to happy fruition, would be the culmination.

She realized that all of the most important events of her life had begun, had taken place, here in New Orleans, her place of birth. She felt quite sure that tonight, yet another momentous cycle would begin, the final circle as it were. At least she prayed it would, with all her heart.

She advanced slowly, her eyes searching the room. She had not yet seen him, but suddenly, with a cry of delight, she recognized Lopasuta and Geraldine. They were in the center

78

of the ballroom, waltzing ever so gracefully. Geraldine's eyes were shining, and her face was lit up by her dazzling smile. Laure looked around the ballroom again, still not locating the costume that Leland had described he would be wearing. She told herself that when they did meet, she would make no discernible display of her affections, even though the masks would ostensibly protect both her and Leland from exposing their true identities and feelings. No, quite the contrary. She would be very casual, and only when they were alone together—and only if she felt that he, too, shared this exultant mood of rapturous reunion after long absence—would she remove the mask and, with it, the outward veneer of insouciance that she would display.

She put her fan to her mouth to hide a smile as a man wearing a remarkably realistic papier-mâché elephant's head and trunk solemnly waltzed by; his beefy frame was overtightly encased in black linen trousers, white spats, and black patent-leather shoes. His partner was a buxom dowager who wore a startling Medusa mask, the artificial hair formed into serpents, some coiled, some straggling. Below the mask, she wore a green velvet evening gown with an old-fashioned long train, which one bejeweled, plump hand kept reaching back to flick up, lest nearby dancers step on it.

A tall man wearing a black domino mask over his eyes came to her side. His face was tinted with a brownish dye to suggest one of the pirates of Hispañola in the days of Captain Kidd and Blackbeard. A cutlass hung from a swordbelt at his waist under a magnificent purple silk coat, out of which the ruffles of his silk shirt peeked. His fawn-colored breeches were tucked into fine brown leather boots, and he doffed his tricornered hat and made Laure a low bow. "Wouldst thou care to trip the light fantastic with a swashbuckling pirate, elegant princess?" He addressed her in a mellow baritone voice.

"I am too gentle and fearful a lady to dare being the consort of a pirate captain, even for so little a time as a waltz, m'sieu," Laure pertly replied, and gave him a roguish glance and tapped her dainty nose with the tip of her folded fan.

"I am bereft! The night is desolate now! I promise I shall not carry you off to my sloop and put out for the Tortugas, if you will but grant me one dance," he pleaded.

"Alas, I am pledged to another, m'sieu. But if I were

alone, surely your gallant attitude might ease my fears. Be content with that—and may this night of Carnival bring you all the realizations of your dreams.''

"How can it, when you have already dashed them to nothingness, beautiful princess!" he eloquently replied, as he donned the buccaneer's hat. Putting his hand to the hilt of his cutlass, he made her another, though less florid, bow, then turned back and was lost in the crowd.

Laure kept her place near the entrance, about twenty paces away from the milling throng of dancers in their inventive costumes. The music and the scene captivated her, and she gave herself totally, sensuously, to the mood of Carnival. Laure had the feeling that what she saw and heard in this panoramic ballroom would remain fixed like a painting in her mind, long years after tonight.

She did not notice that a tall man attired in the costume of a French musketeer and wearing a cocked hat with a white plume had come up behind her until suddenly she heard him say, "I rejoice that you sent the pirate packing, madam. He would be a predator and seek only a greedy capture, whereas I am sworn to the credo of defending a beautiful woman."

She turned, startled at first to hear these words addressed to her. As she faced the masked man, he completed his introduction by doffing the white-plumed hat and making her a low bow.

"But, m'sieu," she coolly protested, "to my uninitiated eyes, I must say I cannot see much difference between a cutlass and a rapier. If, as you say, the pirate with his cutlass was a predator, should not your rapier terrify me equally, for assuredly you might use it to coerce me into submission."

"Your point is well taken—no pun intended, I assure you!" He straightened and gave her a roguish smile, then continued, "Yet the history of the musketeer is that he is sworn to serve the king, and thus, equally, to defend queen or princess or, indeed, even a peasant girl, so long as she is one of the king's subjects."

"You express a lofty sentiment, m'sieu," Laure faced him, maintaining a dignified mien, unflinchingly erect, as if indeed she were the great lady her costume professed. "But on a night such as this, when everyone wears a mask to conceal his or her identity, is it not equally true that this sentiment of yours may be illusory, or even deceptive?"

"Not so, for I have brought with me proof of my devotion to that credo—that is, if you are indeed the one I seek."

"How can I tell if I am the one?"

"Since this is the night of Carnival and of masks, beautiful princess, I must at least till midnight conceal my true identity. Yet I think the rules of the game permit a tiny clue—and this, together with the proof of which I have just spoken, I give you now: I was not always a musketeer of *La Belle France*. I came originally from the land of leprechauns and bewitching colleens—though I declare here and now that, even with your mask, you surpass in beauty any colleen that ever my poor eyes beheld to this moment. And now for the proof. . ."

With this, he unbuttoned his elegant, beribboned coat and put his hand into the broad pocket in the lining. He drew forth two roses, one red, one yellow, wrapped in tissue and tied together with a green ribbon. He made her a low bow, then handed her the bouquet and said very softly, "The red rose is for passion, the yellow is for fidelity. And, finally, the green ribbon symbolizes both your beautiful eyes and the prime color of the flag of my native land."

Her voice trembled a little as, still striving to play the role of haughty princess, wary of a profaning commoner, she replied, "But roses are known to have thorns, m'sieu."

"Not these, beautiful, faraway princess. I saw to it that the thorns were removed. And now, humbly, hopefully, yearningly, I await your answer."

Laure pressed the little bouquet against her heart and, holding out her other hand to him, murmured, "I believe you to be the one who addressed a suppliant letter to me. I am satisfied with the proofs you have thus far shown me. Did you not mention in this letter that you yearned for at least one dance and one glass of champagne?"

"I did indeed, beautiful princess," he whispered huskily.

"Then be my escort for the ball," she eagerly whispered back.

Ten

She felt herself languorously drawn out of the cocoon of darkness, out of the shadowy, nebulous world of dreamless, sating sleep. Lingering in this limbo moment by moment, she drowsily felt the sensate awareness of her body returning to her, with a rarefied sensitivity that foretold a marvelous vibrancy for these first waking moments.

She stirred, uttering a sigh of remembered pleasure. Evanescent, featherlike touches traced her dimpled bare shoulders, the hollow of her throat, the cleft of her gently swelling breasts. How exquisite it was to lie here still immersed in darkness, knowing that joy and fulfillment awaited the opening of her eyes. Laure Bouchard's lips curved into a dreamy smile, and at that moment they were ardently but softly kissed. Her lashes fluttered, and her green eyes took cognizance of her surroundings.

"My faraway princess, come back to me," Leland murmured, his fingers lightly stroking her sides, making them quiver. Propped up on one elbow, he smiled down at her, and the warmth and concern and almost poignant yearning in his look made her shiver with the sudden, sweeping recollection of the night they had shared in bliss, a consummation of the magical state of Carnival in New Orleans.

The shutters were drawn, and she could not yet tell what time of day or night it was. As he kissed her again, his smile deepening in pleasure to find her fully awake, she felt refreshed and replenished, gloriously young again. She was woman incarnate for this man who had blended poetry with wit, charade with passionately arousing wooing, making her rejoice in being the one whom he had chosen as his love. Now she was sure; no lingering doubt remained that Leland Kenniston was her destined husband and lover.

As he kissed her lips for the third time, she piquantly murmured, "But I'm no longer a faraway princess, my darling—I cast off all my royal raiment. With you here, oh so happily with you here, Leland, is a woman of flesh and blood who adores you."

"You are a princess, a goddess, a houri all in one, my Laure," he told her, as his free hand continued to pay tribute to her body, reaching now her satiny bosom. "What a joy it is to lie with you, to hold you, seeing you naked, knowing that you are mine. That is—will you truly be mine? Once again, Laure, I ask you to marry me."

"I will."

"Laure, my darling!" He was speechless for a moment, his mouth open in delight. "It's all I've hoped for, ever since I first met you. I think you know that."

"Yes, I've known it. I think I've felt the same way all along, but last night, when the musketeer I had hoped to see brought me two roses and told me what they meant, that's when I was truly sure. My darling, I'm very blessed to have a man like you care so much for me. Passion and fidelity—few women in all the world ever realize so much from the man with whom they hope to spend the rest of their lives."

"It is my pledge, Laure, and I'll dedicate myself to fulfilling it each day, each night that we're together. Oh, my sweetheart! You will never have any regret about your decision, I promise."

Her eyes had filled with tears, but they were tears of joy, as she wordlessly nodded.

"Laure, do you have any hesitation about coming to live with me in New York?" His voice was anxious now, his face serious. He put his hand to her cheek and bent closer to her, as if impatient to hear her answer.

"To live with you in New York?" she thoughtfully repeated, and her brows were creased by a slight frown.

"Well, obviously, we will have to live there since it's where my headquarters are. I know it's a great change for you and your children, but you'll all be happy there, I promise you will. There's so much more to do there than there ever could be in Alabama or here in New Orleans, and besides, it's certainly a healthier climate in the summer."

"Yes, that's true," she said hesitantly.

"I know." He nodded and moved closer to her, as if he had already read her thoughts. "You're thinking of the plantation and the tenants who depend on you for their livelihood. That's one of the many things I love about you, Laure—that you take your responsibilities so seriously. You're a wonderful employer, in addition to everything else I love about you. Like your delicious mouth, for instance." Debonair and teasing, he turned his head to brush his lips lightly over hers.

Her arm linked around his neck to prolong the embrace, and she returned it ardently. But she then whispered, "I—please, Leland, you mustn't think I'm hesitating because I want to go back on my promise to marry you. Oh, no, it's not that at all! But I've so much to think about! To tell you the truth, I hadn't expected you to ask me to come to live in New York as immediately as this—"

"Then tell me what you do feel and think. If we're going to be married, there must be no barriers between us, no evasions—and certainly no doubts. If you think there are problems about this move, let me help you try to resolve them. I want to be with you the rest of my life, Laure."

"I know that even without your words, dear Leland." Once again, she kissed him, and then he moved away from her, sensing that this was a moment for introspection and sober decision, and not wishing to distract her with caresses or kisses.

She was grateful for this attitude of his, to allow her to concentrate on the eventualities his proposal had unexpectedly roused within her mind. She felt it was still another proof of how much Leland deeply cared for her.

Closing her eyes, locking her fingers behind her head, she lay completely still and pondered what leaving Alabama would entail. Surrendering herself to cold, rational thought, she sensed that some of her almost feverish eagerness in coming to meet him here in New Orleans, after having received that telegram, had been motivated by the gradually intensifying feeling that Windhaven Plantation was no longer truly her home. With Luke gone, the plantation had come to seem more and more like a shrine to his memory. If she remained there, she would always be surrounded by reminders of the past.

Assuredly, she could not expect Leland to begin a life with her in such a place. He was, after all, a man of affairs who was most at home in the great commercial centers of the world. Besides, at Windhaven Plantation, there would be too many ghosts for them both to overcome. Not of guilt, to be sure, for she knew that Luke would have wanted her to find happiness and security and peace after his death. He had never spoken of it—or even mentioned the possibility of his dying before her—but because he had been so considerate and so devoted, she believed that if indeed there was a hereafter, he must now be happy that she had found a man worthy to succeed him. A man completely different from Luke, meaning a completely new life for Laure.

On the other hand, to agree to wed Leland Kenniston and to leave Windhaven Plantation for New York almost immediately would force upon her the contemplation of a decision for which she was not yet ready. Obviously, she would never abandon Windhaven Plantation altogether: It had stood all these years as a memorial to old Lucien Bouchard, the founder of the dynasty, and all his hopes and dreams had come to fruition in the building of that red-brick chateau. It must be continued and remain part of the Bouchard heritage. To dispose of it, simply to eliminate it from her thoughts, would be a betrayal of Luke and all he had believed in.

Also, though she was confident of the capabilities of Marius Thornton and Burt Coleman, she was reluctant to leave the plantation entirely in their hands. Though Marius was still a fairly young man, his increased responsibility over the past few years, together with his own familial obligations, had made him seem older of late and less vigorous. There could be no doubt that he had been trustworthy and intensely loyal all these years, but he had not spared any measure of himself in working with the tenant farmers and the field workers on the plantation. Indeed, now that she reflected upon it, she realized that he had not had an actual vacation in at least three years. Thus, to put the entire weight of running the estate on his shoulders with such short notice would really not be fair to him, or to his family. And as for Burt Coleman, he had Andy Haskins's land to look after, as well as his work in aiding Marius.

Leland slipped out of bed and, donning a dressing robe, went to a taboret near the window. From the table he lifted a decanter of Madeira and poured out two glasses, then brought them back to the bed and handed one to Laure. "Here, my darling, it will refresh you," he murmured.

Opening her eyes, she acknowledged his thoughtfulness with a smile. Drawing the sheet to cover her breasts, she sat up, took the glass, and sipped it, her luminous green eyes sending him a radiant message of love. He lifted his glass to her and inclined his head, in a kind of silent tribute, then turned and went back to the window.

Once again, she was grateful for the unselfish way in which he respected her need to ponder these problems, problems that had to be resolved if the two of them were to have a happy future together.

The brief interlude had in no way broken in upon her reflections, and Laure was able to consider with an almost impartial, matter-of-fact outlook the steps that would have to be taken before she could grasp this wonderful man's hand and say, "I will follow you to the ends of the earth, if such is your desire, my darling."

It was true that she had been very lonely. Now that Geraldine and Lopasuta Bouchard had moved with their children and the young Chinese nurse to settle here in New Orleans, her circle of friends seemed to have dwindled drastically. Those friends that she shared with Luke were for the most part far older than she was, and after they had paid their respects to her martyred husband, they had, for reasons of tact and consideration, made only token calls in the months that followed. And perhaps they were sensitive enough to understand that repeated calls would only remind her of her loss. That was as well. For the truth was that she had very little in common with them. Even people like Andy and Jessica Haskins, dear as they were, could never truly understand her nature. Nor could they ever share in those things that gave her pleasure in life.

Still, to leave Alabama forever—it was a momentous decision! A cosmopolitan upbringing would be good for all of her children. It would expose them to more progressive ideas and to people of a wider and broader culture than rural living and schooling could ever impart. And that was a vital part of the future: the proper mental and spiritual growth of her children by Luke Bouchard. She remembered now that, even as she had sat at the hospital bedside and held Luke's hand and watched him draw his last breath, she had told herself that the one thing she must ensure would be to see that their children would have every opportunity to acquire both theoretical and practical wisdom, so as to be able to take their rightful places in society.

She also realized that if she and the children continued to

live in Alabama, they could not entirely escape the narrow, insular outlook that the Civil War had imposed upon so many Southerners, who in turn conveyed it to their offspring. There would always be the remembrance of the ruthless, oppressive North over a defeated and downtrodden South. Surely that was no wholesome heritage for Luke's children.

She exhaled a deep breath, then finished her wine, and he walked over to take the glass and set it back down on the little taboret. "I'm sorry I've taken so long to think this over, my darling," she apologized. "But you see, I was so eager to be with you, and I was hoping that you would ask me to marry—because I was almost positive I was going to say yes—well, I just didn't stop to think of what would happen after that."

"Of course, my darling. I truly didn't mean to upset you—" he began.

She reached out for his hand and brought it to her lips, then smiled playfully. "You know, I think I'm fondest of you because I'm never wrong in your eyes—although that can be very dangerous once we're married, darling," she teased. "However much a wife feels herself to be loved, there are times when she wants her husband to bring her up short, if she does or says something he doesn't quite approve of. I want you always to do that with me."

He laughed and kissed the tip of her nose. "I should say the same thing to you, my love. Especially since you've already been a wife, but I've never been a husband before. So, being new and untried, I'm certain to display many more irritating traits than ever you will, my dear one."

She laughed happily and again brought his hand to her lips and kissed it, then reached up with both arms to draw him down to her. "For a man who says he's so untried"—her voice was bantering and suggestive now, and her eyes sparkled with mischief—"you somehow manage to say exactly the things I want to hear." Then, her face sobering, she sat up primly and made sure that the sheet continued to cover her bosom. She held it firmly with both hands, as if to signify that this was the time for a decision by Athena, rather than by Venus. "You see, Leland, if I come to New York with you, I have to make plans to leave the stewardship of Windhaven Plantation in the most capable hands possible. My foreman, Marius Thornton, and his assistant, Burt Coleman, are certainly the most trustworthy men you could find anywhere in this country. Luke taught them well for many years—thank God—so they are excellent supervisors now. But you see, if I leave Alabama, the plantation will be without an owner in residence for the first time ever—and that is a big step. Marius and Burt are devoted to the Bouchard family, but I must be sure they would feel able to run things without my being there—for their sakes, as well for my children, who will one day inherit the estate."

"I understand that very well, and I'd call you eminently practical, my darling."

"Please, you mustn't flatter me now. I'm thinking out loud, Leland. Oh, I can see all the advantages of being in New York, especially now that you helped me send Lucien abroad to a school where he can get far more benefits than ever he could in our still very rural and backward Alabama school system. I feel all the other children should have the same advantages, and I'm sure they'd have that in New York."

"Oh, yes, indeed they would."

"So please be patient, my darling, and give me some time to work these problems out—and they're my problems entirely, not yours."

"But that isn't true, dearest." He reached out to take one of her hands and kiss it, then her dimpled shoulder, and then as quickly drew back, so as not to distract her.

"I'll do my very best to work matters out, so that I can leave Alabama without any misgivings. If all goes well, I think I could be ready to marry you by the end of June— would that content you?"

"Of course. But I must say that since you've done me the honor and the great joy of saying that you'll marry me, Laure, you mustn't feel that these are your problems only. I want to be your friend and counselor, not just your lover and companion." He kissed her lightly again. "Well—now that you've set a more or less specific date for our nuptials, let me propose this in return: I'll spend this time finding the perfect residence for us and your children. It'll be a place close to a park, so they can romp outdoors when the weather is fine, and it will be close to the best schools I can find."

"That would be wonderful! All right, then, it's settled.

And I think I'd best get back to Lowndesboro as soon as possible, so that I can work these things out.''

"But not right now, not just yet, my darling. The shutters are still drawn, the room is still dark. Let us pretend that the night has not yet ended, that our carnival is still being celebrated.''

"Oh, yes, yes, my dearest one!" Laure murmured, as her hands let the sheet fall from the sculptured beauty of her body.

Eleven

Having climbed aboard the train bound for Cañon City, Robert Markey moved down the aisle of the car occupied by the contingent from Windhaven Range, doffing his Stetson and smiling at Sister Martha, who paused in her conversation with her three companions to smile graciously back at him. When Lucien Edmond greeted him, he forced a mechanical smile and mumbled some hardly intelligible words of acknowledgment, then took a seat by himself away from all the others, and stared gloomily out of the window. He hadn't at all liked the way that man had kicked the terrier outside the Pueblo depot; anyone who took out his anger on a helpless little dog had something wrong with him, deep inside. He remembered how his father had once told him that the Hindus believed the spirits of one's ancestors were reincarnated in animals, and for that reason, one should always be kind to dumb beasts. That might or might not be so, but he did know that if he hadn't found Tramp, he might have given up and died, long before he got all the way to Texas. He smiled as he recalled how anxious Tramp had been to come along with him on the trip to Leadville. He would sure miss him all these months he'd be away.

He thought again of the dark-haired young man, and could not explain why he had an uneasy feeling about him and his companions. All he knew was that the treatment of the dog had greatly upset him. He sighed, then gave up on this line of thinking and turned his full attention to the scene outside his window. Suddenly something caught his eye, and he peered intently. Far to his left, some three or four hundred yards away from the siding, was a group of men in Stetsons, wearing heavy riding breeches and woolen jackets. They were mounted on horseback, and even as he squinted to try to make them out as clearly as he could, they started off at a gallop and disappeared from view. Northwestward, he thought to himself. From what he could make out, there were perhaps eight to ten of them. He shook his head uneasily and grimaced. Then he heard the conductor coming through the car, booming out, "Folks, we're gonna start for Cañon City in about five minutes. Hope you're all settled comfortably. The Denver & Rio Grande thanks you for riding with us, and we hope we'll see you again right soon!"

"Well," Ramón mused aloud, "we ought to get into Cañon City early this evening, and from there, it's another hundred miles to Leadville by stagecoach. So that means we're going to have to spend the night in Cañon City. We seem to be testing out a lot of hotels along the way," Ramón chuckled mirthlessly.

"True enough," Joe agreed, glancing out of the window. "Look over there, Ramón—I'll bet that mountain is about thirty miles away, although the air's so clear you'd think it was only five."

"Yes," Ramón replied, "and I'll bet the snow on it will stay almost until August. I've heard it said that they've about ten months of winter and two short months of summer up here in Colorado." He sighed wearily. "I'll admit that Mara would go anywhere with me, but now that I've had my first sight of the Rockies by train, I'm beginning to wonder if I really want to move my family all the way from Texas and stay here permanently. Oh, well, time enough to think about that once we get our mine started, right Joe?"

"Right as rain, Ramón." Joe took out his watch and consulted it. "We're about halfway to Cañon City now. Hey, look out there. Looks like a group of horsemen coming along—wonder if they want to halloo the train—"

Before he could finish the sentence, the train came to a screeching halt without warning, and passengers and their parcels tumbled pell-mell in a melee of tangled arms and legs. Sister Martha uttered a cry of alarm as she was flung to the floor, but she quickly righted herself, trying to help Sister

90

Margarita. "Don't be frightened. It will be all right," she consoled the elderly Mexican nun.

Robert Markey sprang to his feet at the back of the car and ran down the aisle. "Look, Mr. Hernandez! Those men out there on the horses—they've got rifles! I've had a bad feeling ever since I saw some guy kick a dog back in Pueblo. He and some cronies boarded the train back there, and I saw them get in a car up ahead. Hey! That was a shot! One of those guys is shooting at us!"

The grim-faced horseman riding alongside the halted train had just triggered his rifle, and the bullet cracked through the glass window only inches away from Ramón's head. It continued across the aisle and hit the window opposite, shattering it, too.

"Everybody get down!" Ramón shouted, as a second bullet whizzed through the broken window, again narrowly missing him. As more bullets were fired in rapid volleys, Robert, crouching low, hurried to where the sisters sat and urgently ordered, "Please, Sisters! Get down on the floor and don't move! It's a holdup. God knows what they're after—oh! Sorry, Sister Martha!"

The mother superior would have laughed at this understandable gaffe had it not been for the seriousness of the situation. Instead, she gently touched Robert on the shoulder, signaling her empathy, then helped Sisters Concepción and Luz lie flat on the floor between their seats. She then scurried across the aisle on her hands and knees to the prone figure of Sister Margarita. The two elderly nuns then raised themselves up slightly, and bent almost double, with their faces nearly touching the dirty, dusty floor, folded their hands, and silently prayed.

As more and more shots were fired, the noise level inside the railroad car became almost intolerable. Women and children screamed at the top of their lungs, and babies howled in protest. Their menfolk, trying desperately to calm them, while themselves fearing the worst, had to shout to be heard, completely nullifying the calming effect of their words.

Many of the passengers had taken out their own pistols or had retrieved their rifles from the overhead luggage racks, but many more were too terrified to do anything but stay flat on the floor. The Windhaven vaqueros, having all too often been bushwhacked on trail drives, were the most effective members of this counterattacking force. Although the train robbers had the advantage of mobility, still a number of shots the vaqueros fired accurately found their marks.

Robert Markey crawled up the aisle to a vacant seat. Drawing his revolver, he smashed the butt against the yet unbroken pane of glass, shattering it. Calmly and carefully, he took aim and fired. One of the riders flung his hands in the air, his rifle dropping to the ground. For a few seconds, he seemed frozen in this agonized pose, then he slid off his horse and tumbled to the ground, rolling down the steep grade until he was lost from view.

"Vaqueros, keep firing!" Ramón shouted in Spanish. Then turning to Joe, he yelled, "You and I will head up front and see what's going on."

From the seat behind him, Lucien Edmond shouted, "I'm coming with you." Tossing his Colt revolver onto the seat, he clenched his Spencer carbine and, crouching low like Ramón and Joe, followed the two men down the aisle as they crossed from their car into the next one.

Frank Scolby reached for the revolver that Lucien Edmond had left for him. After raising himself up for a hasty glance out the window, he slid back down to his knees. "Dammit!" he muttered. "I didn't think the James boys got up this far north!"

"I don't think it's the James gang, Señor Scolby," came the voice of Felipe Sanchez from the seat behind him. "My guess is that this train is carrying a payroll, and somebody found out about it and wants it real bad."

Just after Felipe uttered this pronouncement, a bullet whizzed over his head, and he ducked reflexively. "¡Madre de Dios!" he swore to himself. Lifting his head cautiously, he spied his would-be assailant riding by for another go-around with his reloaded shotgun. Aiming with careful deliberation, Felipe waited until the very moment that the outlaw sighted along his own gun—then the vaquero squeezed the trigger, and the bandit fell to the ground with a sharp cry.

Walter Catlin and Timmy Belcher hunkered down the aisle of the car, keeping their heads below the windows. They tapped Diego Martinez and Santiago Dornado on the shoulders, motioning these men to follow their lead. Walter shouted above the clamor, "We've got to make sure that none of those bastards out there boards the train. There's no telling how the passengers would panic if that happened.

"I suggest," he continued, "that we pair off and station ourselves in each of the other two passenger cars, and if anyone tries to board—shoot him."

The others nodded their agreement with this plan, and Walter and Timmy hurried to the end car while Diego and Santiago positioned themselves at each end of the second car.

Just as Walter and Timmy were about to open the connecting door to the last car, they heard a woman scream. The two Windhaven men dropped to the floor, and after a brief nod to each other, Walter pulled open the door.

The bandit at the far end of the car reacted instantly to this movement and fired—and the bullets whizzed harmlessly way over the cowboys' heads. In that same moment, Walter fired his revolver at the outlaw, hitting the man in the shoulder. Hesitating only a fraction of a second, the man leaped back off the train and fled for safety.

Timmy smiled and clapped his brother-in-law on the shoulder. "Looks like we got here not a moment too soon," the younger man declared. "That was good thinking, Walter. Remind me to ask your advice if I ever need it about anything."

When, by their watches, they had estimated that the train was exactly halfway between Pueblo and Cañon City, Jack Hayes, Reuben Huntley, and Gabe Penrock had left their seats at the front of the first passenger car, where they had been nervously waiting this moment. They had opened the door at the front of the car, which gave them direct access to the coal tender behind the locomotive. Climbing up the tender's ladder, they had cautiously run across the top of the uneven pile of coal. They knew full well that the engineer and his fireman would be intent on their jobs, and any noise the three bandits made would be drowned out by the fierce noise from the engine.

Reaching the front of the tender, the men nodded once at each other, then dropped down just behind the engineer and the fireman, training their revolvers on the men.

The two railroad employees passed a swift glance between themselves, a silent message that said neither of them should do anything foolishly heroic. "We'd better do what they say, Sam," the engineer said to his coworker, who mumbled back, "I told you we should've had a guard with us on this run."

"Shut up, you two!" Hayes snarled. "Now, nice and easy, keepin' your hands where I can see 'em, I want you"—he gestured with his rifle at the engineer—"to bring this train to a nice, quick stop. I mean quick—and I mean right now!"

"But—" the engineer started to protest.

"But nothin', mister. Do it!"

Pulling up on the brake handle, the train came to a screeching, grinding stop. The three outlaws had prepared for the suddenness of this action by bracing themselves firmly against the sides of the car. "Okay, Gabe," Hayes ordered, "you stay with these guys and make sure they don't try nothin' —kill 'em if you have to. Me an' Reuben'll go back through to the baggage car—I found out that's where they've got the payroll. By the time we get there, our men ridin' outside should have all them scared passengers nice an' quiet. Ain't nobody gonna give us no trouble—an' if one of them damn fools feels like playin' hero, he'll get his head blown off afore he can try anything. Come on, Reuben."

The three outlaws had heard all the shooting, but had assumed that most of the firing was being done by their own men. Recklessly, Hayes and Huntley sauntered back through the door into the first passenger car—just as Lucien Edmond, Ramón, and Joe entered the same car at the other end. The Windhaven men, seeing the two desperados, fired simultaneously. Reuben Huntley, reacting out of self-preservation, dropped to his knees. Jack Hayes, however, stood his ground; he triggered one shot from his carbine, which whizzed harmlessly by Lucien Edmond, burying itself in the ceiling. Hayes, coughing a welter of blood from the bullets he took during the fusillade, dropped to his knees, then fell flat on his face, completely still.

"Don't move! We've got the draw on you!" Lucien Edmond shouted to Huntley as he leveled his carbine at the red-bearded man.

Shouting a flurry of curses, Huntley dropped his revolver and reluctantly got to his feet, raising his hands high over his head. He suddenly looked intensely at Ramón, who was standing to Lucien Edmond's right, holding a carbine at waist-level, aimed at him. "Goddamnit, greaser! You got more lives than a goddamn cat!" he growled.

"You apparently know me," Ramón coldly replied. "If so, you also know that I'll not hesitate to use this rifle. Just come toward us, and no tricks—or you'll get what your friend just did."

"All right, all right, greaser. Yeah, I know you. I saw you through the business end of a telescope up near Trinchera Pass."

"So you were one of the men who tried to bushwhack us on our way to Colorado," Ramón interposed.

"That's right. I shoulda picked you off there. He'd have paid me a bounty for your scalp, greaser—" Then, realizing that he was saying too much, Huntley clenched his lips and stared down at the floor, an ugly sneer on his coarse, bearded face.

"Any more of your friends out there in the engine?" Lucien Edmond wanted to know.

"If you're so damned anxious to know, find out for yourself, mister. I ain't sayin' a thing more."

"Joe, march him back into our car and tie him up. There must be a marshal in Cañon City; we'll turn this character over to him when we get there."

"*If* you get there—" Huntley began. But Ramón and Lucien Edmond, putting two and two together, suddenly ran to the front of the car. Meanwhile, Joe Duvray prodded Reuben Huntley in the side with the muzzle of his carbine and ordered, "Grab the back of your neck with your hands, mister, and march ahead of me real slow. I'd just as soon pull the trigger as talk to you. I don't rightly fancy your calling Mr. Hernandez a greaser."

"I could say worse things about that son of a bitch—all right; I'm going, I'm going," Huntley grumbled, as Joe gave him a vicious jab with the muzzle of the carbine.

Gabe Penrock was still covering both the engineer and the fireman with his revolver. The fireman, lanky and white haired, a few months away from his retirement, was begging for his life: "Please, mister, don't kill us! We got families! We stopped the train the way you wanted—don't shoot us!"

"That you did—and we're mighty grateful," he sneered. "But the two of you might talk to the law and describe my pals 'n me." Penrock grinned evilly as he cocked his revolver. Leveling it slowly, he aimed at the engineer's heart and pulled the trigger, and the man crumpled to the floor.

95

The fireman let out a scream and sank down to his knees, clasping his hands. "Oh, please, mister! Please! I won't say anything I promise! I—"

Just then, Lucien Edmond and Ramón opened the door of the engine cab. Like a cat, Penrock whirled and triggered a shot. In his haste, he had aimed high, and the bullet whistled by both Ramón and Lucien Edmond. Before they could fire, he took them by surprise by seizing a shovel as he crouched low, and flinging it up at them. The diversion worked, and he then dived out of the engine, rolling down the steep slope.

"He killed Tom," the fireman sobbed, leaning over to touch the body of his coworker.

Lucien Edmond glanced back at the dead engineer, then raised his carbine and fired after the fleeing outlaw. But Penrock, with the agility of a man bent on saving his life at any cost, had regained his feet and was running like a deer, dodging this way and that, till at last he disappeared into a thick clump of spruce trees.

At the same time, John McCreedy, one of the dozen outlaw riders to fire on the train, saw Penrock escape the fusillade that Ramón and Lucien Edmond sent after him. Having already ridden his horse into the protection of the woods below the tracks, he called out, "Gabe . . . Gabe! Over here! Quick—on my horse!"

"That you, John? Damn! Everything went wrong! Look, you and the others go back to Dodge and tell Mr. Cornish that that damned greaser he's got it in for was on this train. Now how the hell was anybody supposed to know that? Anyway, my guess is that the greaser's on his way to Leadville, so it'll probably be easy enough to find him there—and pay the bastard back!"

Penrock vaulted onto the outlaw's horse and clasped his arms around McCreedy's waist. "I recognized him, 'cause when Reuben, Jack, me, and the other boys tried to bushwhack the Mex, Reuben let me take a squint at him through his telescope. And here he was again, plain as day. They must 'a got Jack and Reuben—I heard gunshots just before I shot the engineer. I didn't have time to kill the damned fireman 'cause the greaser and a tall blond guy came gunning after me."

"Jeb isn't going to like this—not one little bit. We lost at least four men, and a couple others were wounded. And if

96

they took Reuben and Jack, that's real bad," McCreedy
grumbled, and he slackened his horse's gait, now that they
were out of danger and in the protection of the thick woods.

"I'm gonna go to Leadville. You tell Mr. Cornish that I'm
going to stay there, and if that greaser's planning on doin'
business there, I'll stir up plenty of trouble for him. You tell
Jeb Cornish that, you hear, John?"

"I'll tell him—and more 'n likely, he'll send some men up
to help you out. Christ, I know how much he was counting on
this payroll. Nothin' we can do about it now, though. Listen,
I'll get you over to a town just this side of Leadville where
you can get yourself a horse. Hey, think that greaser knows
you by sight?"

"Well, he saw me, but I don't think he saw me long
enough to remember what I look like and come gunning for
me. Don't you worry. I can always grow a beard to make
sure he don't know me. The important thing's *I'll* know
him—no matter where the son of a bitch'll be hangin' out in
Leadville. And I'll get even with him—tell Mr. Cornish he
can count on it!"

Reuben Huntley slumped morosely against the back of an
unoccupied seat in the car where the Windhaven Range crew
rode. Hog-tied hand and foot, his Stetson pulled down over
his face, he morosely reflected on his bad luck. *Poor old
Jack,* he thought to himself, *never had a chance. Maybe
Gabe got away, to get the word to Cornish. Somebody's gotta
do it. This goddamn greaser has a way of turnin' up where
you least expect him. But that'll have to be Jeb's problem
from now on.* When they turned Huntley over to the marshal
in Cañon City and the circuit judge came around, he knew
that the least he could expect would be about ten years in the
penitentiary. The only consolation was that he'd heard a
Colorado prison wouldn't be half so bad as Yuma had been.

Lucien Edmond and Ramón had stayed in the engine to
calm the hysterical fireman and to urge him to try to get the
train started so they could get to the end of the line at Cañon
City. Fortunately, the fireman knew how to operate the controls of the engine, and Ramón, after compassionately carrying the body of the dead engineer into the next car and laying
him gently on a vacant seat, volunteered to help shovel coal
into the still-smoldering furnace. Lucien Edmond pitched in

as well, and soon the engine began to chug and puff, and the fireman blew the whistle to let the conductors in the cars behind him know that they were finally resuming their journey.

Robert Markey helped the nuns back into their seats, anxiously inquiring whether any of them was hurt. Sister Martha smiled at him and shook her head. "Not to worry, Mr. Markey. We've had God watching over us—as He has over you. Now we're sure that He approves of our mission."

Twelve

Hugo Bouchard was completely in love with Chicago, and had thoroughly enjoyed his first wintry Christmas.

He had never imagined that a country boy like himself could feel so totally at home in a city environment. The hustle and bustle, far from distracting and annoying him, proved to be a stimulus. He felt his mind was being ever enriched by all that Chicago had to offer. Cordelia Thornberg, whose brother, Dr. Max Thornberg, was on the staff of Rush Medical College—where Hugo had started his medical studies soon after the Christmas holidays—had swiftly proved to be far more than an ordinary chaperone. Though a single woman of forty-two, she had an utterly contagious zest for life, along with a sense of humor that served to put even the shyest new acquaintance completely at ease. Carla, Hugo's talented, artistic sister, adored her, for Cordelia Thornberg was cultured and in every sense a woman of the world. She was the very opposite of the hidebound, cloistered type one generally associated with spinsterhood.

Cordelia and her brother owned a large brick house across the street from Charles and Laurette Douglas, with whom they were on the friendliest of terms. From the very outset, Carla and Hugo found themselves far from being strangers in this new home, so distant from Windhaven Range.

Laurette Douglas was a Bouchard by birth; her mother had been Maybelle Belcher, who had married Luke's irresolute brother, Mark, and had then been abandoned by him. Laurette had suggested the Chicago schools for Hugo and Carla and had shown them extraordinary kindness and friendship since their arrival. They in turn adored her and her husband, Charles, and Carla and Hugo both noted how exceptionally devoted Charles was to Laurette and their children. The Douglas marriage was solidified not only by their love for their children, but also by the financial success of Charles's growing department store chain—in New York, Galveston, and Houston.

Thus it was that, far from being lonely their first Christmas away from home, Carla and Hugo had been feted and made to feel a welcome part of the Douglas family as well as the Thornberg household. Max Thornberg had been slated to begin a two-year sabbatical to visit leading European hospitals, but this leave had been postponed until early spring. Hugo had not been expecting the presence of the august physician, and he found himself in awe of this man of forty.

Carla and Hugo had spent many happy afternoons skating on the improvised rinks at Lincoln Park, shopping along State Street, enjoying the vaudeville and the theater and the band concerts. Unlike many students who had to live in boarding-houses where the provender was predictably monotonous, the young Bouchards enjoyed superb home-cooked meals from Cordelia Thornberg, who was a *cordon bleu*.

This sunny, cheerful day in April saw Hugo Bouchard about to begin his second semester of the six-term, twenty-one-weeks per term course. During his first semester, he had assiduously attended and made copious notes during the lectures in anatomy (where Dr. Thornberg had been the instructor), physiology, blood circulation, and general circulation, and he found most exciting of all his studies in organic chemistry, with laboratory work presided over by one of the finest young chemists of the time.

Hugo had been so pleased when, after his probationary period to determine his academic proficiency—since his prior education had been less than formal—Rush Medical College informed him that as of the start of the January semester, he would be welcomed as a first-term student. In his letter welcoming all new students, the college president had written: "Our curriculum emphasizes the preparation of physicians who will function chiefly as medical practitioners and who will be dedicated to the delivery of outstanding health care to people in every station of life, including the needy, who so often are not well served by the medical community.

This is why we seek applicants whose qualities of character—above and beyond their intellectual attainments—indicate a dedication toward humanitarian goals. It is our wish that each doctor whom we send forth from this college will become a pillar of strength in his community. The Hippocratic oath is our credo; there is no greater reward than to heal the sick, giving the same thoughtful and judicious health care to all who are in need of our skills.''

This, indeed, was all that Hugo believed a doctor should be. To be sure, because he was so young, he saw only the romance and excitement of medicine; he cared nothing for what might be the material gains of a successful medical practitionership. The letters he was exchanging with Dr. Ben Wilson in Wichita, a man who had selflessly ministered to downtrodden Indians, promoted Hugo's intense idealism. Every time Hugo read one of Ben's letters—in which he detailed his practice in that growing community on the high plains where he was still the only doctor—Hugo felt a tingling excitement over having chosen this profession, to which subconsciously he had been drawn and which, on the cattle drive last year to Colorado, he had learned was his true *métier*.

Though he had always been tall and wiry of build, there was no doubt that the strenuous cattle drive to Colorado had given him greater stamina. It had matured him physically, just as he had been mentally matured by having found that he could be useful in other ways besides the handling of four-footed animals. The rewarding knowledge that he had saved the lives of two vaqueros had remained with him. Whenever he entered the lecture rooms at Rush Medical College, though he was awed by the reputation of his professors, his quiet determination to succeed and to be as useful in his way as Ben Wilson was in his, inspired his studies.

He and Carla had been given separate, beautifully furnished spacious rooms in the large Thornberg house. Carla took full advantage of the garden, now that lovely spring weather had come to Chicago. She took her easel and paintbrushes out to the gazebo and sat there for several hours, until the sun began to fade, sketching the entire landscape, thumbnail studies of individual flowers, the gazebo itself, and even a commendable self-portrait, with the help of a pocket mirror. There was already to her work a quality of impressionism, partly influenced by the attention her teachers at the

100

Chicago Academy of Fine Arts paid to the growing new French school. One of her teachers was Mademoiselle Clothilde Vermier, a woman in her fifties who confided to her students that, as the only child of a wealthy Marseilles industrialist's family, she had refused the traditional fate of an arranged, suitable marriage, and had gone off to Paris for five years to try her skill at painting.

"I did not have the talent or the discipline to be a truly noteworthy artist," she had told her absorbed class that first week. "But I was fortunate in meeting the true greats, such as Pierre Auguste Renoir, Claude Monet, Édouard Manet, and Paul Cézanne. These artists convey their impressions of objects in terms of light and shade. They have set out to record the world of nature as it looks to the human eye, in all its complexity of color. They paint what the eye *sees*, not what the mind suggests ought to be there. Cézanne succinctly summarized the new school when he said, 'For an Impressionist to paint from nature is not to paint the subject but to "realize" sensations.' You too must try to discipline yourselves, to see and record things as they really are, not repeating slavishly the old formulas for rendering objects. In looking at your work—whether it be in ink, or watercolor, or oil—the viewer should be able to say to himself, 'Yes, that is the way it looks—I had not seen it that way, truly, before now.' "

Mademoiselle Vermier, who had come to the Academy just a year ago, had purchased, with her substantial family allowance, several early paintings by these four French masters, and proudly displayed them to her students. Carla was struck by the light and color of these works. Several times during the week, after the other students had politely lingered for a question or two and then departed, she had closeted herself with her teacher. Mademoiselle Vermier was tall, gawky, and plain. Yet Carla recognized an intensity to her, particularly in her piercing and eager dark blue eyes, which made the young woman oblivious to all else save the enthusiasm Mademoiselle Vermier generated in discussing her favored artists. Their works were new to the United States, but already she spoke of them as great masters who would set a new standard for others to follow, to imitate.

Lucien Edmond Bouchard had provided Carla and Hugo with spending money, a portion of which was for their room and board with the Thornbergs. But Cordelia Thornberg, with

101

a rare and delightful camaraderie, insisted—about a month after Carla and Hugo had settled in—that she looked upon them more as friends than as boarders, and that she would much rather have them spend their money on books, the theater, and entertainment, things that young people should enjoy. "Study and self-discipline are all very well, but I've never subscribed to the theory that, to be a good artist, you must starve in a garret," she had told Carla early in January. "You and your brother are young, but I can already see that you're dedicated and not dilettantes. I think, particularly since you're in a strange city, you'll be much more at your ease if you know that you have a few extra dollars to buy on impulse those things you like, and that give you pleasure. You'll earn them, after all, by working so hard in your studies. Besides, Max and I immensely enjoy your company, and we certainly don't need the extra money. So let's have no more talk of paying for room and board. Max and I have already talked it over, and we would like you both to stay here as guests."

"But that isn't fair!" Carla had protested, as she scrutinized the woman standing before her.

Cordelia Thornberg was tall and strikingly handsome. Standing five feet eight inches, this full-blown woman dressed magnificently and wore her auburn hair in a youthful upsweep, with a fringe of curls along the top of her forehead, the knot at the back embellished by a flower from her garden. Her face was angular, but it was softened by the tremendous warmth in her ready smile, and her amiable gray-green eyes were keenly observant. Whenever she did smile—which was often—she revealed traces of exceptional beauty that made Carla secretly wonder why no man had ever won her.

To this unspoken question, Cordelia provided a characteristic, spontaneous answer when she came out to visit Carla in the gazebo on this unseasonably warm mid-April afternoon. She stood for a moment silently observing Carla at the easel, noting that Lucien Edmond's lovely daughter had chosen to paint clumps of early blooming crocuses and hyacinths in oils. When Carla momentarily laid down her brush and stepped back to contemplate her work, Cordelia softly broke in, "I like that very much, Carla, dear. You've managed to instill an individuality to each blossom, yet you've done so simply by utilizing the different plays of light and shadow. Very accomplished, I would say."

102

"Why—why—thank you, Miss Thornberg—"

"Oh, good heavens, girl—please drop the 'Miss' and call me Cordelia!" her chaperone announced. She then intensely continued, "What you're doing with your painting is very close to my own feeling about life, Carla. You see, I never considered myself part of a flock, a garden plot as it were, nor a follower or sycophant. To use a term that you may not be acquainted with, I should call myself a loner. Or even an iconoclast. There are certain obligations to such an outlook on life, but also many rewards for those wise enough to have made their choice. As one day you will make yours—though I'm certain you'll never be like me."

Carla turned, her eyes wide with questioning. "But I do want to lead my own life and find out what I can do best, Miss—I mean, Cordelia," Carla stammered.

Cordelia smiled, put her hand on Carla's shoulder, and urged the young woman to sit down on the bench, then took her place beside her.

"I shall tell you something I don't tell just anyone, but I feel you and I have so much in common. When I was eighteen, I fell madly in love with a young Parisian, who was visiting Chicago. Our parents were wealthy, and they had encouraged the match. We were betrothed, we had made our wedding plans, and then Emile came down with scarlet fever and died. I was heartbroken. I actually didn't want to live for a time. But Max stood by me, comforted me. He tried to point out to me that I had my whole life ahead of me, and how much better it was for Emile's sake that, if he had to die, he died so swiftly and believing he and I would soon be man and wife. Well, Carla, that did comfort me."

"I—I understand."

"I mourned Emile longer than I should have, till Max, who was a resident at a hospital, finally insisted that I forget my own sorrows by appreciating the sorrows of others less fortunate than myself. We had only two or three small hospitals in Chicago in those days, before the Great Fire, and I volunteered to work in them virtually as a scrub woman. I began to appreciate the gifts I had—of youth and of enthusiasm for life. I still mourned Emile, naturally, but I found so many other wonderful interests—painting, music, and books—and I even spend some time in hospitals to this day and do other charitable works for the unfortunates of the city. So you see,

I've come to terms with my life, and I find it totally absorbing."

"And you never—" Carla blurted out before she could stop herself. She blushed furiously.

Cordelia laughed softly and put her arms around the young woman's shoulders, shaking her head. "No, dear, I involved myself so much in other things that I didn't really have time to fall in love. Besides, our parents died when I was only twenty and Max eighteen, and the bulk of their estate was left to me. It was an unusual will because, as a rule, a woman doesn't inherit. But my father and mother had confidence in me, and perhaps, too, they wished to make it up to me for my loss of Emile. Whatever the reason, I was administratrix of the estate, and I helped Max, and we developed a wonderful partnership. That absorbed me, too. So you see, Carla, dear, I love everything that each new day brings— from a sunrise to a sunset, the sight of children playing and the sound of their laughter, to the music of the band concerts we've attended, to good wine and food, to books—poetry, drama—Well, there's so much in this world to absorb and delight that you should determine your own way of living. You can have a wonderful life without a man, I assure you! But then, you and I are probably quite different in personality. One day, you will no doubt find a man—and if he is the right man, he'll want you to go on with your work, because I can see how much talent you already have."

Carla felt a sudden surge of affection for this gracious, sophisticated woman who had begun to treat her almost as if she were a foster daughter. Impulsively, she put her arms around Cordelia and kissed her on the cheek. "Oh! I—I hope I didn't embarrass you—but you're so good to me, I feel so much at home here—" she stammered, self-consciously flushing at her own impetuosity.

"My dear girl, I'm not embarrassed in the least! I'm charmed! And I have exactly the same feeling toward you. But," Cordelia's voice was wry, "I detect a note of sympathy. You're thinking to yourself, 'Here's this wealthy woman who lost her first and only love, and who is sour on the world!' "

"Oh, no!" Carla protested. "I didn't think that at all—"

"That's good, because you mustn't. Oh, yes, I suppose I could have found another suitor after poor Emile, but I discovered rather quickly that I didn't want to give up my freedom. Oh, early on I told myself that I was helping my brother achieve his potential as a doctor. I thought that was a wonderful cause, and because I was the administratrix of the estate, I devoted all my energy and thought to making certain that Max would have every chance to fulfill himself.

"But, truth to tell, I used this as a defense against those people who kept telling me that a proper young lady should have a proper young gentleman to look after her. Ha!" She crowed with laughter. "I would much rather have a large friendly dog looking after me than a husband to whom I would have to justify my time and needs. You can go off and leave a dog and *he* won't complain!" She laughed again and kissed Carla on the forehead. "You mustn't ever have the slightest notion of a thought that I'm a frustrated old maid—"

"Oh, my goodness, I'd never call you that!" Again, Carla protested.

"Good! Because I've certainly never looked upon myself as that—at all! Actually, Carla, I know that you're already sophisticated enough to realize that marriage isn't the be-all, end-all destiny for a woman. That's a conformist attitude, and God knows I'll never be a conformist. But you, you're warmer and more tender, and I think a good deal more vulnerable. So, yes, I think you would be happiest with a man—but you'll hear from me if he's not the type who's understanding enough to let you have a career, as well."

Carla laughed and hugged her new mentor. "That—that's very kind of you, Cordelia. I really—well, the fact is, in Texas where our ranch is, there really weren't any boys I could be interested in."

"I know that, dear. Your mother wrote me a very lovely letter when you were on your way here with Hugo. She hinted that it would be nice if I could introduce you to some eligible young men—but I'm in no hurry to do that, for this isn't yet the time. First, you have to find yourself. You've a whole life ahead of you—why, you're barely twenty! Although you're a year older than your brother, he has much more equanimity. He's a much more conservative, traditional type. Hugo strikes one as already being in his twenties, probably because he's so absorbed with his studies to be a doctor. Incidentally, my brother has been so pleased with Hugo's prowess. He's sure that Hugo has a wonderful future."

"I'm so glad to hear that! I knew he wouldn't ever be

happy taking over the ranch and going out on cattle drives. I can't thank you enough, Cordelia, for taking us both in and giving us such a wonderful chance."

"It's my pleasure. Now, I've taken far too much of your time. You go on with your painting, and this evening, if you and Hugo feel like it, we'll have dinner at the Palmer House. They've a very fine restaurant there, and I'm longing to try the *tournedos*, which is a specialty of theirs." Cordelia patted Carla's cheek and then, with a quick wink, went back into the house.

As Easter neared, Hugo Bouchard was looking forward to the second term at Rush Medical College. His subjects would be general anatomy, *materia medica*, and physiology, with a special emphasis in this last course on alimentation—diet and its absorption into the system.

A few days before Easter, Cordelia Thornberg handed Hugo a letter from his mother. When he opened it, he found a check for one hundred dollars, a present from his parents, and a long letter from Maxine urging him to divide the money with Carla and enjoy whatever special treats they wished:

Your father sends his love from Leadville, and he tells us that he, Ramón, and Joe Duvray have engaged a very capable mining engineer, a John Darwent. He's Kentucky-born, in his mid-thirties, and he's already done some fine work with one of the other major mine owners in Leadville. He and your father are hiring experienced miners at very good wages, and it probably won't be long before we hear about the first yield from dear old Mr. Scolby's mine.

Here at the ranch, the vaqueros have done a wonderful job in rebuilding, and they've finished restoring the church, the bunkhouse, and the classrooms for the children, where the nuns are as busy at work as ever.

All of us send our love to you and Carla, and we prize your letters. I'm so pleased to hear how much the two of you enjoy Chicago and the friendship of that wonderful Cordelia Thornberg. Hugo, I can tell from your last letter that you've truly found yourself. I'm so very proud of you, and I know that one day, when you graduate as a doctor, you will have a rich and wonderful life, knowing that you can contribute to those who are not so fortunate.

Carla wrote me that Miss Thornberg has been generous enough to suggest that the two of you are guests and friends, rather than paying boarders. However, I would suggest you try, since she doesn't want to accept board, to spend the money getting her things she might like for the house, and, of course, being her hosts at dinners at fine restaurants and the like. I leave this to you, because you're so tactful and considerate.

You know, of course, that your father has given some thought to the idea of our eventually moving to Colorado. However, from his last letter to me, I find that he is not quite so enthusiastic, for Leadville is a rough, brawling mining town laid out with no thought to the long-range benefits of family life. But, we'll wait to see what he decides by summer or early fall.

Well, my darlings, I will close now. God bless and keep you both. Your sisters send their love—but Edwina is terribly envious of her big brother and sister living far away in a big city!

Your loving mother

On the morning before Easter, Hugo and Carla went downtown to Charles Douglas's department store. There, Carla selected an elegant parasol with ivory handle as her gift to Cordelia Thornberg, and Hugo purchased a bottle of fine French perfume.

When they returned home Carla wrapped the gifts, which they somewhat nervously presented to their chaperone. They both knew that she had exquisite taste, and hoped their choices would please her. They needn't have worried. Cordelia was deeply touched and dabbed her eyes with her handkerchief. "How thoughtful and kind you both are!" Then, unwrapping the parasol, she exclaimed, "Oh, my! What a wonderful color, just perfect for strolling down State Street!" She hurriedly unwrapped the small package. "Hugo, my dear boy, my compliments on your taste—you couldn't have known, but this happens to be one of my very favorite perfumes. Now, my treat to you will be to take you both to a performance of Bach's Easter Oratorio after we dine at the Palmer House.''

After classes that Monday, Carla and Hugo reached the house at the same time. The lovely young woman tugged on her brother's sleeve and insisted, ''I'd like you to see my latest oil, Hugo.''

''I'd love to, Carla. Gosh, you've sure been working hard at your painting ever since you came here.''

''But that's what I'm here for! Besides, the garden is such a wonderful place to work, especially that charming gazebo. Here, I'll show you.'' She ran up the stairs to her room and quickly found her portfolio, then descended and took her brother into the drawing room. She drew out the completed painting of the flowers that she had been working on for the past week. Like the French Impressionists, Carla had imbued the blossoms with an ethereal quality.

Hugo stared at it, mystified, then scratched his head and said rather dubiously, ''I don't exactly know what I'm supposed to be seeing. I mean, I *think* they're flowers, but they all look so fuzzy and some are dark and light and—''

''Hugo,'' Carla patiently explained, mimicking Clothilde Vermier's words, ''a painting doesn't have to be a photograph. It isn't supposed to be a copy. An artist represents a thought, a feeling about something. This is the flower bed in the garden behind the house, by the gazebo.''

''Oh—I—well, I—I don't know much about painting, but I sure don't recognize these blobs as flowers. I don't understand the style. I haven't seen too many paintings—but what you used to do back home in Texas was a lot different. I—well, I could recognize what you were painting then.''

Carla was furious, but she tried to control her anger. ''Honestly, Hugo, that's just the point! At the Academy, thanks to Mademoiselle Vermier, I'm learning to express myself, trying to find my own style. In a way, it's like you; when you finally get to be a doctor, won't you specialize in some particular form of medicine?''

Hugo pondered a moment, then said, ''Well, sure, but that's not the same thing. I mean, what I'll have to make a decision about one day will be rooted in physical reality; what you're talking about is merely an abstract concept of no real importance.''

Carla said nothing. She simply placed the painting slowly and carefully back into the portfolio, then turned on her heel and stalked out of the room.

Thirteen

After the memorable but exhausting festivities of Mardi Gras, Lopasuta Bouchard and his wife, Geraldine, were happy to resume the normal pattern of their days. Geraldine had come to love her new home in New Orleans, for she felt exactly as Laure Bouchard did about leaving her home in Alabama and moving to New York. Such a change of surroundings provided the opportunity to bid farewell, once and for all, to all those things that might serve to recall past unhappiness.

Three years before, when—unknown to Geraldine—Lopasuta had been kidnapped and spirited off to Hong Kong by a group of scurrilous men seeking revenge against the Comanche lawyer, as well as attempting to gain ownership of Windhaven Plantation after Luke Bouchard's death, Geraldine had felt desolate and abandoned. Even after her husband's eventual return to Montgomery, Geraldine realized that approval and goodwill would never replace enmity and hostility in the hearts of so many of the town's citizens—hostility directed against Lopasuta for his outspoken championship of the downtrodden and the poor, and against her for having married a half-breed.

Now all of that was behind them at last, owing to a fortuituous meeting on board the ship carrying Lopasuta home to America after he had lived in penury in Hong Kong for almost a year and a half. Indeed, Geraldine thought to herself, that meeting had proved to be not only the answer to her prayers, but to her dearest friend's, as well. ''My goodness,'' she said half-aloud to her infant daughter, as she sat rocking with Marta in the gazebo in their garden, ''think of the sweeping changes Leland Kenniston has caused in all our lives! We now have a charming new home here in New Orleans—yes, my darling, it's much nicer than the one we had in Montgomery!—your daddy is so excited about his new work as Leland's attorney, and your beautiful godmother, Laure, is going to marry that wonderful man. But, shhh! Don't tell anyone just yet, Marta, because it's a secret that Laure shared with me just before she went back home." Geraldine giggled, and her infant daughter giggled back at her. "My lovely child," she sighed, "I guess I'll have to stop confiding these things to you as soon as you learn how to talk! I'm sure my little secrets wouldn't be secrets very long, would they?" She lifted the child from her lap and kissed her on the forehead.

As she sat enjoying the afternoon air, Geraldine contentedly rocked, humming a tune. A mockingbird perched at the top of the magnolia tree started going through its repertoire, and Geraldine started to whistle the song she had been humming, wondering if the bird would pick it up and add it to its list of songs. The scent of lilacs drifted by on the warm breeze, the sun enveloped her in its soothing rays. Mei Luong had gone out shopping, and Dennis and Luke were napping in the house. Except for the birdsong, it was utterly quiet, and she felt utterly at peace.

She smiled when she thought back to Lopasuta's reaction to something she had said to him. When they had learned that Marta would have to be their last child, since Geraldine was physically unable to bear any others, she had told Lopasuta that she thought of Luke as *their* son, and he had been almost overwhelmed with surprise—and joy. "Sometimes," she mused wryly, "I think my dear husband doesn't know me very well."

Luke was Lopasuta's son by Lu Choy, a Chinese sampan woman who had saved the young Comanche's life when he had been abandoned in a fetid alleyway in Hong Kong, and left for dead. Owing to his poverty-striken circumstances, Lopasuta had been obliged to live with the young woman on her boat, and during a fearful typhoon, in the act of comforting Lu Choy, they had shared one night of love. The woman had died giving birth to Luke, and shortly after her death, Lopasuta had finally managed to gain passage back to America, with his infant son and his nurse, Mei Luong.

Geraldine had completely understood the circumstances lead-

110

ing to Luke's birth and had felt that, indeed, had Lopasuta not been taken from her, that child would have been theirs. Luke would be two years old in August, but he was big for his age, and he and three-year-old Dennis had great times together—with only an occasional spat over a favorite toy.

Geraldine contentedly sighed once more as she looked down at her daughter and smoothed her fine, silken hair. "Truly, Marta," she whispered, "it seems like a miracle that we have finally found such happiness."

It was a week after Leland Kenniston had returned to New York, and Lopasuta was hard at work in his office. He had by now won a number of favorable legal judgments on behalf of the import-export business, and Leland had been so impressed by his work that just before he left New Orleans he told the young lawyer that from now on he could expect a large increase in salary.

As Lopasuta and René Laurent, the Creole factor for the firm, were conferring about some bills of lading from the latest shipments of Irish lace and whiskey, René asked him if he had seen the morning paper.

"I glanced at it over breakfast, but I didn't really read it thoroughly. Was there something in there that I should know about?" Lopasuta asked.

"Yes, as a matter of fact—" René walked over to his desk and picked up the newspaper, riffling the pages. "Ah, here it is. Look here, on page five." He pointed with his finger to two small paragraphs halfway down the page.

Lopasuta took the paper and studiously read it. Then he looked up sharply at René and said, "Why, this is very important! This could have a drastic effect on Leland's business, René." He looked down at the news item once again and reread it to himself:

The Board of Trade will convene next week on Monday, March 22. One of the items on the agenda that will be discussed is the proposal to increase the tariff rate in the Port of New Orleans. It is expected that the voting on this issue will be very close, for while some of the members feel an increase in the levy is justified on the basis of continually increasing expenditures that

111

the city must meet, others are taking the position that such a measure would surely amount to "biting the hand that feeds you."

The vote will take place in a closed hearing, as the board wishes to minimize public intervention. However, this publication will be apprised of the details, and will report them in next Tuesday's edition.

Lopasuta whistled soundlessly. "I'm very glad you pointed this out to me now, René, because it just so happens that I'm having lunch today with two port officials I've become friendly with. You probably know them—Daniel Harkinson and Harold Dumary. Nice men, both of them, and diligently interested in keeping the port operating smoothly. I'll state our case to them, and I'll hope they understand how important it is that the tariff not be increased."

"Well, that is a happy coincidence," René smiled. "Let's finish up these invoices quickly, then, so you won't be late for your engagement."

An hour later, Lopasuta walked hurriedly to the small restaurant where the three men were to meet. After being seated and placing their orders, they relaxed over a glass of white wine. Both Dan Harkinson and Hal Dumary were in their mid-thirties and had lived in New Orleans all their lives. They were also impeccably honest, much to the dismay of many shippers and traders who had fruitlessly tried to bribe them. Unlike some of their colleagues, therefore, both men had to make do on their somewhat meager wages. They would ordinarily have brought sandwiches from home for lunch, and this restaurant meal was considered a rare and lavish treat—although, indeed, by Lopasuta's recent standards, it was only moderately expensive.

As they ate, they talked about the steadily increasing amount of shipping in the Port of New Orleans. Lopasuta brought their conversation around to the impending vote by the Board of Trade.

"I appreciate the board members' concern, because the old wharves are in continual need of repair, due to the increase in traffic—not to mention the fact that the present wharfs are really too small for some of the newer ships using the port, so that new, larger ones will have to be built. Such construction and repairs are very costly, of course—but it's necessary nevertheless to look at the other side of the coin.

"I ask you to consider, gentlemen," he continued, "if the tariffs are substantially increased next year, many shippers and importers may decide to take their business elsewhere, perhaps shipping their goods by rail from other, less expensive ports of call—or to them, as the case may be. I understand that the railroads are very interested in increasing the amount of freight they handle, and they are offering very attractive rates. For convenience's sake, most of the businessmen operating here in New Orleans would, I'm sure, prefer to continue to use this port. But if the levy is raised, that might not be economically feasible."

He paused and took a few bites of his chicken. Dan Harkinson nodded his head in understanding and said, "That's well put, Lopasuta. Please go on."

"Well," Lopasuta said, "looking at it from the businessman's point of view, as I said, it would be imperative that the rate remain where it currently is. And looking at it from the port officials' point of view, more revenues are needed to keep everything running up to snuff. However, if you think about it, both ends can be accomplished by the one mean. That is to say, if the tariff rate is kept reasonable, we can afford to keep operating here—and more and more people will feel this way. As people come to know about the efficient and low-cost operation that New Orleans offers, shipping will constantly increase. And that, of course, will mean increased revenues for the city. And as for the more costly repairs to the wharves: I'm sure there are better ways of raising the money. My guess is you could easily persuade the banks and the leading businessmen—like my employer, Mr. Kenniston—to support a bond issue to cover the costs . . . *if*, that is, the tariff rates have been kept favorable all along."

The two port officials had thoughtful expressions on their faces, and Hal Dumary declared, "I certainly see what you mean. Obviously, there's been a lot of talk along these same lines, but to actually know that a major shipper like Mr. Kenniston might pack up and leave—well, certainly that's not the effect any of the board members were looking for! Tell you what, Lopasuta," Hal suggested, "we'll both be giving testimony at the hearing next week, since the board knows

113

that we're deeply involved in things down here on the docks and is interested in what we think. I'm sure Dan agrees with me that we all have the same interest at heart—the survival of the Port of New Orleans—and we're going to do our darndest to insure that survival. I just hope the members who are leaning the other way will see our—perhaps I should say *your*—point, and will vote to maintain the current tariff."

"That would be wonderful!" Lopasuta declared effusively.

"And now, I think I've bent your ears long enough—and probably given you indigestion in the bargain," he laughed. He then called the waiter over and asked what they had for dessert. "My treat, gentlemen," Lopasuta told his friends when they started to protest over this added expense. "It's the least I can do for your help."

The following week, after the vote was taken and it had been decided to hold the line on any increase in tariffs, Lopasuta triumphantly wired Leland Kenniston in New York, giving him all the details. "I'd like very much," he had written, "to be able to do something for these two men, because I'm sure that if it hadn't been for their testimony, the vote might very well have gone against the shippers. If it's all right with you, Leland (and if you don't feel that it's ethically inappropriate), I'd like to treat them to a night, as our guests, at Laure's casino. These men and their wives have very little chance for any luxury in their lives, and I thought this would be a nice gesture, a way of saying thanks for their thoughtfulness."

Lopasuta received a wire back from Leland the following morning, expressing his appreciation for all the lawyer had done and giving his approval for Lopasuta's suggestion. "I think it's an excellent idea! Absolutely excellent! Once again, you've proved how invaluable your acumen and insight are to me, quite apart from your legal abilities. Well done!"

At noontime, Lopasuta walked over to the port offices and shook hands with his two friends. "Dan, Hal, I want to propose something—and I warn you, I won't take no for an answer."

The two men looked at him curiously. "Don't leave us in suspense, Lopasuta," Dan laughed. "Go on."

"Gentlemen, you've probably heard of the Maison de Bonne Chance over on Rampart Street. And I venture to say

114

you've never had an opportunity to spend an evening there. Well, I'd like to take you and your wives there as my guests Saturday night. My wife will join us, of course, and the six of us can have a delightful time—the food is excellent, the wine unsurpassable, and the gambling, if I do say so myself, a good deal of fun. We've only been there a few times, and I know my wife would welcome an evening there again. What do you say?"

"I'd say sounds great to me!" Hal grinned. "How about you, Dan? I'm sure Eloise would adore a treat like that—and Julie would positively kill me if I said no!"

Dan laughed and readily agreed. "Sounds great to me, too, Lopasuta. Shall we meet you there at seven o'clock?"

"Perfect. Well, gentlemen," Lopasuta said, rising to his feet, "I'd best be getting back to the office. Till Saturday, then." He waved his hand in farewell and sauntered down the wharf.

The evening was a complete success, and the Harkinsons and the Dumarys were thoroughly enchanted and delighted by the courtesy shown them by the casino's staff. Even better, both men won handsomely with the stakes Lopasuta had given them to play with. They parlayed a small number of chips into over two hundred dollars each by the end of the evening.

"This is certainly more than I ever imagined I'd be getting out of a night on the town," Dan laughed gleefully. "This sure boosts my yearly salary!"

"I don't know about you, Dan," Hal interjected, "but I'd sure like to get something special for Julie with this unexpected bonus. She's never once complained to me that I earn too little, never once wished out loud that she could have a fancy, special dress—although I've seen the longing in her eyes when we've passed the shops. Trouble is," he confided, "I'm not much for women's trifles, and I wouldn't know where to begin to buy something as a surprise that would really make her happy."

Lopasuta glanced over to where Geraldine and the other two women were wrapped up in their play at a *chemin de fer* table, then put his head together with his friends. "I've an idea. My secretary, Judith Marquard—you know her of course—has excellent taste, and she once mentioned in passing that she has a friend who's a dressmaker—very exclusive, very *chic*, as the women like to say." He grinned, then went on, "I'm sure if you tell Judith what your wives' favorite colors are and their sizes, she'll come up with the perfect choices for you."

"Lopasuta, you're a lifesaver! That's a terrific idea. We'll stop by your office first thing Monday morning," Dan exclaimed. He looked at the gilt clock standing on a mantle at the far side of the room. "Good grief, look at the time! I haven't been up this late in years. I'd like to have one more glass of wine, then call it an evening."

A few months after the birth of her last child, Judith Marquard had gone to work for Lopasuta. She thoroughly enjoyed her duties, and seldom missed her old job at the former Brunton & Barntry Bank, since taken over by new management. Keen of mind and quick of wit, Judith swiftly assimilated the operation of the business and enthusiastically plunged herself into her work.

Indeed, because during her association with the bank she had won a great deal of respect from influential businessmen throughout New Orleans, she had had an effect on Leland Kenniston's business as well. For when these men learned that she was now associated with the import-export firm, they spread the word of her new association. As a result, a number of new accounts—who had heard of the Kenniston operation but were as yet undecided as to whom to do business with—approached René regarding the purchase of merchandise from the Kenniston cargoes. They knew that Judith was totally reliable and trustworthy regarding financial recommendations, and presumed that she would only work for a company that met her high standards. Lopasuta and Leland had been so pleased by this unexpected turn of events that very shortly after she started with them, they increased her salary and gave her the new title of assistant.

Now nearly twenty-nine, Judith—a willowy, beautiful blonde—neither felt nor exhibited any signs that would indicate she had lived through a period of wretched unjustness that had very nearly permanently blighted her life.

After the death of her parents four years earlier, a dissolute, impecunious Southern aristocrat, David Fales, had promised to marry Judith. Instead, he had arranged for her to be

116

brutally gang-raped, and then callously proposed that as she was now "damaged goods" and therefore no longer fit for any gentleman, she should become his mistress—for as much as Fales desired her, his plans called for marriage to a wealthy heiress, not a penniless farmer's daughter.

Her self-esteem had reached bottom, and she had made her way to Montgomery, where she prostituted herself for unscrupulous land speculators. There, through a series of events that had involved attempting to blackmail then-Representative Andy Haskins to vote for a fraudulent land scheme, Judith met Luke Bouchard, who arranged for her to work at the Brunton & Barntry Bank in New Orleans. It was while employed there that she met Bernard Marquard, a blind former army officer, and his love for her had fully restored her pride. Bernard completely understood and respected her need for independence—both intellectually and financially—and had encouraged her in her decision to continue working after the birth of their two daughters. He was extremely proud that highly respected industrialists admired Judith for her rare intelligence, not merely for her beauty.

Now, early on this Monday morning, Judith was already hard at work, preparing all the basic information for a new contract that Lopasuta would be discussing with the principals later that day. When Lopasuta strode into the office a little after nine o'clock, he greeted her warmly, then bade her to come sit at his desk.

"Judith, I need your help with something," he began, and proceeded to explain about the surprise gifts for Eloise Harkinson and Julie Dumary, and how he thought Judith's dressmaker friend would be the perfect solution.

"I agree," she declared. "Her garments are beautifully made and very high fashion. They're the kind of dresses that most women only get to dream about owning! Oh, yes, I'd be glad to do it for them. I've seen both of them on occasion visiting their husbands at the port office, and they're lovely ladies. Oh, indeed," she exclaimed enthusiastically, "it would make them both so happy!"

"Thank you, Judith," Lopasuta said with a smile. "I can always count on you for just about anything, can't I? Incidentally, I think it's high time you and Geraldine became better acquainted. I think the two of you would really enjoy each other—each of you has an independence that sets you off

117

from most other women. What would you say to coming to dinner with Bernard on Saturday evening?''

"I'd say absolutely! We'd love to come, Mr. Bouchard," Judith replied.

"Wonderful. But there's one condition to this invitation," he said with a mock-solemn expression on his face.

"And what's that?"

"That you stop calling me Mr. Bouchard and start calling me Lopasuta."

"Done!" she said with a laugh.

Shortly after their conversation, the bells on their office door jangled, and Lopasuta and Judith looked up to see Dan Harkinson and Hal Dumary entering.

"Good morning, gentlemen," Lopasuta said as he walked over to greet them with an outstretched hand. "I've just been talking to Judith about our plan, and she's in complete agreement. If you'll excuse me, I've got some work that I have to get to, so I'll leave you in her capable hands."

"Thanks, Lopasuta," Dan and Hal chorused.

Judith bade them to sit, and fifteen minutes later the men were all smiles as Judith finished telling them in great detail about Mademoiselle Victorine's clothes. She had carefully noted their wives' sizes and color preferences, and assured the men that she would choose dresses for their wives that they would be sure to love.

"I'm not sure whether she will have anything already made up in their sizes and colors, so it may take a week or two." Then, noticing the crestfallen expressions on their faces, she quickly went on, "Don't worry. I'm sure Mademoiselle Victorine will come up with something. I'll stop by your office at the end of the day."

Profusely expressing their gratitude, Dan and Hal rose and left.

Just before noon the next day, Judith hailed a carriage and went to the dress shop on Chartres Street. Judith had first met the dressmaker when, on their first anniversary, Bernard had insisted on buying her a special ball gown and had taken her to Mademoiselle Victorine's shop. The Frenchwoman had taken an immediate fancy to Judith and had shown such respect and admiration for Bernard that a friendship had blossomed from that initial meeting.

Mademoiselle Victorine had come to New Orleans from Paris two years before the outbreak of the Civil War. She had married a Creole when she was just twenty-one, and when two months later he went off with his Louisiana regiment as its captain, he was killed during his very first battle. Because her marriage had been so short-lived, she had sorrowfully decided to revert to her maiden name.

Through the guidance of an older cousin, she had been apprenticed to a well-known dressmaker. Hoping to suppress her grief, Victorine had become absorbed in the work, and by the time her employer had retired five years later, she had become a master designer. Her cousin, Emmaline, some seven years older, was a gifted seamstress, and it was she who translated Victorine's designs into shimmering reality, creations that captivated the fancy of New Orleans's social set.

As Judith entered the dress shop, Mademoiselle Victorine, a stout woman with an amiable face, hurried forward with cries of delight to welcome her. "*Ma chérie!* How good it is to see you!" Then she kissed her friend, saying, "I hope this visit is not simply a social call, and that you have decided it is time for a new dress."

Judith laughed at this by-now old joke and said, "As a matter of fact it is—but not for me personally, because I am still getting excellent use out of the beautiful blue taffeta."

"*Tu te moques de moi, vraiment, chérie!*" the dressmaker affectionately chided, wagging a plump forefinger at the tall young woman, her coppery-red pompadour bobbing as she gestured.

"Mam'selle Victorine, you may be the answer to a bit of a problem," Judith declared, changing the subject. "At least I hope you can help."

"You've only to ask, *chérie*. Come, I was just making Creole coffee, with a drop of cognac. And this morning my cousin Emmaline baked some *petits fours*. I should like your opinion of them."

"How could I possibly eat dinner tonight if—oh, very well, I can't resist. I know how wonderful your cousin's *petits fours* are. But just one, and a small one, mind you!"

"Let us go, then, into the private salon. There we can be at our ease, you can tell me what you have in mind, and I shall see how I may best serve you."

Twenty minutes later, after Judith had laughingly protested

that she absolutely could not eat another crumb—having consumed not one, but two of the richest of the *petit fours*—she set down her second cup of coffee. The dress designer leaned forward and, with an engaging look, asked, "Now then, *chérie*, I take it you are in need of a dress for someone other than yourself?"

"Yes, Mam'selle Victorine. Actually, not one dress, but two. You see, they are surprise gifts for two young women whose husbands have just, unexpectedly, come into some money. They have never had anything extra with which to buy such extravagances, and now that these men can afford it, they want to show their love and gratitude to their wives by buying them dresses such as yours—dresses their wives have always longed for, but have never been able to own."

"That is a beautiful sentiment," Mademoiselle Victorine sighed. "These two men sound like ideal husbands. It is a pleasurable thought that my gowns will be worn by women who sound very deserving. A nice change," she said somewhat cynically, "from the *demi-mondaines* and arrogant matrons who too frequently come into my shop."

Judith giggled into her hand, then demanded with a smile, "I hope I do not fall into either of those categories!"

"Ah, *ma chérie*! I assure you, you have your own, very special category. But I am talking too much. I am sure you are very anxious to see my dresses. It just so happens that I have two lovely evening gowns that were not sold for the Mardi Gras balls. I was in no hurry because our things—Emmaline's and mine—always sell. It is a stroke of good luck for both of us, you and I, that I still have them at a time when you need them. Come, let me show them to you."

Rising, she led Judith to a closet and, opening the door, exhibited two magnificent evening gowns. One was of white organdy, hand embroidered with purple flowers, the other was of rose silk, trimmed with delicate lace flounces at the bodice and at the edges of the short puffed sleeves. Judith exclaimed over their beauty. "They're exquisite—but they must cost a fortune."

"For you, I will make a special price. One hundred dollars for them both, and we do not make a *sou*. But then, you and I are dear friends, *n'est-ce pas, chérie*? Incidentally, I'm sure the dresses will need alterations, so tell the ladies they may

120

stop in any afternoon this week. I will make the necessary changes free of charge."

"I can't thank you enough," Judith declared. "And I'm sure neither will their grateful husbands be able to."

Fourteen

Mei Luong, the young Chinese nurse, had become deeply attached to Lopasuta Bouchard and his beautiful wife, Geraldine, and felt even closer to the three children. Every morning, when she awoke in her soft, warm featherbed, she could hardly believe her good fortune. Here she was in this beautiful house and in her very own room, never knowing cold and hunger—never knowing any hardship, in fact. She was also given affection and respect, aside from any material wants.

She had been a sampan girl, her vessel moored not far from Lu Choy's fishing boat in the village of Aberdeen, on the south side of Hong Kong Island. Indeed, she had known Lu Choy, though at first only as one of the many almost nameless, impoverished girls who, in China, were cast out by their families. Such girls supported themselves as best they could from their meager earnings derived from the catch and sale of fish, crabs, and sometimes—though rarely—baby squid.

For herself, Mei Luong had been born after two sons to a couple who farmed on the mainland. The farm yielded scant harvests, and her father and mother, like so many thousands of poor Chinese, arranged for the sale of their daughter. When she was twelve, her father sold her to a brothel keeper in Canton. She managed to escape late at night a month later, to make her way out of the city, along the narrow, dusty road toward the British colony of Hong Kong—for she had heard that the British authorities there prohibited slavery.

When she reached Kowloon, she inveigled passage aboard a boat that was heading for the Hong Kong Island, and when she landed, she spent days looking for work.

For nearly three years, Mei Luong sewed garments in a dingy, airless shop, earning a few pennies a day. Then at fifteen, she met a young coolie who had come to the shop to pick up some garments for his mistress, and he had fallen in love with her. It had been a wondrous feeling, she later told Lopasuta and Geraldine, to be loved—she, whom even her own family had considered worthless trouble.

Her young lover recommended her to the steward of the wealthy household where he worked, which belonged to a dealer in precious jade. After working there for a year, she had been overjoyed when the coolie, Li Kuo, was given a generous gift by his employer so that he might marry her. At her urging, with this money he bought a sampan in Aberdeen, when she had pointed out that they could earn an independent living by fishing.

Then, four months after she found herself pregnant by Li Kuo, Mei Luong's life was blighted once again: Her husband slipped and fell off the sampan in deep water and drowned. To add to this crushing blow, when her child was born it was malformed, but mercifully, it died a day later. Scarcely a week after her baby's birth and death, an old midwife had come for her and told her there was a foreign devil who needed a wet nurse for his newly born child.

There had been much talk in the village when Lu Choy had rescued a tall, very unusual *wai kuo jen*, a foreigner from far across the seas, and had nursed him back to health. It was said also that he was a good, kind man, who seemed to respect the ancient customs. So it was not looked upon as surprising when the news came that Lu Choy was with child by this foreigner. And when Lu Choy died in childbirth, Mei Luong had gladly accepted the role of wet nurse to the infant, trusting the foreigner, even as Lu Choy had done.

And now she was in America.

She was devoted to Lopasuta and also his family, and it was exactly because of this that she was determined to master the English language. Although she had proved a very fast learner during the trip back from Hong Kong—so that by the time they reached Montgomery, she could understand the language quite well and speak it passably—she hoped eventually to speak it as well as any native-born American. While they were still in Montgomery, she had asked for an hour or two every other day for herself and was readily granted it. During that time, unbeknownst to both Geraldine and Lopasuta, she went down the street some three blocks to a house where, in exchange for a paltry sum, she was given English lessons by an elderly retired schoolteacher.

Hazel Murchison had only pleasant memories of the many children she had taught at a rural school some twenty miles east of Montgomery. She was virtually a recluse in her cottage, but one afternoon, while rocking on her porch, she had seen Mei Luong with Dennis and Luke, and had been struck by the Chinese woman's obvious adoration of the children. With an impulsiveness that was uncharacteristic of her, she had introduced herself to Mei Luong, and during their conversation the elderly teacher discovered that Mei Luong wanted to become completely proficient in English, so that she could please her employers still more.

Mei Luong had finally told the Bouchards of her lessons when they were readying to leave for New Orleans. They praised her for her determination to improve her linguistic skill, and promised Mei Luong they would find a new tutor for her, one who would give her a sound basic education in other subjects, as well. This had made Mei Luong weep with joy, for she could scarcely believe she would finally receive formal schooling.

Mei Luong was soft-spoken, humble, and self-effacing in manner. She wore her black hair in traditional Chinese fashion, with bangs framing her forehead in the front and drawn back into a single queue that hung down her back. She had soft, dark brown eyes, and her smile set off her high cheekbones, making her exceptionally pretty.

When she walked down the street pushing the large perambulator in which the two boys sat side by side, men paused and stared at her. To be sure, Mei Luong well understood that sometimes such attentions were denigrating and not at all flattering, but even so, they reminded her of the few happy months she had with Li Kuo. Her loneliness was all the greater because she was in a foreign land, even though she was with people she loved. She hoped that, one day, she might meet a man who would want her, marry her, and give her children of her own.

On the last Thursday in April, toward the end of the afternoon, as Lopasuta Bouchard sat alone in his office signing letters, the door was tentatively opened, and a tall, good-looking man crossed the threshold. He was neatly dressed in white linen trousers and jacket, as befitted the already hot and humid weather in the Queen City. He had a high-arching forehead, a strikingly prominent Roman nose, a firm, sensuous mouth, and his complexion was what was customarily called cafe au lait.

Lopasuta rose from his desk and came forward to greet his visitor. "I—I hope it isn't too late to come to see you, Mr. Bouchard. I realize that it's after hours, but—well, one of my friends recommended you as the best lawyer in New Orleans and I had to come and see you," the man apologetically declared. "My name is Eugene DuBois, and I—I want to engage your services to defend me on a contract for work."

"Make yourself at home, Mr. DuBois. It's not too late at all. Here, take this chair by my desk. Now then, sir, suppose you tell me what's on your mind," the Comanche lawyer proposed.

"I got your name from Aurelio Jefferson, Mr. Bouchard. Maybe you remember—his father was a freed black who had a transport business. As a matter of fact, that's how Mr. Jefferson met Aurelio's mother. She was a Mexican living in Laredo, where Mr. Jefferson was taking goods."

"Oh, yes, I do remember that case. Isn't that the one where your friend inherited his father's transport company and acted as an independent contractor to New Orleans businesses who wished to ship merchandise across the Rio Grande?"

"Yes, sir, that's it exactly."

"Let's see, I recall your friend Aurelio had an understanding with the owner of a dry goods shop here on Portchartrain Lane," Lopasuta went on, "only, after he got back from the journey, the owner refused to pay him what they had agreed upon and said that he had taken too long in conveying the goods to their destination."

"You have a very fine memory, Mr. Bouchard," Eugene DuBois declared with a smile.

"Not really, Mr. DuBois. I happen to remember this case very vividly because I had to deal with an extremely biased judge. The man had made it quite clear that his sympathies were on the side of the storekeeper. I'm not quite sure how I finally persuaded him to the contrary. Perhaps I was just lucky that day in court."

"No, sir; with all due respect, I beg to differ with you. Aurelio could have been put out of business if it hadn't been

124

for you. I'm sure the jury found for him, thanks to your defense. At any rate, Mr. Bouchard, I'm in something of the same predicament. That's why, after Aurelio told me how well you'd done for him, I swore to myself that I would offer you the case.''

"I'm glad you did, Mr. DuBois. I like to stand up for people who don't have too much influence and might otherwise get unjust treatment before a local judge. You see, Mr. DuBois, I'm basically a civil lawyer. Although I'm working for a private company as a corporate lawyer, I've an agreement with my employer that allows me what free time I have left over to devote to defending people like you and your friend Aurelio. So, please take your time and tell me the facts of the case. We can always talk about what my services are worth after I learn whether I can really be of help to you.''

Eugene DuBois settled himself, crossed his legs, nervously plucked at his cravat, and was silent for a moment as he tried to marshal the facts for his interlocutor. At last, he began, "First of all, I should tell you a little of my background, Mr. Bouchard. My father was a Creole born here in New Orleans, and my mother was a quadroon—no, this is not the usual story of a man who makes arrangements with the girl's mother to keep her as a kind of mistress.''

"I understand. Take your time, Mr. DuBois.''

"Thank you, Mr. Bouchard. Well, my father married my mother because he loved her, and also because he felt very sorry for the way she was treated. You see, she was a slave on a sugarcane plantation, upriver from New Orleans. As frequently happened to young, beautiful slaves, the owner took her as his mistress. When he died, his wife, who had resented his affair with my mother, took out her spite on her to pay her dead husband back for his infidelity. She was whipped for the least mistake and very often simply because the wife wanted to show how vindictive she could be. Well, the plantation owner and his wife had a son, and when he was twenty-one, he persuaded his mother to give him the slave for his own use. He even managed to get a bill of sale for her, making him the legal owner. Actually, this son—my father— had long been in love with my mother, who was two years younger than he. Once he legally owned her, they ran off together, and were married. My grandmother—I'm sure she

125

would be appalled to hear me call her that—disinherited my father and never spoke to him again. It caused quite a scandal at the time.''

"I can see how it would," Lopasuta dryly commented.

"So you see, Mr. Bouchard, I have an eighth of black blood in my veins, and I'm proud of it—just as I'm proud of my father. Of course, equality is often still a long way off in the South; inferior status is still the lot of anyone who has the slightest bit of black blood in his veins, despite the Emancipation Act.''

"I can understand your feelings. I myself have a Comanche father and a Mexican mother. The name of Bouchard was given to me by my adoptive father, who saw to it that I was given legal training by a kind and very wise old man," Lopasuta explained.

"Then you know what racial enmity and prejudice can be, I'm quite certain.''

"I had more than my share of it back in Montgomery, Mr. DuBois. But now, why don't you tell me how I can help you?''

"Oh, forgive me for taking up so much of your time! I wanted to give you some background information so you would know a bit about me. And my story is tied into this, in a way. You see, when he left home, my father taught himself carpentry as a trade. My father saw to it that I became skillful with my hands, too, when I was a little boy, encouraging me not only to study books and acquire a good education, but also to be able to earn my own living with manual skills. Over the last two or three years, my business has been quite good because there is a good deal of construction of new houses in New Orleans, as you probably know.''

Lopasuta nodded his understanding, and Eugene DuBois went on, "I've been able to hire two workers, one a white man in his forties who, when he lost his wife and two sons to yellow fever a few years ago, started to drink and ruin his life. I chanced to meet him last year on St. Louis Avenue, when he was being put out of a tavern because he had run out of money. They threw him into the gutter, mocking him, and I thought to myself that here was a white man who understood how brutal his fellow man could be. It made me feel both humble and grateful that I had fared so much better than he had. I took him to a men's bath house to sober him up,

126

and then I bought him some food. We talked almost all night long. It turned out that he was a fairly good carpenter himself, so I hired him at once. The other worker is black, and the three of us get along together very well. My business was doing very well, too—that is, it was until this problem arose."

"I assume that you've been victimized in your work by someone who disputed an agreed-upon price for your services and those of your coworkers," the young Comanche lawyer proffered.

"That's exactly how it was, Mr. Bouchard." Eugene DuBois leaned back in his chair and frowned, then shook his head. "Here's what happened. About four months ago, a M'sieu Georges Carrolier, who owns property about fifteen miles upriver from New Orleans, came into my shop and told me that one of his friends, whom I'd done work for, had recommended me. I remembered that man's name, and I also remembered that I had some difficulty collecting my fee. But I thought to myself that at least it was a recommendation, and that if I did a good job for him, this M'sieu Carrolier might himself refer me to others. That is the way a small business grows, as you understand."

"Of course. Do go on, Mr. DuBois."

"Well, sir, Jim Hearns and Tom Jackson—those are my two workers—came out with me to inspect the job. It was an old white-columned mansion, one of those traditional ones you find so often upriver. A lot of work had to be done on the columns themselves, because the wood was rotting, and there was work to be done on the cornices and the eaves, as well. The owner asked me what I would charge, and I told him that I would give him a fair estimate after I'd thoroughly inspected the job and had taken the time to determine the materials and labor costs."

Lopasuta nodded and leaned back, attentive to the pleasant-natured young man before him. Eugene DuBois had already made a considerable impression on the Comanche lawyer, and he had struck a sympathetic chord in Luke Bouchard's adopted son.

"Well, Mr. Bouchard, I gave him an estimate, and he told me to go ahead. I told him I would have to have some money up front to pay a painter whom I knew, and he gave me the money for that well enough. The work took about three weeks, and when I had finished it, I submitted a bill on my letterhead. Immediately, Carrolier began to criticize my work and to say that I had charged far too much. Well, in the end he gave me only a third of the money and said I could whistle for the rest. Finally, when I rather politely tried to tell him that he had readily agreed to my estimate, he came out and said, 'Look, I could have had a white man do it, so be satisfied with what you've got. I don't really care to deal with *nigras*, and if it hadn't been for the fact that my good friend Matthew Simonson spoke highly of you, I'd certainly have picked a white carpenter for my work.' And that, Mr. Bouchard, is where the matter stands. I've met him two or three times on the street, but he completely ignores me. I can see him talking to his companions and glancing back at me, and then the others laugh—so I'm afraid that he is adding slander to the injury he has done not only to me, but to my two men by denying them their share of pay for their labors on that job.''

"Let me ask you a question, Mr. DuBois. Was this price, this estimate of yours, ever discussed in the hearing of your two workers?''

"Oh, yes. They were with me when I first went out, and when I went back to give him the price. I wanted them to double check that I hadn't left anything out of my calculations. Yes, Hearns and Jackson heard me quote the price and heard Carrolier say—as best I can remember right now—'That sounds reasonable enough. Go ahead and get it over with. I expect to be entertaining within the next month, and I'd like to have you finish it up quickly.' ''

Lopasuta nodded almost absently, then rose and went to an old mahogany bookcase to the left of his desk. Thoughtfully frowning, he put out his hand and touched one or two of the volumes on the second shelf, then chose a thick volume bound in blue buckram and carried it back to his desk. "I want to see exactly what the Louisiana courts have ruled in the way of oral contracts, Mr. DuBois,'' he explained. "Bear with me for a moment. Now, just so that I can be certain as to your legal grounds, you say that there was never any written contract? You know, of course, that it is customary to draw one up, when work of a prolonged nature is involved?''

"That's true,'' the handsome young Creole ruefully admitted, "and I should have had brains enough to insist upon it. But you see, my finances were not too good at the time. I owed my two workers a week's pay in back wages, and I was so anxious to get the job—''

"Of course. Just the same, I think you are reasonably protected. Ah, here we are. Now, probably, Mr. DuBois, your client's defense will be based upon the fact that there is black blood in your veins. He would do so, you see, because this state is backward as regards the civil rights of minority groups. However, you did tell me that your white worker was present at the time and heard the client agree to the terms?''

"I did, sir. And it's true.''

"Very good.'' Lopasuta closed the book with a satisfied smile, walked back to the shelf, and replaced it. "In that case, unless for some reason Carrolier's attorney succeeds in throwing out your witness's testimony—on the grounds that he is not reliable, or is guilty of some act of moral turpitude, or whatever would influence the court in Carrolier's favor— you had a legal contract. The case I just checked was one that was heard before the Louisiana Appellate Court three years ago—*Martieri* v. *Hunt*—which parallels your own situation. In that case, the court upheld the oral contract because there was a witness of good standing who swore under oath that he had heard the two parties agree to terms.''

"That's a great relief to me, Mr. Bouchard, I don't mind telling you.'' Eugene DuBois leaned back in his chair, took out a cotton handkerchief, and mopped his brow. "I'm very much beholden to you. Incidentally, I haven't come to you for free legal service, because I'm quite able to pay you. It's only that I wanted a lawyer who would be sympathetic to the kind of difficulty I found myself in simply because my client looked down upon my ancestry.''

Lopasuta left his desk and stood beside the young Creole, put his hand on the latter's shoulder, and reassuringly smiled at him. "Even if you were penniless and with no prospects of any revenue in the near future, Mr. DuBois, I would take your case because of the satisfaction it would give me to see a rascal punished for trying to trick an honest man. What I propose to do is to write a letter to this client of yours. I shall inform him that Louisiana law has established—and the courts have upheld—the principle that if a white man is witness to an oral agreement between another white man and a third party whose social status is 'inferior' because of race, that agreement is deemed to have been validly witnessed and is in force. I shall also tell your client that if he lets this matter go to court, he will surely lose and will be liable for court costs, and that it would be expedient for him to settle this matter out of court. In addition, a court case would surely attract publicity that would be detrimental to him.''

"I can't begin to thank you enough, Mr. Bouchard.'' The young Creole gratefully held out his hand, which Lopasuta shook with a gracious smile.

"Wait until I have the reply from your client before you congratulate me. But I'm reasonably sure that we have a winning case here. If you'll give me his address, I'll have my assistant, Mrs. Marquard, deliver the letter to him tomorrow at his residence. And unless I miss my guess, if he has common sense, he'll want to avoid the court confrontation, which not only would add legal costs to what he already owes you, but perhaps also would cost him more; I might even go so far as to sue for punitive damages.''

"I'll be very anxious to hear from you. Here is my invoice with his address, Mr. Bouchard. Thank you so much again.''

"You're quite welcome. Do you know, Mr. DuBois, I find such a scholarly bend in your nature that it's too bad you couldn't have pursued a more academic career.''

"Well,'' Eugene DuBois philosophically shrugged, "since it wasn't financially feasible for me to obtain higher education, I—like so many other sons have done—followed in my father's footsteps. But I'll admit to you that I'd love to be able to increase my education and work at something that gives me a greater challenge.''

Lopasuta had a thoughtful expression on his face. "I have something in mind. Are you free tomorrow evening for supper, by the by? You hadn't mentioned that you were married, so I assume that you—''

"No, I'm single, Mr. Bouchard,'' Eugene DuBois interrupted. "I've been much too busy trying to make a decent livelihood for myself to have much time to spare for courting.''

"Well then, I'd very much like to have you as my guest tomorrow evening at my house. Here's my address. I want to talk with you about something that's just come to mind. It may well be that I can help you realize your ambition.''

"That's very good of you, Mr. Bouchard. I'd be delighted to come.'' Eugene DuBois wryly smiled and said, "The prospect of a home-cooked meal is wonderful. I eat out very sparingly, so most of the time I cook for myself—and I'm none too fond of my own cooking, I'll be frank with you.''

Lopasuta tilted back his head and laughed. "I know what you mean! I can barely boil water myself. Fortunately, my wife is a superb cook. And we've a nurse for our children who could put many a famous New Orleans chef to shame. Mei Luong sometimes pampers us with dishes like Mandarin duck, a beef with vegetables and almonds, or again with little black mushrooms that are absolutely mouthwatering.''

"Mei Luong? That's an uncommon name, one I hadn't heard before, Mr. Bouchard.''

"Well, she's Chinese, you see. It happened that I spent time in Hong Kong, and there employed Mei Luong as a nurse. My wife and I have three children, two boys, and a girl born last winter. As a matter of fact, when I get home this evening, I'll tell Mei Luong that I'd be very grateful if she would take over the kitchen tomorrow evening, in honor of your coming.''

"Really, I don't know how to thank you. It's most kind of you." He was silent a moment, then asked, "It's none of my affair, of course, but haven't you run into some antagonism by hiring a Chinese? I've so frequently read that in some areas, like out west, the Chinese are very shabbily treated.''

"You're quite right, they are. But so far, perhaps because she's known to be part of my household and has been accepted by our community, I've encountered no problems with her, for which I'm very grateful. I know there is talk of a treaty between China and the United States that would regulate the number of Chinese laborers coming into this country. I'm basically opposed to this kind of treaty; the only good effect it could have would be to put on a formal basis the right of a certain limited number of Chinese to live and work here—educating people to understand that, if our government accepts a quota of Chinese, then there is no justification for treating them like pariahs. Naturally, I fear that the framers of the treaty have no such intention; I think they mean ultimately to exclude as many Chinese as they can.''

"Mr. Bouchard, I have to tell you how much I respect you and how happy I am that I took Aurelio's recommendation to confer with you. I was just a small boy when the Civil War began, but I can remember telling my father that if people only followed the way of life they were taught in church, we wouldn't have so much hatred and distrust."

"Mr. DuBois, you and I have a good deal in common. I'm looking forward to your being my guest as well as my client—and, hopefully, my friend."

Fifteen

Eugene DuBois set down his coffee cup, exhaled a sigh of contentment, and turned toward Geraldine. "I can't remember when I've had a more delicious dinner, Mrs. Bouchard—or a more exotic one. I've never had duck prepared that way before, and those spareribs with sweet and sour sauce—and the fried rice with onion—I'm afraid I've disgraced myself by agreeing to second helpings all too easily."

"I assure you, Mr. DuBois, it was our pleasure." Geraldine laughed happily and gave Lopasuta, at her left, an almost imperceptible nod of her head to show that she thoroughly approved of their visitor. "After all, it's my opinion that the enjoyment of good food can only be a sign of a discriminating palate," she said in a mock-solemn tone, then added, "Besides, I joined you in having seconds—and would have had more if there'd been anything left!"

"I heartily agree," Lopasuta laughed. "It's quite true, Mei Luong surpassed herself. With your permission, I'd like to call her in, so that you can tell her personally how much you enjoyed what she prepared. For she did all of it, you know."

"I feel so honored! By all means, I would love to compliment her."

Lopasuta reached for the silver handbell beside his plate and rang it several times. The kitchen door opened, and Mei Luong appeared. She was dressed in a cream-colored cheongsam slit at the sides to mid-calf, and her feet were encased in embroidered slippers. But this evening, she was not wearing her hair in a queue, as was her wont. Instead, the sides were gathered into a knot at the back, and the rest of her lustrous black hair hung down her back like a thick ebony curtain falling almost to her waist.

Last night, Lopasuta had told both Geraldine and Mei Luong that they were to have a guest for dinner the next evening and had gone on to explain what empathy he felt toward the young Creole. Then Geraldine had taken Mei Luong aside while Lopasuta went to his study to write some notes on the case he would be handling for Eugene DuBois.

"I've never heard my husband speak quite so warmly of a person he's met only once before," she said to the lovely Chinese woman.

"Then I must take special pains with the meal I am to prepare," Mei Luong rejoined softly.

"I'm sure that whatever you cook will be delicious," Geraldine replied. "You always do your utmost for us. But— that makes me think of something I've had on my mind—now that you're here in this country, I want you to begin thinking of making a new life for yourself."

"But, Mrs. Bouchard," Mei Luong had protested, "my life is to serve you and your husband and to look after your wonderful children. That makes me very happy, and I am trying very hard to be worthy of the responsibility you have given me."

Geraldine remarked offhandedly, "It's really remarkable, dear, how much English you've learned. I sometimes think," she said with a teasing smile, "that you really speak it better than I do."

"Oh, no, this humble person would never even think of a thing like that, and it is not true," Mei Luong again protested, blushing furiously.

"You're just adorable—and I'm sure you know you're very pretty. There is one thing I would like you to do for me tomorrow."

"And what is that, Mrs. Bouchard?"

"Now that you are your own woman—or at least as free as *any* woman is in America, though we still have a long way to go," Geraldine airily explained, as she took Mei Luong's hands and smiled at her, "I'd like you to let down your hair, like the rest of us American women. Your braid is so severe— and besides," she giggled, "feeling a breeze playing through your hair feels so good."

"But—but I am a nurse, and tomorrow I shall be the

cook—there is no need for me to seek to make myself look like someone beyond her station," Mei Luong countered.

"I'll shake you good and hard if you keep on saying silly things like that, Mei Luong," Geraldine scolded. "You don't suppose for a minute that Lopasuta and I expect you to take care of the children and to cook for us the rest of your life. No, indeed! One of these days, Mei Luong, you're going to find the right man, someone who will make you very happy. No, don't interrupt—I know all about the terrible things that happened to you, but you are still very young, and now that you are here it's as if you were given a new life, a new birth in a way, and you must make the most of it. One of these days, a young man will see how sweet and good and lovely you are, and he will fall in love with you. At least, that is what Lopasuta and I would like to have happen."

"My gracious—do you mean that I am to make myself look like an empress tomorrow evening because a man is coming? You surely do not think that this stranger will be the one to notice humble me?" Mei Luong breathlessly exclaimed.

Geraldine could not suppress a most unladylike burst of laughter as she put her hand to Mei Luong's soft, rounded shoulders and playfully shook her. "I told you what I was going to do, if you kept downgrading yourself. Now that's the end of it, do you hear? No, I don't say that our guest tomorrow night is going to be the one who sweeps you off your feet and carries you away on his white charger to live happily ever after—"

"Please? I do not quite understand—" Mei Luong's eyes were wide and questioning.

"That's just an expression we have. You see, many American girls are brought up on the fairy stories that promise one day, if they are very good and sweet and proper, gallant, dashing young men, knights in shining armor riding white horses, will ride into their lives. They will reach down, pick them up, and ride off into the sunset and marry them—and live happily ever after. It's not such a bad idea, either," she laughed.

"But I do not think that any man in this country would want to marry a poor Chinese girl, a girl who was sold to an evil house, and then who fished on a little boat so that she could buy her food."

134

Geraldine shook a warning forefinger at the Chinese girl. "Now that's the last, the very last time you're to put yourself down, Mei Luong. You're not just a nurse, or a cook, or a servant here. You're part of our family—and if I have anything to say about it, you'll always be a part of our family."

Mei Luong had burst into tears, overcome with joy at such unexpected affection. Sympathetically, Geraldine had put an arm around the Chinese girl's shoulders and murmured, "Now tomorrow, before our visitor comes, I'm going to take you into my bedroom and fix your hair myself. And you're going to wear your prettiest cheongsam."

The next evening, as Mei Luong emerged from the kitchen after dinner, Eugene DuBois stared incredulously at her, and then stammered as he rose to his feet. "I—I want to thank you for the most wonderful meal I've ever had, Miss Mei Luong."

"You are most kind to say that, sir." She inclined her head deferentially, but her cheeks had begun to flame at the admiring look in his eyes as they first exchanged glances.

"No, I'm not being kind, I'm just telling the truth. It was wonderful," Eugene replied.

"Mei Luong," Geraldine interposed softly, "this is Eugene DuBois."

"I'm pleased to meet you, sir." Lu Choy said with a shy smile.

At this moment, Lopasuta excused himself. "I'd like to go into my study to look up a few references that might have a bearing on your case," he said to Eugene. "But please—sit and enjoy your coffee. I'll be back in a few minutes."

When he had left, Eugene turned to Mei Luong. "I really meant what I said about dinner," he assured her.

The young Chinese woman raised her eyes to his and blushed again. "Thank you, Mr. DuBois, for all your praise for my humble work in the kitchen. I am so very glad you enjoyed it. Now you must excuse me, for I must go back to clean things up, as that is my work." Mei Luong, beside herself with confusion yet pleased at finding herself the center of attention, had begun to walk backward toward the kitchen, her head bowed in deference.

Geraldine quickly rose. "The dishes can wait, Mei Luong.

I think Mr. DuBois would like to know something about your beautiful country. I tell you what, I'm going into the study and see if I can help my husband find the books he needs and make some notes for your case, Mr. DuBois, so why don't you just sit here and chat with Mei Luong. Please sit down, Mei Luong—go ahead, please.''

With this, she left the two young people standing looking at each other and closed the door behind her. There was an arch smile on her face, and her eyes were shining with mischief. But it was a romantic mischief, for she, too, had been very impressed by the demeanor and sincerity of Eugene DuBois.

"Please sit down, Miss Mei Luong," Eugene courteously urged.

Mei Luong entwined her fingers, nervously twisting them before her, her cheeks rosy with blushes. She glanced helplessly at the door through which Geraldine had gone, then shyly and almost fearfully glanced at the tall young Creole. "You are sure you do not mind?" she timidly inquired.

"Mind?" he almost exploded. "I told Mr. Bouchard yesterday afternoon, that I seldom have any time to go out with girls because I am so busy trying to make a living—but I swear, Miss Mei Luong, you're the loveliest girl I've ever seen.''

"Oh, no, you must not say such a thing! You do not even know me—and—and—and—I am Chinese—from a very poor family!'' Mei Luong was beside herself, wishing that the earth would suddenly open and swallow her up. Yet when she dared glance up at him and saw that he was staring with open admiration at her, she could not help but be delighted—yet embarrassed, all at the same time.

"I know that the Chinese people are treated badly out in California and Seattle and other places, Miss Mei Luong. But you see, I am much in the same position here in the South. My father was white, but my mother was a quadroon, that is one having one-fourth black blood. So many people look down on me, too, you see.''

"Oh, Mr. DuBois, *I* would never do such a thing! You are a very good man, and you said such kind things to me—''

"And I meant every word of them, too!" he almost fiercely insisted. "Now please sit down. Really, I'd like to know about your life in China. *Please*.''

She gave an encapsulated version of her short, unhappy life in Hong Kong, and then told him how she had met Lopasuta—a meeting that had utterly changed the path her life would normally have taken. "So you see," she concluded, "Mr. and Mrs. Bouchard have been so very kind to me, there is nothing I would not do for them."

Eugene DuBois grinned boyishly. "Well, if that's the way you feel, Miss Mei Luong, then I think you should do as Mrs. Bouchard requested and stay and talk with me. Maybe we could each have another cup of your wonderful coffee, if there's any left?"

"Yes—there—there is some. I will bring it. You are sure? I mean, that you wish me to continue to sit with you?"

"I wouldn't have asked if I hadn't meant it. Please, Miss Mei Luong, it will make me very happy."

"All—all right, then. I will go get the coffee." She walked slowly to the kitchen door, then turned back and saw him looking after her with the same light of admiration in his eyes; she could not suppress her blushes. Uncharacteristically, because of the excitement of this meeting and the surprising kindliness he had shown her, she blurted out, "I think you are a very good man. I would be proud and honored to have coffee with you, Mr. DuBois."

The letter that Lopasuta Bouchard drafted and Judith Marquard took to Georges Carrolier bore immediate results. By the following Monday, the Comanche lawyer received a note by messenger to the effect that its sender stood ready to pay the rest of the disputed fee and formally offer his apology for the slur on Eugene DuBois's birth.

When Eugene came the following day, to learn what action his recalcitrant client intended to take, Lopasuta gestured him to a chair by the desk and, without a word, handed the note across the desk.

"Why, Mr. Bouchard, this is wonderful news! Now we'll be able to avoid a court confrontation."

"Yes, and I'll see to it that the money gets here by the end of this week, or know the reason for a delay," Lopasuta promised. "Well now," he went on, "that's disposed of, isn't it? Incidentally, I somehow never got around to discussing what I intended to discuss with you at dinner last week. You're a very intelligent man, Mr. DuBois. I think you might

137

have a future as a lawyer. And certainly, feeling as you do that there's too much injustice, you could strike a valiant blow in defense of all people of mixed blood who presently can't afford a spokesman, or who are afraid to test the law because they are sure it will be on the side of whites. What would you think, Mr. DuBois, if I offered to engage you as a law clerk? I've been needing one for some time now, and I think you'd do admirably. I'd train you myself; we'd spend an hour or two every day reading the law until you had a solid foundation in it. Also, you could make yourself useful to me in many other ways. For example, you could help Mrs. Marquard considerably by going to some business meetings, or the stock exchange, and getting the latest news. As I told you, what time I can spare from this import-export firm I devote to civil law. If there were two of us, we could handle that many more cases. And if you were diligent, you could very easily become a lawyer within a year, or a little more than that. How does the idea strike you?''

Eugene sat with his mouth open. "I'm flabbergasted! I never thought of myself in that way—but—but I'd certainly like to try it, Mr. Bouchard!" He leaned back in his chair and mused aloud, "Hearns and Jackson could probably handle all the work for my company—besides, they're both excellent carpenters in their own right. Of course, I'd want to supervise the initial stages of any new jobs and maybe put my hand in at times—''

"That could be arranged. We could work out any of these details. But I really think you'd make an excellent lawyer. You're articulate, you handle yourself well, and I believe you're a hard worker.''

"Mr. Bouchard, you've opened up a brand-new world to me by making an offer like this. The fact is, I'd like to try it, just to see if I could make the grade.''

"Then it's settled. Perhaps you could start next Monday. We'll go slowly at first, till you work out your schedule between your carpentry firm and this office. Oh, by the way, there's something else—''

"Yes, Mr. Bouchard?''

"This is supposed to be a secret, but my wife told me just this morning, before I came to the office, that Mei Luong thinks you are very wonderful and a good man. I rather think

138

she'd like to see you again. Maybe this is none of my business, but how do you feel about her?''

"I—I told her she was the loveliest girl I'd ever seen, and I meant it. I also think she's a very warm, intelligent person—and I'm awfully pleased that she thinks well of me, I must say!''

"Why don't you come to dinner tomorrow evening, and we'll talk further about some of the work that I expect you to do here in the office and give you some primary legal texts to read. I think I mentioned I got *my* legal training from a dear old man who was a wonderful lawyer and a pillar of justice. All I know about law I learned from him—and I hope I'll be half as good a teacher with you, Eugene."

Lopasuta Bouchard offered his hand, and Eugene DuBois shook it, his face aglow.

Sixteen

Easter Sunday morning of this year of 1880 found Andy and Jessica Haskins entering a large, white clapboard church. They were attending services with their children and the middle-aged nurse Andy had engaged a week after he had gone to Tuscaloosa, Alabama, to accept the post of director of the sanatorium in that town. Mrs. Emma Parsons had been recommended to him by his predecessor at the sanatorium, Edmond Philippet.

Andy had first come in contact with the sanatorium seven years earlier, when he and Luke Bouchard had been the targets of an assassination attempt by a deranged, former Confederate captain. Luke had arranged for the man to be cared for in the Tuscaloosa sanatorium—a private rather than state-run institution, which had been under the directorship of Edmond Philippet.

Last year, when Philippet had been told by his doctor that his health demanded a move to a drier climate, he had written to Laure Bouchard, asking her if she could recommend someone to take over the position. Laure immediately thought of Andy, knowing that the one-armed state senator would be sympathetic and compassionate—not to mention the fact that he had already stated he was quite fed up with the vagaries of politics and his fellow politicians.

Apprised of the opening at the sanatorium, Andy had discussed it with Jessica, who had eagerly urged him to accept the new position. Burt Coleman had promised to assume the stewardship over the land that Luke Bouchard had deeded to Jessica's now-dead father. He said, "Mr. Haskins, you've got my word I'll look after it as if you were here watching me every minute of the day. I'll send letters to you nearly every week to let you know how the crops are coming, and Amelia will help me keep the books, and we'll send you checks on the profits after we've paid expenses. You can depend on me."

Andy had taken over the sanatorium post—first on a part-time basis and then, when his term as senator had ended with the summer recess, full-time. By now, he was thoroughly familiar and comfortable with his duties and hoped that his progressive ideas would bear fruit among the patients.

Tuscaloosa, which had once been the capital of Alabama, was a pleasant, quiet town. Its serenity, in contrast to the political chicanery that went on in Montgomery, considerably eased Andy's nerves, tautened and exacerbated as they were by the death of his benefactor, Luke Bouchard.

The large, airy two-story house on the outskirts of Tuscaloosa had a huge yard and was ideal for their three children—Horatio, seven and a half, Andrew, who had his fourth birthday in January, and their little sisters Ardith, three, and Margaret, eighteen months. There were separate bedrooms for each child and for Mrs. Parsons. The nurse was a widow in her mid-fifties; she had lost her husband and two sons during the war. Her devotion to the Haskins children gave Jessica and Andy ample time to rediscover each other, just as in the early days when they were courting. In addition, Emma Parsons often insisted on relieving Jessica of the chore of cooking, and she had proved to be an excellent cook.

On this sunny Easter Sunday, Andy and Jessica wished to give fervent thanks for the changes in their lives that had let them be closer than ever before, and had allowed Andy the opportunity to help people more directly and definitely than he could have done in the senate. The sanatorium was endowed through private means and had a state license to operate. Andy Haskins, as director, could exercise influence and investigate cases far more thoroughly than any state institution for the insane.

One of the first things Andy had done when he arrived at the institution was to confer with the physician in charge, an enthusiastic young man in his early thirties. Calvin Torrance, a Birmingham-born bachelor with three years of general practice in one of the poorest rural communities in all of Alabama, had decided to turn to the care of the mentally deranged. He had a personal reason for that choice, which demanded an unflinching, strong-willed nature, coupled with gentle sympathy: His father, while serving as a corporal in the Alabama infantry, had lost a leg and suffered shell shock when a Union howitzer's shell exploded in a trench just a few feet away from him. Though he had ostensibly recuperated and adjusted himself to an artificial leg, and though his mind seemed to have recovered from the shock, Dr. Torrance saw his father's mind and health grow more and more unstable with the passing years until finally, five years ago, Magnus Torrance had tried to kill himself. After being certified as insane, it had been his son's painful and agonizing duty to have him committed to a state sanatorium.

As a result of this, after hearing of Edmond Philippet's fine work in Tuscaloosa, the doctor had applied for a position, and had been accepted. Andy had found him so conscientious and dedicated, that last August, he appointed Dr. Torrance assistant director and increased his salary. One fall day when they were having lunch together in the dining hall, Andy observed the behavior of the more lucid patients, who were given greater freedom than others. He turned to Calvin Torrance and remarked, "You know, sometimes it's hard to be realistic, and realize that we're dealing here with people who have gone into little worlds all their own. Sadly, too often their families are so troubled and bewildered by their behavior that they dismiss them, say they're insane, and probably wish they were dead so they wouldn't have to think about them. But we must keep them comfortable and make them as happy as possible, because it isn't for us to judge whether their lives should end or not."

Calvin nodded his head in agreement, "Just think—it wasn't all that long ago that in England, for example, the people would have been chained to the walls and given slop to eat.

141

The gentry visited Bedlam, Newgate, and Bridewell to make sport and to laugh over these unfortunate souls' antics. I sincerely hope that kind of practice has been completely abolished."

"That's for certain!" Andy almost shouted in his vehemence. "But there's another practice that I suggest occurs frequently, and it's just as abhorrent. Mr. Philippet told me that he suspected a few of his patients had been committed here by greedy relatives, who hoped they would die as quickly as possible so they could legally inherit whatever money there was to take. In one shocking case—the man's since died—Mr. Philippet said that he suspected this old man's son and daughter-in-law actually tried to poison him; when they didn't succeed, they had him committed and more or less told Mr. Philippet that it would be a blessing if the father died."

"It's hard for me to stomach such greed, Andy. But I hope you and I will be perceptive enough to ensure that nobody will be committed here who really isn't insane," Dr. Torrance said. "Incidentally, I've just received an application from Dr. John Salisbury of the state insane asylum. He's heard of our institution and would much prefer to be associated with us—and I think it would be good to have him here. He's a man in his late forties, and he's had years of experience in certifying mentally unstable patients. It would be good to have as many qualified doctors who've had a great deal of experience with the insane on our own staff as possible, as a sort of counterbalance in case you or I should be misled by rapacious people."

"I agree. Why don't you ask him to come down here for an interview?"

A week later, Dr. Salisbury inspected the sanatorium, spent three days conferring with Andy Haskins and Dr. Torrance, and enthusiastically reaffirmed his desire to work there.

As they walked down the aisle to a pew that had enough empty places to accommodate them all, Andy put his hand protectively on the small of Jessica's back. They reached an appropriate pew, made sure the children were seated on either side of Mrs. Parsons, and took their own seats. Andy wasn't really a church-going man, but he did believe in the Almighty and he was grateful that He had sent Jessica his way. No man in this world could ask for a better wife, and their boys, aside

142

from the usual mischief children of that age got into, were a delight. Ardith was a quiet little girl, while the baby was still too young to determine what she would be like when older.

Yes, he had a lot to be grateful for, and this holiday, celebrating as it did the resurrection of His only Son, had a special meaning for Andy Haskins. He hadn't felt quite confident at first that he was cut out to be director of the sanatorium, but in the time that he spent there since last summer, he felt as if this job had been waiting for him all of his life. It made him even more aware of the fact that although he'd lost an arm in the war, he still had his wits about him. For all around him were pathetic, unhappy people who'd had one piece of bad luck or another in their lives, and they just hadn't been able to stand up against it.

Andy had made a point of reading up on these mental disorders—not that he'd ever be smart enough to discuss medical matters with Dr. Torrance, or this new fellow, Dr. Salisbury, but he could see what a complicated piece of machinery the human mind was. He came to appreciate that sometimes when people had a shock or a tragedy, they wanted to retreat into a tiny, dark little world, where nothing could bother them, and where they could pretend that none of their troubles had happened.

Jessica reached for Andy's hand, as the minister in the pulpit, looking up from the huge Bible spread open before him on the lectern, began to conclude his sermon: "Blessed are the meek, for they shall inherit the earth. The Lord our God, who sees the fall of the tiniest sparrow from the heavens, witnesses those small deeds of Christian kindness equally as He does the unjust deeds of those who work in shadows and think to go unseen. He weighs minutely the tiniest sands in the balance scale of our lives, and He forgives those who have conspired against others who are contrite in the knowledge of their misdeeds, as He forgives the loyal servant who errs out of zeal."

He paused a last moment. "On this Easter, this blessed day of the resurrection of the Son of our dear Lord, I ask each of you to look in upon his secret heart and admit those errors he has made, and to pray for redemption through faith and good works. For only thus can hatred and evil, suspicion and greed, prejudice and wickedness be defeated for all time, so that He may have His coming again into our temporal world.

God bless all of you, and may you enjoy His bounteous blessings. Amen.''

After church, while sitting in the buggy waiting for Mrs. Parsons and the children—who had stopped to say hello to friends—Jessica turned to Andy. ''It was a beautiful sermon, Andy, wasn't it? And I think the pastor had you in mind, when he spoke of good deeds.''

''Oh, no, Jessica,'' the one-armed man deprecatingly protested. ''I'm sure he was speaking in generalities.''

''Nonetheless, your good works are well known.'' She kissed him lightly on the cheek. ''The children were good as gold; I was a bit surprised. They didn't cry even a little bit, and they barely fidgeted. Mrs. Parsons is such a wonderful nurse, isn't she? What a stroke of luck it was to find her—and to find that we got a wonderful cook in the bargain!'' She looked at her husband and whispered, ''I love you so, Andy Haskins.''

The following afternoon as he sat going over some papers on his desk, Andy heard a knock on his office door. He automatically put the pages back into their file and called, ''Come in.''

Harriet Bowles, a stout, middle-aged woman who had entered the nursing profession at the start of the Civil War, smiled and approached Andy's desk. ''Good afternoon, sir,'' she said. ''There's a gentleman here to see you—he said he has an appointment. A Mr. Roger Winters. He has his aged father with him.''

''Ah, yes. Thank you, Nurse Bowles. I'll be out directly.'' As she withdrew from the room, Andy walked to the file cabinet and extracted a slim folder. He refreshed his memory by reading the letter Mr. Winters had written a few weeks earlier, plus the copy of his reply, setting up this appointment.

There were chairs lining each side of the wide entryway, which served as waiting and reception area for the sanatorium. A large desk dominated the center, and radiating off this area were carpeted hallways leading to other offices and the dining hall. A broad staircase led up to the second and third floors on which the patients' rooms were located. There were three floors in all to the sanatorium, housing some sixty patients. Those who were either senile or nonviolent, the two doctors had assured Andy, could safely be quartered two or even three to a room so long as there were attendants who were solicitous and efficient in their duties. Padded walls lined other rooms in which violent or hyperactive patients were lodged individually. On the third floor were larger, airier rooms for those who seemed to be on the threshold of regaining their facilities and were scheduled to be release within the next several months. Also on the third floor were five large rooms for the staff attendants.

As Andy entered the reception area, he saw a frail, white-haired old man, sitting with his head bowed, his arms folded across his chest so tightly that, at first glance, he appeared to be hugging himself. The old man's eyes were closed, his mouth was partly open, and his lips were moving soundlessly.

"Mr. Haskins?" The young man who stood before him was six feet tall, with well-groomed black hair, short side-burns, and a small, neatly trimmed mustache. He was impeccably dressed in a light gray spring suit with a high collar, above which the starched tips of his white shirt showed. His face was handsome, and his voice was cultured, though with a note of superciliousness to it. His arrogant, dark blue eyes fixed Andy with a quizzical look.

"Yes, I'm Andrew Haskins, Mr. Winters. This is your father, I presume."

"That is correct. As you can see, I believe I described his condition accurately in my letter. Although, to be fair, the journey from our home in Bessemer—which is roughly fifty miles northeast of here—was a bit trying."

"I'm sure it was, Mr. Winters. Please, sit down won't you?" As Andy seated himself, he said, "I've just been refreshing my memory by rereading your letter. You said your father is sixty-seven."

"That's correct. He was sixty-seven in January. I'm afraid—" Roger Winters loudly sighed and shook his head, then looked down at the floor before again fixing Andy with an intent gaze, "—I'm afraid the poor old thing is completely senile. I'd be obliged to you if you could attest to this, for I believe my father is no longer capable of handling his own affairs."

"I see. Well, Mr. Winters, while I am the director of this institution, I have no medical qualifications to issue such a judgment. This is done by my two associates, who are physicians with no mean experience in the field of mental instability.''

"Mr. Haskins, I'm sure that your two colleagues would confirm my verdict."

"That may well be, but since we are licensed by the state, Mr. Winters, things must be done properly. My medical aides can hardly certify that a man is senile and mentally incompetent without a thorough examination."

"Of course, of course," the young man hastily broke in. "I read about you in the papers when you took over this institution—which already had an excellent reputation from your predecessor—so I wouldn't expect one of your honest reputation to do anything that isn't absolutely aboveboard." He gave Andy an unctuous smile.

"That's kind of you to say. However, shall we get back to your father? Would you give me a comprehensive account of his behavior?"

"Of course. You see—well—" again Roger Winters looked down at the floor and sighed, "—I'm afraid my poor father's behavior has suddenly become extremely erratic. Some days he behaves as you see him today; other days he's very eccentric, unpredictable. So it would obviously be for his own good to have him committed here, where he can't get into trouble—or cause trouble for anyone else. And I'm sure your colleagues will find that anyone in my father's present mental condition must surely be declared mentally incompetent."

Andy Haskins frowned. Though Winters's attitude seemed a trifle harsh and brusque, Andy could not deny that the elder Winters was displaying ominous symptoms: He sat huddled on the bench, still hugging himself, head still bowed, eyes still closed, and lips still silently moving.

"I think you'll agree, Mr. Haskins, that my father should be under observation. I'm sure that you and your doctors will concur with me that he can't fend for himself and would be much better off under your excellent supervision here at the sanatorium," Winters persisted.

"Yes, Mr. Winters, I daresay that the best thing for us to do is to examine him thoroughly—although the science of determining the degree of mental instability still hasn't been developed much beyond guesswork in a great many cases, you know." Andy was beginning to wonder whether this young man cared about his father at all. From his demeanor and dress, the family was obviously well-off. Surely they had the means to hire a private nurse who could look after the old man at home, where he could live out his days surrounded by comfort, instead of being shunted away to be consigned for the rest of his days to a sanatorium for the insane. Obviously, the best thing to do was to get Roger Winters out from under his heels so his colleagues could properly examine the poor old fellow.

He finally said, with an attempt at a sympathetic smile, which he felt was far from convincing but apparently satisified his listener, "Very well, Mr. Winters. If you'll come into my office and sign an agreement to have your father committed to us for preliminary examination, we can go on from there."

"Of course, if that's the way you prefer it done." Winters followed Andy to his office and seated himself. Leaning forward, he boldly declared, "I want to confide in you, Mr. Haskins. You see, I'm hoping to get married, and my cousin, who lives with us, he's also courting a girl. To be frank, Mr. Haskins, Father is in the way—excuse me. I didn't quite mean to put it that way; please don't misunderstand me. I should say, rather, we're all so helpless at home. We have a few servants, yes, but when our fiancées come to visit us, they get so upset when they see poor Father sitting in the corner with his face turned to the wall, not speaking to anyone. Then there've been times when he starts ranting and raving, when he starts threatening me and saying that I don't care about him at all. Most assuredly, quite the opposite is true. My cousin and I have leaned over backwards trying to make it pleasant for him in his declining years, but he's just beyond help—I mean, a family can do just so much, don't you agree, Mr. Haskins?"

Andy Haskins found himself feeling rather uncomfortable, wondering why Winters was so eager to make his point at such length. But once again, he forebore to offer any comment, deciding to postpone all judgments about the situation until examination of the patient was completed. "If you'll just sign this paper," he said, "then we can proceed. We'll be in touch with you as soon as we have the results of our examination."

"Oh, er—well, yes, of course." Winters impatiently leaned forward, took the pen Andy handed him, and signed the paper of temporary commitment. The former state senator wryly thought that for all the emotion the young man displayed, this drastic action was, for him, not really very different from writing out a bill of lading for goods shipped, or for the delivery of a cow to its new owner.

"Is that all I have to do now? When do you think you can let Cousin Dalton and me know what the doctors think about leaving Father here for good? Of course, I wouldn't want to put him in a state institution—that's too cold and inhumane, you understand. But you see, when age starts to hit some men, they really begin going downhill fast." Winters paused and took out a linen handkerchief, mopped his brow, and uttered a heartrending sigh. "I'm sorry to see it end like this. Well then, you'll be in touch with me, I presume?"

"Yes, Mr. Winters. I'll have the doctors examine your father in the morning. I think it's important now to get him placed into a room, see to it that he's made as comfortable as he can be, and then arrange for his dinner—by the way, do you have any suggestions to make as to his diet? If he has any lingering maladies, it might call for a very different menu from what we usually give stable patients."

"No, he eats about anything—he's especially fond of chocolate candies, as a matter of fact. Although when I mentioned Father's symptoms to our family physician, the doctor did mention to me that perhaps Father might be having a severe allergic reaction to such confections and that it would be best if his diet were to exclude such things until the exact cause for his condition is determined." The young man regarded Andy with a humorous expression, then declared, "Frankly, I find that idea utter nonsense. Why, the very idea that something as harmless—and delicious—as chocolate could induce such a state in Father, is patently absurd!"

"Not at all, sir," Andy assured Winters. "On the contrary, I believe it is entirely possible that severe reactions can occur from the simplest sources. I find your doctor's suggestion to make perfect sense, and I shall issue strict instructions that your father is to receive no chocolate until we have given him a thorough examination."

Roger Winters sighed poignantly. "Do whatever you must, Mr. Haskins. I appreciate your concern. Father's condition really worries Cousin Dalton and me."

"Well, by signing this paper, Mr. Winters, you've transferred the worries over to us. You can call here in about a week, by which time we ought to have our preliminary findings completed.''

"That long? I shouldn't think it would take a week to determine that he'll really never be able to return to his house and conduct a normal life again, Mr. Haskins.''

Andy was nettled at the way the younger man kept harping on his father's deficiencies before even the most scanty preliminary examination had been made of the old man. "I'm sure that if there's any chance of restoring him to good mental and physical health, you'd be the last person in the world to want to callously abandon him," he said rather testily. "Perhaps next week we might have some sort of answer for you. Or perhaps it will take a good deal longer. It all depends on what we're able to determine from our observations. It isn't at all like diagnosing a physical ailment, sir.''

"That will have to do, I suppose. I do so hope that Father will be happy here. I mean, it's terrible to have to end your days in an insane asylum, but Cousin Dalton and I just couldn't cope with this from day to day with no hope in sight that he would ever get any better. Well then, Mr. Haskins, I'm indebted to you. However, I'd like to see how Father is getting on here, so may I stop in again? I'll call on you, shall we say in four days?''

"That would be fine. I'll show you out.''

As soon as Roger Winters had left, Andy called Nurse Bowles into his office. "Will you get Jim and Mack please, Nurse? I'd like them to help Thomas Winters into a room. Put him in a room where he'll have a good view of the garden in the back.''

"Very well, Mr. Haskins. I'll get them right away.''

Andy went out to the reception area and seated himself beside the old man, who still sat morosely, his arms still unyieldingly folded across his chest. "Mr. Winters, my name is Andy Haskins, and I'm director of this institution. Your son tells me you've been ill. We're going to give you a nice room where you can rest a bit, and then we'll bring you your dinner.''

Thomas Winters slowly turned his head and, through lackluster eyes, contemplated the one-armed man seated beside him. Then he shrugged and closed his eyes again, without uttering a word.

In that momentary glimpse, Andy had discerned that the

old man's pupils were glassy and dilated. He made a mental note to call this to Dr. Salisbury's attention at the preliminary examination the next morning.

Jim Castle and Mack Garten, two sturdy young men in their late twenties, both displayed a genial nature. As orderlies in the hospital, they worked long hours, without complaint, and with total dedication to the welfare of the patients of the institution. They came into the reception hall and, seeing the old man, glanced questioningly at Andy, who nodded. He rose now and said gently, "Mr. Winters, I know you're tired, and these attendants will take you to your room. Don't worry about a thing. Tomorrow, we'll have a nice talk. Will that be all right?"

This time, the old man slowly raised his head, opened his eyes, and stared almost beseechingly at Andy. His Adam's apple shifted, and there was a faint sound, as if he were struggling to speak.

"Don't tax yourself, please, Mr. Winters," Andy soothed. "We'll talk tomorrow morning, after you've had a good night's sleep. Will that be all right?"

Once again, a choked, strained sound emerged from the old man's mouth. His eyes were glassy, and his arms began to tremble as he finally unfolded them and let them fall to his sides. The two attendants flanked him on either side and led him gently up the stairs.

The young attendants reported to Andy Haskins that Thomas Winters had given them no trouble, but rather had looked around the room and given a brief nod, as if to signify that he approved of it.

Andy inquired, "Was he still hugging himself when you left him?"

"I'm afraid so, Mr. Haskins," Jim spoke up. "He's sure a sad-looking old fellow."

"Thank you for telling me," Andy said, and sighed. "You might look in on him every now and again. If anything develops tonight, you let me know, no matter how late it is. I'll go home early to eat, but I plan to come back. I'll frankly admit I'm a little worried about our new patient. I don't know—maybe it's just because he seems so helpless."

*　　*　　*

At noon the next day, Dr. Salisbury went to Andy Haskins's office to report his findings. Choosing his words carefully, he declared, "I noticed from the very outset that Mr. Winters's eyes were dilated and glassy. This lethargy of his, and this business of the protective clenching of his arms around himself, led me to believe that he might be suffering from something other than senility."

"What are you getting at, Doctor?" Andy asked, his brows raised in question.

"He seems to be in fairly good general health, but he's a little weak, and I believe that he might have a touch of malnutrition. That might—and I emphasize *might*—account for his listlessness. . . ."

"Go on," Andy suspiciously demanded.

"This is only speculation, you understand, but I believe he is under the influence of a type of opiate. What Dr. Torrance and I would like to do is to keep him under very close observation for the next two or three days, and then we'll be better able to give you an accurate report as to our diagnosis."

"I wouldn't have it any other way! I'm absolutely shocked, though—to think this old man might be addicted to opiates. I confess, I had suspected that the son just wanted to get rid of his father—but, obviously, it wasn't that way at all. No wonder he thought the old man was going insane, or at least senile. I hope I wasn't too rude to him when he practically begged me to take his father off his hands."

As the days passed, Thomas Winters seemed to respond to his treatment—which consisted of little more than a good deal of loving attention and hearty, nutritious meals. Slowly, his faculties seemed to be returning, and the glassy stare that had characterized his expression seemed to wane.

When his son, Roger, returned at the end of the week, Andy was pleased to report to him that the old man was improving, and if the senior Winters continued on this path toward recovery, he could probably be released shortly.

"I see," young Winters replied tersely. "I presume it is permitted for me to see him."

"Of course!" Andy personally escorted the young man up to his father's room. "Incidentally, Mr. Winters, I wish to apologize for any abruptness on my part when I first met you. I hope I didn't offend you in any way."

"Not at all, Mr. Haskins. I understand that there are many unscrupulous people in this world, and that—because of my concern for my father—my actions may have been misinterpreted. You needn't apologize, I assure you, and no offense was taken."

Andy left the two men alone and returned to his office. He was busy enough so that he did not have time to concern himself with Thomas Winters for the remainder of the afternoon—besides which, the old man was probably thoroughly enjoying his visit with his son.

Just before Andy was preparing to leave the sanatorium the following afternoon, a worried-looking Nurse Bowles appeared at his door.

"Mr. Haskins, Thomas Winters has had a relapse. I've already called Dr. Salisbury, but I thought you would like to know, sir."

"Thank you, Nurse. Yes, I'll go right up to his room. I'm sorry to hear that—he seemed to be doing so well. This morning he was even socializing—even laughing—with some of the other patients. I wonder what could have happened."

"I don't know, sir," the nurse replied. "But he's back to just sitting there, hugging himself like he was when he first came here. Poor old man . . ."

When Andy reached Thomas Winters's room, he was just as the nurse had described him. The doctor was solicitously hovering over him, examining him with his medical instruments.

"It's most peculiar, Mr. Haskins," the doctor finally said, taking the stethoscope out of his ears. "I would swear that this man is drugged again. Obviously, my diagnosis was incorrect, for although he exhibits all the symptoms of opiate use—this stupor, for example, and the glazed look in his eyes—we haven't prescribed any drugs whatsoever. Therefore, since his condition mirrors that as it was initially, these symptoms must be completely emotionally induced.

"I would say, under the circumstances, that we continue to watch him closely and try to ascertain if there is a pattern to these mood alterations. Perhaps that will give us some clues as to the proper treatment."

"That seems a sound course, Dr. Salisbury." Andy stood looking down at the old man, stroking his chin. "I shall have to inform his son, of course. I'm sure he will be most disappointed to learn that his father won't be rejoining him soon after all. In fact, it may be that young Winters is right, and the logical thing to do is to certify old Thomas, and just try to make his last days as pleasant as possible here in the sanatorium.''

Seventeen

Just over a year ago, in March 1879, Charles Douglas had taken his young junior partner with him to New York City with the intention of opening a branch of the Douglas Department Store there. Charles viewed this project as the culmination of a dream, and the fact that he wanted Alexander Gorth to manage the New York branch indicated the extent of Charles's faith in Alex's abilities—abilities that he had shown repeatedly in the Galveston store.

During their stay in New York Charles had signed a fifteen-year lease with the real estate broker Daniel Terry on a vacant lot on Twenty-first Street and Broadway. Astute merchant that he was, he had finally prevailed upon Terry and his partner, Cornelius Johnson, to alter the rental agreement, adding a clause allowing Charles to buy the land outright after five years—with the stipulation that half of the annual rental fee paid out over this initial five-year period could be applied to the agreed-upon purchase price.

"This is really a steal, Alex," Charles Douglas had confided to his ambitious young store manager, "and I think one of the reasons Terry and his partner, Johnson, let me have it at such a bargain rental was that they didn't think I could make it through the five years. But I'm going to show them, with your help. Perhaps it's not as large a piece of property as I would have liked, but the location is perfect. Its proximity to the Lord & Taylor and Constable & Company stores means that if our store is stocked with a variety of good merchandise, we'll have immediate traffic to start with in the customers heading for those two establishments. Once we get them to stop here first, which we hope to accomplish through advertising, we'll take them away from those two merchant princes, just see if we don't!''

"I'm going to try my darndest, Charles," Alexander had enthusiastically promised.

Upon signing the agreement for the land, Charles had retained a contractor, Jerry Stevenson, who was to work with an architect and draftsmen, drawing up plans for the store. In order to provide these professionals with the best estimate of his needs, Charles at once sat down with Alex to go over the layout they anticipated they would desire.

"We have four stories to fill with the best merchandise available, Alex. On the first floor, let's place the items that will appeal most to women: perfumes, sachets, cosmetics and toiletries, as well as jewelry," Charles had suggested. "There should be a special department for sewing gadgets and dress materials for the homemaker who wants to make her own clothes and those of her children."

Alex was equally enthusiastic. "We should consider having a floor for furniture," he declared. "Plus mirrors, table linens, and service—fine chinaware and Sheffield silverware if we can get them at a decent price. And, on the same floor we can have a special department featuring cooking equipment, especially for the new homemaker who doesn't know much about such things."

"That sounds like just the ticket, Alex," Charles had said with a broad grin.

Several months later, when Charles had received word from Jerry Stevenson that the basic four-story structure was in place and only the interiors remained to be finished, he once again summoned Alex Gorth. The young man traveled to Chicago and spent the night at Charles's home, then the two partners took the train to New York the following morning, to view the partially completed building and to spend time refining the interior layout.

After admiring the impressively ornate facade of their new building on Broadway, Charles and Alex entered the store and spent the next few hours walking around from floor to floor, making careful notes and sketches. In one section of the third floor, Charles announced, "This would be just the place for a very large display of men's ready-made outerwear, and—let's see—oh, yes. Over there we can show ties and shirts, and undergarments. I'm glad we decided that the store won't be entirely for women. I know it's somewhat unusual to feature men's apparel along with women's, but I think our customers will welcome the convenience of having everything under one roof. Especially since the ladies are likely to bring their husbands or sweethearts shopping with them on occasion. With this in mind, we should also consider branching out into sporting goods. We could add them in our second or third season. Things like bicycles and tricycles, machines the couples can take around Central Park. And croquet sets, badminton, tennis racquets, and even golf clubs. The English and the Scotch are great golf players, and the interest is growing in this country for that outdoor game. Oh, yes, speaking of the English, we should have a section with fine gourmet foods like English biscuits, imported teas and coffees, perhaps even quality candies. You see, Alex, my vision is of an all-around store that stresses quality, variety—and of course includes your own personal brand of attentive customer service."

"That—that's very flattering of you, Charles." Alex had crimsoned with pardonable pride.

Jerry Stevenson had assured his clients that the store would almost certainly be finished by early November, three weeks ahead of schedule. Armed with this encouraging news, Charles Douglas and Alexander Gorth spent another few days in New York City, going over interior plans with decorators, ordering merchandise for later delivery, and in fact managing to compress weeks of work into seven days. By the end of the week, thoroughly exhausted, they had gone to Grand Central Station to board the train to Chicago.

On the trip back, Charles made suggestions about likely neighborhoods for Alex and his wife and children to live in, and expressed the hope that the move could be accomplished quickly and painlessly. "I know it will be a wrench to leave your home, Alex," the older man had said solicitously, "but it's essential that the move be made as quickly as possible. We want to make sure, of course, that you're all settled in by the time the store has its grand opening the first week in December."

"Don't worry Charles," Alex had assured him. "As soon as I get back to Galveston, the first thing I'm going to do is find a suitable replacement for me at the store there. I'm hoping that won't take longer than a couple of weeks, because I've already been interviewing candidates for the position, and I've narrowed the choices down to three men. I'll see them each one final time, and then I'll make my decision—with your approval, of course.''

"I've every confidence in your choice, Alex," Charles said sincerely. "You've proved to be an excellent judge of character—and frankly, you've learned so much about this business, so quickly, that I'm quite astounded. No, any decisions about personnel will be entirely yours, and that goes for the new store, as well. However, I would like you to hire that fellow Patrick Keogh—you remember him, don't you? The cab driver we met when we first went to New York? As I promised him, I think he'd make an excellent floorwalker—and I intend to keep that promise.

"You know, Alex," Charles had continued, "a good floorwalker can be invaluable for business. If he's courteous and helpful, he can give the customers the impression that the store goes out of its way to give service. Since the floorwalker is generally the first employee a customer deals with, it's important that we have someone like Mr. Keogh who is, indeed, anxious to please and who does more than he's asked.''

By the time they had reached Chicago, all of the final details had been worked out. When they parted at Union Station, where Alex would catch a later train on to Galveston, Charles had told his junior partner that he would plan to meet him in New York a few days before the official opening. They had shaken hands, and Alex went to inquire which track his train would be departing from.

For three weeks, Alex and Katie had been plunged into virtual nonstop activity—interviewing, packing, shipping, arranging for some of their possessions to be put into storage for later retrieval, others to be sent to a New York warehouse. As they sat on the floor of their living room surrounded by half-filled boxes and a sea of newspaper to protect their breakables, the two of them were acting like children at Christmas. Laughing and talking excitedly and animatedly about their impending future, they somehow managed to get the last of their packing done, and by the end of the afternoon, they were sitting there dirty and exhausted but feeling that they had accomplished the seemingly impossible.

Alex reached over and, with his handkerchief, gently removed a smudge of newsprint from Katie's cheek. Katie was just about to plant a kiss on her husband's cheek in return when, instead, she burst out laughing. Alex gave her a curious look, then followed her gaze.

"No, no, Patrick!" she called over to their sixteen-month-old son. "You don't have to be packed away like the dishes."

Patrick was happily wrapping himself up in some of the newspaper while intently eyeing an empty box. When Jennifer heard all the laughing, the four-year-old girl came running into the room to see what was so funny. She started giggling and declared to her parents, "I think it's a good idea. That way, we won't have to worry about him crying on the train ride to New York."

Alex laughed with his daughter and teased, "That might be a pretty good idea. As a matter of fact, if we pack *both* of you, then your mother and I won't have to worry about you complaining that you're hungry every five minutes."

"Oh, Daddy!" Jennifer said, a rueful expression on her face. "You wouldn't dare!"

Alex walked over to her, picked her up, and gave her a hug. "You're absolutely right; I wouldn't dare. I also wouldn't want to. Part of the fun of this move will be seeing the excitement on not only Mommy's face, but yours, too." He gave her a kiss, then set her back on the floor, and she ran to assist her little brother in his play.

"Gosh, Katie," Alex murmured. "Just think of all the changes that have taken place in my life in the last six years, I can hardly believe it. I know the way I was back then—a hopelessly shy, pimply-faced kid who never expected to amount to anything more than what I was: a clerk for a dishonest storekeeper. You know, when I think about it, I'm not really sure where I got up the nerve to tell that McNamara cad that I'd buy his store on time when he was forced to leave Galveston. Truth is, I really didn't know that I would be able to pay him back." His face broke into a sudden grin. "But I did, didn't I? I suppose most of my determination came from the fact that I wanted you as my wife so badly—I mean, I felt that if I was a successful store owner, then you would want me."

Katie stood up and walked over to her husband. Putting her arms around his neck, she declared, "Alex, I knew what a wonderful person you were from just about the first time you ever came into the bakery." She suddenly giggled. "I must say, I'm not sorry to have left that job. By the end of the day my hands looked more like dough than the dough did!"

He kissed her lightly, then said, "Still, I think I've had more than my share of luck."

"Pshaw!" Katie stood back, hands on her hips. "Luck had nothing to do with it. Why, how many men would have gone out of their way to help out a rival storeowner like you did for Charles Douglas after the hurricane made such a mess of his store? Not to mention risking your life to save his late partner's wife and daughter, Arabella Hunter and Joy? No, Alex. Luck had nothing to do with it. Charles recognized your pluck and goodness, and that's why he made you a junior partner—and that's why he's given you this opportunity in New York." She kissed him on his cheek and said softly, "*I'm* the one who's been incredibly lucky, Alex. Whoever thought a poor Irish immigrant like me would end up becoming a grand lady living in New York with her wonderful husband and two beautiful children? I just wish my parents were still alive to be able to share my happiness."

The opening of the Douglas Department Store took place on October 20, although a few of the items they had planned on displaying had not yet arrived—some imported items that had been held up by a storm in the Atlantic. Still, the majority of goods they had purchased were offered for sale, and the opening day business had been very brisk.

Word had quickly spread about the new store offering a wide variety of quality merchandise, and within weeks—at the height of the Christmas buying season—the crowds were as thick as they could ever have wished for. Much to Alex's delight and surprise, their business slacked off only slightly after the Christmas rush—which Charles had generously attributed to the way the store was being managed by his partner.

Now, on this Easter of 1880, Alexander, Katie, Jennifer, and Patrick had gone to mass at St. Patrick's Cathedral to rejoice in their blessings. Katie was a devout but not overly zealous Catholic; Alex had been raised a Presbyterian, but he had readily converted to his wife's faith as a symbolic way of expressing his gratitude for her having come into his life.

With them was their housekeeper, Moira Donegal, whom they had hired soon after arriving in New York. Charles Douglas has suggested an employment agency that specialized in domestics, and there Alex and Katie had interviewed a dozen or more applicants. Finally the Gorths had decided on hiring a smiling, freckle-faced, twenty-year-old girl from County Cork. Not only was Moira personable and of sunny disposition, but she also was better educated than most of the immigrant Irish girls who had come to New York in droves to find work to escape the economic poverty that was gripping their native land. The young woman had scrimped for four years until she had finally managed to save up enough to pay for passage in steerage.

By now Moira was almost as much a fixture in the new Gorth home as the rest of the family. Katie had discovered that the resourceful, charmingly candid girl had a droll sense of humor and a superb natural gift of mimicry, so that she could hold Jennifer and Patrick—although he was too young to really understand—spellbound with bedtime stories about leprechauns, trolls, and benign witches who granted fortunate mortals the fulfillment of their dreams. The children idolized her after just a few weeks, and this alone made Katie quite happy that she had decided to pull up stakes and settle in bustling New York City.

After Easter services, they strolled up Fifth Avenue with the rest of the people who were dressed in their finery and were enjoying the lovely day. It was only a short distance to their apartment building, located at Park Avenue and Fifty-sixth Street.

Alex had been surprised when Katie had opted for this particular location, so far uptown from most of the shops. But Katie had declared that from what she had been reading in the newspapers, this was one of the nicest parts of town—still fairly sparsely settled; even if it eventually was all built up, which was inevitable considering how fast the city was growing, the children would always have nearby Central Park to play in. "I know it's a bit far from the store, but the Fifth Avenue coach will take you only a block away from Broadway, and it only costs ten cents."

Alex had agreed, especially since the apartment itself of-

159

fered them everything they could have wanted: a large living room, dining room, four bedrooms, and two bathrooms, with large windows affording excellent cross ventilation—a necessity in the hot, humid summer months.

There was also a garden in the back, and Katie made it her business to meet the wives of the other tenants, urging them to work with her in creating a setting that would be pleasant to the eye. Perhaps it was true that some of the neighbors in this building were more affluent than the Gorths, but Katie's irresistible charm soon won them over against any reservations they might have had because her husband was "in trade."

While the munificent salary of two thousand dollars a year as manager of Charles Douglas's New York store was more money than he had ever earned before in all his life, the apartment alone took almost a quarter of his salary for the entire year. Added to this were Moira's wages of twenty-five dollars a month, and Katie discovered that they would have to pay unheard-of prices for foodstuffs: twenty cents a pound for butter, the same for a dozen eggs, twelve cents a pound for crushed sugar, a quarter for a pound of chicken, and thirty-five cents a pound for choice cuts of beef. On the other hand, she had always been a fine cook and knew how to make leftovers, as her adoring husband fondly put it, "taste just like a banquet."

However, just last week, because after five months business had been so brisk, Charles Douglas had sent Alexander a telegraph declaring that he was raising Alexander's salary by another five hundred dollars a year.

Crossing to the east side of Fifth Avenue at Fifty-sixth Street to head over to Park, Katie declared, "Well, I must say, it surely was fun skating in Central Park this winter, and just think of all the band concerts we've heard. And now that it's getting warmer, we can take the children out to Coney Island. Do you know, I'm just dying to visit the Brighton Beach Fair Grounds, and I bet you'd enjoy clamming in Coney Island Creek. I hear they have the most wonderful fireworks displays, too."

"I'll be happy when summer's here, too, and as for Coney Island, I'll admit I can't wait to see you in a stylish bathing dress—from our store, of course."

"Alexander Gorth!" Katie exclaimed, but her lips twitched with merriment, belying her rebuke.

Moira, who was following just behind them, holding Jennifer by one hand and pushing Patrick's pram with the other, heard this interchange and had to suppress a giggle of amusement. She adored her new employers, and what she liked best were the obvious ways in which they displayed their love for each other. Her mother had once told her that when parents loved each other, their children would grow up believing in gentleness and romance, and thus it would become easier for them to find true love when they came of age. Of course, she was hoping that, one day, in this bustling, noisy but fascinating city, there would be a man whose eyes would meet hers from across the street and with whom she would fall instantly and lastingly in love. Meanwhile, it was very pleasant to see Mr. and Mrs. Gorth enjoy life so much and play with their children the way they did. She didn't at all have the feeling of being just a lowly domestic servant like all the other girls in the agency, who were fearful and curtsied and minded their manners and took care not to say a single word that might meet with disfavor. Not, to be sure, that she would ever forget her place with the Gorths, but they were so easygoing themselves that one didn't have to feel that one was treading on eggs around them.

That evening, before they went to bed and well after Moira had put the children to sleep, Katie turned to her husband and said, "You know, darling, there are just two things I want, although one of them can really wait."

"Oh, is that so? And what have you in mind, my lovely colleen?" Alex beamed at her.

"Well, the thing that can wait is a nice house and a garden all our own. Even though our neighbors are very nice, with our own house I'd feel more the way I did back in Galveston."

"I'd like a house too, Katie, honey," he confessed, sitting on the couch and putting an arm around her shoulders as he drew her to him for a very satisfying kiss. "With the raise, I can begin to save more, so maybe in a couple of years we can have that house. I've already written it down on my agenda for future reference, Katie. Now the next question is, what's the thing that you really want quickly?"

"Maybe you think I'm silly, but I like to keep active.

161

Sitting around the apartment, even considering that I've chores to do, isn't my idea of being a really helpful wife.''

"I've no complaints on the subject. I like everything about you and everything you do for me.''

"You're a sweet man, Alexander Gorth, and you warm the cockles of a girl's heart, you do for fair. But let me finish: What I've got in mind is helping you at your work.''

"But you do help me, darling," he reassured her, as he drew her close to him and kissed her again, even more lingeringly this time.

"Now that's enough of that at the moment, Alexander, dear. Right now, this is a serious conversation, young man. And I want you to pay particular attention.''

"Of course, I will. But I don't understand why you say you want to help me, because if it hadn't been for you, I wouldn't be here in New York today," he uncomprehendingly protested.

"Alexander Gorth, you're the dearest man, yet you can also be the most exasperating. Now that we have Moira—and she's a perfect treasure—I have lots of time on my hands. And I hate to sit around doing nothing and just feeling that I'm justifying my existence simply because I'm a wife and mother.''

"But, good gracious, Katie, darling, that's good enough for most women!" again he protested.

"But it's not for me, Alex! Look, you were telling me just the other day that you've had some problems with people who try to slip jewelry or perfume or handkerchiefs into their purses, or the pockets of their coats.''

"That's true. That's one of the hazards of running a department store.''

"I know that—and that's what I'm getting at, if you'll only pay some attention. I think I could cut down your losses from shoplifting, if you'd let me work in the store—as a detective.''

"A detective?" he incredulously echoed. "Katie Gorth, what's gotten into you today?''

"I've been thinking about this for some time, Alex. Now you listen till I've had my say. Isn't it logical to assume that, if I posed as a shopper myself, a woman shoplifter would never in the world dream that I was really working for the store? She wouldn't pay any attention. And exactly because

I'm a woman, I know just how a woman acts, especially when she's trying to be sneaky.''

"I'll admit it's not a bad idea," Alex mused, thoughtfully frowning. "But I'd have to ask Charles what he thought about it. It's certainly something new, and I don't know that department stores have ever done anything like that—I mean, hire a woman detective. There are lots of security guards and private detectives, but they're almost always men, and of course, I've instructed Patrick Keogh, who's the best floorwalker I've ever seen, to keep his eyes open for any shenanigans.''

"Yes, he's a dear, and he's very conscientious, but all the same, he isn't a fellow woman customer. Where you need me is where there are small items that are all too easy to slip into a pocket or a purse, and make away with. I do wish you'd let me give it a try. I'd feel so much more useful, and I could save the store money, too.''

"Well of course, if I hired you, honey, I'd arrange to pay you a salary. It wouldn't be right to let you work for free.''

"That *would* be nice!" Katie purred. "Now why don't you send Charles Douglas a telegram first thing tomorrow and see what he thinks? I promise that if he doesn't like the idea, I won't bother you about it again. But I bet he'll go along with me. Be sure you stress the angle of how a woman can usually anticipate what another woman's going to do better than any man can.''

"That I won't argue with you about, and I will send the telegram.''

"You're a perfect angel!''

Eighteen

Somewhat to Alexander Gorth's surprise, Charles Douglas responded to his young partner's wire on the same day. The Chicago merchant declared that he heartily endorsed Katie's idea, and he authorized Alex to put her on the payroll at a token twenty dollars a month. "You see what a smart man you're in business with, Alexander Gorth?" his wife teased,

163

standing with her arms akimbo and giving him a roguish look.

"Of course I do," he dryly replied. "He made me his partner, didn't he?"

Katie laughed appreciatively. "Touché!" she replied as she came close to him, hugged him, and then gave him a long, very tender kiss. "Now let's get down to serious business. What I think I ought to do initially is to go down with you this Thursday and Friday, which are the busiest shopping days. I'll just wander around the store and see what I can see. I want to deduce ideas of just what to look for and how I should behave in order to catch shoplifters in the act. Oh, it's going to be exciting—and I'll save you and Charles lots of money, you just watch and see!"

Moira thought the idea a fine one and was only too eager to help out by looking after Patrick and Jennifer for those entire days. "I plan to put in at least two or three hours every day. But some days, especially toward the end of the week when they have the most store traffic, I'd like to be there most of the day. Would it be too much trouble for you to look after the children and maybe even do the cooking for us on those days?" Katie anxiously asked. "I'll be able to make it up to you, because I'll be getting a small wage for my work, so I'm going to give you five dollars a month more."

"Oh, goodness, that's very generous of you, Mrs. Gorth!" Moira's eyes shone with pleasure. "But I'm so happy here with you, I hadn't even thought of wanting anything for any extra work."

"You're sweet, but I'm not going to take advantage of you. I insist you accept the raise."

"I really don't know what to say, Mrs. Gorth. You're so very nice to me, you and Mr. Gorth both!" Moira shot Katie a look of intense gratitude and affection, then hurried off to the children's bedroom when she heard Patrick crying.

Katie went with her husband the next day on the Fifth Avenue coach, enjoying the long drive down to the department store. It was a warm, sunny day, but there were few elegantly dressed women strolling on the Avenue. Alex had discovered that the fashionable women—those who wanted the best quality of merchandise and spent the most money in his store—were not attracted by bargains so much as to lose their beauty sleep, and that traffic really began closer to noon than at the store's ten o'clock opening. For the middle-class shopper, however, ten o'clock was ideal, since often husbands working uptown would escort their wives to the shops and then go on to their jobs.

For her experimental sortie, Katie wore a pretty beribboned bonnet and a simple blue dress. She carried an enormous reticule and walked leisurely from counter to counter, examining the displays of merchandise. Covertly, she glanced around to see what other shoppers were doing. That noon, when Alexander took her to lunch at an inexpensive restaurant around the corner, she excitedly confided, ''I'm sure I'm going to be a big help to you and Charles. I was just keeping my eyes open today, but I believe that one beautifully dressed woman slipped something into the pocket of her coat. She was at the jewelry counter, and, I was across the room, but just as I turned and saw her, I noticed her hand did something very quick behind her back. There was a very sweet clerk helping her, but she didn't keep her eyes on what the customer was doing. You might just tell your clerks, Alex, that they can help a lot themselves by not taking anything or anyone for granted.''

''That's not a bad idea. We're going to have a store meeting Saturday before we open, because next Monday we have a big white-goods sale; after-Easter clearance, you might call it.''

''Maybe you'd like me to talk to them? I told you, because I'm a woman, I know pretty much how a woman's going to act, and I could tell your clerks what to be on the lookout for.''

''All right, but you'll have to get up bright and early because I want to be down at the store at least a good hour early to go over certain things I want the store personnel to do.'' Alex wore his most serious look.

''Alex, I just love you when you get that intense look on your face,'' Katie giggled. ''You're becoming a regular tycoon, now that you're here in New York. And I'm very proud of you.''

He reached across the table, took her hand, and drew it to his lips. Katie flushed a most becoming crimson and gently disengaged her hand, admonishing, ''My gracious, Alexander Gorth, not in a public place!''

165

The waitress came over and took their order, then returned to the kitchen. As soon as she had gone, Katie went on, "I don't mind at all getting up early, and Moira and I have already arranged a schedule for my cooking hours. I hope you don't mind too much, but I gave her a five-dollar raise—naturally, I'm going to pay her that out of my own salary from the store."

"That's very thoughtful, but *I* can afford to give Moira a raise, you know," he reproached her with a smile.

"I know you can—but I won't let you. Please let me do it my way, just once. After all, I gave you the idea—and I'm going to earn my salary, you can bet your boots on it, Alex, dear."

"There's one thing you have to remember, though, honey," he admonished her. 'You have to be absolutely sure before you accuse someone of shoplifting. I think I'd better ask Morrison Talmadge, the lawyer who looks after our suppliers' contracts, about the fine points of the law. His office isn't very far from the store; I might just run over there today before closing time. I'm pretty sure you really don't dare stop and search a customer right in the store. If I remember, you can only suggest to them that perhaps they picked up a piece of merchandise by mistake, implying that they should put it back on the shelf, or else run the risk of being charged with theft."

"Don't you worry, I'll be very careful, Alex."

The waitress had by this time brought their lunch, and Alex and Katie enjoyed the delicious hot entree, following which Alex insisted that his wife indulge herself with a strawberry tart for dessert. When they had finished the meal, Katie sighed, "My, that was delicious, Alex. Now I think I'll spend another hour in the store, and then I'll go on home by myself."

They rose, and Alex paid the check, adding a tip for the friendly waitress. As they turned to go, he gave Katie a quick kiss on her cheek.

"That's very sweet, Alex," she whispered, "only you'd better not do that in the store. I won't be able to catch any shoplifters if they see the boss kissing me."

Patrick Keogh had been taken into Alexander's confidence and, so that Katie's debut as an actress would not be blatantly given away, promised not to recognize her when she came into the store to shop. The former carriage driver, resplendent in a fine new suit of Scotch tweed—one of the many excellent imports Charles Douglas had ordered for New York's demanding clientele—charmed dowagers and debutantes alike by his gracious manner and his solicitous attention and response to their most trivial questions as to where this or that merchandise was located.

Secretly, Katie's enterprising young husband's curiosity was piqued by the challenge that his effervescent wife had set for herself. Since shoplifting had already become a noticeable problem in the operation of the new store, he was hoping that her tactics would help put a stop to it.

He had already learned, even in Henry McNamara's dilapidated little store, that it was not only the poor who tried to steal because they had no money to pay for what they needed, nor was it food alone that was stolen. His own feeling was that he would pardon a shoplifter if the motivation for the theft was to prevent starvation. He had read Victor Hugo's *Les Misérables,* which had first appeared in Paris in 1862, and subsequently had been translated into a popular-priced English version. He was sure that there were many Jean Valjeans in the world, and he knew from his own experience that he was too softhearted to prosecute someone who stole because he was hungry. Though he had never told Katie, once during his employment with Henry McNamara, while the owner had been absent, an elderly woman had come into the shop. She had quaveringly inquired the price of a can of beans and then nodded sadly when informed of what it was. He stooped down to retrieve something that had fallen off the counter, and as he straightened, he was just in time to see her slip the can into her tattered reticule and hobble out of the shop. Conscientiously, he had put the price of that can of beans into the till and rung it up, taking the hard-earned money out of his own pocket.

That night, instead of buying a fresh loaf of bread at Gottlieb's, he bought a stale one. That stale bread had tasted like a banquet to him, and he said to himself, "That poor woman is far worse off than I am. At least I have a job and I'm young and healthy."

But Charles Douglas's New York City store did not attract the poor, or even the lower-middle class; thus far, the customers appeared to be from the middle and the upper levels of society, being well dressed and apparently having abundant spending money for their purchases. All the same, he had estimated that shoplifting accounted for losses of about two percent of the gross intake from all departments in a month. That was too large a figure to be ignored.

Meanwhile, his attractive wife appeared to be delighted by her new role as a casual shopper. She had never been happier in all her life than she was this Monday, as she sauntered down the aisles, going from floor to floor, touching this or that piece of merchandise, and sometimes stopping to ask the sales clerk its price or information about its manufacture. When she had worked at the bakery, she had done her share of wishful dreaming and window-shopping, and now those dreams had become a reality.

She casually watched the stylishly dressed wives of the affluent as they were deciding whether this store was a worthy competitor to Lord & Taylor, Constable and Company, and J. T. Stewart's. Thus far—to judge from this Monday morning traffic—it appeared that they basically approved of it, and the sales figures that Alexander Gorth forwarded to Charles Douglas more than bore out this premise.

Katie viewed these women almost cynically. She understood that well-to-do women might look upon store pilferage as a kind of lark, testing their own ingenuity against the vigilance of the wary merchant. She told herself she would not be surprised at all if she found some well-known dowager slipping a watch or bracelet or bottle of cologne into her garments or reticule. To be sure, she understood also that it was a touchy point on how best to make the would-be thief surrender the merchandise. If the culprit were indeed from one of the socially prominent families of the city, it could be not only embarrassing, but also costly in the long run: A woman who was made to suffer embarrassment over what she had considered a harmless little prank would spread the word to her friends, and they, in turn, would boycott the store. This meant that she, Katie Gorth, would have to exercise her tact, diplomacy, and her own inherent ingenuity to outwit those women who thought themselves smarter than her husband.

She found it a fascinating game, pretending to be a woman with money to spend for anything her heart desired, all the while observing how other women, from their twenties to fifties, were fashionably dressed and noticing what most interested them. As she meandered from counter to counter, sometimes going to another floor to other rooms of merchandise—then returning suddenly, as if by whim—she caught snatches of conversation that gave her an insight into the problems these affluent women faced. She concluded that, by and large, their concerns were no different from those of women at any social level: a faithless lover or husband, a dreary marriage that might be brightened by the acquisition of a new dress, a hat, or a pair of chic gloves; or again on a more banal plane, the fretting over some rival who had stolen a march on her by hiring a perfect jewel of a cook or a lady's maid. These conversations ran the gamut from high tragedy and brooding frustration to petty impatience, selfish bickering, and shallow trivia. And she found it amusing to conjecture what sort of woman really existed behind the facade of an elegant gown and bonnet and what depths—or lack—of character these overheard remarks portended.

Conscientiously, she stayed away from her husband whenever she saw him come out of his office on the fourth floor and go to this or that department. She turned away, pretending to be intently absorbed in fingering a piece of lace, or an Oriental rug, or the upholstery of a loveseat. As for himself, Alex was well aware of his wife's presence, and thus far his reports (from none other than Patrick Keogh himself) were highly favorable. Katie was playing her role to perfection, and no one suspected that she was anything more than a capricious shopper with plenty of time and money on her hands, seeking to be diverted from boredom in this new and already popular New York department store.

By her third day on the job, Katie was well acquainted with those counters that featured merchandise that could be easily pocketed. She had picked out spots from where she could keep these counters in plain sight without being obvious. That morning, she entered the store and, walking slowly to the right, ignored Patrick Keogh, whose face remained impassive, though he noticed her, as he busied himself instructing a stout, bejeweled dowager on where to find Oriental rugs.

Once past Patrick, she went slowly by the counter where perfumes and colognes were sold and moved on to the costume jewelry department. Here, Katie knew, was one of the choicer opportunities for pilferage. The objects themselves were small, and a quick movement of the hand sufficed to make them disappear into the pocket or purse of the thief.

She paused, diagonally across the way from the costume jewelry section, and slowly glanced around just in time to see a stunningly handsome woman in her early forties approach the counter and request of the sales clerk a closer, in-the-hand look at particular items. Standing with her back to Katie, she examined the costume jewelry in a small, velvet-lined box that the busy sales girl had taken from the display case and placed before her. The clerk's attention had been engaged by a shrewish elderly woman whose shrill, peevish voice arrogantly pronounced her wish to be served swiftly, so that she might keep an already delayed appointment.

Suddenly the handsome matron placed her right hand on the open display box and then moved it down to her hip. Katie's watchful eye had intercepted this transfer of a piece of costume jewelry into the pocket of the woman's cape. She waited to see what would happen. The harassed young clerk at last finished her sale, then moved back to the matron and pleasantly inquired, "Is there anything you fancy, madam?"

"No, I really don't think so, but thank you for showing them to me, miss."

With this, the matron turned and moved toward Katie's right, walking on toward another department. Katie hurried over to the counter just as the clerk lifted the case and prepared to replace it on the counter shelf. "Just a moment—I want to take a look at that myself, if you don't mind," she requested. Immediately she could see that the matron had very ingeniously shifted the other items, so that the missing piece would leave no noticeable gap on the velvet surface of the jewelry box. She pursed her lips. "Thank you very much." The clerk, who like all the other sales help knew who Katie was and what she was doing in the store, gave her a curious look but said nothing.

Katie now walked toward the matron, who had stopped to examine a neat stack of fine Irish lace handkerchiefs. Moving alongside the woman, she murmured, "Excuse me, but I think you'd better come along with me to the office."

The matron started and, coloring slightly, turned and regarded Katie Gorth with widened, large brown eyes as she indignantly retorted, "What are you talking about, young lady? And who, may I ask, are you, to speak to me in this fashion?''

"I'm sorry to bother you, madam," Katie was sweetly polite, "but I happen to be a detective employed by this store. Would you kindly follow me?"

"Whatever for? Surely you don't mean to imply—oh, this is outrageous—the very idea!—do you know who I am? I am Mrs. Vanderpool! My husband is with the Stock Exchange.''

"I don't mean to offend you, but I have reason to believe that you have on your person an article that has not been paid for. I'm sure it can be explained. Please, Mrs. Vanderpool, don't make a scene. We can handle this quite calmly and properly in a private office," Katie gently insisted.

"But this is unheard of! It's ridiculous! My huband and I are extremely wealthy; certainly you can see from my attire that I am not the type of person who needs to steal a mere bauble!'' the matron blustered.

"Please, madam," Katie murmured, glancing around, "you don't want to make a scene, I'm sure. Why don't you come to the office, and we'll talk it over quietly? Please come this way.''

"Very well! But I warn you, you've made a false accusation against me, and my husband is very prominent. I demand that you call him at once! I'm sure that he will wish to bring suit against you people who dare to think that I would stoop to such a childish prank!'' Again, the matron's voice rose shrilly, and people were turning to stare at her. As Katie gestured toward the direction of the elevator at the rear of the store, Mrs. Vanderpool indignantly drew herself up and, with great poise and dignity, went on ahead with Katie following.

When they reached Alex's office, he had already been advised by the floorwalker of what had taken place, and was there seated at his desk when Mrs. Harold Vanderpool angrily strode in. Katie quietly moved in behind her, closing the door so that there could be complete privacy for this potentially unpleasant scene.

The store manager rose and politely greeted the fuming matron. "Good afternoon, madam," Then, eyeing his wife, he asked, "Is something wrong, Katie?"

"There's a great deal wrong, sir!'' the matron angrily broke in. "This young woman had the effrontery to accuse me of shoplifting. I told her—as I shall tell you now, sir—

171

that my name is Mrs. Harold Vanderpool. My husband is with the New York Stock Exchange. If you know anything about that organization, you must know that we are quite well-to-do. I am hardly the sort of person who should be apprehended on the ridiculous charge of shoplifting. I assure you that I have enough money to buy out most of the merchandise in this store, if I wished. However, after the treatment I've received today, I doubt that I shall ever come here again!''

"You have my sympathies, Mrs. Vanderpool." Alex was gently conciliatory. "Katie, would you mind telling me exactly what happened?"

His wife detailed what she had seen, but before she had finished, the matron again indignantly interrupted, "That's a lie! I insist, sir, that you send for my husband. If your establishment does not yet have a telephone, you must have some messenger who could go to the Stock Exchange. When he gets here, I warn you, I'm going to tell him to bring suit against your store, particularly this offensive young woman who dared to accost me and accuse me of such an unbelievable crime!"

"I'll be glad to send a messenger to bring your husband here, Mrs. Vanderpool. I assure you, the Douglas Department Store wants to make friends, not enemies. If the charge proves to be erroneous, I'll see to it that proper apology is made," Alex placatingly offered.

"Indeed!" Mrs. Vanderpool drew herself up and glared at him, then turned to send a baleful glance at Katie, who maintained a bland, innocent face and remained silent.

Going outside, Alex beckoned to one of the young stock clerks and whispered to him. Forty minutes later, an impeccably dressed, dignified-looking man in his mid-fifties, with thinning, graying hair, hurried into the office and went directly to his wife. "Lila, dear, what's the meaning of this?"

Lila Vanderpool burst into tears and clung to her husband, her face pressed against his chest. "It's just dreadful, Harold," she sobbed. "That horrible woman there had the nerve to say that I stole a piece of their costume jewelry!"

"There, there, my darling, don't cry. Sit down now, and I'll handle this." The broker consoled her and helped her to sit down. Then he turned to confront Alexander Gorth. "Now then, sir, you realize that in making an accusation of this kind, you must be able to prove it. If you can't, I'm prepared to tell my attorney to bring suit against the store, and you and this woman personally. As I have one of the best lawyers in all of New York City, you'll have reason to regret your rash action if it proves to be unfounded."

"Mr. Vanderpool, I regret this as much as you do," Katie Gorth spoke up, her quick tongue and Irish temper coming to the fore. "All I ask you to do is to look into the pocket of your wife's cape. You'll find a piece of costume jewelry there, because I saw her take it. I'm not making it up; I certainly have no reason to do so."

"Harold, are you going to believe this woman, or are you going to take my word for it?" Lila Vanderpool almost hysterically sobbed, taking her hands away from her tear-stained face and piteously staring up at her husband.

"Lila, I'm afraid I'm going to have to ask you to allow me to do it. If the charge is false, I'll see that you get full restitution from these people. But in all fairness, it has to be done."

"Harold! How could you ask such a thing? Don't you trust your own wife?"

"Of course I do, my dearest. But this is a legal matter, and they've made a charge, and we have to disprove it. I'll look in the pockets for you."

"Go ahead. You won't find anything. It's merely an outrageous accusation!"

"Please stand up, Lila, dear," he gently urged. Lila Vanderpool rose and again buried her face in her hands, sobbing, "Oh this is just disgraceful! Never in my life have I been so ashamed and humiliated!"

Harold Vanderpool sent Alex and Katie a stern look, then put his hands into the pockets of her cape. His eyes widened with surprise as he drew out the piece of costume jewelry. "Lila—there *is* a piece of jewelry in your pocket."

"Oh, no—but I couldn't have—oh, please, oh, this is just awful—I don't understand it—" She bowed her head, covered her face with her hands, and helplessly sobbed. Vanderpool looked uncomfortable and cleared his throat: "I'm afraid I'm the one to apologize. I can't believe this—"

"Mr. Vanderpool," Katie gently suggested, "perhaps your

173

wife had no intention of taking it; maybe she was compelled to."

"I—I'm afraid I don't understand you, miss."

"It may be what they call kleptomania. Mr. Vanderpool, people who suffer from it—and I say 'suffer' because it's just like a sickness—unknowingly steal. There's a psychological reason for it, from what I've read about such things." Then, turning to her husband, she said, "Mr. Gorth, I really don't think that any charges should be pressed, if you want my opinion."

"I'm inclined to agree with you, Katie," Alex nodded.

Harold Vanderpool adjusted his collar, took out a fine linen handkerchief, and mopped his brow. Then he bent to his wife—who had collapsed, sobbing, into a chair—and whispered something to her, put an arm around her shoulders, and kissed her forehead. Turning to Katie, he said in a voice that trembled with unsteadiness, "You may well be right, miss. Of course, I owe you every sort of apology, and I apologize for Lila, too. If what you say is true, miss, then I think I'll take my wife to a doctor who perhaps can find out why she does a thing like this."

"It's not her fault, really, Mr. Vanderpool," Katie reassured him with a smile. "I'm terribly sorry if we distressed you and your wife. But you see, sir, we've had a good deal of pilferage, and I was only trying to do my duty."

"I quite understand. You're to be commended." He turned to face Alex. "I must say, it's most generous of you not to press charges. I'm not without influence in this city, and I can assure you that I shall tell my friends that the Douglas Department Store treats people properly."

"I should be most grateful to you for that, Mr. Vanderpool," Alex said with a smile, extending his hand, which the broker energetically shook.

Mr. Vanderpool turned back to his wife and helped her rise from the chair. "Come on, Lila dear. I'm going to take you to Dr. Murray. I'm sure he'll be able to find out the reason for this."

"Harold—I—I'm so ashamed—I can't understand why—my mind just went blank—I didn't mean to—"

"There, there, my dear, it's all right." Once again, he faced Alex. "Thank you again for your forbearance. I shan't forget it."

Two weeks later, Alexander Gorth received a personal note from Harold Vanderpool. It read as follows:

Dear Mr. Gorth:

I am in your debt for your sympathetic understanding of the misadventure involving my wife. My family physician, Dr. John Murray, has a background in psychological problems, and when I mentioned to him the suggestion of kleptomania, he queried my wife and determined that she indeed is suffering from this malady.

Although these things apparently take a good deal of time to see through, he is confident that in due course, his treatment will be effective.

My wife wishes me to express her apologies for having brought about this unpleasant situation and thanks you, as I do, for your decision to let the matter rest. As I promised you, we have already told a number of our good friends and close acquaintances of the excellence of your fine department store, and I think you may expect an upsurge in your business from them.

Cordially yours,
Harold Vanderpool

Harold Vanderpool was as good as his word. A month after receiving that letter, when Alex went over the accountant's statement of sales and net profits, he was delighted to find that Douglas Department Store had registered a full ten percent increase in volume over any preceding month, including even that of the Christmas season. He sent the report off with an enthusiastic letter to Charles Douglas in Chicago, and that night he and Katie treated themselves to a festive dinner at Delmonico's.

Nineteen

It had taken some time for the passengers of the Cañon City-bound train to be calmed for the resumption of the journey following the attempted payroll robbery. Finally, however, they had all taken their seats, some huddling in borrowed coats and blankets in a feeble attempt to ward off the chill winds coming in through the broken windows. When the train slowly limped into the station under the hesitant hands of the fireman at the controls, a great sigh of relief could be heard throughout the cars.

Reuben Huntley was hustled off to the marshal's office, where Lucien Edmond and Ramón gave their testimony of the events. The two men then hurried back to the train, where they conferred with the rest of the members of their party.

"Fortunately," Lucien Edmond began, "the stages have waited for the train to arrive. The conductor told me that there are often delays—sometimes they're due to the weather, sometimes mechanical failures—so the drivers don't just give up and go home." His face broke into a rueful grin. "I guess in this part of the country it's the unexpected that's normal."

Ramón broke in, "Did you ask the conductor about lodgings in Leadville, Lucien Edmond?"

"Yes, I did," he replied. "He told me about several reasonably priced boardinghouses where all of us men can stay, and apparently there's a well-respected widow who operates a rooming house for ladies on the outskirts of town. He said we'd be able to recognize the place easily enough; it's the only place on the west end of Leadville that has a gabled attic and white lace curtains in the parlor window. The conductor said the sisters will be safe and comfortable there."

The Windhaven party boarded the procession of stagecoaches, and as they wound their way along the defile, the words of Carlyle Channing Davis, the editor of the Leadville *Evening Chronicle*, were recalled by Lucien Edmond. He had been reading Davis's account of his own introduction to Leadville in the newspaper that his San Antonio banker had given him, and the tall, blond Texan found himself agreeing with every word of the description of that journey: "The coach rolled like a crippled vessel in the trough of the sea, lurching from one side to the other, bumping over boulders and into ruts and quagmires, plunging and swaying down the winding, tortuous road. . . ."

In the deepening gloom, Lucien Edmond looked down into the gaping maw of the ravine, just inches away from the wheels of the coach. He shuddered to imagine the disastrous results if one of the horses should lose its footing, or if the harness should break, or—most dangerous of all—if in the unlikely event that an inexperienced driver was at the reins, he hesitated a fraction too long one way or pulled a bit too much the other. He was glad that most of the journey would be made in darkness; the drivers and their horses knew the way so well that they needed no more than the lantern light thrown out ahead to guide them, and the passengers were spared the terrifying view. Lucien Edmond decided the wisest course was not even to think about this trip, so he pulled his Stetson down over his eyes and forced himself to sleep for the remainder of the ride.

Although it was almost midnight when the stagecoaches finally pulled into Leadville, it seemed as if it were twelve o'clock noon instead. Lights blazed from just about every window, and the streets were crowded with all types of humanity. Miners elbowed businessmen out of their way; gamblers and bunco artists wended their way in and out of saloons and hotels; ladies of the evening walked arm in arm with bankers from the East; street urchins begged for pennies in front of dance halls. While the Windhaven travelers had been expecting a wide-open town, they were completely unprepared for the sights and sounds of Leadville.

Called the "Magic City" by Carlyle Davis, Leadville never slept. Every inch along the town's main thoroughfares had been built up, the dusty streets lined shoulder-to-shoulder with multistory brick buildings, log cabins, and clapboard structures of every architectural description.

As the party walked along the wooden sidewalks in front of the Grand Hotel—where a ten-foot by ten-foot chamber could be rented, and where, chances were, a fellow seeking a place to sleep would have to share the bed with a total stranger already occupying it—Lucien Edmond sighed wearily. He glanced over at the nuns, trying to assess their reactions.

The Leadville inhabitants were staring as curiously at the nuns as Lucien Edmond was—albeit for different reasons. People of every walk of life and every ethnic origin were commonplace here; still, the sight of four sisters of the church standing out in front of a fleabag hotel well after midnight caused many a passerby to cast puzzled looks in the sisters' direction.

Sister Martha's equanimity, however, held fast; indeed, she was mildly amused to see the reactions that she and her nuns elicited. Yet she knew the women were not as used to worldly sights as she was, and she felt it would be wisest to have them indoors and safely abed as quickly as possible. She turned to Lucien Edmond and anxiously inquired, "I wonder if we might find that boardinghouse, Mr. Bouchard."

"Of course, Sister Martha. Let's see, we're on Chestnut Street, and the conductor said the boardinghouse is over on First Avenue. . . ." He scratched his head, trying to figure out where exactly the boardinghouse was in relation to where they stood. He approached a young man standing by a buckboard in front of the hotel and asked, "Would you like to make some money taking our baggage to a boardinghouse? I'll pay a dollar."

"Sure thing, mister." The bearded, lanky young man in his late twenties straightened and, his eyes brightening, sprang forward with alacrity.

"That's fine," Lucien Edmond smiled, then he turned back to Sister Martha. "We'll get you and the sisters settled first, then we'll find our lodgings." As he stared down the street, he shook his head and added, "I must say, my first impression of Leadville isn't too encouraging. It's sure noisy and dirty."

Ramón Hernandez concurred as he took off his sombrero and slapped it against his thigh. "And here it is April, but there's still plenty of snow around. Apparently winters last a good long time here, and my vaqueros and I are not too used to cold weather."

"But it sharpens the senses and increases one's energy, Ramón," Lucien Edmond bantered, "and it gives a man a good appetite after a hard day's work. After the hot spells we've had at Windhaven Range the past ten years, the cold

178

weather in Leadville doesn't disturb me. But just about any-thing else I can see from right here does—look over there," he disgustedly commented. A drunken man was swaying down the street, and as he reached an open window, a gaudily painted prostitute purloined his hat, forcing the man to go inside to retrieve it. Such open prostitution—totally accepted in this city—was a way of life completely antithetical to the moral lives of the Windhaven men. The corruption of Leadville seemed to exceed even what the men had seen and experi-enced in Kansas cow towns—nor did Lucien Edmond recall observing Leadville to be so violent when he had been here the previous fall.

Lucien Edmond turned to the mother superior. "I'm afraid, Sister Martha, that you and your sisters may be distressed by the violence and godlessness here. I confess I'm beginning to wonder if your zeal might not be misplaced."

But the imperturbable woman merely smiled and shook her head, gently reproving him: "You must have more faith, my son. In Mexico, we often had to deal with *bandidos,* as well as *peones,* who rebelled against their masters. And yet, our belief sustained us, and the dear Lord kept us from harm. These men are rough, perhaps like children who have had no love or schooling, and I know that they are drawn here by a desire for material wealth. Yet I am certain that there are many poor souls who have neither wealth nor friendship—and it is for these, who need us most, that we have come. We shall manage, my son. Have no fear of that."

"I stand rebuked, Sister Martha," Lucien Edmond declared. "But, at any rate, the first order of business is to get you over to that boardinghouse, so that you can refresh yourselves and have a good night's sleep after our long, tiring journey."

Sister Martha brightly responded, "It has been a wonderful opportunity to see this country, my son, with some of the most picturesque and inspiring landscapes any of us have seen. And the mountain air is rarefied and invigorating. Never fear, we shall thrive. Do you not know the parable of Job, my son? The discomforts God sent to him were to test his faith and his loyal adherence to the Divine laws. Though he was harshly set upon and impoverished, he was restored unto more than he had at the beginning of his trials and tribulations." She suddenly yawned, then smiled. "And speaking of tribula-

179

tions, I do hope this woman of whom the conductor spoke will put us up."

"I am glad to know that you can admit to physical weariness. For I confess I am exhausted, and I was beginning to think that you were immune to such human frailties," Lucien Edmond chuckled. Striding forward, he showed the driver what pieces of luggage to take and then helped each of the sisters into the buggy. "I'm told there's a boardinghouse on First Avenue run by a widow—"

"Sure, I know the place, mister," the bearded young man broke in. "It's Widow Boyd's place. She's a good soul, she is, mister. The sisters will be fine with her."

"There, you see?" Lucien Edmond turned to Sister Martha. Then, to the driver, he said, "Thanks for your help. The rest of us will wait here for you, and I'll pay you after you drop us off at our lodgings—if that's agreeable to you, my good fellow."

"Sure is, mister. My name's Jack Farley, by the way." He clambered up into the driver's seat, took the reins, then called, "Giddyap!" and the wagon lumbered up the street.

"Well, that's fortunate," Ramón told his brother-in-law. "What's your plan for tomorrow, Lucien Edmond? Joe told me the mine is up on Stray Horse Gulch; and it might be a wise idea to hire a crew immediately and get some temporary house built near the mine, so we can live there and be right on hand for our work. Otherwise, we'll have to go to the bother of renting or buying horses and driving out there from the boardinghouse we'll have to stay in. I personally would rather live at the site of the mine—that way, if there should be any trouble, we'd be right there to guard it."

"I agree with you completely, Ramón. First thing tomorrow, after we've rested and had a good breakfast, you, Joe, and I will go out and hire ourselves a good mining engineer, so we can soon find out how rich we're all going to be."

Standing nearby, the old prospector, Frank Scolby, stared down the street and soberly declared, "I'd say you're right about not wantin' to live in this town, Mr. Bouchard. It wouldn't take long for your men and anybody else you hire to get a house built where it could be right comfortable. I also never want to leave a mine once it's operating, because that's just invitin' trouble."

"Then we're all in agreement, Mr. Scolby," Lucien Edmond declared. "I'm sure there are enough unemployed miners and hopefuls in this town who'd jump at the chance to help us build a house. Well, as soon as the sisters are quartered, we'll find our own boardinghouse and get a good night's sleep. There's plenty to be done starting first thing tomorrow."

"Here's the Boyd house, Sisters." The driver drew on the mare's reins and then quickly climbed down from his perch to help the sisters descend. "I'll just stay here till I'm sure Mrs. Boyd's gonna be able to accommodate you. Then I'll go back for the men."

"You're very kind, my son," Sister Martha said in a thin, tired voice. "I'll find out just as quickly as I can if we'll be welcome here. Do please watch our luggage, and we'd be much obliged if you'd bring it in, if Mrs. Boyd can take us."

"Of course I'll do that, Sister."

Sister Martha sent him a grateful look and ascended the short flight of wooden steps to the door, hesitating for just a moment because of the late hour. But she took hold of the knocker and rapped three times, and the door was opened almost instantly by a plump, gray-haired woman. Seeing the habit of Sister Martha, she almost unconsciously inclined her head and made the sign of the cross as she stammered, "Sister! I never expected to see someone like you here in Leadville, that's for certain."

"You are Mrs. Boyd?"

"That's right, Sister. Phyllis Boyd. How can I help you?"

Sister Martha averred, "The conductor on the train that brought us to Cañon City told us that you have a very fine boardinghouse here. We were wondering if you could put us up, as we hope to stay here for quite some time. We feel that perhaps we can bring comfort and assistance to the needy and the sick of this mining town."

"It would be my great honor to have you here as my boarders, Sister—Sister—"

"It is Sister Martha, Mrs. Boyd," the elderly nun put in.

"If you wouldn't mind sharing sleeping quarters, Sister Martha, I've got two nice rooms in the back of the second floor. You'll find them fairly quiet, if I do say so myself. Come in; I'd be pleased to show you the rooms."

181

"Thank you so much, Mrs. Boyd." Sister Martha turned to her three companions and beckoned them to follow her into the house.

At the conclusion of her inspection, she nodded and declared, "They are perfect for us. How much are you asking, Mrs. Boyd?"

"You'd take meals with me, I daresay?"

"That would be most convenient, yes." Again Sister Martha smiled. "And I can assure you that we should appreciate home-cooked food."

"The two rooms will be thirteen dollars a week, including meals for the four of you. I set out a hearty breakfast, and cold meats and cheese for lunch. And dinner is always filling. Mr. Boyd used to joke and say that the real reason he married me was because I could cook lamb stew and roast chicken better than he ever tasted in all his life."

"If I weren't so tired, my mouth would be watering," Sister Martha said with a laugh. "If it's convenient, we'll take the rooms right now. We have been traveling for some weeks all the way from southeastern Texas."

"I do declare!" Mrs. Boyd exclaimed. "You must be exhausted after a journey like that. I won't delay your rest one minute longer." She looked around the parlor. "I didn't notice you carrying luggage, Sister Martha. Is it at the stage depot?"

"A young driver carried us and our luggage here. He's very patiently waiting outside," the nun told her.

"Well, you all wait right here and I'll go ask the driver to bring the luggage along to your rooms." Phyllis Boyd's voice was disarmingly cordial.

While the luggage was taken to the nuns' rooms, Mrs. Boyd invited Sister Martha and the others to have tea and cake with her in her parlor. Although they were terribly tired, they felt obligated to keep this kind woman company after disturbing her at such a late hour.

"I just can't get over it, Sister Martha," the genial widow exclaimed as she served the nuns. "You say you've come all the way from Texas! Father Robinson will be so pleased to meet you, I'm sure—he's the Catholic priest here, the only one in town. Frankly, I wouldn't have picked Leadville, if I'd had my choice. But I loved my man, and we were close to each other, and then he got the gold fever, you see." Here

182

she uttered a pathetic sigh. "He found a little, enough to set me up in this house, which after his death I made into a boardinghouse. You see, Sister Martha, after Hugh died, well, I didn't have any relatives or he either, so I decided to stay on and at least try to provide a decent place for women who didn't have too much money to spend and try to give them the comforts of home, as you might say."

"That is a very Christian act, Mrs. Boyd," Sister Martha warmly approved. "Actually, there may be others of us who would be in need of your hospitality. You see, others in our order plan to come up later on and start a school for the miners' children. The four of us," she nodded to Sisters Luz, Concepción, and Margarita, "hope to start an institution for the needy—especially the wives and children of miners who have been killed."

"There are enough of them here, all right. Mining is dangerous, and it doesn't pay well, either. Most of the wealth belongs to a few lucky souls. Take Horace Tabor, for example: That man has had the most extraordinary luck!"

"Mr. Bouchard, who brought us here from Texas, has mentioned him several times. I'm sure the sisters would like to hear about him as much as I."

"You might say that this town really belongs to him, in a way, Sister Martha," Phyllis Boyd explained as she helped the nuns to more tea and cake. "They found gold here about twenty years ago, in California Gulch, and the town that sprang up was called Oro City. But about two years later, the gold sands were worked out, and the town dropped from above five thousand people to almost a ghost town, from what some of the old timers have told me. Then, about five years ago, a Minnesota prospector reworked some of the abandoned claims and got himself a metallurgist as a partner. They found the heavy red sands that got in the way of the sluicing were just about pure carbonate of lead, with lots of silver in them. Miners immediately started pouring back in, prospecting for strikes on Iron and Carbonate Hills. And little over two years ago, this town—it's near a city now—was renamed Leadville, and Horace Tabor was elected mayor."

"And how did Mr. Tabor come into all this good fortune?" Sister Martha pursued.

"It's an interesting story. He was born in Vermont and was originally a stonecutter. He and his wife, Augusta, and their young son came out here in the gold rush, but he never really made anything, and his wife made expenses by taking in boarders. He'd just about given up on his hopes of any kind of decent strike, but one April morning in 1878, he grub-staked two German shoemakers who came into the general store he owned. They told Tabor that they had staked a claim on a plot of land, and in exchange for provisions—which came to $64.75, including a jug of whiskey—they would cut Tabor in for a one-third share. Almost at once they struck a lode they called the Little Pittsburg. It was said that they made the strike at the only point on the hill where the vein of silver was so near the surface. But that wasn't all," Mrs. Boyd paused and sipped some tea.

"Well now, out of the Little Pittsburg Mr. Tabor made half a million dollars, and he invested it in yet another mine." She laughed and continued, "A man had decided to play a trick on him by salting that mine—that means, Sisters, that you sprinkle some silver down the shaft of a mine that hasn't produced anything, and then try to sell it off to somebody who doesn't know anything about it. Only, Mr. Tabor had his men go on digging and, sure enough, after digging just eight feet after they'd pumped out the mine, they struck pure ore. Mr. Tabor christened it the Chrysolite, and the ore taken from that mine brought in $100,000 a month. And then he bought the Matchless Mine on Fryer's Hill for $117,000, and that's turning out to be the best of them all. It's said he's worth over nine million dollars! You may have seen the Tabor Opera House on Harrison Avenue, as well as the bank he built. Last year, he was elected lieutenant governor, and there's talk that he might get to be governor and then go on to be a United States senator."

"He would appear to have the Midas touch," Sister Martha thoughtfully observed.

"Yes, that's what they're saying all over this state. Unfortunately, according to the talk, Horace Tabor is, shall we say, outgrowing his wife, Augusta. I don't mean to shock you, but it's well known around here that he's taken up with a pretty young thing not much more than twenty years old, herself divorced, who came from a small Wisconsin town with her husband—he tried to find gold, too. Her name is Elizabeth Doe, and the miners call her Baby Doe. I'm not one to

184

gossip, but from all I've heard, I'm afraid that poor Augusta Tabor is going to play second fiddle before much longer.''

"That would be reprehensible indeed.''

"Indeed, Sister Martha. I was brought up to believe marriage was for life and divorce was sinful. But that's enough about Horace Tabor. I'm sure you're all very tired, so I'll go turn down your bedding and bring you some extra pillows, so you can get a good night's sleep.''

"You're very kind, Mrs. Boyd, and speaking for my companions, I want to thank you for the way you've made us feel at home.''

"That's nice of you to say, Sister Martha. It's hard for a body to do all that much when there are so many poor people in this town who haven't had any luck at all.''

"You have a good heart, Mrs. Boyd,'' Sister Martha observed. "I should like to talk to you again about the plans I told you about. The man who brought us here has a claim on a mine, just outside Leadville, which has been determined to be very profitable. And he will give a large contribution in the name of charity to the unfortunates. Perhaps you might wish to help us offer food and clothing to those who are in desperate circumstances.''

"I would love to do that. It would make me feel I was being useful, and it would be a way of being thankful for the blessings I've had.'' Phyllis Boyd's face was aglow with happiness.

Twenty

The driver of the buggy reported to Lucien Edmond that he had taken the nuns to Phyllis Boyd's boardinghouse and that they seemed to be quite content with their quarters. Greatly heartened, Lucien Edmond directed that half of the men and their luggage should go with Jack Farley to a rooming house, and he and the rest would wait for a second run. When the driver returned for him and his men, they climbed aboard and leaned back, crowded as they were, to await the last lap of their long, arduous journey. Each of the men was silent, preoccupied with his own thoughts about the locale of this new Windhaven Range endeavor. Watching the people pass by, seeing the lights of the dance halls and saloons and the lurid yellow flares from the constantly working smelters, Lucien Edmond thought that it could be a scene out of Dante's *Inferno*. The frequent sounds of gunshots and cries of rage and pain were mingled with the sudden gusts of wind that attacked this mountain town and stirred the patches of snow still clinging to the dark earth.

There were few trees on the barren hills, whose jagged crests were discolored by the sluice drippings. A nauseous smell clung to the town, and the full moon was obscured by a smoky glaze from the smelters. There was no beauty to Leadville—only the outward signs of a ferocious struggle for survival, in which some would make untold riches while others starved and sought charity in vain. Lucien Edmond and his men had come to this Colorado mining town at the very zenith of its boom. Even before another year would pass, it would begin to decline; there would be more and more impoverished men and women, people who had come here with the dream of being economically free, yet who would become prisoners of privation.

Frank Scolby's mine was located two miles northeast of Leadville, and the morning after the men had found boardinghouses and enjoyed a good night's sleep after their exhausting journey, Lucien Edmond and Ramón walked over to the office of the Leadville *Chronicle*. There, the peppery, thirty-two-year old editor brought them up to date on what was taking place in this thriving city.

Carlyle Davis, the tireless reporter-editor of the *Chronicle*, listened to Lucien Edmond's explanation of why they had come to Leadville and then shrugged. "You men have as much chance of becoming millionaires overnight as a lot of men in this town. Or as much chance of ending up broke. Last winter, there was an old prospector who died from the cold, and his friends put him in a snow bank in the cemetery until they could hire somebody to dig a grave in the frozen ground. After some months, his friends visited the cemetery, only to find that a rich silver lode had been struck while excavating the grave. The cemetery had been staked out, and the dead man, quite forgotten, remained in the snow bank until the spring thaw. That's what you can expect here in Leadville.''

"That's appalling!" Lucien Edmond shook his head and eyed Ramón. "We're from Texas, Mr. Davis. The reason we're here is because we helped an old prospector whom we found on the way back from a cattle drive. He'd been left to die, so to reward us, he insisted on sharing his claim up here with us.''

"There are a hundred stories like that here in Leadville, Mr. Bouchard,'' Carlyle Davis chuckled. "Mines, even shallow holes in the ground, have been sold and resold many times a day, and always at a profit. There are countless stories of millions being made from grubstakes of just a few dollars. Absolute yokels out of the cornfields back in Iowa have dug in ground that experienced prospectors considered valueless, and they have turned wealthy overnight. Usually, not knowing what to do with their newly found wealth, they fritter it away and go back to the poorhouse.'' He paused to let his words sink in, then asked, "Now, what can I do for you?''

"Well, first, we want to get a good mining engineer and a capable crew to build a smelter on our claim.''

"I can put you in touch with an honest contractor, who will get you miners enough—if you're willing to pay a decent price. You may or may not know that Leadville is going through a crisis right now. A lot of the miners are talking strike, and the Carbonate Kings—that's our cynical newspaper term for these men who have become millionaires overnight—don't want to pay a decent wage, or shorten work hours.''

"I'm prepared to pay more than the going rate for capable, trustworthy men,'' Lucien Edmond calmly observed.

"Then you'll certainly be a different type of newcomer from the kind we've been accustomed to, Mr. Bouchard. And what else?''

"We have an immediate need to hire some men to help build a house near our claim. It'll house the men we brought with us, as well as my partners and myself.''

"That, too, I can help you with.''

"I'm grateful to you, Mr. Davis. Tell me, is there a Catholic church in town? I wasn't certain that there was.''

"Actually, yes. Two years ago, a priest named Father Robinson ordered the first load of brick, and Irish miners built his church and topped it off with a tall steeple. A little

187

later, the railroad company presented the congregation with a bell you can still hear on Sundays. There are other denominations in town, but all they really worship is money—that again is a cynical observation. Father Robinson is doing rather poorly, and his health isn't the best.''

"I asked that because, on our ranch in Texas, Mr. Davis, we gave shelter to a party of nuns who had been driven away from Mexico, and they established a school for the children of our vaqueros. Four of them, including the mother superior, have come to Leadville, hoping to help the poor and the needy. They're staying with a Mrs. Boyd.''

"Oh, yes, Phyllis Boyd. A fine woman. I'm sure that she goes to Father Robinson's church and has told the nuns about it—I'm also sure the poor old man will be only too happy to have their help. I feel sorry for Mrs. Boyd—she lost her husband here about ten months ago, buried when a mine caved in. There haven't been too many good women coming into town, of the sort that would appreciate a decent house like hers and want to stay there. I'm sure she's grateful for the company of your nuns.''

"Thank you for telling me. I'll make sure she's adequately compensated. Well then, I'll take the names you mentioned as being the best sources for the crew I'll need and the engineer. I'm obliged to you," Lucien Edmond replied, as he reached into his pocket for a notebook in which to record the names.

Within a week of their arrival in town, thanks to the suggestions of the *Chronicle* editor, Lucien Edmond Bouchard and Ramón had hired a dozen carpenters, who had been only too happy to accept his unusually high wages to build a sturdy frame house some two city blocks distant from Frank Scolby's mine.

Furnishing the house was a costly matter, for as could have been expected in a mining town, there was ruthless profiteering by local storekeepers. Even staple groceries like cans of beans and sacks of flour sold at four and five times what they cost in Denver; a barrel of whiskey brought a dealer a $1,500 profit, and hay was priced at $200 a ton. For the simple beds, chairs, and tables, sufficient to give the men of Windhaven places to sleep and to eat from, Lucien Edmond paid the exorbitant price of nearly $800.

188

The cold weather persisted, and coal lamps and kerosene stoves were all that provided heat in this desolate, two-mile-high locale. It was a singular contrast, Lucien Edmond wrote Maxine a week after he had come to Leadville, between the warm, fertile valley of Windhaven Range and this snow-packed camp. And yet, he told her, here was a chance to make a fortune almost overnight, something impossible to be done through honest industry and planning at Windhaven Range. It was a turn of industrial enterprise, the like of which he had never before encountered—but it was only the beginning of what was in store for this young nation, which had just begun its second hundred years of life.

Lucien Edmond had engaged the services of John Darwent, a mining engineer in his mid-thirties. He had taken his degree in archaeology at an Eastern university, and then had become fascinated with the far more modern and exciting prospect of discovering wealth beneath the earth, rather than in ancient cities and artifacts. He had, indeed, helped Horace Tabor develop one of the smaller profitable mines last year.

"I've some time on my hands now, Mr. Bouchard," he had declared at their first interview, "and Horace Tabor has become like a man trying to live a kind of fairy tale—he's caught up in it so deeply that he might never come back to reality. Truth is, I'm pretty tired of his ways. At any rate, I'm at liberty now, and I'll be happy to investigate Mr. Scolby's claim and determine how large a holding you have here. Whatever its extent, it'll take hard work to extract the ore, but you don't strike me, Mr. Bouchard, as the type of man who, like Mr. Tabor, wants quick easy riches and doesn't care how he arrives at the end he seeks."

"Thank you for the compliment, Mr. Darwent. I guess I've had to work hard all my life and expect the reward after labor, as was true of my father and my great-grandfather. I'll admit that the prospect of extra capital will help me develop some plans I have about my own ranch and the people on it, and also I'd like to see Frank Scolby enjoy some luxury in his old age. But you do what you think necessary, Mr. Darwent. Hire a good crew—and I'll pay top wages and ensure good working conditions. I've already heard that a lot of the miners are thinking of striking over those issues."

"And small wonder. Too many of them have been killed or badly injured in accidents that happened only because the

189

mine owners took no safety precautions and just wanted to get as much ore out as quickly as they could. I'll admit I'm on the miners' side, and I'd like to work for you."

By the second week of May, the crew that John Darwent had hired had completed the first mine shaft, and they, together with the Windhaven men, had completed the building of a small smelter, to serve until such time as a larger, more permanent facility could be constructed.

When John came out of the cave with the first ore samples, his eyes were shining with excitement as he approached Lucien Edmond. "I've taken samples, Mr. Bouchard, at the rate of two pounds per foot of vein. And, to give it a fair test, I've used eight-foot intervals between the test holes. I can tell you that you have an immensely rich lode here. Tomorrow, we'll put the men to work at the smelter, processing your ore. I'm afraid, though, you'll have a problem about shipping the silver out. The express companies are afraid to come in here and transport bullion because ruffians have banded together and have erected toll gates on some of the main roads. Those who won't pay the toll are simply robbed outright.

"Of course, you can deposit the bullion in the banks," he went on, "but they're getting overcrowded. Many of the miners, Mr. Bouchard, because they don't trust the banks, use the post office and buy money orders payable to themselves, renewing them when they expire. The good news is that I've heard by August, the Denver & Rio Grande Railroad will have completed its line into Leadville, which will solve your shipping problem."

"I thank you for your advice, Mr. Darwent. It's quite possible I may decide to take some of the bullion back to Texas with me in a solidly made wagon, with my men armed to guard it. There may be other possibilities as well. But first, let's see how rich this vein really is."

"It's very rich. And there's danger, too. Although I picked the very best men I could find in town, some of them may boast of the work they're doing to less fortunate fellows. And that might attract the kind of riffraff who'll make trouble," John told him.

"I think my men can handle any trouble. They've had to drive off bandits and hostile Indians all too often. I don't want to resort to violence, but I'll see that this mine is protected."

190

"Mr. Bouchard, I might tell you that while you were in town buying supplies, a number of rough-looking fellows walked over here and asked me a few questions. I told them we were prospecting, but hadn't struck anything rich yet. I only hope they believed me. There was one young fellow, slick and smooth as a whistle, with a neatly trimmed beard, who asked a lot of impertinent questions. Even wanted to know who owned this mine. Well, I just thought I'd tell you. Tomorrow, we'll start melting down the first ore."

When Lucien Edmond Bouchard had called on Sister Martha and her three companions to learn how they were getting along at Mrs. Boyd's boardinghouse, he casually mentioned the church of Father Robinson. Sister Martha briefly mentioned that Mrs. Boyd had told her of Father Robinson, but made no further comment about this; after he had left, however, she went to the kitchen where Mrs. Boyd was preparing the evening meal.

"I have been thinking about how all of us here can help the poor," the elderly nun declared. "Let me go to Father Robinson and ask him if he would come over here, and all of us can plan something worthwhile together."

"I could donate some food to those who don't have money to buy any," Phyllis Boyd proffered.

"That's a splendid idea, Mrs. Boyd!" Sister Martha enthusiastically agreed. "It has come to me that we can have two bases of operation for our work—the church itself or the rectory, and your boardinghouse. Of course, Father Robinson must approve our plan, and you, too, must feel comfortable with it—and not put yourself out at all."

"No, go on, Sister Martha. So far your idea makes perfect sense to me. After all, I have quite a few spare rooms here, as you know, and I would be more than willing to give them over to those who need them if your benefactor is willing to finance this operation," the middle-aged widow declared.

"Excellent! Tomorrow, then, we shall all meet with Father Robinson and hopefully set our operation in motion. For the moment, however," the nun said with a wry smile, "I think the only operation that needs attention is our dinner. I believe your stew could do with a bit of stirring!"

Twenty-One

Over in Dodge City, on this Friday night in the second week of May, business was booming. At the Comique, largest of the town's saloons and gambling halls, all of the tables were in operation—packed with cowboys who had ridden in with the first cattle drives of the season. The green baize curtain had been raised on the stage—for the Comique was also a theater—and the patrons at the bar, as well as at the tables, were enjoying the suggestive dancing and bawdy songs of a bevy of chorines. When they were not performing on the stage, these women plied their usual trade of cadging drinks and arranging to sell their favors in the rows of small, comfortably furnished cubicles upstairs.

The long, wide, polished walnut bar was crowded this evening not only with cowboys and stagecoach hands, but with patrons drawn from the better strata of Dodge City society as well. They drank their whiskey, alternately eyeing the provocatively attired girls on the stage and the oil painting above them, with its opulent naked blonde languorously offering herself on a chaise longue. Four bartenders were kept busy filling glasses and cleaning the used ones to accommodate the gratifying rush of business.

At a table far to the left and at the back, some thirty feet from the stage, Jeb Cornish lolled in his chair, pouring himself a second glass of Maryland rye whiskey while he chewed at his unlit cigar; his watery blue eyes squinted at the dancers, cynically appraising them. One of them, a long-legged chestnut-haired girl of eighteen, named Flossie, had come to Dodge City from Missouri just a week ago, having run away from a stern Presbyterian stepfather, who delighted in sermonizing over her wickedness, concluding each harangue with a strapping. Flossie had been pathetically grateful when Cornish had magnanimously given her a job at ten dollars a week "plus all the tips you can earn by just being nice to the customers, Flossie, honey." Tonight he intended to put her gratitude to the test. Besides, it was high time she was broken in. She had a fresh, almost childish charm to her, which should bring a great deal of money from the regular patrons who periodically demanded new girls, seeking variety to gratify their amorous outings.

Having filled his glass, he set the bottle down and took a greedy swallow; he belched, then lit his cigar, and leaned back, squinting at the dancers. Flossie sent him a covert wave of her hand and a tremulous smile. He chuckled to himself. There was nothing he liked better than teaching a young girl all the tricks she would need to wheedle an extra dollar or two from her future customers.

In this pleasant frame of mind, he took out his watch, studied it carefully, then turned slowly to stare at the door. It was time Gabe Penrock was reporting in—his train from Pueblo had been due at six o'clock tonight. Ever since John McCreedy had come back from Cañon City to tell him of the failure of his planned train robbery, Cornish had been anxiously awaiting Penrock's return. He had highly approved of Penrock's decision to stay in Leadville and learn if that damned Mex, Ramón Hernandez, was actually going into the mining business there. Something was going to have to be done once and for all to settle that greaser's hash. He'd been the monkey wrench in Cornish's works too often now to be allowed to live a day longer.

He swore under his breath. More than likely, Penrock was saying hello to his wife, Rhea, instead of coming right to the Comique to tell him all the news. Not that he blamed Gabe for that; hell, he'd take Rhea into his own bed any night of the week.

There was something about Rhea Penrock that got under his skin. That cold snottiness of hers, that willowy body, and those luscious long legs and deep gray eyes could make a man's insides turn over just thinking about what he'd like to do with her.

The baize curtain fell now as the girls concluded their final number. Along with scattered applause came bawdy shouts and catcalls directed at one or another of the dancers as the girls, still in their costumes, emerged from one wing of the stage to mingle with the patrons. Cornish observed that Flossie hung back, her large blue eyes wide with timid apprehension. He chuckled to himself again. He'd teach her how to solicit business, once he'd broken her in his way. The thought

193

warmed him, and he reached for his glass and finished the whiskey, setting it down with a clatter, and then turned again to the door as he heard it open.

The tall, wiry, black-haired man he had been waiting for sauntered in, although his appearance had been altered by a neatly trimmed beard. That was good thinking, a good disguise to throw the greaser off the track while Penrock had been nosing around Leadville to find out exactly what Hernandez was up to. Well, he could almost forgive Penrock for keeping him waiting like this.

Cornish's eyes narrowed, and he swore under his breath, for he saw that just behind Penrock, following him into the saloon, was the man's statuesque wife, Rhea. She closed the door behind her, and came to stand beside her husband, as she looked around the dance hall with a studied air of insolent contempt that both excited and angered the corrupt Indian agent. One of these days, Cornish said to himself, he'd have a little talk with Gabe, tell him that it wasn't smart to mix pleasure with business, and certainly not to let Rhea flaunt herself all over the place. It was only bound to stir up trouble. Suppose one of the drunken cowboys at the bar took a notion to sidle over to that long-legged piece and ask her to go upstairs with him—there'd be a row for fair, and the danger of that was that Gabe Penrock might get shot defending his wife's honor. Honor! Jeb Cornish nearly laughed aloud at the thought. But then, there was no accounting for taste. Who would have thought that Rhea, with what had happened to her and the way she'd grown up, would fall head over heels in love with this young desperado, who'd had a price on his head ever since he'd turned fourteen.

Rhea Penrock was wearing a sombrero tilted down over one side of her face, cowboy boots, Levi's, and a dark blue cotton shirt that strained against her magnificent breasts. Even from here, Cornish could make out the points of her nipples, as the fabric tightened with every slow, calculated breath she took, making her dramatic entrance. The cunning bitch! What he wouldn't give to make her go down on her knees to him and call him master—but right now, he needed Gabe Penrock a lot more than he needed that man's young slut of a wife.

And so, as the couple made their way toward his table, he grandiosely beckoned to one of the pretty girls serving as a waitress and bade her bring a fresh bottle of rye, as well as a bottle of the French champagne he'd had sent in from New Orleans. Rhea liked to drink champagne, he remembered.

With a false joviality, he made an expansive gesture. "Sit down, both of you! Gabe, I've been waiting to hear from you ever since you sent me that telegraph wire from Pueblo. Was that stupid operator the one who soured our plan?"

"No, Mr. Cornish, he swore on a stack of Bibles he didn't know anything about it—I mean, that the greaser and his partners from Texas were going to be on that train with their men. You know by now that old Jack Hayes got his, and Reuben Huntley got sentenced to a twenty-year stretch at hard labor."

"That adds to the greaser's score! What have you found out about him and his pals?" the fat Indian agent demanded, as the dance-hall girl set down fresh glasses and the two bottles, then proceeded to open them. He turned his attention to her, leering as she leaned over the table in a way that offered an expansive view of her overly ripe bosom.

There was a sudden explosive sound, and with a startled cry, the waitress began to pour the gushing golden liquid into the glass set before Rhea Penrock. As she set down the bottle and straightened, Cornish reached out and, with a vicious smile, pinched her thigh with his pudgy right thumb and forefinger, till she let out a shrill scream of pain. "Aw, Gawd, please, Mr. Cornish, I didn't spill it on purpose, honest! I couldn't help it! It came out so fast!"

"That's just to teach you to be careful next time, Lizzie. Now get the hell back to your work."

Rhea Penrock gave him a disdainful look. "You're quite a man with the ladies, Mr. Cornish. I can't say as I approve of your ways, though."

He assumed his most hypocritically benevolent smile. "When I'm in the presence of a real lady, my dear, you'll find me a totally different person. Lizzie's no lady; she's a crummy little tramp from Iowa who's been here three months, and she isn't worth her feed yet. But now let's talk about more pleasant things—like settling that greaser's score, and it's a mighty big one. Gabe, boy, what are they doing out there? Are they in Leadville for sure?"

"For sure, Mr. Cornish," Penrock nodded confirmation. Rhea, drawing her chair closer to him, slid her arm around his waist and provocatively eyed him. "I sent word by

195

McCreedy I was going to stay around till I found out what this Lucien Edmond Bouchard and Hernandez were up to. Well, I don't know how they did it, but they've stumbled onto a rich lode. The talk around town is that some old hard-rock prospector on his uppers found it by accident. They've hired themselves a crack mining engineer, got a smelter built, and got themselves a pretty good crew of miners. I hear tell they're offering better wages than they're getting anywhere else.''

"I've never seen a man with as much damned luck as that greaser!" Cornish growled. "Ambush him, and he wipes out some of our best men. Plan a train robbery to get the payroll, and what happens but he's on the same damned train! He's got more lives than a cat. Now what's your idea of taking him out of the picture so all we read about him in the newspaper is a death notice?"

"I've been thinking about that, Mr. Cornish. You know, there's a lot of trouble up there with the miners. Just before I got on the train to come here, I was talking to an old coot who's working as a slagman in one of Tabor's mines. He says last year they had trouble at the Malta smelter, where the fellows who worked in the furnaces and their helpers wanted an eight-hour day and some safety devices put in. He told me he'd seen three men burned alive when a slag pot spilled. They're working twelve hours a day and overtime, and the smell in those mines from all the gases and the heat, why, it's enough to kill a horse."

"What's this got to do with the greaser?" Jeb Cornish interrupted in an irritated tone.

"I'm getting to that, Mr. Cornish. Like I said, I've been figuring things out for you. And I think that maybe we can use these miners to do the job for us."

Cornish blinked, considered the bearded young lieutenant who sat opposite him, then grinned. "You've got a brain in you, Gabe, so all right—let's hear it. At this point, after all that greaser's got away with, I'll try just about anything if I can be sure of getting rid of him so I never hear his goddamned name again."

"Well, this same old guy told me they wanted only a quarter more a day. He said that these miners take their chances when they go down those overnight mines, that they can get hit from falling rocks, and the shafts and tunnels don't

196

have enough timber to stand firm. When they ride up and down in iron-ore buckets, the things bang against the walls of the shafts and tip over. And that's to say nothing of all the blasting powder they use, which goes off before it should—why, they've had a dozen miners killed the last couple of months. Then there's the danger of coming down sick with pneumonia or lead poisoning when the miners put in all those long hours in the cold, wet mines that don't have any air in them—''

''You're making my heart bleed for those miners, but I still don't hear anything about Hernandez,'' Cornish broke in with a snarl.

Gabe Penrock held up a propitiatory hand and chuckled. Rhea smiled at him and slid her hand along the inside of his thigh, and she moved still closer to him, sending Cornish a defiant, bold look that made him flush angrily. ''Hold your water, Mr. Cornish, I'm coming to the point right now. This same old slagman told me that the miners are going to strike sometime toward the end of the month. What I'm going to do is to get right back to Leadville, and if I can spread enough dollars around for beer and whiskey, I can get them riled up enough to attack the mine. Sure, Mr. Bouchard's men and the working crew there will put up a battle, and they've got those repeating rifles and carbines that did in poor Jack Hayes and the others you sent to attack the train—but maybe if I can get those miners angry enough, I can sneak in there, lay some dynamite, and blow up their shaft. And in the middle of all that, it'll be easy to do away with Hernandez.''

''That sounds great! Use the mob to be your weapon, or at least to divert the attention of the greaser and his men away from what you're really going to do to him—I'll go along with that, Gabe boy!'' Cornish exulted.

''Well, if it's okay with you, Mr. Cornish, I'll go back tomorrow on the five o'clock train. It'll take about three days to get back into Leadville.''

''I see you're sporting a beard, Gabe. My guess is that you grew it so Hernandez wouldn't recognize you, am I right?''

''Right as rain, Mr. Cornish.''

''He looks good in it,'' Rhea spoke up, giving the fat Indian agent a mockingly sultry look. ''And it tickles, too. It's real nice. I've got me a different hubby with a beard on.'' She turned and gave her husband a sly grin. ''Let's get out of

197

here, honey. You know what you have to do, so why waste more time talking when I haven't seen you in all this time? After all, our honeymoon isn't over yet. See you around, Mr. Cornish.''

Gulping down her champagne, she turned and flung the glass against the wall, shattering it. While Cornish goggled at her, she rose and, her arm around her husband's waist, sauntered off with him, looking up at him with narrowed, smoldering eyes, rubbing her hip against his, as they walked out of the dance hall.

Jeb Cornish poured himself another glass of Maryland rye, glowering at the departing couple. "What I wouldn't give to teach her manners, that uppity bitch," he muttered to himself. "But if she's what Gabe needs to get the job done, I've no complaints—not yet, anyhow.''

Twenty-Two

The affable mining engineer, John Darwent, hurried up to the house that served as living quarters for the Windhaven men in Leadville and eagerly pounded on the front door. "Mr. Bouchard, Mr. Hernandez, you're not going to believe this! There's a carriage outside and some men in kilts are climbing out of it!''

Lucien Edmond and Ramón had slept late, having put in long hours in the mine shaft examining samples of ore from the lode, which continued to be richer than had originally been believed. From the small well at the base of the white-hot furnace far above, lead and silver came gurgling up, which the workers ladled out into iron molds and cooled off into forty-pound "pigs." John had exulted over the fact that the silver was so rich that it exceeded six pounds per total. "Lots of the owners are shipping their pigs to New Jersey to be refined, Mr. Bouchard," he had told Lucien Edmond a week before. "If you'll give me the authority to buy some more equipment, we can do a fair job here." Lucien Edmond had readily assented to the additional purchases.

He turned to Ramón now, upon hearing John's imperious

summons. "I wonder what's up, Ramón. Who could our visitors be?"

"Well," his brother-in-law smiled, "I guess there's just one way to find out." He opened the door and stood momentarily spellbound.

John Darwent had not exaggerated. The carriage was one of the most elegant Ramón had ever seen. The two men flanking it were indeed dressed in Scottish kilts, the likes of which Ramón had never encountered. They were pleated garments of red, green, and black plaid cloth. Nor had Ramón ever seen anything like the sporrans they wore—the pouches, made of goat's hide and hair, which hung from their belts. Their red and green stockings only added to their ludicrous appearance, in Ramón's eyes, for they were topped by knobby knees, and the Mexican had to suppress a nervous laugh not to seem rude.

"That's the classic Highlanders' garb," Lucien Edmond whispered to his brother-in-law, and Ramón was relieved that he had not laughed aloud.

Six guards, who also wore colorful clothes but of a cut less surprising to Ramón, stood at the rear of the carriage, their brass helmets gleaming in the sunlight. In the driver's seat was perched a chubby man in a black top hat and red frock coat. He had gathered the reins tightly in his hands, halting the two spirited geldings that had drawn the carriage from town along the winding road that led to the mine.

Upon seeing Lucien Edmond and Ramón appear, one of the Highlanders opened the door of the carriage, saluted, and stepped back. Out of it emerged a stocky man in his fifties, with a scraggly walrus mustache, his hair receding almost to the middle of his skull, leaving his high-domed forehead glisteningly bare under the bright Colorado sun. A large diamond solitaire graced each pudgy finger, and his shirt cuffs, of the purest silk, were decorated with square cuff buttons of diamond and onyx almost the size of postage stamps. On his shirt front, there was a huge diamond stickpin, which caught the sun's rays. He turned to gesture impatiently at the individual who was descending from the carriage after him: a handsome, smiling man in his thirties who promptly whispered something in the older man's ear and then strode up to Lucien Edmond and Ramón. "Gentlemen, my name is William H. Bush. I'm Lieutenant Governor Tabor's aide-de-camp.

The lieutenant governor has heard of your new mine and comes prepared to make you an offer.'' Then he turned back to the portly Carbonate King and obsequiously added, ''Your Excellency, these are the gentlemen I was telling you about. Do you want me to conduct the negotiations?''

''Hell no, Billy, I can sure as hell speak for myself,'' Horace A.W. Tabor grumbled, as he moved slowly and portentously toward the bemused Lucien Edmond and Ramón. ''Billy, you go back into the carriage and tell Maxcy he's to stay there and not open his mouth. He may be my assistant, but he's only twenty-two and doesn't have the finesse his old dad has when it comes to buying a mine.''

''Right, Your Excellency!'' Billy Bush, the manager of Tabor's luxurious Clarendon Hotel in Leadville, saluted the silver tycoon as if the latter were a field marshal and hurried back into the carriage, closing the door behind him.

''Well, you men are new to Leadville, I hear tell,'' Horace Tabor began. Glancing back over his shoulder, he added with a kind of sheepish grin, ''Perhaps my Highlanders and guards look a bit odd out here. But you see, it's always good for a man who's high up the ladder in politics and finances—I plan to be governor soon enough of this new state and, after that, a U.S. senator, by God!—well, as I said, it's a good idea to have men around you can trust, in case of any trouble.''

''A very sensible precaution, Mr. Lieutenant Governor,'' Lucien Edmond Bouchard pleasantly agreed.

Ramón spoke up. ''A pleasure to meet you at last, sir. We've both heard a great deal about you.''

''That's hardly surprising, considering I own practically all of this town. Built some of it myself, too. By the by, have you gentlemen been to my opera house yet? The best thing to come to Leadville since the discovery of silver or gold, I'd say. Why, our newspaper editor calls it the finest theater house west of the Mississippi.''

''We've been too busy working to take much advantage of the social life of Leadville, I'm afraid, Mr. Tabor,'' Lucien Edmond parried with a smile.

''Well, just 'cause I'm the impresario, I don't think I'm in the least biased. It's really top-notch. All the seats are upholstered in plush, and it's got a frescoed ceiling. And for lights, seventy-two gas jets—count 'em when you come. All you have to do is mention my name and say that I gave you an invite. They're repeating *The Rough Diamond,* and seats are scarce and selling at a premium—even though you can put nearly nine hundred people in my opera house."

"It's very kind of you to offer us an invitation, Lieutenant Governor," Lucien Edmond murmured. "Perhaps in a few weeks, after we've got everything under control, we'll have some time to spend relaxing."

"Well, I'm here right now to help you relax starting this minute, because if you're smart, you'll pull out now. Maybe you haven't heard that the miners around here think they're being badly treated. Damned fools don't know when they're well off. There's talk of a strike, and if they pull that off, they'll stop all the mining operation in the area. That's why I think you'd be wise to take my offer. You've got that fellow Darwent working for your engineer, I hear tell. He's a good man, worked hard for me—don't know why he came over to you Texans. You *are* from Texas, aren't you?"

"That's right, sir," Ramón spoke up this time. "We have a cattle ranch there. As it happened, we saved a prospector's life when we came back from a drive bringing cattle up to this state, and he was kind enough to cut us in on this mine."

"Hell, if I buy this mine from you, you can divvy it up between you. I'm prepared to make you a damn good offer. Anyone'll tell you I pay good prices for what I want. Actually, I've got more money coming out of all the mines I've got than I know what to do with, but I want your mine, and I'm willing to give you the best market price you'll find anywhere around here. I've never cheated anybody yet, and you can't say that of a lot of the mine owners."

"I think we'd rather take our chances, Mr. Tabor," Lucien Edmond soberly answered. "I don't think the miners have any cause for hostility against us. We pay fairly and honestly in our operation, so I think we'll be spared what some mine owners are probably going to get."

"I don't like your tone, mister. You're the Bouchard fellow, aren't you?" Tabor truculently countered.

"That's correct, sir." Lucien Edmond's voice was steely. "Now if you've nothing else to discuss, you'll have to excuse us. We have to get up to our mine. You see, we're right on the spot every day with Mr. Darwent. We want to continue to ensure that our mine's as safe as it's possible to be under the circumstances. We haven't had an accident yet."

"Maybe so. But that doesn't mean it's not possible," Tabor growled. Ostentatiously, he unbuttoned his frock coat to let them see the diamond stickpin, adjusted his cuffs, cleared his throat, and spat just beyond his expensive leather boots.

"I'm sure that's true, Mr. Tabor," Lucien Edmond firmly replied, "but that's our problem, not yours. Since you have so many mines, I'm sure you won't be too disappointed if you don't add ours to your string. This is new for us, it's exciting, and it's a welcome change after all the cattle drives we've run the last few years. We plan to keep it and take our chances."

"Well, if that's the way you feel, so be it. I won't wish you any bad luck, but I'll tell you that you'd better be on your guard if those miners go out on strike. You don't have a private army the way I do."

"That's true, we haven't. Good day to you, sir." Lucien Edmond had the last word.

Horace Tabor snorted, glared at both of them, and then walked back to his carriage, the door of which was swiftly and unctuously opened by one of the Highlanders. Lining up in two platoons, the Highlanders and bodyguards alike marched off, whistling "John Brown's body lies a-moldering in the grave."

Ramón turned to his brother-in-law and shook his head. "All the things I've heard about Mr. Tabor, I can now believe."

John Darwent was chuckling with ill-concealed humor. "I kept my mouth shut because I was afraid I'd burst out laughing. I don't think old Horace has been talked to like that since the last time Augusta gave him hell for grubstaking vagrants—grubstakes that turned into millions. But it did my heart good to hear you talk back to him." Then, his face shadowing, he glumly added, "But I'm pretty sure there's going to be a strike after all. I just hope there won't be any trouble, and that the miners I've hired to work here get back into town and tell everybody how decently you treat them."

"Amen to that," Ramón solemnly agreed.

Twenty-Three

Elizabeth McCourt, born in 1854 in Oshkosh, Wisconsin, was the daughter of devout Irish Catholic immigrants. Her father, Peter, was a tailor who had settled in this lumber center after first emigrating to Canada and then upper New York State. Oshkosh was then as Leadville would become: a boomtown whose inhabitants realized overnight fortunes and—just as suddenly—overnight privation after several disastrous fires swept this "Sawdust City." Peter McCourt was the victim of one of these fires.

He had invested heavily in real estate, and after the last fire not only did his holdings vanish, but his usual clientele could no longer afford custom tailoring. Nonetheless, as Elizabeth was the apple of his eye, the favorite of all his children (of whom there had been fourteen, with several dying in infancy) nothing was too good for her. Her father's doting attitude was the major influence on Elizabeth's subsequent behavior.

At the age of twenty-three, Elizabeth married William Harvey Doe, a handsome and wealthy young man. His father had accumulated a large stake from Colorado mining properties and then returned to Oshkosh to invest heavily in the lumber industry.

After the wedding, Elizabeth and Harvey, as he was called, left by train for Colorado. Harvey's father, meanwhile, had begun to lose money as the timber market deteriorated, so he decided to accompany the newlyweds on their honeymoon, hoping to strike it rich again in the gold fields.

Five feet two inches in height, with golden hair and dazzling blue eyes, Elizabeth attracted considerable attention when she arrived in Denver, from where the happy couple went on to Central City, Colorado, and the Teller House. That city had been the heart of an earlier gold rush, and Elizabeth's father-in-law was certain that he could recoup his dwindling fortune.

Elizabeth's husband, however, proved to be a romantic dawdler and did little work for his father with the new mine shaft, which was in Blackhawk, near Central City. Elizabeth began to feel that she had made a mistake and that, if the mine was not successful, she would be destined to the drab life of a day laborer's wife. There were either the very rich or the very poor in these Colorado mountain towns.

When the news came that the quartz lodes that Harvey and his father had struck were too low-grade to bother working, her restlessness grew. By 1878, the young couple was estranged, and "Baby Doe" (the name the miners had applied to her) had met a clothing-store owner, Jacob Sandelowsky, a handsome, black-haired, thirty-year-old Polish Jew. He had in fact been a friend to both Harvey and Baby Doe, lending the couple money in order to assist them during Harvey's increasingly frequent periods of shiftlessness. The knowledge of this bounty—and the obvious attraction Jacob manifested for his wife—so irritated Harvey Doe that toward the end of 1878 he disappeared. Baby Doe took a job as manager of the ladies' wear department in Sandelowsky's store, to cover her living expenses until her negligent husband should reappear.

In November of that year, with Harvey still out of town, Baby Doe learned that she was pregnant. At about the same time, everyone was electrified by the news of the silver strikes in Leadville, and the ambitious young woman believed that that was where she could seek the fortune destined her. But she held off making this move when her father-in-law provided her with funds and organized a search for his still-absent son. When the errant Harvey was found and brought back to Central City, a brief period of reconciliation ensued; Harvey found himself a job on the night shift in a mine. But soon the couple was quarreling bitterly again, leading to yet another disappearance followed by another reconciliation.

After the stillbirth of Baby Doe's child in 1879, a child which, as she wrote in her scrapbook, "had dark, dark hair, very curly, and large blue eyes," Harvey Doe's behavior became even more erratic, and he continued to absent himself repeatedly, at more frequent intervals. Finally, his wife decided to take the daring step of divorcing him, despite their Catholic marriage.

She had originally planned to bring suit against him on charges of adultery and nonsupport, but Harvey's father persuaded her to seek the divorce in Denver on the charge of nonsupport only. In return for obtaining the divorce with a minimum of scandal and without a demand for alimony, she was given a sum from a mine claim that her husband had signed over to her. She was never to see Harvey or his parents again.

By now, Jake Sandelowsky—who would soon change his name to Sands—had urged her to move to Leadville, which was exactly in her plans. Once there, her ambition led her to single out the middle-aged Horace Tabor.

Tabor had constantly argued with his dour, circumspect wife, Augusta, that she must live up to their new position in life, but she had rejected such suggestions. She regarded with contempt his ambitions to play the host to sycophantic friends, refused to be his hostess, and called these friends "no better than parasites." He had her move from Leadville to Denver, ostensibly because, as lieutenant governor, he needed to maintain a residence in Colorado's capital city, and his wife should be in charge of it. But in fact, he was glad to have Augusta out of the way.

Augusta suspected that her husband was not particularly faithful to her, and that was his main reason for wanting to put distance between them. However, somewhat to her husband's credit, at least his dalliances with loose-living women were conducted with complete discretion. That is, until now.

A few months before the miners' strike of May 26, 1880, Baby Doe entered the Saddle Rock Cafe for supper, knowing that Horace Tabor would be there. She took a nearby table, and from time to time she glanced over at the portly millionaire—and soon he was staring back at her with mounting interest. It did not take long before the waiter brought a note over to her table asking her to join the Silver King and his aide, Billy Bush.

By contrast with the forbidding mien of his wife, Augusta, this woman, with her curly blond hair and beautiful blue eyes set in a round face, looked enticing and fresh. Horace Tabor had been smitten.

On that very first night, Baby Doe told Horace about herself and her indebtedness to Jake Sands. The following morning, the storekeeper received a note from Baby Doe, brought by Billy Bush: It broke off their relationship. With the note, Sands found the money Baby owed him—plus interest. Thus Baby Doe became Horace Tabor's mistress. She had hopes of ultimately becoming his wife.

*   *   *

Within a few days, Horace Tabor had installed Elizabeth Doe in her personal suite at the Clarendon Hotel on Harrison Avenue. The three-storied frame building was garishly furnished with the most luxurious carpeting, decor, and bric-a-brac, rivaling even New York City's most luxurious hostelries. The food offered in the hotel dining room, prepared by a chef from Delmonico's in New York, was famous throughout the region. The lobby and bar areas had by now become more or less the private preserve of the Carbonate Kings—those millionaires who had made fortunes almost overnight from silver, and who now presented a solid front of opposition to the pleas of the miners for better pay and working conditions.

It was fate that had brought Baby Doe to Leadville at this time of unrest. If Augusta Tabor—with her shrewd, practical knowledge gleaned from years of hardship running boarding-houses and grocery stores to support her husband during his prospecting days—had been with him in Leadville, the bloody strike of May 26, 1880, might never have taken place. But Horace Tabor, a coarse man of whom it was said that dance-hall girls had to ply themselves with liquor to be able to endure his amours, had become so madly infatuated by Elizabeth Doe's youth—and felt himself so rejuvenated by her obvious adoration of him—that he found courage to defy the luckless, impoverished miners.

Theirs were legitimate grievances, to be sure. Miners had to work twelve hours a day, six days a week, under the most appalling conditions—for a paltry three dollars a day. It was virtually impossible for workers to survive on such wages in an economy in which all food and housing were highly inflated. Their demands—which had begun to surface a year earlier with the initial unionization talks—were few: an increase of their wages to $3.75 per day, safer conditions in the mines themselves, and a hospital where miners suffering the ill effects of lead poisoning—caused by constant exposure to the carbonate ore—could receive treatment.

Tabor himself had been a miner, a slagman, and he had risen from the ranks of the miners—yet he was outraged by their demands, as were his colleagues. They banded together to warn the miners that unionization would be met by force. He summoned his vigilantes—who already had lynched ne'er-do-wells and supposed murderers on little more than circumstantial evidence—and sanctioned their violence by dubbing them militia companies called Tabor Tigers.

The mine owners then met for a sumptuous dinner at the Clarendon and said that they would lower wages to $2.75 a day if the miners did not give up their intolerable demands. Unfortunately for the miners, there were many unemployed in town at this time, eager to take the place of those who refused to work.

Baby Doe told her doting lover that she admired him for his forthrightness and courage. "Don't you bow down to them, Horace, darling," she advised him late one night, just before the strike. "You're so forceful that you'll surely beat them. Just stand up to them and don't give in."

Augusta Tabor would have argued compromise, foreseeing the bloody riots that could ensue, but Horace Tabor saw only the encouragement of his beautiful young mistress. He had already determined that his unattractive, cranky wife would stay in Denver while he took unto himself this delectable promise of a new and exciting life.

Thus emboldened, he issued an outrageous order just a week before the strike. Anyone found smoking or talking down in the workings of the Chrysolite Mine was to be discharged. The foremen knew it would be impossible to uphold such an order and quit rather than try. After naming fiery Michael Mooney their spokesman, the miners staged a walkout and called for a general strike.

Instead of agreeing to meet with Mooney, Tabor—remaining in Baby Doe's suite, living out his fantasy of restored and renewed youth—counted on the presence of hired thugs and the opposition of armed citizens to keep the miners from getting their demands.

Meanwhile, Phyllis Boyd and Sister Martha had organized a free soup kitchen after the elderly nun had gone to the Catholic church and brought back Father Robinson, who had given his blessing to this benevolent action. Mrs. Boyd had plunged into the humanitarian work of feeding the starving miners and their families to the utmost of her physical abilities. Father Robinson, gratefully accepting the money offered to him by Lucien Edmond Bouchard, started a similar soup kitchen in one of the rooms of the church rectory. Two of the nuns worked there, while Sister Luz assisted Sister Martha at the Boyd boardinghouse. While this effort did little to alleviate the deprivation the miners endured, word spread quickly of the endeavor, and the sisters were heartened by their acceptance.

Twenty-Four

Gabe Penrock had returned to Leadville a week before the strike, and he had been busily and profitably spending his time. John McCreedy, the burly desperado who had ridden the younger man away from the thwarted train robbery and then had gone back to Dodge City to inform Jeb Cornish of the failure of that attack, had accompanied Penrock with four other members of the Cornish gang. These five men had taken accommodations in a couple of the less reputable lodging places in town. Two of the men put up at the Mammoth Palace, a huge shed that could house five hundred men. It offered hard bunks, which guests could occupy at a fee of fifty cents for eight hours.

The desperados found no difficulty finding decent meals in town. Some of the saloons served ten- and fifteen-cent dinners, and Cornish's men—having been given advances on their wages—took full advantage of these simple repasts. They were lucky: Many of the miners around town were literally starving, and some in desperation resorted to ordering large meals in restaurants that they were unable to pay for, preferring to face a jail sentence rather than go hungry. Few of these miners, however, were actually arrested.

Penrock himself checked into a boardinghouse not far from the Clarendon, registering under the assumed name of Mordecai Haines. Two nights later, as he stopped by the parlor of his elderly landlady, Mrs. Bedloe, to pay her something on account, she lamented that things in Leadville were going from bad to worse. "Would you believe, Mr. Haines," she sighed, "my man Tom, he was fair crippled last year, when his leg was smashed by a falling ore bucket—and the owner said it was because Tom was lazy and not keeping his wits about him, so they wouldn't pay a cent for his doctor or hospital bill. Now he's laid up here, nagging me and raising a riot because he's out of work. Poor old fool, he couldn't work even if he wanted to. And food goes up and clothing, too—what's going to become of us all, Mr. Haines?''

"Why, Mrs. Bedloe, we miners surely do need a union." Penrock oratorically declared. "It's not right for the mine owners to make all the profits and not pay their workers a living wage. You see, Mrs. Bedloe, I worked in a mine back in Missouri, and I know what it is to be done in at the end of a week with hardly enough cash to buy bread and beer and ham. Damned if I'm not going out and see what I can do to stir things up myself.''

"Please be careful, Mr. Haines. You're a nice young man, and Tom and I don't want you to get hurt. That rotten Horace Tabor and his friends, they've called in troops and vigilantes, and you could get beat up real bad.''

"Don't you worry about me, Mrs. Bedloe. I can take care of myself. Tell you what, when I get back from the meeting tonight, I'll bring your Tom a bucket of beer.''

"That's mighty kind of you, mighty generous, Mr. Haines. God knows poor old Tom doesn't have much to look forward to in this silver town. Why, they're charging five cents for a schooner of beer, would you believe it, Mr. Haines?''

"Well, I've had me a little luck, and I want to treat you and your man. I'll bring the bucket directly on back from the union meeting." And with that, Gabe Penrock buttoned his woolen jacket, left the warm parlor, and went out into the gray, chilly evening.

There had been a fire a few weeks back along the timberline just above the boomtown, and the townspeople had been afraid the fire would spread down to the town itself, with its rickety wooden frame buildings. Ironically, however, the chief problem right now was a lack of wood; there just weren't many trees left up in the hills, to use as fuel for the smelters. And coal was so expensive that a lot of mine owners were thinking of closing down anyway—it would be one certain way of breaking the strike.

Penrock chuckled to himself because even the elements seemed to be cooperating with his ingenious plan to eliminate Ramón Hernandez forever from Jeb Cornish's widespread enterprises. Bad weather, the general strike set for tomorrow, and the unwitting accomplices he had so ingeniously bribed, should combine not only to dispose of Ramón Hernandez and the high and mighty Mr. Lucien Edmond Bouchard, but also to recoup the money that had been lost to the gang when those two meddlers had almost single-handedly prevented the robbery on the Denver & Rio Grande train. Paying those two back would also settle the score for Jack Hayes and Reuben Huntley.

Penrock had learned that hundreds of Mexicans had come to Leadville to work in the mines, along with Poles, Germans, and Irish. On this evening before the general strike, he made his way to one of the saloons to meet with John McCreedy and the other four gang members to plan their strategy.

Penrock, posing as Mordecai Haines, claimed to have put in a year or two as a miner back in his native Missouri. To win the sympathy of the many striking miners for whom he had bought drinks and even meals, he told the tearful story of how his father had died of consumption after twenty years in a mine, and how the ruthless mine owner not only had refused to pay his widowed mother the last week of his father's wages on the grounds that the man had been ailing and not put in a full shift during those few days of that final week of his life, but also had sent neither condolences nor even a few dollars to help with the burial.

It was a story that many of these starving and ill-paid miners could appreciate, for it reminded them of the tactics of many of the so-called Carbonate Kings.

A few days after arriving in Leadville, Penrock had befriended a middle-aged German from Pennsylvania, Wolfgang Heimroth, whose wife and children had died a decade ago. He had come to Leadville, in his loneliness, with the illusory hope of striking it rich, and had bitterly spoken out against the inhuman conditions of the Leadville mines: the paltry wages, the ever-present danger of death by accident or illness, the rickety structures of the shafts themselves, and the dilapidated equipment. *"Herrgott, mein Freund,"* he had vehemently declared to Penrock on the evening of their first meeting, "those *Gottverdammt* owners, they treat us like *Schweinhunde, wirklich!* My poor Anna and the *drei Kinder* died so long ago, but when I see all *meine Freunde* having little *Geld* for their wives and children, paying what they must for food and *Bier*, sick and with no doctors, no one to help them"—his flushed, heavily veined face mottled with

210

impotent anger—"I would do anything to get back at those greedy bosses. We had similar conditions in the old country, Herr Haines, and sometimes poor men did brave things to strike back. They made bombs, and they used dynamite—"

Penrock had leaned forward across the table, his eyes narrowing with interest at this last, half-drunken allusion. "Tell me, Wolfgang," he tried to keep his voice casual, "have you ever worked with dynamite yourself?"

"*Aber natürlich*. I did it in my *Heimat* before I came here. *Ja*, I was a miner, too, like you, Herr Haines."

"Wolfgang, I think I know how you can get back at someone who is one of the worst of the Carbonate Kings. He's a Mexican, what we call a greaser here in the States. There are lots of Mexes working in the mines here, and they're just like you, either broke or sick of slaving away for nothing. But this Mex has a rich silver mine and he's living on the blood of good men. Hell, he's even too proud to live here in town—why, even Horace Tabor stays here."

"*Ja*," the German growled, emptying his glass.

"Bartender, another bottle of your best whiskey for my friend Wolfgang here," Penrock had called out to the bald, thickly mustached bartender. The man grunted an assent, brought a bottle of rye whiskey over to the table, and stolidly waited until Penrock had fished five dollars out of his wallet to pay for it.

"That is kind of you, *mein Freund*. I do not often have the chance to drink whiskey; I have no *Geld* for it," the middle-aged German declared, then rubbed his swollen, bleary eyes with his dirty knuckles. "I do not know why you are so kind to an old man whose life is nothing."

"But it can be something, Wolfgang. You can help me and you can get back at the bosses by helping me fix this Mex bastard—and I'll see that you get good money for doing it," Penrock muttered.

"How?" Heimroth was greedily uncorking the bottle and, with an unsteady hand, pouring out a large libation for himself.

"If you were to take some sticks of dynamite and connect them to a plunger, you could blow up a mine shaft, couldn't you, Wolfgang?"

"Of course, I could. That is no trick at all. The trick would

211

be to get the dynamite in the mine shaft when no one is watching.''

"I'll see to that. Look, Wolfgang, I'll give you money to buy the dynamite and a bonus for yourself of a hundred dollars.''

"You will?'' The German's eyes widened and brightened with greed. "But why do you hate this man? Has he hurt you in some way? Why not try to blow up Tabor's mine? That would make more sense.''

"No, Wolfgang.'' Penrock shook his head. He gave a deep, theatrical sigh, then said, "I had a girl friend back in Missouri, you see. This mine owner, Ramón Hernandez, he came through town once a couple of years ago and he took my girl away from me. And then, just last year, I had a letter from her saying that she was down and out, that the greaser had kicked her out when he was done with her, and she was sick. Well, I later found out that she died.''

"My poor friend!'' Heimroth sighed heavily, then helped himself to half of the whiskey, almost at a single gulp. "Now I understand it, you want *Rache,* revenge, *nicht wahr?*''

"Yes. Will you help me? Will you be my friend?''

"For that reason most of all, yes, I will help you.''

John Darwent's swiftly constructed refining plant had temporarily solved the immediate problem of converting the ore to silver bullion, without a delay of several months in shipping it eastward. Already a delivery had been made to the Denver National Bank in the Colorado state capital: Felipe Sanchez and Narciso Duarte, the most experienced of the six vaqueros who had come from Windhaven Range, had been chosen to drive the specially constructed wagons that conveyed the bullion out of town to the railhead of the Denver, South Park & Pacific Railroad, where it was transferred to a secured freight car for the balance of the journey to Denver. Walter Catlin and Timmy Belcher had accompanied the two vaqueros; all four men—well armed, yet dressed like miners in old, dirty, tattered clothes—had made the trip and returned from Denver last week, with a receipt from the bank for $123,000 in redeemable silver, deposited to the account of the mine's partners.

Lucien Edmond, Ramón, and Joe Duvray sat in the small office of the engineer, a low, squat, wooden frame hut about a hundred yards south of the opening of the mine shaft, and were excited that these first excavations proved the richness of the lode.

"The assistant engineer who came out from Central City to work with John," Lucien Edmond recounted, "estimates that we should draw at least half a million the first year, and perhaps double that the second. According to both of them, the vein goes very deep, and we should sink the shaft another twenty or thirty feet before the end of the year." He grinned and shook his head. "It's hard to believe! We've already earned a very handsome stake that will enable us to expand in any way we choose."

"It's amazing." Joe shook his head. "If you'd told me about fifteen years ago, when Andy Haskins and I were sitting on a levee in New Orleans, waiting for anybody to hire us who had an extra dollar or so to spend, that this would have happened, I'd have told you that you were drunk on either mint juleps or tafia. But you know, Lucien Edmond, I have to tell you that I don't much care for Leadville, despite the money it's given me."

"I've come to that conclusion myself, Joe. The corruption, decay, and poverty don't sit well with me. At any rate, we've all learned something, and we've made money doing it. Also, we've been lucky that our shipment to Denver wasn't intercepted by road agents."

"If you ask me," Ramón put in, "I wish we'd brought two dozen men along, and twice as many weapons and ammunition. This strike has me worried. There are so many out of work and just starving, it could get very ugly. I've a very uneasy feeling about all this."

"One that I share, Ramón," Lucien Edmond declared. "From what I heard in town, the strike's going to be tomorrow. There's going to be a big march, and Mike Mooney, who's trying to unionize the workers, is going to lead it through town. All of us will have to be ready in case there's trouble."

"But I thought that paying top wages as we do and letting it be understood that we're not mine owners who want to have everything our way would keep trouble from our door," Joe proffered.

"When people are starving, when they're out of work, when somebody feeds them liquor and they think they have

213

grievances, there's no accounting for what can happen," Lucien Edmond soberly commented. "When John hired our crew, he told them exactly where we stood on the matter: that we wanted to pay wages beyond what the miners asked for, that we had staked an old man who had struck it rich near the end of his life, and that we were giving him a fair share. I assume they've spread the word around town. All the same, it'll do us no harm to keep our eyes open tomorrow and to watch everything that goes on. When people are in a temper, they don't act according to reason, just emotion."

"We should be especially careful, Lucien Edmond," Joe spoke up again, "because tomorrow is also the day that we're going to pay off our workers. Some of the malcontents, fired up on whiskey and the like, might just come out here to see if they can get some easy pickings."

"That's also occurred to me." Lucien Edmond frowned and scratched the tip of his chin as he pondered a moment. "I've been talking to most of the miners who work for us, and they seem to be a friendly, cooperative lot. Some, of course, were down on their uppers when we hired them, but John recommended them because of their experience. The only problem, as I see it, is that when they're finished with their work, they might go to a saloon and hear some of the striking miners' retaliation talk. Also, if they get liquored up, they'll get to talking to the other miners about how much they're making. That could cause trouble, too. My feeling is it's always wise to be prepared for the worst; then you can be pleasantly surprised."

Robert Markey had come in during this conference, and said nothing thus far, assimilating it all. Lucien Edmond looked over at him, acknowledged his presence with a smile, then asked, "And you, Robert, do you have any thoughts to contribute?"

"I—well, no, not really, outside of what you already said—that we ought to be armed and ready, just in case there's trouble. You know, I haven't forgotten that train ride we had coming here."

"That could have been coincidence," Lucien Edmond casually drawled. "The conductor told me that there was a big payroll, and that's what the robbers were after. It just happened that we were on the same train—I don't attach any special significance to that."

214

"I just don't know. I've had a nagging feeling all along—well, I don't care what you call it, Mr. Bouchard, but I think that maybe those robbers knew us."

"It's possible it could be the work of that Indian agent back in Dodge City," Ramón Hernandez grimly declared, recalling his encounters with the man who had denigrated him, calling him a greaser the first time they had met. "Remember, Lucien Edmond, when we caught that fellow Reuben Huntley on the train after you killed his partner, he admitted that he'd been one of the gang that tried to bushwhack us when we went to Colorado with the cattle for Maxwell Grantham. I wonder if they won't try to get back at us for foiling their plans again."

"Well, you might be right at that, Ramón, but they lost a lot of men. My feeling is that after the train robbery and what happened to them, they're not going to come back for more," Lucien Edmond confidently declared.

"You're probably right. This is all just theory. We'll just be a little more careful tomorrow than usual," Ramón concluded. "Now, do you plan to pay the miners off at noon tomorrow as always?"

"Why not? Those that have families need the money for their wives and kids. And those who aren't married, well, we can't deny them the pleasures of whiskey or women, if that's their fancy, after they've put in a hard week in our mine," Lucien Edmond said with a shrug.

"No, I suppose not. Well, let's turn in and get a good night's sleep. It's going to be quite a day tomorrow, from all I've heard in town," Ramón gloomily declared.

Twenty-Five

When Gabe Penrock had reported to Jeb Cornish that the partners of Windhaven Range had come to Leadville to work a silver mine, he told the Indian agent that he had seen many Mexican mine workers in the town. Cornish had insisted that he take two Mexican desperados, Diego Santorces and Juan

Corales, who were both wanted for murder, arson, and assault in the province of Chihuahua.

These men had proved themselves invaluable in spy work. More important to Penrock's plan was their native Spanish; part of the scheme had been to sow seeds of dissension and hostility among the Mexican workers of the Scolby mine by having Santorces and Corales spread false rumors about Ramón Hernandez—based on the fictitious story he had already told the old German miner, Wolfgang Heimroth.

The two desperados were seated in a noisy, crowded saloon this evening before the strike. The waitresses were harassed as they pushed their way through the throng, skillfully swerving and tilting trays laden with schooners of foaming beer to set down before the polyglot crowd of miners, of all races and ages, who had come here to air their grievances among their brothers and to inveigh against the ruthless mine owners. Santorces and Corales beckoned to a plump, raven-haired girl, and Corales waved a five-dollar bill at her, grinning and muttering, "Those others won't miss the beer, *querida*. This is for you if you'll put your tray down right on this table, *por favor*."

The girl's eyes widened with greed. She giggled as, glancing hastily over to a far table where this order had been destined, she slyly set the tray down and then hurried back to the bar, after tucking the bill into her bodice.

Santorces reached for two foaming glasses and set them before two of John Darwent's Mexican mining crew. *"Por ustedes, señores,"* he expansively declared.

"Muchas gracias, amigo." Pedro Comingo effusively thanked him as he reached for one of the schooners and, putting it to his mouth, gulped down nearly half of its contents, then belched with satisfaction: *"Bueno.* This is excellent *cerveza.* But, señores, I do not quite understand why you want us to strike against our *patrones,* Señor Hernandez and Señor Bouchard. They are good men, not like Señor Tabor and those others who want us to die for nothing in their dirty mines. Our *patrones* pay us very good wages, four dollars and a half a day—"

"Yes, but a man works for honor as well as *dinero,* Pedro," Corales slyly intimated. "What would you think of a man from your own country who stole the *novia* of an

216

amigo of mine and then, when she was ill, turned her out to die? A man like that has neither *corazón* nor *cojones*."

Comingo was from Guadalupe, having come with his cousin, Paco Miramar, to Leadville eighteen months ago. Both bachelors in their late twenties, hoping to earn enough so they might one day go back to Mexico and marry their sweethearts, they had most recently worked in Tabor's Chrysolite Mine. After they were laid off, John Darwent had promptly hired them both for the Bouchard enterprise. Softspoken, hardworking, encouraged by the prospect of better wages, they had already been marked down by the young mining engineer as men who could be trusted with greater responsibility and perhaps even supervisory jobs in the next month or two.

Pedro Comingo glanced at his cousin, and shook his head. "I would never have dreamed that of the *patrón*," he muttered. "That is disgusting!"

"I tell you this, *mi amigo*," Santorces unctuously went on, "because I know you are men of honor."

"That is true," Paco Miramar solemnly nodded as he took a hearty swig from his schooner of beer.

"There will be a big march tomorrow of many thousands of miners," Santorces continued, "and some of them will come to see about this outsider, this *mejicano*, who owns a mine and does not take part in the community."

"But, Señor Santorces," Pedro protested, "the fact is, he pays us much more than Señor Tabor, or any of the others."

"It is only a dollar fifty cents more a day. What is that, but about twelve cents or so an hour—it is blood money, Pedro," Corales heatedly spoke up.

"But what do you wish us to do?" Pedro helplessly demanded.

"Are you not being paid tomorrow?" Santorces insinuated.

"Yes—" Pedro's eyes narrowed.

"Who pays you your wages, Pedro?" Corales wanted to know.

"Señor Darwent, the engineer. He is in charge," Paco spoke up.

"Is it after the noontime *comida*?"

"*Pero sí.*" Pedro nodded.

The Mexican desperados exchanged a covert glance and

stealthily concealed their satisfaction at hearing this important piece of news. Gabe Penrock would want to know about the payroll. A week's wages of six days a week at four dollars fifty cents was twenty-seven dollars. Multiplied by some thirty workers, this meant over eight hundred dollars, plus bonuses for overtime. Darwent should have on hand well over a thousand dollars, a tidy stake to be pilfered when the uprising against the mine took place.

"When they pay you your wages, Paco," Corales now asked, "are all the men summoned from the mine? Is there anyone left to guard it?"

"Oh, no, señor. There is no reason for anyone to be in the mine. We line up in front of the construction shed, where Señor Darwent keeps his office. Usually the *patrón* Señor Hernandez is there to wish us well and to say good things to us," Pedro eagerly volunteered.

"I understand. All I ask of you, and you too, Paco," Santorces solemnly remarked, "is that you do not try to risk your lives, if anyone should attempt to spread the strike to the mine of your *patrón*. You will understand that there are many of us, your *compañeros*, who think that it is unfair for one of our people to come here and set himself up as a Carbonate King. It is time that all of us shared in the profits for which we dig, for which we risk our lives. They could easily pay you much more, and this business of giving you a dollar and a half a day more is only to blind you so you do not see how you are being used just as badly as Señor Tabor and the others treat their workers."

"I do not wish to fight. I did not come here all this way from Guadalupe to strike, or to fight with anyone," Paco exclaimed.

"Good. I ask nothing more of both of you than that you stay away from what may happen tomorrow. *El Señor Dios* will judge your *patrón*, and He will know how to punish a man who has no honor, either to his workers or to a *novia* stolen from a man to whom she was promised, then driven out."

"We did not know this, truly, señores," Paco protested, exchanging a wondering look with his cousin. "Very well, so long as you do not wish us to fight. We will stay out of the way if there is trouble—but then, we would do this anyhow, so that we may go back to Guadalupe."

"You have my promise," Santorces leaned across the table and emphatically declared, "that if you both do exactly that, you will take back to Guadalupe much more money than you could ever save."

Twenty-Six

At midnight on May 25, Gabe Penrock met with his five accomplices in a dance hall across the street from the Clarendon Hotel, to draw up the final plan of action for the next day's general strike. When Diego Santorces and Juan Corales reported what they had learned from the two cousins who worked in the Bouchard silver mine, Penrock congratulated them on their work. He leaned back in his chair and beckoned to one of the saloon girls to bring a bottle of the best whiskey in the house.

The young outlaw looked around the crowded, noisy saloon, reeking with the smell of stale beer, whiskey, and cigars. The air was so thick with a smoky haze that he could barely see to the other end of the room. The place was packed with miners bolstering their courage for the strike by downing glass after glass of alcohol in every variety.

Every now and again, angry shouts rose above the general din, piercing the air with their ferocity. On the whole, though, the miners kept their conversations low and private, fearful of company spies in their midst.

A roar of laughter went up from a table near the back of the saloon, as three miners, well oiled by the boilermakers—beer with whiskey chasers—they had been consuming in vast quantities, leaped onto their table. Arms raised defiantly, they damned all the Carbonate Kings, and each of the trio tried to outdo the others in his boasts of what he personally would do during the strike to even the gap between the rich and the poor.

Penrock smiled to himself, pleased with the way things were going. With the miners fired up the way they were, it was almost certain that none of the mines would escape the workers' wrath—including the Scolby mine. Yes, he thought, this strike would be the perfect cover for his real purpose: the murder of Ramón Hernandez.

Penrock leaned forward across the table and the men with him leaned toward him so they could hear words meant only for them. "Now, we know they're going to dish out the payroll in the engineer's shed right after lunch," he told his colleagues, "so that'll sweeten the pie that much more. Incidentally, I've got me a German who knows everything about dynamite, and he's going to—shall we say—give us some expert help." The five men laughed, then Penrock held up his hand for quiet. "Now listen, we're going to accomplish three things tomorrow: We're going to get some ready cash, blow up the mine, and dispose of that greaser once and for all, so that Jeb Cornish will give us all a big bonus."

The men nodded, their eyes shining with avarice at the prospect. Taking a quick sip of his whiskey, Penrock outlined his devious plan.

Wolfgang Heimroth had spent the night making a dynamite charge and attaching it to a metal plunger. Three hours before Mike Mooney's march began, Penrock went to see the German at his rooming house, and gave him instructions as to where to locate the plunger. His face flaccid and covered with a thick gray stubble, Heimroth carried the explosives and the plunger in a worn knapsack, which he clutched tightly in his thick, swollen fingers. Heimroth had made his way in the inky darkness to the Scolby-Bouchard mine, where, because many hours were expected to elapse before the strike began, only Manuel Olivera and Pablo Bensares were standing guard.

The German climbed surreptitiously to the site, where he found a secondary entry to the main mine shaft. Here were kept ore carts, loaded with various samples, taken periodically, that John Darwent inspected to determine the longevity and richness of the vein.

Heimroth hid the oilcloth-covered package of dynamite, and played out wire for about two hundred feet. He then crept out of the narrow entrance and went up behind the mine to hide the plunger.

About an hour after dawn, when Ramón Hernandez and Lucien Edmond Bouchard came out of the house, they were

220

told by the two vaqueros who had stood guard that night that nothing unusual had happened and that all was quiet—except that sporadically throughout the long night, there had been the distant sound of gunfire.

"The miners are going to start stirring soon," Ramón said to his brother-in-law. "Let's hope they have no reason for coming out this way."

"Yes, I'll feel much happier when this day is over," Lucien Edmond reflected. "Yesterday, Santiago Dornado told me that he'd heard in town that Tabor and some of the other bigwigs of the mining community had a meeting at the opera house to review their Committee of Safety. Apparently, they've got vigilantes to use violence against the strikers, as well as a regiment of amateur soldiers to smash the strike. All the stores are supposed to be closed today, and the owners and the employees are all enrolled in that militia to reinforce Tabor's own private army."

Lucien Edmond was silent for a few minutes before continuing. "You know, Ramón, when we first planned to come here, I thought that a number of us—myself included—might want to get away from Texas for a time, might move up here and settle down with our families. Now I'm not so sure. It's an awfully rough town, and it doesn't seem to have much hope of redemption. Also, I somehow have the feeling that when this strike is all over, no matter who wins, things are going to get worse."

"I share your feeling, *mi amigo*," Ramón nodded. "I think it best for us to let John Darwent hire additional reliable men and look after the mine for us. Or else, if you wish, I'll be glad to stay here through the year—even though I'll miss Mara and the children."

"We can talk about that later, Ramón. Right now, we'd better prepare the men to stand guard. But I want them to be friendly and to keep their weapons concealed as best they can. I don't want to incite any of the miners if they come out this way—and I'm praying they won't," Lucien Edmond solemnly declared.

Mike Mooney, head of the Miners' Cooperative Union, rode ahead of a silent mass of four thousand men marching to Fryer's Hill. When they reached their destination, Mooney halted the column and the miners crowded around him in a huge circle. "Men, I want it absolutely understood that any guards at the Little Pittsburg, the Little Chief, and the Chrysolite aren't to be hurt," he shouted. "We want these damned greedy owners to see that we can put our point across without any bloodshed. We all know perfectly well they're already calling out thugs and gunslingers, and they'll kill us if we give them any show of force. Those guards, like ourselves, have families, and they're working for those owners because they've got wives and kids to support. Just don't pay any attention to them, but let the big shots like Horace Tabor see that we mean business. We're not asking much, just four dollars a day for eight hours of honest hard work. Now let's march!"

Gabe Penrock and his five accomplices, dressed in tattered old clothes, mingled with the marchers. As the crowd started to move, the outlaws began buttonholing the miners, whispering to them, inciting them to attack the mine that Ramón Hernandez and Lucien Edmond Bouchard had developed. "Come on, fellows, don't be fooled by the fact that these two are paying you a little more than the other owners. It must mean their mine is more dangerous than any of the others. Besides, just as soon as they see you're depending on them for a living and have no place else to go, they'll cut back your wages to nothing."

When the march broke up shortly before noon, Penrock and his cohorts had assembled a group of some hundred miners, leading them along the road that led to where Frank Scolby had found the rich silver lode.

At Penrock's instructions, his companions had filled their knapsacks with bottles of whiskey, and freely passed them around to the miners. By the time they neared the Scolby-Bouchard mine, most of them were drunk, abusive, and belligerent. It was easy to rouse their sympathies over imagined wage injustices and his lie about Ramón having stolen his woman. And particularly when Penrock slyly intimated that if they were successful in taking over the mine and driving away the Mexican and his co-owner—whom he described as a heartless cattle baron who seized land and drove rightful settlers from it—the miners would operate it themselves, each man receiving a share of profit.

Twenty-Seven

Minutes before the crowd of angry, drunken miners led by Gabe Penrock and his cohorts reached the Scolby mine, Lucien Edmond and Ramón entered the shaft. The engineer, John Darwent, had suggested they examine an outcropping of the main vein. "It looks as though this vein, too, is extremely rich, gentlemen." John was highly excited. "It's absolutely mandatory that we sink an additional shaft. I'm quite sure that if we go down as far with this subsidiary shaft as we did with the first one, we'll unearth an even richer haul than we've already gotten. I'm pleased with the way it's gone so far, gentlemen, and even more pleased with the confidence you've placed in me."

"You've earned it, John," Lucien Edmond told him, clapping him on the back. "You've hired an exceptional crew, and there's been no friction at all. And we've been very lucky in being able to get off a very profitable shipment to the Denver bank. I hesitate to send any more right now, at least for the next week or two, till things are settled between the miners and the owners."

"That may not be so easy. I've heard rumors in town," John asserted with a grave look, "that Tabor and his crew are determined to break the backs of the miners, to punish those who cause the most trouble, like that Mike Mooney. They've even gone so far as to talk of lynching mobs."

"That's very dangerous talk. I hope to God the governor of the state or the army get wind of this and send some help, before there's outright murder," Lucien Edmond indignantly declared. "Something like this brings out all the bad blood and all the old grievances. It seems to me they want to use the strike as an excuse to settle old debts and pay back people they don't like."

Just then, Walter Catlin and Timmy Belcher hurried into the mine, and Walter called out, "Mr. Bouchard, Mr. Hernandez, are you there? It looks like trouble!"

Lucien Edmond called back, "Stay where you are, both of

you, we're coming out." He turned to John Darwent. "If there's trouble, you'd best stay inside. Do some more checking on that subsidiary vein you were just telling us about. I'm perfectly willing to sink another shaft and to pay even higher wages than I'm now offering. If you see any of our workers coming up, try to keep them inside so they won't be subjected to hassling by this mob. And tell them about my offer. Tell them I appreciate their loyalty, and let's keep them out of trouble. Besides maybe this will blow over peacefully—at least, I pray to God that it will."

Seizing his Spencer carbine, which was propped by the side of the entrance of the shaft, Lucien Edmond moved to the main entrance. Ramón, similarly armed, was just beside him. Timmy Belcher and Walter Catlin, hands over the pistols that were holstered at their sides, anxiously awaited them. "Look," Walter yelled, "there's a large group of men coming up the road toward the hill here, Mr. Bouchard. I can hear them cursing, and they're saying something about a dirty greaser and blowing up his mine, or setting fire to it—"

"My God!" Lucien Edmond ejaculated. "Timmy, go to the house and tell Narciso, Felipe, Diego, and Santiago to forget about breakfast for now. And wake Pablo and Manuel up, and tell them I'm terribly sorry, but they'll have to catch up on their sleep once this damned strike is over. But tell Mr. Scolby to stay put! I know he'll want to be heroic, but he's too old to be involved in a fight. Good Lord!" he shouted suddenly. "There are over a hundred men there! I don't like the looks of this at all!"

"I'm on my way, Mr. Bouchard," Timmy shouted, as he hurried down the road to the house.

Gabe Penrock, holding up his hand, turned to the unruly group of drunken, angry miners. "This is the place, men. There's the dirty Mexican bastard I was telling you about. He's got a carbine, and he'd just as soon shoot you down as look at you. Are we going to let him get away with that? Are we going to let him make a fortune here and then go back to Mexico and boast how he cheated decent men out of their rightful money?"

"No, by God!"

"Kill the son of a bitch!"

"Lynch him!"

The shouts were coarse and angry. Penrock and his men had done an excellent job of inciting these miserable men.

Four of the vaqueros came out of the house, and walked quickly to the mine entrance, armed with pistols and carbines and rifles, but having heard Lucien Edmond's warning to hold these weapons in readiness and not to incite violence by flaunting them openly, they concealed them behind their backs or at their sides and tried to smile at the approaching group of men.

Gabe Penrock turned to one of his henchmen, Dave Martin, and in a low voice muttered, "See up there, on top of the hill, just over the mine? That's where Wolfgang planted the plunger. Look, in a couple of minutes, stage a sort of a fight. Have some of the men rush the bastards. I'll get up there and prime the plunger. I'm almost certain the greaser and Bouchard will run into the mine for safety, and then I'll blow them to kingdom come!"

"We'll do it," Martin muttered with a grin. Then, beckoning to Santorces and Corales, he whispered, "Remind the Mexicans in this crowd about Hernandez and the girl. Pass out some more of the whiskey—give them a few bucks, too, and tell them to cause trouble. If we keep those fellers busy, we can get into that construction shed and steal that payroll. Since they pay off around noon, they must have the money in there already, probably in a satchel or something."

"*Comprendo, mi compañero,*" Diego Santorces chuckled, and touched the brim of his sombrero.

"All right, men, what's the problem here?" Lucien Edmond moved forward to accost the group of angry miners, a forced smile on his face, his arms outstretched in a gesture of tolerant friendship. "None of you fellows works for me, so I don't know why you want to strike my mine. Maybe you haven't heard that I'm paying better wages than any mine owner in Leadville—"

"We'll believe that when your miners tell us. They aren't around now, are they?" one of the strikers called.

Lucien Edmond turned to the miner who had angrily shouted out that question. "They're all busy working in the mine, as a matter of fact. They don't have any grievance with me, so why should you?"

"That's what you say, mister!" the truculent man snarled.

Suddenly stooping down, he picked up a jagged rock and flung it at Lucien Edmond, and then he stepped aside.

"Now wait a minute, there's no need for that. Do any of you know the mining engineer, John Darwent? He used to work for Horace Tabor. He'll tell you that my crew's satisfied, because he's the one who hired them," Lucien Edmond indignantly protested.

"Oh, sure. All you mine owners are alike, having somebody else tell your lies for you. What the hell do we care about a mining engineer, mister?" The man bent to pick up another rock and hefted it in his hand, sneering at Lucien Edmond. "Just stand there peaceful-like, mister; I'll open a hole in your skull."

Gabe Penrock, who had detached himself from the group and walked around the area, assessing the situation, slowly sidled up to Dave Martin, whispering to the outlaw, "Cover me. If anybody takes a shot, kill him! I'm going to get me to that plunger and be ready. Have the men start that fight. Go ahead, give them the signal!"

"Sure, Gabe!" Martin nodded his understanding. Turning to the angry crowd, he bawled, "Are we going to stand here palaverin' with that Texas skunk and his Mex pal? Let's rush 'em!"

At this, a dozen of the men in the front row started toward Lucien Edmond, but Ramón Hernandez, lifting his carbine, fired a warning shot into the air and called out, "That'll be enough of that! We don't want to hurt any of you fellows, we've nothing against you, and there's no reason you should try to attack us. For God's sake, show some sense! It's the other mine owners who are putting you in unsafe mines and paying you skimpy wages, not us. Why don't you tackle them?"

"You shut your mouth! You ain't got no right to talk about sense and justice, you bastard!"

Rocks began to fly, and Lucien Edmond was hit in the face and uttered a gasp of pain. When he fired his carbine in the air, the men facing him drew back. Muttering among themselves, glaring at him sullenly, they stood there deciding what to do next.

Penrock had taken advantage of this diversion to climb the slope and to fling himself flat on his belly near the plunger, concealed just where Heimroth had described it. Just at this moment, Robert Markey came out of the house, a hundred yards below the mine. He was followed by Pablo Bensares and Manuel Olivera, who after only a few hours of sleep stared bleary-eyed and incredulous at the mob of angry miners who confronted them.

Lucien Edmond made a final appeal to the drunken, irascible group of strikers: "What will it take to convince you fellows that you don't have any beef with us? That we're paying high wages? Look, we're going to be opening up a subsidiary shaft, and we'll be hiring more men. Any of you who want to come here tomorrow, I'll have my mining engineer talk to you, signing you up—for good wages!"

Heedless of Lucien Edmond's words, the miners started to rush toward the mine shaft, and Narciso and Felipe hurried to bar the way. Two of the miners seized rocks and flung them at the two vaqueros, hitting Felipe in the chest and stunning him, so that he sank to all fours, groaning with pain, while Narciso was hit in the side of the head and sprawled unconscious on the ground.

"I warn you, I won't tolerate this any longer!" Lucien Edmond angrily cried out. "These men have done nothing to you! Now be off about your business; we don't want to shoot and hurt anyone, but we will if we have to."

At this, a volley of jeers rang out; rocks and pebbles were hurled at him, hitting him in the neck and the chest and the leg. Determined not to hurt any of these striking miners, with whom he was in full sympathy, Lucien Edmond retreated to the entrance of the mine, along with Ramón.

Gabe Penrock, from above, licked his lips in anticipation and murmured to himself, "Just go all the way inside, you bastards. I'll send you both to hell in a blaze of glory! Just go a little farther in, and that dynamite can do its work!"

Ramón, frightened by the strikers' ferocious show of hostility, believed, as Lucien Edmond did, that discretion was the better part of valor. He accompanied his brother-in-law back to the mine entrance, and they disappeared from view.

"What are we going to do? If they get any bolder, our men will have to shoot—but if there's anyone badly hurt or killed, it'll be on our conscience. Not only that, but the rest of the miners will go back to town and tell more of these lies to hurt us," Ramón remarked to Lucien Edmond.

John Darwent, who had been just inside the shaft, came

227

rushing out of the entrance and ran down to the miners. One of the men flung himself at the engineer and tackled him. "Just stay where you are, mister. We don't want to hurt you. You've got nothing to do with this, so just stay there and you'll be all right!"

"This is wrong. You men can't get away with it! You— Henry McAdams," John pleaded, "I remember you from the days when I worked for Tabor. Look, I'll give you a job, I'll give you *five* dollars a day. But don't do this! We're all friends of yours; we're on your side!"

Manuel and Pablo, recognizing some of their own countrymen among the group, called out in Spanish, "We are your friends, señores! You are being told lies about our *patrones*! They are good men, and they want to hurt no one!"

Walter Catlin and Timmy Belcher, crouching low at the side of the porch of the house, had their weapons drawn and ready as twenty of the miners came toward the building. One had lighted a pine torch covered with tar, and was holding it aloft, drawing back his arm and ready to throw it at the building.

Walter Catlin drew off a snap shot, which struck the miner's hand. "You son of a bitch! You broke my wrist!" the miner yelled as he doubled over, clamping his other hand around the bleeding wound.

"Look, I don't want to hurt you and I won't kill you, but for God's sake, get away from here! This is all wrong!" Walter cried in desperation.

Robert looked up toward the mine, and as he did so, he happened to see Gabe Penrock's crouching figure. He frowned in concentration, a memory tugging at his brain. This man had a beard and yet he was very much like that one—of course! The one who kicked the dog at the Pueblo station!

Heedless of the danger around him, Robert ran through the mob and hurried up the side of the slope. Pausing every now and again to conceal himself from the man above him, who seemed to be intently concentrating on something, he zigzagged his way up to the crest of the hill, flinging himself behind a clump of bushes. Robert cautiously peered around the side of this camouflage, then let out an audible gasp as he saw what Penrock was up to.

The outlaw was kneeling beside a pile of slag, and he looked up sharply when he heard Robert's cry. Cursing under his breath, he stood up and placed both of his hands on the handle of the plunger and started to push. Shouting over to where Robert knelt, he warned, "It's too late to do anything, mister, so just stay where you are! I don't mean you any harm—or any of the other workers here. It's your boss I'm after, and he's got about fifteen more seconds to live—"

"No!" Robert screamed, and stood up, drawing his pistol from his holster. It would be a long shot—for about one hundred feet separated him from his foe—but it was the only chance Ramón and Lucien Edmond would have. Steadying his shaking hand, Robert let off six rapid shots in succession.

Penrock screamed and clutched his head, then he stiffened. For what seemed to Robert an eternity, Penrock stayed on his feet, swaying back and forth over the plunger. Robert could barely stand the suspense a second longer, wondering if Penrock would accomplish in death what he failed to carry out while alive. Finally, the man's body fell, just barely missing the handle of the plunger.

Robert exhaled, realizing that he had been holding his breath all the while that this macabre dance had been taking place. The young man sat down on a pile of rock, for his legs were so shaky that they could barely hold up his weight.

From below came angry shouts. Weakly, Robert stood up and looked down on the mob of miners. Their attention was riveted on the pistol, still smoking, in Robert's hand and on Gabe Penrock's lifeless body.

"He had dynamite there," Robert called down to the miners. "He was going to blow up the mine! That man's an outlaw! He was part of a gang from Dodge City that once tried to bushwhack us! Listen, you men, you've been fed lies! Look, I'm a farmer from Indiana. I went out to Kansas with my wife and kid, and this Mexican that you hate so much, well, he saved me from being lynched by his cowboys when I tried to steal a cow for beef for my family! And later he gave me a good job in Texas. Is that the sort of man you want to hurt? For God's sake, listen to reason!"

"He's a liar," one of Penrock's cronies shouted. Glancing worriedly at his cohorts, he whispered, "The son of a bitch, he's killed Gabe! Wait till Jeb Cornish hears about this!"

"The jig's up, we better beat it!" Dave Martin muttered. "We've gotta get back to Dodge City and tell Jeb everything went wrong again! I don't think he'll like the news—and Rhea sure as hell won't!''

The miners had drawn back now, stunned by the realization that they might have been duped, appalled by the sudden violent death of the young man who had led them to this riot. When Robert Markey had told them that Gabe Penrock had tried to blow up the mine with men in it, even their inebriated, angry, and befuddled brains grasped the wrong of what had been done, and one of them now called out, ''Somebody's been using us! They wanted to blow up the mine and have us blamed for it! Let's get the hell out of here! Let's strike Tabor and Fryer; they're the ones who deserve it!''

''Thank God for that,'' Walter Catlin muttered to Timmy Belcher as he holstered his gun.

The rest of the miners headed toward town, without so much as a backward glance. The five remaining outlaws mingled with the miners, escaping detection—but Jeb Cornish's plot had failed again.

Timmy rushed to the mine to call out, ''They've gone, Mr. Bouchard, Mr. Hernandez! It's all right to come out now!''

Ramón and Lucien Edmond emerged from the mine shaft just as Robert Markey reached the entrance.

''What happened, *amigo*?'' Ramón demanded of the young cowhand.

Robert told them what had happened, grinning widely with relief as he described the terrifying seconds that followed the shooting. ''I've gotta tell you, Mr. Hernandez, I was about ready to faint dead away!'' He wiped the perspiration that still clung to his forehead, despite the fact that it was a cold morning.

Ramón looked at his brother-in-law, then exhaled a long sigh of relief. Then he turned back to Robert and, impulsively, flung his arms around the young cowhand, embracing him. ''You've not only saved our mine, but you've saved our lives. *Por Dios*, you are *muy hombre*! I know that you came to Windhaven Range to pay off a debt. Well, you paid off that debt long ago. Now you have put me in yours.''

Then he offered his hand and Robert shook it, and there were tears in the young man's eyes as he straightened, a smile on his face. He was thinking of Marcy and their child, grateful that now he had paid his debt—and he had given back two lives for those that had been taken from him.

230

Twenty-Eight

Though the danger to the Scolby-Bouchard mine had been averted by the men from Windhaven Range, the threat of violence continued to hang over Leadville during the next few weeks. Horace Tabor continued to bluster his defiance of the miners, though even he began to realize that a lieutenant governor leading a pitched battle against men striking his own properties was hardly good public policy. It contributed nothing to the appearance of decorum that, as a public figure, he wished to maintain—particularly since he hoped one day to become governor of Colorado and even ultimately a United States senator. Nonetheless, for the defense of his mines, he created the Committee of Safety and then convinced Governor Frederick R. Pitkin to back the mine owners by sending in the state militia and declaring martial law.

The city marshal, Matt Duggan, was a notorious bully—and a killer. He terrorized the innocent and guilty alike, and he was completely fearless. Together with the militia, Duggan and his men were sent out to patrol the streets with orders to arrest any group of three or more. At ten o'clock curfew was established—with all saloons ordered to remain closed round the clock. Anyone having no visible means of support was declared a vagrant and fined, and over four hundred men—including a few of the union leaders under Mooney—were sent to jail.

Governor Pitkin was a forceful man in his own right, and in the present crisis he was determined to exert his authority. He was not about to let it appear that his lieutenant governor was running the show. He gave clear and specific orders to Major General David J. Cook, head of the militia, that order was to be restored in Leadville. Cook, who had earlier rid the territory of outlaw bands and had also served as city marshal in Denver, had no fear of Tabor and his wealthy cronies.

When he arrived in Leadville with his forces on June 13, the major general saw that the situation had reached the boiling point. And in addition to the immediate threat of violence between workers and mine owners, Cook realized that the town faced danger from another quarter: The criminal element was ready to go on an orgy of looting as soon as violence erupted.

Cook did not come into this situation unprepared. At his orders, several officers of the Rocky Mountain Detective Association, who had accompanied him to Leadville, undertook to circulate among the townspeople to size up the situation. Their report was ominous: The Committee of Safety, they said, was plotting to kill Mooney and several strike leaders. The Committee's plan was an elaborate one: Mooney and his friends would be seized and handed over to a squad of soldiers who were on the side of the Committee. Then, out of nowhere, a mob would appear, rushing the guards holding the prisoners; the soldiers would put up a perfunctory show of resistance, then they would hand over Mooney and his colleagues to the mob.

Major General Cook acted quickly. He took over Tabor's militia companies, selecting from them those men who opposed lynching. These were enrolled in Cook's own forces; the others were discharged. The Committee of Safety was thereby dissolved, the plan to kill Mooney thwarted, and Leadville spared an outbreak of unprecedented violence. Cook also enforced to the letter the regulations of martial law, in spite of cries of outrage from Tabor, who saw that his own authority in the town was being undermined.

About a week after taking over the militia, Major General Cook called for a meeting between the two warring factions in the strike. The mine owners were adamant and intractable, and the miners realized that their efforts had been totally fruitless. The mine owners could maintain the upper hand for as long as they wished, and there were no courts to force them to compromise. The union leaders finally suggested that the miners would return to work at the old three-dollar-a-day rate if they could realize a working day shortened from twelve to eight hours.

Tabor and his friends issued a flat "Never!" Either the striking miners could work the same hours at the wages they had been receiving, or they would be fired. The owners declared that the mines were their property and, therefore, no one had the right to tell them how to run them.

Thus the strike ended in total failure. For the dubious

232

privilege of earning three dollars a day, the miners had to endure horrible working conditions that all too frequently resulted in sickness or injury—many times with fatal results. Though the strike had been termed by some of the more eloquent newspaper writers as a storm "full of sound and fury, signifying nothing," it was symbolic in foretelling the ultimate demise of this boom mining town.

It was a scorching Friday afternoon in the second week of June, and Jeb Cornish was sitting playing faro with a few of his cronies, his shirt sleeves rolled up, his fat, florid face dripping with sweat, which he frequently mopped with a red bandanna. From time to time, he reached over to take a swig of whiskey and paused to relight his cigar.

His mouth was twisted into a petulant grimace, and in a whining voice he was complaining of the bad run of cards he had had all afternoon. "Dammit, you guys are going to clean me out—and you're not such good players, any one of you. It's just another example of this run of lousy luck I've been having here in Dodge. Sometimes I wish I was down in South America, where I could start things fresh and get what I want."

"Look, Jeb," Abel Pendergast, one of Penrock's fellow outlaws, tried to cheer him up, "it's not your fault—but it's not ours, either. Dammit, we did all we could to fix that greaser once and for all, and his fine Texas pal with him. As I told you, if only Gabe had been able to hit that plunger before that damned young punk of a cowhand shot him, we'd have been back here with good news instead of having to tell you of another failed scheme and the loss of one of our best men."

"I haven't spoken to Rhea yet," Cornish confessed as he took a pull at his cigar and then another sip of whiskey. "I didn't want to break the bad news myself. Wonder how she's taking it."

"Not good, you can bet your boots on that, Jeb." Pendergast sighed and shook his head. He studied his cards, then declared, "I guess I'm out. My luck's no better than yours."

"Yeah, nothin' but lousy luck," Cornish complained. "Like I said, it wouldn't take much to move me out of here and leave the good old United States for new territory. Hell, with nothin' but stupid greasers south of the border, I betcha I

233

could pull off my deals every time." He paused and reflected, "What is it about this Bouchard and this Hernandez? Why do they always have to be where they're not supposed to be when I'm plannin' somethin'?"

"Hey, boss," Pendergast suddenly muttered under his breath, his eyes fixed on the saloon's swinging doors, "I think you've got a visitor. Want us to take off and leave you with her?"

"Yeah, why don't you skedaddle? Leave me to finish the dirty work—I always have to anyhow." Cornish heaved a long, dolorous sigh. With an obsequious smile, he shoved back his chair and rose, not without a grunt of exertion.

"Why, Rhea, honey, it's a treat for sore eyes to—"

"Save your crap for your sluts, Cornish." Rhea Penrock came slowly toward his table. As usual, she was wearing a man's shirt, riding breeches, boots, and a Stetson pulled down over one side of her head. Her cold, gray eyes were narrow, her lips tight, and her bosom rose and fell with vehemence as she stood facing the fat Indian agent. "So you muffed it again, the way you've been muffing things for the last couple of years. And the worst of it is you lost me the only man I ever cared for. I've been likkering up to try to forget what happened, deciding whether I ought to shoot you down for the fat pig you are—"

"Now, Rhea, honey, I know how you must be feelin'—"

"Don't honey me, you fat, no-good louse!" She hissed petulantly.

"Aw, Rhea, there's no need to be insultin'," Cornish protested with an oily smile, spreading his hands out on either side of him. "I swear to God I sent along some of my best men. They had everything planned. We had Diego and Juan stirring up the Mexes, and we had Dave and Abel and John along with Gabe to rile those miners and get them drunk, so's they'd start a fight. We were gonna haul off the payroll, and kill that greaser and that fellow Bouchard along with him— and Gabe was gonna be made captain of my crew, I mean it, honey."

"Well, John told me sort of how it happened. Why don't you give me the rest of it?" She drew up a chair and flipped it around, seating herself with her legs spread on either side of the back. She unflinchingly stared at him, till he lowered his eyes and coughed, then took another swig of whiskey.

234

"There—there's not really much to tell, honey—I mean, Rhea. Look, it was all set." He started off on an elaborate recapitulation of the events as they had been told to him by the survivors of the failed plot. Occasionally punctuating the narrative with curses for Ramón and Lucien Edmond, Cornish rambled on.

"Get to the point!" Rhea broke in.

"Sure, sure, Rhea, I am. Well, some damned cowhand they've got along with them—well, just by luck, the damndest luck there ever was, saw Gabe and fired at him. He was lucky—in a million years he oughtn't to have hit your man, you know? If Gabe had only kept hold of that plunger, why, maybe he could have sent them both to hell—at least, you'd have had that to make up for Gabe."

"Nothing's gonna make up for Gabe. I told you, he was the only man I ever gave a damn about." She leaned forward, studying his face, as if to memorize it, her lips curled in a sneer. "Me, I'm gonna take things into my own hands. I'll get some satisfaction, if it's the last thing I ever do! Only this time, I'm not letting it be handled by your stupid men. They've bungled everything—first the bushwhacking, then the train robbery, and now this—and that's the last straw, Jeb Cornish."

"What's on your mind, Rhea? You know I'll give you all the help I can—I miss him just as much as you do."

"Like hell you do, you fat slug!" she bellowed. "All you have is your sluts; you've never been in love in your life. But Gabe, he was a real man. He had a hard time of it, just like me. But we got together, and it was good, damn good. And I don't take kindly to some punk killing my man."

"But, Rhea, I'd like to help you out—I'll give you all the men you want—"

"Skip it. And I know what you're thinking. You think you can get into my britches now that I've got no hubby to look after me." Swiftly, she drew a knife from the pocket of her jeans and, reaching across the table, seized Jeb Cornish's unbuttoned shirtneck with her left hand, while she poised the tip of the sharp knife against his double chin. "See how easy it would be? And I've half a mind to do it, though it wouldn't bring poor Gabe back."

"Come on, R-Rhea, you—you know you don't mean that. Look, I was always a friend to him—I promoted him, gave him more money—I helped him—well, so he could marry you. It isn't my fault—''

''I like to see you sweat, you fat pig,'' she grinned mirthlessly, ''but, from now on, I'll go my way. I'll pay that greaser back—that Bouchard fellow too—and I don't need your help. And if you've got any ideas about shacking up with me, get them out of your stupid mind, Jeb Cornish—you make me sick!''

She straightened and rose, pocketing the knife. She gave him a last look and then walked slowly to the swinging door of the saloon. Just as she was about to open the door, she turned back and, in an angry voice, demanded, ''Where does this Bouchard fellow call home? I hope you know that much anyhow.''

''Oh, sure I do, Rhea. Sure I do. They call it Windhaven Range—it's down in Texas, about a hundred miles southwest of San Antonio. Anyone in those parts knows of it. Don't tell me you're going out there and try to knife the greaser and Bouchard, though. You'd never make it—''

''I didn't say I was going to knife them. I'm gonna come up with another plan. Maybe you'll read about it in the paper. Maybe I'll send you a letter—but just leave me be. I've got an idea or two, and I'll handle things my own way, for a change.''

She swung the doors behind her, and Cornish took his bandanna and rubbed his sweaty face again, then he uttered a long, unhappy sigh. He reached for the bottle of whiskey, but when he lifted it up, he saw that it was almost empty. Putting it to his lips, he drank it down almost at a gulp, then flung the empty bottle against the wall, shattering it into scores of pieces. ''Goddamnit anyway!'' he swore. ''How does that bitch figger she'll rid me of that devil's whelp of a Mex and his partner, when my best men have tried it a couple of times and got themselves a place six feet under for all their trouble?'' He beckoned to a waitress, and his oily smile fixed on her as she approached. ''Honey, turn your tray over to Joe and tell him I'm taking you over to my place for a little foolin' around. If you treat me right, you'll make a helluva lot more 'n you will cadgin' drinks from most of these cowhands.''

She gave him a sickly smile, trying to nod with some show of enthusiasm, and walked slowly back to the bar and laid the tray down. She leaned over to whisper to the bartender, who guffawed and whispered a piece of advice. Her face was flaming, and her head was bowed in mute subjection when she approached Jeb Cornish's table. He rose steadily, embraced her in a bear hug, then whispering lewd endearments into her ear, led her out of the Comique.

To Jeb Cornish, a woman was a convenience, an exasperation, a foil, or a decoy to be used or expended to his own advantage. He was domineering and bent only on pleasure, grudgingly tolerating any irritation and exasperation. Generally, he had used his dance-hall girls only to entrap an unsuspecting cowhand so as to fleece him of hard-earned cash. (That, indeed, was how he had first run afoul of Ramón Hernandez. He had attempted to set a woman against the handsome Mexican in a version of the ancient ''badger game'' in order to trick him out of the cash that Cornish had paid Ramón for a herd from Windhaven Range.) But there his imagination stopped, for in his opinion, the usefulness of a woman as his weapon or ally was limited to the persuasiveness of her sexual favors. That was precisely why he was inwardly scoffing at Rhea Penrock's cold, incisive vow that she would avenge her outlaw husband's death.

Though she was only twenty-two years old, Rhea had already lived an arduous, dangerous life that would have spiritually or physically crushed many others. She had been born in Natchez, the illegitimate daughter of a red-haired slattern, Lucille Galloway, who was the only child of a poor Tennessee sharecropper. Fleeing her impoverished, uncaring parents, Lucille had been happy to take a job as a scullery maid in the elegant house of a wealthy cotton planter who lived near Chattanooga.

Because she was alluringly desirable, Lucille captured the fancy of the planter's dissolute son, who took pleasure in boasting of his amorous conquests to his equally amoral cronies. When she discovered that she was pregnant by him, his answer to her tearful entreaties was to revile her and then to tell his father that this lowly kitchen helper had dared to try to seduce him and now claimed that she was carrying his child.

Upon her immediate discharge, Lucille ran away to the only place that offered refuge to an unfortunate like her—a

237

brothel on the outskirts of Chattanooga. There, she gave birth to Rhea, and insisted on keeping her child. For years Rhea observed the squalid goings-on of life in a bordello, and pitied and yet loved her mother for her weakness. Nonetheless, Lucille manifested full maternal concern, lavishing genuine affection on her daughter and giving her presents whenever she could afford them.

When Rhea was fourteen, her mother entered a Natchez brothel. Two days after Rhea's fifteenth birthday, one of her mother's regular patrons, a riverboat pirate, quarreled with Lucille over her fee and knifed her. Afterward, having previously observed the beautiful, nubile Rhea, he broke into the young girl's room as she lay sleeping and brutally raped her.

When Rhea ran to the police, tearfully recounting these events, she was told that the world was well rid of just another whore and that, after all, she had not been present at the actual scene of her mother's death, and so could not identify the murderer except by unacceptable circumstantial evidence.

This brutal tragedy hardened her already resolute nature. The madam urged Rhea to take her mother's place, and Rhea, disillusioned yet practical, saw there was no other immediate future for her. Moreover, she had sworn to kill the man who had knifed her mother, and she believed that if she worked in the brothel, she might get her chance.

Rhea determined that the man who had murdered her mother—whom she had heard boast of his prowess on the Mississippi and of the booty he had taken—would return again. And five months later on a stormy November evening, she saw him in the salon, where she and the other girls were on parade for him to make his choice.

She no longer wore her jet-black hair hanging loose. Rather, she pulled it back from the top of her high forehead into a chignon, which made her look older. Yet she had retained a kind of girlish innocence, and watching the pirate's face, the madam boasted, "She's one of our best, Cap'n Sorley; just fifteen—but she's better than Mamie, or Helen there, take my word for it."

The swarthy, black-bearded pirate chuckled. Walking over to Rhea, he locked a thick arm around her neck and dropped a five-dollar gold piece down the front of her bodice. "That's for coming with me, bitch, and there's another five if you please me. Now, let's see if you're as good as Madam Cora says you are."

Once inside her room, Rhea slowly and provocatively undressed while the bearded ruffian, after undressing down to his smallclothes, sprawled on the bed and lecherously watched her. Wearing only a black corset and hose, held up by elastic garters high on her slim, lissome thighs, with her hands on her hips—flaunting her lithe, supple body—she moved deliberately toward the bed. He seized her with a roar of salacious laughter and pulled her down and mounted her, while she locked one arm around his neck and pretended to be passionately aroused, honeyed words of praise coming from her lips. With her other hand, she sought under her pillow for a knife she had secreted there. At the height of his climax, she lifted her right hand and, with all her strength, plunged the knife down into his back. He let out a frantic, high-pitched scream; his eyes rolled, and as they glazed in death, he stared incredulously at her.

Swiftly dressing, she looted his pockets and found three hundred dollars in gold and greenbacks. Cleansing her knife, she tucked it into her garter and then went to find Madam Cora. She explained what had happened, and the horrified woman agreed to help fling the body into the river in the dead of night. "But you'd best beat it, kid. The police may come around here asking questions and put two and two together—and that would get us all into trouble. I can't say as I blame you, Rhea. He had it coming—hell, maybe there's even a reward, but you don't want to stay around here to find out," the madam advised her.

At six o'clock in the morning, wearing her prettiest bonnet and dress, Rhea Galloway made her way to the dock and there boarded a riverboat heading up to St. Louis.

In St. Louis, she hoped that at last she might find honest employment and begin a new life. But again, fate was against her, and when her money ran out she was forced to take low-paying jobs, first in a factory and then as a kitchen domestic. She hastily left both places of employment after being harassed by the ardent men in charge, who coveted her provocative young body.

At the age of seventeen, she made her way to Dodge City, working first at one of the smaller saloons as a dance-hall girl. There she met Gabe Penrock, who took her over to the Comique and had Jeb Cornish hire her.

She was grateful to the tall young outlaw, and a mutual attraction grew between them, culminating in their marriage. He was always tender with her, not brutal as most of her lovers had been; that was why, when she learned of his death, she swore a vow that those who had been responsible would pay with their own lives.

Now, sitting alone in the boardinghouse where she and Gabe had lived, she poured herself glass after glass of whiskey and pondered—till at last an evil glint came into her eyes. She said aloud, "I think I've just thought of a way to do that greaser in—my way."

Twenty-Nine

When, at the middle of March, Laure Bouchard had returned to Windhaven Plantation, her mind and heart were filled with Leland Kenniston's proposal of marriage. Taking the ferry from the Queen City to Mobile, and thence up the river on the leisurely steamboat, she had stood at the rail looking eastward, her eyes dreamy and her mood hauntingly nostalgic.

There was so much to be gained—in joy, in the serenity her maturing years would now know, in the knowledge that her children would again have a father who would be as concerned for them as she was—and, as a very special dividend, the awareness that Leland had rekindled all her dreams of romantic and passionate love.

And yet, from a moral standpoint, she had difficulty reaching the decision to pull up her roots. The tenant owners who lived on the land that old Lucien Bouchard had gained from the mighty Creeks nearly a century ago depended on her. Marius Thornton and Burt Coleman came again to her mind—could they completely take charge of the estate, with all its attendant responsibilities?

Her mind had shifted to how her children would react to such a drastic alteration in their lives. The younger children—Celestine, Clarissa, and John—would almost assuredly enjoy the change of scene and be enthralled with the many wonders of New York. Paul, who at twelve was showing more signs of manliness and seriousness each day—but with the added nuance of a wry sense of humor that at times reminded her uncannily of Luke—was surely as adaptable as his older brother Lucien was.

Then, too, there was the matter of the children's governess, Clarabelle Hendry. How loyal, how devoted and loving she was, serving as surrogate mother in the times when Laure had most needed her. Would Clarabelle accompany her to New York?

Returning from this meeting with Leland, she felt more sure of herself than ever before. The feverish anguish of her widowhood following Luke's heroic martyrdom was now over. The solicitude and the tenderness that her friends had shown her had restored her spirits; leaving her now simply with memories that were bittersweet. And now, against the oncoming years, Laure Bouchard held within her heart an imperishable treasure, the knowledge that a man who represented all that she admired and respected and loved, cared for her deeply enough to want to spend the rest of his life with her.

She had kept the Mardi Gras costume, and she would treasure it always, even if she never wore it again. She would put it away, but whenever he was in Europe, or otherwise away from her—after they were married, naturally!—she would take it out and look at it, and she would recall each wonderful moment, each soft caress in the darkness, the sound of his voice, the feel of his lips on hers, the touch of his hands, the reassurance and the contentment, the passion and the desire, which had merged into consummate love.

And so she came back to Windhaven Plantation in a mood that was joyous and yet tinged with a bit of sorrow. She had longed to go with Leland, even to the ends of the earth—yet, of course, she could not. She had known it from the first. Still, it delighted her to know that he would have taken her with him then and there, had she been ready.

When she had reached Windhaven Plantation, stepping slowly down the gangplank, helped by the solicitous gray-haired captain of the *Dulcimer*, she found Clarabelle Hendry and the children awaiting her—and in the background, his eyes red and swollen, Marius Thornton.

241

Her eyes widened with surprise at this sight, for she knew that he rarely showed emotion of a personal kind, only diligence and concern for all that the Bouchards had created here on this land of red clay and towering bluffs by the Alabama River.

She gathered the children into her arms. Paul stood off to the side, somewhat aloof, waiting his turn. She hugged and kissed him, then murmured, "I've brought you back something. I decided that it's high time you learned how to play chess—it's a wonderful game. I got you a board and chessmen, and a book that has some of Paul Morphy's games. He was born in New Orleans, and he was the greatest player in the world for a time; everyone was afraid to challenge him."

"Thank you, Mother," Paul took her hand, "but Marius—it's awfully bad—he has something to tell you."

"What's wrong, dear Marius?" Laure turned to face the handsome black man whom Luke Bouchard had saved from a mob during a riot in New Orleans, the man who was her trusted foreman on the plantation.

"It's my Clemmie, Miz Laure. She was taken ill with a fever a few days after you left, and she passed away in forty-eight hours. There wasn't any pain, thank God. But I'm all alone now, with the children she gave me. I'm feeling mighty poorly, Miz Laure. Please forgive me—I know it's no way to welcome you back—"

She put her arms around him and cried. "Oh, Marius! Oh, I'm so sorry! Oh, God, sweet Clemmie, how I loved her, how good she was for all of us—" She stood back and took out a handkerchief from her purse. After wiping her eyes, she stammered, "I had something important to talk about with you, but—but this isn't the time."

"It's all right, Miz Laure. I don't mind talking. In fact, working hard and keeping my mind occupied is a way of trying to forget what happened—you know."

"Don't I just," Laure sighed heavily. She looked at the man's grief-stricken face and touched his arm. "Please, dear Marius, I want you to take your ease. We can meet later on—perhaps this evening, if that will be all right."

"I'm at your service always, Miz Laure, you know that."

"Dear Marius! You've been such a wonderful steward—you've looked after us here sometimes more than we realize and we can never pay the debt we owe you. I know it's hard

242

to accept Clemmie's death, but at least you have the memories of all your happy years together—and that you were the one who took her away from New Orleans and slavery—" She stopped. "I'm going to cry again; please, Marius, let's meet later in Luke's study."

"I'll be there, Miz Laure." He turned, and with his shoulders slumped, he walked slowly back to the chateau.

She sighed heavily and gathered her children to her, kissing each of them again. Taking the girls by their hands, she went into the house and upstairs to her bedroom. Opening her valise, she brought out presents for Celestine, Clarissa, and John. Paul's chess set and the instruction book were also extracted, and she promised that, before dinnertime, she would teach him the rudiments of the game.

The children went off to their rooms, and Laure began to unpack. Alone, she again took out her handkerchief and cried. The sorrowful news of Clemmie's death moved her very deeply, and it made her wonder if this unforeseen calamity might not force her to alter her own plans for moving to New York to marry Leland Kenniston.

After lunch, Laure climbed up to the topmost tower at the south wing of the red-brick chateau. She stood there for nearly an hour, staring at the tall bluff where her martyred husband lay beside his adored grandfather and the beloved woman, Dimarte. In a sense, she felt she communed with his spirit, and though she was not a believer in cryptic and mystic signs, nonetheless she was almost in a mood to receive one. She was a devout believer in a God who saw every act, every deed. If her Catholicism was not an abject and unthinking acceptance of every tenet of the faith, she was nevertheless moved by the spirit of the Mass—embracing what she considered to be its essential meaning and striving in her own life to share, to give, to be generous to all who were in need. . . .

The sun had now begun to descend behind the bluff, and the green foliage and trees of this early spring were tinged with shadows. As she watched, it seemed to her that she could see the shadows of Indians moving along the slope that led to the crest of the bluff—the spirits of those Creeks who had welcomed Lucien Bouchard when he had come from France to seek a new life, a new country, a new hope for the future. They lived in spirit here, where once they had ruled—

243

kindly spirits that looked down on her through the decades and judged her to be a Bouchard who was imbued with the belief that all men are brothers on this earth, no matter what their race or creed, or the color of their skin.

This feeling had been comforting to her, telling her that the cycle of life renewed itself eternally. And it was in this mood of consolation and gentle peace that she went to the study to meet with Marius Thornton.

He was waiting for her in the hall, and she put a hand on his shoulder and looked into his eyes as she murmured, "My dear old friend, how hard it must be for you. I know exactly what you're feeling."

"Thank you, Miz Laure." He unconsciously straightened and tried to compose his features.

"Sit down in that rocking chair and make yourself comfortable. Perhaps you'd like a glass of sherry?"

"Yes—I—I'd like one very much, Miz Laure. It's kind of you to—"

"Don't say it. You and I are friends of many years, and there's no need to stand on ceremony or feel yourself a servant here. You're as much a part of this family as anyone in this house."

He turned away, too moved to speak. She looked away also, respecting his anguish. After a few moments, in a distant voice that he tried to control, he said at last, "Miz Laure—I—I've been thinking—since, well—what happened. I'd like to get some additional help—with your permission, of course."

"Of course, Marius. I want you to have any help or equipment you feel you need to keep Windhaven running smoothly. You see—" She stopped speaking abruptly, then smiled awkwardly. She was about to tell Marius of her decision to marry Leland, but she realized that with his own recent bereavement on his mind, this was hardly the time to place so much additional pressure on his already burdened shoulders. "You see," she began again, "I've been thinking about the future of the plantation a good deal on the way back home, and what you feel may have bearing on all of our plans. You're so much a part of the life here, yet you've never really expressed to me how you feel about all the responsibility that you've had to bear since Luke died. I want you to feel absolutely sure that this is what you wish."

"Miz Laure, that's about the kindest thing anyone has said to me in all my life. You can't know what I feel for Mr. Luke and for you, what I'll always feel till the day I die. Nobody was ever kinder to me, and I loved him. And when he died, I said to myself that I was going to work even harder to make things easier for you. Only now, now that I've lost Clemmie, I—well, I have to take a good, long look and see what I have to do and what's best for our children."

"I understand all that. Tell me what you have in mind, Marius. If you want to leave, I'll understand. Perhaps I can help find you a different job, if you want that—"

"No, ma'am, it's not that. It's—like I said, I could use some help now. You see, I met a young fellow in Montgomery. He's a fine black boy who's been teaching himself agriculture— he's been studying all the technical publications and tracts he can get. He's eager to take up agriculture at a new school they're trying to start up over in Tuskegee—I think they're calling it Tuskegee Institute. It's going to be an advanced school for blacks, and if all goes as planned, it's going to be opened next year."

"I see, Marius. That sounds like a wonderful thing."

"In the meantime, until school opens, he wants work. I'd like to hire him. You see, Miz Laure, I think that this young man can really be of help here, because although I've been learning a lot—especially since Mr. Luke died and I had to take on lots more responsibilities—I'm sure this young fellow could teach me more things I need to know. Of course, I'd want your permission first, Miz Laure."

"Why, Marius, you should know by now that I trust your judgment in these matters," she had responded with a warm smile, "and I agree with you, it sounds like a wonderful idea. Let's see what happens before either of us makes—" she hesitated, "—makes certain decisions."

Three weeks later, Marius brought his young protégé to meet with Laure Bouchard in the study. "Miz Laure, this is Benjamin Franklin Brown. He's the young man I was telling you about. He's very smart, he's eager to learn, and he's done more reading than I ever did at his age, I'll tell you that." Marius smiled at the tall, affable-looking black.

"I'm delighted to meet you. Marius has spoken so highly of you that I've already decided we should hire you."

"That's very kind of you, Mrs. Bouchard!" Ben Brown smiled gratefully, and his voice was soft and pleasant. Laure was somewhat surprised by his excellent diction, which far surpassed Marius's. She realized, with a start, that times had changed. Marius Thornton, born well before the Civil War, had had little chance for education—the norm for a man with black blood in his veins in those days. But Ben Brown represented a new generation; now there were opportunities for education and work and becoming a part of the community.

"Marius will put you to work, Mr. Brown. As for wages, I'll pay you one hundred dollars a month and, of course, your room and board here will be provided."

"That's very generous of you, Mrs. Bouchard, and I hope to justify your faith in me. I'll work very hard, although I'll want to use my spare time in the evenings studying. I received a letter from the Institute's director—Mr. Washington—and they've accepted my application. I'm very excited about the school, because it'll give us blacks a chance to help our own people and let us stand up as free men and make decisions that affect us all," the young man proudly declared.

"I admire your spirit, your goals, and your ambitions. Marius will find you a room here—and it's good to have you as a member of our little community." Laure extended her hand.

The next day, Dalbert and Mitzi Sattersfield and their children paid a visit to Laure. Mitzi and Laure recalled old times, while Dalbert watched all of the children playing together. Laure recounted to Mitzi all the splendors of Mardi Gras, and the lovely, petite wife of Lowndesboro's mayor enviously sighed. "How I do wish I could have been with you, Laure! But the children keep me so busy, and dear Dalbert is working harder than he ever worked before. Why, you should see how he's enlarged the store and brought in new customers! It's really wonderful!"

"Then you don't miss New Orleans too much, *ma petite*?" Laure demanded, a smile on her lips.

Mitzi defiantly shook her head as she glanced over at her husband, who had Laure's two girls enthralled, telling them a story. "Oh, no, not with a husband like that—he's the most wonderful man, Laure! We share each other's thoughts, and there's never anything hidden between us. That's the way a marriage—''

She caught herself and flushed apologetically. "Oh, dear! I didn't mean to go on like that. Please forgive me—I know how you—''

Laure waved her hand and declared, "Never mind, Mitzi. Come to the study with me. I've something to tell you.''

"Girl talk? Oh, my, I'm so anxious to hear some. That's one thing I miss around my house," Mitzi confided with a giggle.

Once the door of the study was closed behind them, Laure took Mitzi's hands in hers and whispered, "I only hope you can keep a secret, you naughty minx! Even though you're an old married woman now, I know how irrepressible you can be! Why, I do believe that if Abraham Lincoln himself had confided in you that he was going to free the slaves—but no one was to know it yet because it was a state secret—the first thing you would have done would have been to run down the street, shouting the news joyfully!''

Mitzi burst into peals of laughter, and the two women hugged each other. When she had recovered her composure, the former soubrette of the Union House murmured, "I do go on, sometimes, I know it. But tell me your secret, and I swear I'll keep it. Not even Dalbert shall know, if you don't want me to tell him.''

"He'll know soon enough, darling. The fact is, you know how I've been telling you about Leland Kenniston, that wonderful businessman whom Lopasuta works for?''

"I remember very well. Oh, I declare! Is he the one you saw at Mardi Gras, Laure, dear?'

"He is, indeed." Laure had the grace to blush before she added, "We're engaged. He wants me to marry him and to move to New York.''

"Oh, my gracious! That *is* quite a secret, Laure! Are you going to do it?''

"If I can work things out with the plantation, yes. New York would be a wonderful place for the children—and frankly, I'd enjoy the change, too. You know how I feel about Windhaven since Luke died. . . .'' Her voice trailed off and she let her gaze wander to the window.

"I know, dear Laure. Tell me, do you really love him?''

"With all my heart and soul. He's never been married

247

before, you know, and he's only five or six years older than I am. How youthful he is, and what an imagination; and he's so tender and considerate!''

''Oh, yes!'' Mitzi giggled, ''You really do love him. And don't worry, I'll keep your secret. When do you plan to move, and what *will* you do with the chateau?'' she wanted to know.

Laure frowned and walked over to the window, drew the curtain aside, and stared out at Pintilalla Creek. ''I told him I could be ready by June. Of course, I've been counting on Marius Thornton more or less running things for me here. But when I got back and learned the news—I felt so dreadfully sorry for poor Marius. You did know Clemmie died, didn't you?''

''Yes, one of your field hands rode into Lowndesboro to buy supplies from Dalbert, and he told him. Isn't it dreadful? She was still so very young. He must be crushed!'' Mitzi sympathetically exclaimed.

''Yes, it was absolutely unexpected, darling, and it's given me a lot more to think about. Marius is so terribly depressed over losing Clemmie—they were so close. And, although he's only in his middle years, I notice that he fatigues easily, and he seems to be aging rapidly. I've no doubt it's his grief that brought this on. He needs someone else to stand side by side with him to help handle all the affairs of the plantation— the crops, the livestock, the sales to different stores both in Lowndesboro and Montgomery, the books—'' She sighed, adding, ''It is a great deal of responsibility. But, for the time being at least, Marius has found someone to help him. I do so hope I can still plan to leave for New York in June.''

''That means I won't see you again—'' Mitzi began to sniffle.

''Now, Mitzi, you know I'd never let our friendship die. You, Dalbert, and the children can come visit us in New York, and we'll be back to the plantation whenever we can—certainly for Christmas every year. Oh, I'm so excited!''

Mitzi hugged her friend, then kissed her cheek. ''We'd better be getting back to Dalbert—and I won't breathe a word of what you just told me till you tell me to.'' With a final hug and a kiss, they left the study.

* * *

The warm spring sunshine of April—so harmonious with Laure's mood of contentment over her pending nuptials—had, by the second week of May, yielded to an onslaught of rain. The entire state of Alabama was beset by a series of unusual thunderstorms, and the Alabama River, usually well below its banks at this time of year, began to rise ominously. Even horseback riders did not dare venture too close to the edge of the bank, lest their mounts slip and throw them into the swirling waters.

By the beginning of the third week of the month, there had been six successive days of torrential rain, and Burt Coleman, assistant overseer, said to Marius Thornton, "I'm saying prayers of thanks that Andy Haskins's land is on higher ground, so I don't have to worry about being in two places at the same time. I'll stay here as long as you want me. I've asked three of Andy's workers to come over here to help us build dikes around the dock and strengthen some of the levees where the land lies low and could be easily overrun by the Alabama."

"I'm much obliged to you," Marius gratefully declared. "Now is the time when we know what good friends we have."

Benjamin Franklin Brown had already proved his mettle: Having reported to work, at once familiarizing himself with the various crops and animals being prepared for market, he foresaw the threat by flood as gray skies greeted every new day and the rain kept up almost without pause. "I can help you build some fortifications, Mr. Thornton," he respectfully suggested.

Marius was only too happy to put him to work, and the newest worker at Windhaven Plantation worked side by side with Marius and Burt far beyond sundown as the situation grew more ominous daily.

By Thursday of this third week of May, the levees were constantly being strained, with breaches in the fortifications occurring almost hourly. Laure, Clarabelle Hendry, and the children were greatly concerned, for the chateau itself seemed certain to be inundated by flood waters. There was no abatement of the rain, and even the Montgomery *Advertiser* gloomily declared that this was the most unusual year in Alabama history, so far as weather was concerned. It was to be hoped, the editor added, that there might be a cessation by the morrow.

But the next day, the water level had risen still more, and water coursing over the dikes reached out for the stables, the barns, and even some of the workers' cottages.

Ben supervised the removal of the cows and horses from their stalls in the threatened barns and pens. He and three other men worked for hours, tramping back and forth through thick, heavy mud that sucked at their boots and the animals' hooves, making walking almost impossible. They wore a slimy, slick path from the barns to the fields on high ground, and some of the young calves and foals had to be hoisted to the men's shoulders and carried.

Marius, using some of Burt's reliable workers, ordered the furniture on the ground floor of the chateau moved to the second and the third floors. Laure, Clarabelle, and the older children hurriedly rolled up the rugs so that they could be carried up the broad staircase and laid in a spare bedroom.

Hearing of the plight of his good friends, Dalbert Sattersfield sent two of his clerks over to Windhaven Plantation with orders that they were to stay there, help all they could, and not return until the flood danger had completely ended.

Marius and Burt delegated some of the women to see to the removal of the workers' personal goods in those cottages threatened by the oncoming water. The rest of the women, and their older children, worked alongside their husbands, piling sandbags onto the levee, praying that the waters would crest no higher than this man-made embankment.

By Saturday noon, the conditions seemed even more perilous. A teenaged boy hurried up to Marius, anxiety and fear showing on his face. "Mistah Marius, suh, Mistah Brown needs your help real bad. He's in the birthin' pen."

Marius wearily wiped his brow. "All right, son, I'm coming." The boy hurried ahead of the foreman and led him to the pen. Ben was squatting down, working over a cow who was starting to calve.

"Mary picked a helluva time to have her calf, Mr. Thornton." The young black looked up, his forehead creased in worry. "It's going to be a hard birth. One of the calf's front hooves is angled back, and there's no way it can be born naturally. Can you find a chain?"

250

"I think so—what are you going to do, Ben?" Marius earnestly demanded.

"The only hope we have to save them is if we can loop the chain over the calf's hoof, pulling it out," the young man explained.

Marius turned to the boy who had accompanied him. "Davey, go to the tool shed by the back of the barn way over near the creek. There's a length of chain hanging on the door. Bring it back as fast as you can!"

"Right away, suh!" The lanky boy bobbed his head and sprinted off.

Just as the boy returned and handed Marius the chain, they heard Burt Coleman shout: "The river! The water's broken through the levee!" Marius poked his head out of the birthing pen and involuntarily gasped. "My God! It's heading right for us—we've got to get out of here real soon! My God, I never saw such water!"

Looking over to the pen, Burt could see the desperate situation his friend was in, and he ran to help Marius and Ben Brown. Marius tied the cow's head to a post, as she fought against the pain, then he grabbed hold of her hind legs and her tail, keeping them out of Ben's way. Ben reached into her uterus with the chain, and after many unsuccessful attempts he finally succeeded in looping it over the calf's hoof, just as water started to ooze into the pen.

"I got it, now! This poor little one isn't going to last much longer. It can't get enough air in its lungs. Mr. Coleman, you pull slowly on the chain while I ease the calf out. Hold it—the chain's slipping! Okay, now! That's it—it's coming—a little more—there! We got it!"

With a final tug, the calf was brought free of its mother's body, and Ben unhitched the chain from the calf's leg. He ripped off his shirt, and quickly wiped the membrane from the newborn calf's head, reaching into its mouth to clear the air passage. But the calf lay still.

"Damn!" Pinching the calf's nostrils shut, he bent down to blow into its mouth. Steadily breathing and pressing on the animal's lungs, his life-giving breath began the calf's breathing on its own.

Marius, Burt, and Davey gave a simultaneous shout of triumph, but Ben was more reserved. He cautioned, "We're not out of the woods yet. The cow's paralyzed from this

251

ordeal; her hind legs won't hold her, and she'll stay that way for some hours. We can't move her, and look at those waters—they're rising every minute!''

Marius and Burt rushed back to the levee and joined the group of ten men who were fighting the breach in the dike.

"All we can do now is pray," Burt groaned to Marius, although he was certain their efforts would be fruitless.

And then suddenly, the water stopped its incessant rise. The rain that had been falling in a steady downpour stopped. The Alabama River had reached its crest; the men of Windhaven Plantation, fighting against the power of the elements, had won their battle.

It was a week later, but already the intrepid Windhaven workers, supplemented by temporary laborers whom Marius Thornton had hired in Montgomery and Lowndesboro at double wages because of the arduous work involved, had made swift progress in the restoration of the plantation. The downstairs rooms of the chateau had been drenched with the overflow from the Alabama River, but the mud had soon dried and been swept out, and now all the floors had been washed and polished, and the furniture and rugs were back in place. Even Luke's old *escritoire*, which Laure was so fond of using, was back—unharmed—in its accustomed place in the study.

Parts of the barns and the stables had been damaged by water, but able carpenters were working ten-hour days replacing the waterlogged timbers and reinforcing the buildings themselves. Only one or two of the workers' cottages at the back of the fields had been damaged by water, but the pigpen and the fences needed almost complete rebuilding.

As if to offset the damaging blow that the elements had dealt to her home, Laure received a telegram from Jesse Jacklin, whom she had appointed manager of her casino in New Orleans. This wire reported that in the first quarter of the year the casino had netted ten thousand dollars in revenue over expenses, taxes, and wages, and that this money was being deposited in the former Brunton & Barntry Bank. Jason Barntry had sold his stock in the bank to Henry Kessling, president of the New Orleans Alliance Bank, whose reputation for integrity and honor stood high in New Orleans. Mr. Kessling had wired Laure Bouchard at the time of the merger that out of deference to her first husband, John Brunton, who had so valiantly continued the bank against almost incredible odds during the Civil War, he was renaming the new institution the Brunton & Alliance Bank of New Orleans.

Thus the unexpected windfall from the casino came at a most propitious time, since it enabled Laure to proceed with full repairs and, indeed, to improve the physical accoutrements of this farming commune.

It was also fortunate that this money came when it did, for the cotton, feed corn, most of the vegetables, and nearly all of the fruit were ruined by the torrential rains and subsequent flood. The losses in livestock amounted to several pigs, two cows, and a prize bull, as well as a flock of laying hens. Laure sent a telegraph wire for new stock to her recently appointed factor in Mobile. Edgar Stewart—a Florida-born, good-natured, industrious bachelor of forty-two—arranged for the shipment of the stock on a cargo steamboat. Crates of laying hens and two fine roosters, as well as a new bull, six heifers, two sows, and a studding boar were scheduled to arrive by the first week of July. By then the fences and pigpens, as well as the chicken house, would have been rebuilt and vastly improved. Under the instructions of Marius Thornton, the workers were to rebuild both structures on foundations raised from the ground, so as to elevate them against the possibility of future floods.

On this last Friday of the month of May, Laure accompanied Marius and Ben on a tour of the plantation. With them was Hughie Mendicott, who came along to point out some of the details the other two men might forget to mention. She expressed herself delighted with their accomplishments. "I can hardly believe my eyes, Marius, Hughie, and you, too, Ben. How wonderful it is to have such loyal, faithful associates and friends as you are. I know Luke, if he had been alive today, would have held a dinner in your honor for all your efforts for Windhaven Plantation. What you've done has enabled my children to retain their legacy and enabled me to retain this, my pride and joy."

"That's kind of you to say, Miz Laure." Marius lowered his head and shifted from foot to foot uncomfortably, for he was always embarrassed in the face of praise.

Sensitive to Marius's feelings of awkwardness, Laure turned to the young black man and said, "Ben, I can't thank you enough for the help you've given us. Marius was certainly right about your expertise. You obviously intuitively understand about farming and breeding—as well as building. The way you saved that breeding cow was a stroke of genius, truly it was. I wish you all the luck in the world in your career—but I have to admit that I'm selfish enough to wish that you could stay on here permanently, as an assistant to Marius."

"Well, ma'am," Ben thoughtfully replied, "I've been thinking that perhaps I could do both things at once. You see, I've been talking with Marius a great deal, and he tells me that he'd really like to work less hard than he's been doing—and, of course, what with his wife passing to her reward, he hasn't quite the enthusiasm for work that he once had—"

"I understand. All of us miss Clemmie so," Laure softly interposed. With this, she put out her hand and grasped Marius's arm and sent him a look of deep compassion.

"Well, ma'am," Ben went on, "what I suggested to Marius is that I stay on here at Windhaven Plantation and study only part time. Then, eventually, when Marius and Mr. Colemen have taught me all I need to know about your plantation, and we increase our yield with some of the new ideas I'll be learning about at Tuskegee, I can take over as foreman." Then, not certain how Laure Bouchard would take to this somewhat brash-sounding proposal, he humbly added, "Of course, ma'am, I'd be the last one in the world to say that I belong in the same league with Marius. He knows so much, and I've so much to learn." With this, he gave a brief nod, and he and Hughie discreetly stepped away a few paces so that Laure and Marius could speak privately.

Laure put an arm around Marius's waist and hugged him affectionately. Her eyes were clouded with tears as she said to him, "Marius, this plan does more for me than you can possibly realize. You know, for a long time I've been thinking that you and Clemmie should have had some of the leisure the rest of you so richly deserved—but, alas, she was taken from you far too soon. But you yourself, with your children to care for, and the job of shaping of their lives thrust on your shoulders alone, you must be ready to do less for me and think more of yourself, for you've already more than earned your permanent place of honor here."

"That's very kind of you to say, Miz Laure." Marius

blinked his eyes rapidly and pretended to look up at the bluff, adding inconsequentially, "I don't think we're going to have any more rain for a spell."

"Let's hope not," she airily laughed, to break the mood. Then, smiling, she stepped back and said, "You know, of course, I've been seeing a good deal of Mr. Leland Kenniston. As a matter of fact, I met him in New Orleans."

"I know that, Miz Laure. Actually, I was hoping—but it's not for me to say—"

"You say what's on your mind, Marius. I'll bet you already can guess what I'm going to tell you, can't you, because you're so wise!" she laughed gaily.

"That you're going to marry him?" Marius hazarded.

Laure nodded delightedly. "I didn't think I could keep secrets from you, Marius! This plan of yours and Ben's frees my mind about leaving Windhaven Plantation and going to New York when I marry Mr. Kenniston—you see, he's asked me to live there. But I see now that there would be no more capable hands than yours to leave Windhaven in."

"God bless you for having such faith in me. Clemmie would have been awfully proud to hear you say this." Marius himself could no longer control his tears and turned away, covering his face with his hands.

Laure walked over to Ben Brown. "I like your spirit, your attitude, Ben, your desire to educate yourself and to improve. That's what all of us must do in this life. It doesn't matter where we come from and what our background is, so long as we try to make ourselves better citizens, better help in the community where we live. You're going to have a wonderful future. And I'm glad that Marius found you and we hired you."

"Ma'am, I don't think I've ever met a woman like you, and I'm delighted to work for you. I've heard about your late husband and about all the Bouchards and what they stood for here in Alabama—you might say they're almost legendary. I guess you also might say I'm proud to be a part of Windhaven Plantation."

The next morning, Laure Bouchard sent a stable boy to Montgomery to send off two telegraph wires. One was to Leland Kenniston and read as follows:

255

Dear Leland:

I have wonderful news! We can proceed with our plans. Will you come to Windhaven in a month's time, so that we can be married here? It is my dearest wish to be married in this chateau, the place that has been my home since I left my native New Orleans. I await your answer eagerly, and I send you all my love.

Laure

The second telegram was to Geraldine and Lopasuta Bouchard:

Dear Geraldine and Lopasuta:

We've had a flood, but thanks to Marius and a new man, we suffered very little permanent damage.

I've just wired Leland, asking him to come here in a month and marry me. My fondest wish is at last coming true, my dear ones, and I want you both here to share this occasion with me. As soon as we set a definite date, I'll wire you at once.

Your loving Laure

Thirty

Two days later, Leland Kenniston's reply was delivered to Laure Bouchard by courier from Montgomery:

My dearest:

Your news has made me the happiest man in the world. I must be in San Francisco next week for a while, since I may be opening a new branch there. Relying on train schedules and sending a prayer to the Almighty, may I set June 26th for this most important event in my life? Wire me at the Palace Hotel, San Francisco, if this is satisfactory.

A telegram is much too public to set forth my feelings. Suffice it to say, they are rapturous, anticipatory, and adoring.

Leland

Laure was radiant after she had opened the wire and read it. Clarabelle Hendry, who was preparing lunch for the children in the kitchen, turned to see her employer standing there, the wire in her hand, and exclaimed, "Why, Laure, you must have had the most wonderful news!"

"I have, Clarabelle—and it involves you too. You remember how after I returned from New Orleans I told you that Leland Kenniston proposed to me, and asked me to live in New York. Well, now that I've completely turned over the stewardship of the plantation to Marius and Ben Brown, I can at last think seriously of making such a drastic change in my life. The question is, dear Clarabelle, will you come with me? You're so indispensable, you're part of the family, and the children adore you."

"Oh, yes, I'd already decided to come if you asked me," the pleasant-featured widow smiled. "I don't want to leave you, either, Laure. Personally, I'm looking forward to the new surroundings. I've heard so much about New York, how it's growing by leaps and bounds—all the entertainment and the restaurants and the wonderful outdoor activities—" She stopped, a bit breathless. "It'll be so wonderful for the children, now that they're getting to be of an age when they can enjoy it all."

"Oh, I'm so pleased, dear Clarabelle!" Laure hugged the woman affectionately, then her face sobered. "But there's just one thing I worry about—tell me seriously, Clarabelle, do you think it's a mistake for me to marry again so soon?"

"Indeed it is *not*!" Clarabelle emphatically declared, placing her hands on her hips. But her eyes were shining with tenderness at the news that this romance would culminate in a wedding. She had secretly felt all along that Laure should remarry, and quickly; otherwise she might remain bereft and lonely, with the problems of the plantation and the children consuming all of her energies. "Nobody who knows you, nobody at all, will ever think you're acting hastily, and certainly you're not being disrespectful to Mr. Bouchard's memory. I know how much you loved him and how he loved you. But he passed on three years ago—and you can't live in the past. He lived just for your happiness, and, if you're happy now, if Mr. Kenniston is all you say he is—and he sounds just wonderful—then I know Mr. Bouchard would be very happy for you."

"Thank you for saying that, Clarabelle."

"You know what happened to me, how much I loved my husband till he was taken from me—well, my feeling is that we have to take our opportunities when and where we find them. You can be sure that everyone will wish you all the happiness there is, and long years to enjoy it with your man, Laure," she concluded.

"My gracious, Leland said the twenty-sixth! We've so much to do! You just have to help me, or I'll be lost!" Laure happily averred.

"It'll be grand, and I'm looking forward to it!" the governess declared. "Are you going to have a big wedding?"

"You know, I've thought about that, ever since Leland proposed to me," Laure confessed. "First, I thought we'd just have a small, intimate wedding, with just my immediate family—like Geraldine and Lopasuta, and their children—and everyone here at the chateau, of course. Incidentally, I want you to be one of my matrons of honor; I insist upon it, Clarabelle."

"Thank you, my dear. That's quite an honor, and I appreciate it very much."

"But getting back to your question, I'm so happy that I found Leland, and because he's such a wonderful man that I want everyone to meet him and share in my happiness, I've decided to have a gala ceremony. I know that when all my friends get to know him, they'll understand I'm not acting impulsively. I'm sure they'll realize that no one could ever take Luke's place in any of our hearts, but as you say, they'll know that life must go on. By marrying Leland, who'll be a wonderful father to the children, it'll show that I'm still devoted to Luke in that very special way."

"Of course it will!" Clarabelle heartily agreed.

"My gracious, when I begin to think of how much work there is—I'm almost frightened of it," Laure giggled. "We'll have to clean this place from top to bottom. We'll order armfuls of flowers. And nobody's going to cook, because I'm going to hire the best caterer in the county. Oh, my—we have

258

invitations to send out to all of our friends and neighbors—
and oh, yes, I mustn't forget that Mitzi has to be a matron of
honor, too—that'll delight her! You know, Mitzi really has a
horror of growing old, and it's so silly because she's going to
be lovely for many years—and Dalbert will always think so.
Indeed, Clarabelle, it's seeing how happy they are, and Lopasuta
and Geraldine, that's made me realize all the more the loneliness I've felt since Luke was taken from me.''

Clarabelle wiped her eyes with her handkerchief and nodded. She put a hand on Laure's shoulder and reaffirmed,
''I'm so very happy for you, dear Laure.'' Then, matter-of-
factly, she added, ''I know Amelia will help us. And we'd
best get started immediately. If you like, I can have Amelia
go into town and talk to the florist and the caterer.''

''That's a wonderful idea. Perhaps we both can look after
her children while she's doing that; we can have a luncheon
party and play games in the nursery,'' Laure proposed, her
face beaming with joy.

Laure sent a telegraph wire to Leland at the Palace Hotel in
San Francisco, joyously agreeing to the date that he had
suggested. She received a wire back late the next day, in
which Leland assured her that he approved of her sentimental
selection of the red-brick chateau as the site of their marriage.
He said that he would do everything possible to arrive a day
or two beforehand so that, if need be, he could help her iron
out any last remaining details. Here was another proof, Laure
thought, of his devoted consideration.

Now that the date had been confirmed, she sent off another
telegram to Geraldine and Lopasuta in New Orleans telling
them when the wedding would take place, and asking Geraldine if she would be her third matron of honor.

The dining room, being the largest and most spacious room
of the chateau, seemed to be the ideal locale for the ceremony. Accordingly, Benjamin Franklin Brown and Marius Thornton, together with several of the other tenant farmers, removed all but the most essential furniture and prepared the
room for the seating and floral decorations for the festive
occasion.

Amelia took letters from Laure to both the florist and the
restaurant that would stock the banquet tables, explaining
what the bride-to-be wished in the way of floral arrange-

ments, food, and libations for the wedding feast. Laure and Clarabelle Hendry began to mail out invitations, using the more personal form of handwritten notes rather than formal printed requests for attendance. Some of them were even delivered by courier, rather than through the auspices of the Postal Service.

Lopasuta and Geraldine arrived from New Orleans on the twentieth of June, professing a willingness to help in the arrangements, and both of them proved to be indispensable. Lopasuta even went to Montgomery to invite an elderly, retired priest, Father Joseph Macklin, to perform the ceremony. Father Macklin had known Lopasuta's mentor, Jedidiah Danforth, and the two old men had frequently played chess together. Now nearly eighty, the frail, gentle priest expressed his delight at being asked to perform the ceremony, and he assured Lopasuta that it was no trouble at all for him—indeed it would be a pleasure—to return now by carriage with the young lawyer, though the ceremony was still a few days off. It would be a beautiful one, in which Laure and Leland would affirm their desire to share, to live in joy and harmony, and to instill in their children the love of God and His beloved Son.

After meeting with the priest, Laure thought to herself that in many ways he resembled Friar Bartoloméo Alicante, for both men had a benevolent, compassionately tolerant outlook on the force of religious belief as it was adaptable to modern circumstances. They upheld tradition, while at the same time understanding the foibles and weaknesses of mankind, and they spoke always of the forgiving and understanding God who had indulgence for those who showed contrition for their peccadilloes and their sins.

Dalbert Sattersfield and his wife, Mitzi, visited Laure two days before the wedding, and Dalbert brought a buggy filled with provisions to be added to the wedding feast, as well as a pair of solid silver candlesticks that his grandmother had left him, which he wished to offer to Laure and Leland for the mantelpiece in their New York City home.

The handsome Irishman arrived at the landing near the chateau a day before the wedding, and it was Amelia Coleman who opened the door to his knock. Leland's rap on the brass knocker—which had been duplicated after the burning of the chateau by Union troops just before Appomattox—now

260

symbolized the coming of the man who would assume the heritage of Windhaven Plantation, a man who would guard and uphold its traditions. For in choosing Leland Kenniston to succeed old Lucien's beloved grandson Luke, Laure had been convinced that, after Luke, no truer, more steadfast and devoted husband could exist for her. It would be Leland who would assume the mantel of paternity to guide her children into maturity, their coming of age, so that—in their turn— they would carry on the traditions of the first Bouchard.

The chateau was bright with flowers: daisies, white Cherokee roses, black-eyed susans, yellow and blue flag irises, and Virginia bluebells—bouquets representing many of the species of wildflowers that Lucien Bouchard would have seen when he had made his way by packhorse from Mobile along the winding Alabama River to Enconchate.

On the day of the wedding, the photographer of the *Advertiser* came to take pictures of the wedding chamber and of the ceremony itself, and the caterer and two assistants arrived to serve the banquet at five o'clock, immediately after Father Macklin had joined Laure Bouchard and Leland Kenniston in holy matrimony.

All of the tenant farmers and their families were present, and Laure had invited Jedidiah Danforth's housekeeper and others whom she had known in Montgomery, associates of Luke's—blacks as well as whites. In Luke's mind, in hers, and she knew also in Leland Kenniston's, there was no difference in social status because of race; all of them were friends and companions, and they came to wish joy to the happy couple.

Andy and Jessica Haskins sent their profound regrets that they could not get away from the sanatorium for this memorable occasion, but they sent a lovely wedding gift and promised that they would meet again soon.

Music was provided by the cheerful spinster who played each Sunday in the Lowndesboro Episcopal Church. The small pedal organ at which she sat had been transported by carriage from town. Glancing back to the old priest for her cue, she saw him nod, and Agatha Murtroyd began to play the "Wedding March" from Wagner's *Lohengrin*.

Young Paul stood solemnly viewing the proceedings, but Celestine and Clarissa, dressed in their very best, were excitedly participating as flower girls. As they walked down the improvised aisle, they conscientiously strewed flower petals in the path that their mother and stepfather-to-be would be treading.

Leland entered the room, and people made way for him, whispering congratulations to him and best wishes. He took his place beside Lopasuta, who was his employer's best man. The priest, in his white robes, stood before a mahogany lectern on which was posed the gold cross from his private chapel.

Large as it was, the dining room could just barely hold all the guests who now waited impatiently, turning in their seats occasionally to catch a glimpse of Laure Bouchard. Suddenly, she came into view, descending the stairway into the main hall and thence into the dining room. A veil covered her golden hair, which was coiffed in a simple chignon. Her organdy gown was of a pale green, and her kid shoes had been dyed to match. She held a nosegay of delicate white swamp lilies, which she nervously kept glancing down at. Just ahead of her walked Clarabelle, Mitzi, and Geraldine, her matrons of honor, each holding a bouquet of yellow roses, which Leland himself had had sent from Montgomery for this memorable day.

Laure covertly cast a glance at Leland and her heart beat faster. Tall and strong, his eyes shining, a smile on his lips, he was elegantly clad in a suit of pearl gray broadcloth that he had had tailored in New York for this occasion.

At Father Macklin's request, Laure and Leland joined hands, exchanging looks of devotion, promise, and trust. She read the adoration in his eyes, and she felt her years slipping away.

Lopasuta produced the ring, and Father Macklin spoke at last the words that united Laure and Leland.

As the ceremony concluded, Agatha Murtroyd began to play an Irish love ballad, and Leland started, turning to Laure to whisper, "Now how in heaven's name did she know that song, my darling?"

"Because in one of your letters, Leland, you mentioned you were very fond of that tune. So I coached her and told her to play it after Father Macklin had made us husband and wife. Darling, since my oldest son is in Ireland and you were born there, it's my way of saying God bless the land of your birth."

"Oh, Laure, my sweet wife, my darling one," he murmured. He drew her into his arms for a long kiss, which sent a delighted buzz of whispers through the room.

They left the very next noon, riding to Lowndesboro to take the train for New York with Clarabelle Hendry and the children. Marius Thornton and Ben Brown drove the buggies that conveyed them to the railroad station, and Geraldine and Lopasuta were also there to see them off.

After the children said their good-byes to Marius, Ben, Geraldine, and Lopasuta, Laure turned to Marius, with tears in her eyes. "This isn't good-bye forever, Marius; you mustn't think that for a minute. Nor you, either, Ben. And you can tell all the others back at Windhaven Plantation that my husband and I and our children will spend our summers, as well as the Christmas and New Year holidays, here at Windhaven Plantation. Thank you, God bless you all, and please write often. Just as soon as we've settled in, I'll write all of you about our exciting new life."

She turned to Geraldine and Lopasuta, hugging and kissing them. "And you, my darlings, see if you can't get off to New York once in a while—if your boss can spare you in New Orleans." They all laughed—Leland hardest of all—and he gave Lopasuta a hearty handshake, then impetuously clasped him around the shoulders.

They boarded the train, and Marius and Ben stood there waving to Laure, then turned to each other with a long, knowing look. "She's a great lady, Ben," Marius Thornton said. "And you and I are going to keep this place running just as smoothly as if she were here to supervise every single detail."

"I swear to you I'm going to do everything I can to make that promise come true, Marius."

Thirty-One

The first week of May 1880 in Chicago was cold, dreary, and rainy—a total contrast to the sunny, cheerful month of April and all the more disconcerting because of its sudden change. But that dreary weather daunted neither Carla nor Hugo Bouchard, each of whom was deeply involved in studies.

For Carla, her time at the Chicago Academy of Fine Arts was a heaven-sent chance to develop her latent artistic talents. She preferred to work with watercolors, rather than oils; however, Cordelia Thornberg urged her to broaden her technique by exploring as many media as possible, telling the young woman that she might be surprised how quickly she could advance.

Hugo Bouchard, meanwhile, was fascinated by the new horizon that his first term at Rush Medical College had opened up for him. He was engrossed in his intensified studies in physiology and anatomy and had come now to the dissection of cadavers. To listen to the professor's explanation of where to find the sensitive nerve structure, then to take a scalpel and probe and discover the realities for himself, was fascinating.

It was understandable that he had only the faintest appreciation of art, for his interests lay in completely different directions. If anything, he regarded Carla's daubing with paints and making charcoal and pencil sketches as little more than a pleasant, diverting hobby. That she could make a career of it was, at least to his mind, impractical and unthinkable. His uncharitable criticism of her floral painting had affected Carla deeply, and she had become cooler toward him than ever before in their lives.

He, however, was absorbed in his studies. His fellow students sat on every side of him, working out the same problems—sometimes exchanging glances with a sigh or a shake of the head to indicate the complexity of the problem—and this gave him a feeling of belonging. That was perhaps why Hugo was not fully cognizant of the subtle alteration

264

between himself and his sister that had begun; indeed, he had already forgotten the criticism he had made of her work. But to the contrary, Carla had not, would not, forget the slighting remarks her brother had offered when she had so proudly and hopefully shown him her work.

To be sure, a word or two on his part might have made all the difference. Carla often said to herself that if Hugo were to tell her about the various projects he faced in his medical studies, she would have nothing but kind words, for she valued the long-range profession of the physician, the surgeon. Illness was the inevitable enemy, and if her brother could help lessen death's grim harvest even by a few, he would in her opinion be performing a noble service.

Still, Carla had great pride in her own work, too, and also the self-esteem understandable in a beautiful young woman of twenty; she intrepidly sought to emulate Cordelia Thornberg's independence and attitude of *je m'en fiche*. Hugo had met few women in his life, apart from his sister, his mother, and those females who dwelt on Windhaven Range. He could hardly be expected to comprehend, therefore, the emotional struggle seething in Carla, who strove to find not only her own calling in life, but also the talents she might bring to it—thereby enriching her experiences and expanding her friendships in a lasting way.

Cordelia, unlike most women of her generation, understood all too well what Carla was enduring—what loneliness there must be, yet what satisfaction, in finding oneself and caring nothing for the opinions of the majority. That, to be sure, had been her own philosophy of life since her girlhood.

She had made equally incomparable friends, the meeting of whose minds with hers meant far more than the conventional ties of marriage and children. And, it logically followed, she was zealously determined to live long enough to see women recognized as equals, not only given the vote in every state of the Union, but also admitted to jobs on the same intellectual level as men if they could qualify.

On the Tuesday of the second week of May, Cordelia invited Carla to attend an opening at a gallery located on North Dearborn Street, near Chicago Avenue. "We'll have lunch at the Palmer House, dear," the handsome, auburn-haired woman promised, "and then we'll spend a good part of the afternoon at the Henriot Gallery. I may tell you, dear

Carla, I'm a patroness of it; I've contributed some money to it and helped a few of the gifted artists who've shown there, though are not yet really known, so that they could have the economic freedom necessary to do creative work. I'm a firm believer in sponsoring creativity in my own back yard, so to speak. It's all very well to respect the Old World—after all, they've had centuries of achievement before this country ever came into being. But I don't want American artists to be imitative; I want them to stand on their own feet. There's something to be said for the United States artistically and culturally; there's a new way of seeing things here, a new point of view that Europe can in no way imitate."

"I agree with you completely, Cordelia," Carla animatedly exclaimed, her eyes shining. "I don't think we ought to be slaves to tradition."

"Now, my dear," the striking woman laughed as she put an arm around Carla's shoulders, "you're beginning to think and talk like me—and that's very flattering. But you're also beginning to think for yourself, and that's exactly what anybody who is endowed with a mind like yours ought to do. There's an old French proverb to the effect that *si jeunesse savait, si vieillesse pouvait.* You know what that means, of course?"

"Yes, Cordelia. 'If youth but knew, if age but could.' "

"Exactly! Well, my dear, the only thing I envy about you is that you're twenty-two years younger than I am. If I had that many more years ahead of me and had your looks and your potential talent, I could just about hold the world in my hands!" She laughed exuberantly, and Carla couldn't help laughing with her, for Cordelia's zest for life was so contagious that it imbued all within her presence with the same eager and ambitious spirit. "Well, what do you say to my plans for today?"

"They sound wonderful, Cordelia."

"All right, then. Wear that slate-blue frock of yours; it does wonders for your black hair and your beautiful blue eyes. Who knows? You could very possibly meet a young man with a great deal of talent. I'm a firm believer in bringing talents together," Cordelia twitted the lovely young brunette.

"Do you know, it's strange, Cordelia, but I haven't really thought about—well—boys—" Carla began.

"Pish-tush!" Cordelia sniffed and made a deprecating gesture with her slim hand. "I'm not going to introduce you to any *boys*, Carla. You're a woman, and if I introduce you to any members of the opposite sex, you can be sure they'll be *men*, men with brains and talent. The mating game is a time-honored pursuit, but I've never been one to believe that merely bringing a young man and a young woman together solves the world's problems. If anything, it seems to have caused a great many. No, my dear, allow me common sense enough to know what sort of man I think might be attractive to you—even if it's only for a temporary flirtation. Don't look so shocked. There's absolutely nothing wrong with brief romances, if they bring you pleasure. But I've felt that you're a young woman of extraordinary sensitivity and very secretive, guarded emotions, so I'm not going to put you into any jeopardy, to find that you've become infatuated with some young scoundrel. All right now, you go dress; make yourself outstandingly lovely."

"You do say the nicest things to me, Cordelia! Do you know, I've almost forgotten what it was like in Texas, I'm so happy here with you," Carla confided.

Cordelia's face shone with pleasure. "And that, young lady, is the very nicest compliment you could ever have paid me. I feel the same way toward you, as if you're the daughter that I never had. Now, let's go dress. I want to allow plenty of time for the wonderful luncheon buffet they have at the Palmer House. This miserably cold weather, so unexpected in May after the lovely warm time we had last month, has given me quite an appetite. Isn't it nice that we don't have to worry about our figures—I'm too old to care, and you were born with the sort of bones that will *never* put on too much flesh! Now hurry!"

Whenever Cordelia took Carla to the Palmer House at State and Monroe streets, the young woman was always fascinated by the place. She had read that the design of this hotel, based on plans by John van Osdel, had been expanded by C. M. Palmer, a noted architect who did much work in Chicago in the decade following the Great Fire. The Palmer House was famous for the thirty-four varieties of marble used in its structure, a twenty-five-foot-high rotunda, an Egyptian parlor, and furniture imported from France and Italy. Its management claimed that it was the world's first fireproof hotel—surely a strong selling point in Chicago after the catastrophe of 1871—and over six hundred tons of Belgian iron had been used in its construction.

Lunch in the Grand Dining Room, which was sixty-four feet wide and seventy-six feet long, was a visual as well as a gastronomic treat. Carla never ceased to be amazed by the gilded Corinthian columns, the marble floor, and the frescoes painted by contemporary Italian artists. Even the damask table linen had been made in Belfast, especially for the Palmer House. The year before, a great banquet had been held there for former President Ulysses S. Grant, with Mark Twain as the principal speaker. Wild game had been featured on the menu: The tables had groaned with saddle of venison, roast prairie chicken, buffalo steak, breast of duck, and filet of wild turkey; these had been accompanied by lavish wines and liqueurs, vegetables, salads, fruits, and a mélange of rich desserts.

Following a leisurely and savory buffet lunch this May afternoon, Cordelia Thornberg summoned a hansom cab to convey Carla and herself to the new art gallery. It was on the first floor of a four-story building that had been erected six months after the Great Fire, and it had been elegantly furnished as a salon, with private rooms for patrons of the arts to meet over tea and cakes and liqueurs to discuss the purchase of whatever paintings had taken their fancy.

Cordelia and Carla were welcomed by a charming man in his early fifties, whom Carla's hostess introduced as Leonard Henriot. Though born in New Hampshire, he had been educated in Paris and had, for several years, run an art and antique shop in that city.

To Carla's delight, she recognized him as a recent lecturer at the Academy, where he had given a most illuminating address on the new school of French Impressionism. To cap her pleasure, he remembered her, and taking her hand and kissing it, he said to Cordelia, "This young lady is not only a perceptive student, but I sense that she will go on to great things. Her instructor showed me some of her watercolors"— he turned to Carla—"and I think that you have extraordinary ability. It remains for you to channel it and to accept advice, but not to swallow it wholeheartedly. An artist is very much like a musician: You must learn your own style."

He led them over to some chairs, and they all sat before he continued. "If an artist dogmatically does what he is told to do or what not to do, he will wind up being a pallid imitation of somebody else. My opinion, for what it's worth, Miss Bouchard, is that you must strike out and find yourself in your own medium of expression—and then perfect it. It's all we have in life to offer, and we give it all we have because we are different, we are individuals, and, above all else, we are creative artists."

"That's a wonderful philosophy!" Carla breathed, totally enraptured.

"Isn't he a darling!" Cordelia exclaimed after the gallery owner had gone off to welcome some new guests. "Unfortunately, he didn't take his own advice. As a young man, he had a superb skill with woodcuts, along the lines of Albrecht Dürer. By the way, Carla, I must get you a copy of *The Death, the Knight, and the Devil*—it's one of the most powerful, vital things I've ever seen, done through the simple medium of relief printing. Even though it was created hundreds of years ago, you'll find a powerful impressionism there. Tinged with religious feeling, of course, but nonetheless very definitely impressionistic. I suppose, whether it be writing, music, or painting, or sculpture, the term 'impressionist' simply means that you are expressing your own impression of what you see and showing it to others through your skills."

"That's very well put, Cordelia. You know, I showed—" Carla caught herself short, not wishing to seem petty in mentioning the recent disparaging commentary of her brother, Hugo. She looked around the gallery, and her attention was taken by a superb painting, that hung on the wall directly opposite from her. "Oh, my! That's absolutely marvelous!"

"That is a work by Mary Cassatt," Cordelia volunteered. "She was born in this country thirty-five years ago, but she's spent most of her life in France. You can tell that she's been greatly influenced by Manet and Degas, and yet she has a marvelously coherent and vigorous idiom all her own. I must confess I admire her still more for her accomplishments because she's a woman."

"It's absolutely amazing how much detail, how much life and color and shading there is in this," Carla breathed, as she stared at the work. "Such delicate lines, and yet they're more powerful than if they were bold strokes."

"Suggestion, intimation, allusion; those are the keys to impressionism. Incidentally, Mary Cassatt has a very dear friend here in this city, you know—Mrs. Potter Palmer, whose husband owns the Palmer House."

"Really? How interesting," Carla exclaimed, wide-eyed, as she noticed the elegantly dressed men and women coming into the salon, talking among themselves in hushed tones, standing before paintings and etchings, and making notes on pads of paper. "This is a very large crowd for an art gallery, isn't it?"

"Well, I like that!" Cordelia said with a laugh. "You mustn't think that just because Chicago isn't thought of as a cultural center as, say, New York is that we're not interested in creative work. There's an earthiness, a rough and eager vitality to Chicago, which, mark my words, is going to make its mark in the creative arts—it already has, for that matter. I must show you the houses on Prairie Avenue, where the most elegant and wealthy socialites of Chicago are building now. They're having them constructed by very brilliant young architects, such as Daniel Burnham, John Wellborn Root, and Louis Sullivan. And by the way, speaking of Mrs. Potter Palmer, the word is that in a year or so, her husband is going to build her a castle on Lake Shore Drive that will rival Buckingham Palace in its sumptuousness."

"It couldn't be any more beautiful than the Palmer House, Cordelia," Carla declared. Every day, she was learning new things about the city in which she was beginning her new life, and it was so exciting that she only hoped she could remember to put all the details down in her lengthy letters back home to her parents and sisters.

As she turned now to study a recent painting by Claude Monet that, as Cordelia told her, had just been received three months ago, Carla's eyes widened. She had just recognized a slim, brown-haired, bespectacled young man whom she had seen frequently in the building where she took her art classes. Cordelia saw how her protégée's gaze had turned from her and smiled knowingly. "Oh, I know that nice young man, Carla. He comes from an excellent family in Boston. You're looking at him as if you'd met him before."

"Well, not formally, but I have seen him at the Academy,

Cordelia," Carla admitted, her face suffusing with a blush.

"I thoroughly approve of your attraction. Now, now! The look on your face tells all! Yes, Thomas Lockwood not only was born to wealth, but he happens to have brains and sensitivity—which I admire even in a male," Cordelia sardonically commented. "Why not go say hello to him?"

"If I didn't know you so well, Cordelia, I'd believe you were trying to be a matchmaker!" Carla had discovered that she, too, had a wry sense of humor; her association with this iconoclastic, zestful woman had allowed it to surface. Cordelia was delighted with it, as she showed by tilting back her head and laughing loudly. "Touché! You've made considerable progress since you came all the way from desolate Texas. Go amuse yourself. I'll go talk to Leonard."

The bespectacled young man was standing in front of the Mary Cassatt painting that Carla had admired upon first entering the gallery. She approached slowly, not wanting to break in on his contemplation. Sensing her presence, he suddenly turned to look at her, and a smile appeared on his lips: "Why, what a nice coincidence, Miss Bouchard."

"You know who I am!" she declared in surprise.

"Why yes. I've seen you often at the Academy—and I was curious enough about you to inquire of your name. I'm not a matriculating student, though. I'm really a dabbler, and I don't want so much to paint as to collect the works of really fine painters. Perhaps I'll run a museum one day—or, barring that, open a gallery in Boston as fine as this one. By the by, my name is Thomas Lockwood."

"A pleasure to meet you, Mr. Lockwood."

"I wish you would call me Thomas. I suppose at the age of twenty-six I should be supporting and upholding proprieties—certainly my parents on Beacon Hill would be appalled at my desire for informality!—but here in Chicago, where it's much more friendly and uninhibited, I think I can dare be a bit unconventional." He smiled at his own speech, then asked, "May I call you Carla?"

The lovely young woman found this opening gambit particularly refreshing. At the Academy, she had already been accosted by several would-be suitors, but infallibly, each of those importunate gentlemen had floridly paid her compliments whose sincerity she doubted and whose motives, unworldly though she was, she nonetheless suspected. "I'd always heard that people from Boston were very stuffy. Isn't there a saying that the Lowells talk only to the Cabots, and the Cabots only to God?'' she ventured boldly, but was unable to suppress the sudden rise of color in her lovely ivory cheeks. The deep tan she so easily acquired back in Texas had faded completely in the past six months, and now her skin had now resumed its natural ivory tinting, giving her beauty a new fragility.

"I suppose that's an accurate saying—knowing both families,'' he said dryly. "I don't think either of them would go so far as to hold that to be the truth, but they probably would not take offense,'' he chuckled. "But enough of the pride of old Boston families. There are much more interesting subjects—for example, what do you think of this Cassatt? I find it so fine, so full of detail, and it says so much. The brush strokes are so free and flowing. I suppose that since she's lived most of her life in France, she has acquired the same discipline and economy of style that characterizes many French artists and composers. Like Fauré—have you ever heard any of his music?''

"No, I must confess I haven't,'' Carla admitted.

"He's only thirty-five, but he's made a name for himself in French musical circles already. He's written a sonata for violin and piano that is simply enchanting. It's so gentle, lovely, and lyrical. You know, I'm rooming with two fellows from my home town who are accomplished musicians. One is Max Radier, a wonderful pianist, and the other is Philip Gardner, a really marvelous violinist. Perhaps some day we could play for you—I myself play an indifferent cello.''

"I'd love that. Are your parents artists or musicians?''

"Hardly! My father doesn't approve of my being here in Chicago dabbling in art—he thinks it's a complete waste of time. But he and Mother have—reluctantly, I assure you—agreed that I might have some time to pursue my interests. Father heads a very conservative, long-established, and very reputable insurance firm. I guess the reason Bostonians are thought to be a bit stuffy is no doubt because after the Revolutionary War and the break with England, they wanted to prove that they could build a solid and lasting nation, so they founded firms notable for stability, durability—and conservatism. Conservatism is, I'd say, the ethos of the genuine, dyed-in-the-wool Bostonian.'' He smiled again, a look of mischief in his gray eyes. "It's probably not a bad thing—for others."

Carla was really enchanted with young Lockwood's whimsical dissertation, and she liked that he did not take himself too seriously. She could read between the lines to understand that he was undoubtedly from an extremely wealthy and distinguished family, but it had given him no snobbery whatsoever. The fact that he was personable, handsome, and did not behave in the usual manner of young men, ogling or ostentatiously complimenting her on her looks, gave him added points in her secret scoring of his potential.

As they had walked to the other end of the gallery to rejoin Cordelia, Thomas Lockwood had asked Carla if he might call upon her and take her out to dinner or, when the weather was pleasant, treat her to a picnic lunch on the shore of Lake Michigan. "Ah—I know!" he had declared before she could give an answer. "Lunch with me tomorrow, won't you? I know the perfect place." He then told her about Kranz's, at State and Washington, with its marble-topped tables, its coffee with rich whipped cream Viennese style, and its elegant pastries and finger sandwiches.

She readily accepted, and the next day she thoroughly enjoyed their rendezvous. At the conclusion of their luncheon, Thomas, in quite proper Bostonian fashion, invited her to a musicale, a soiree at his apartment, which was on the second floor of an elegant house on Prairie Avenue of which Louis Sullivan had been the consulting architect. Again quite properly, he included Cordelia in the invitation, as chaperone, particularly since her munificence as a patroness of the arts he thoroughly applauded.

Cordelia readily consented, and she and Carla were treated to an excellent amateur performance of the Fauré violin sonata that Thomas had spoken of. After this, Thomas took the two women and his roommates to Henrici's, where they dined on roast duck with applesauce, wild rice with almonds browned in butter, sweet yams, and a gigantic German-type apple pancake, which overflowed a large, circular pie tin.

The witty conversation, the discussions of art, poetry, music, and literature enchanted Carla, and when they returned home, Cordelia remarked, "I thoroughly approve of young Mr.

273

Lockwood. He's certainly not one of those hidebound New Englanders. And I daresay he's in love with you."

"Oh, impossible, Cordelia! We've only just met!" Carla protested, blushingly.

"Take it from me, my dear—I know men, and I know what goes on in their heads!" Cordelia beamed. "And I'll tell you this: If you were to decide you wanted him, I wouldn't object. But take caution, Carla. You must decide whether this, the first man whom you've met so far away from your isolated home in Texas, is the one and only for the rest of your life."

"I like your being so candid and frank with me, Cordelia," Carla avowed. She hugged her chaperone. "I've often been told that life is wonderful when one is young, and at a time like this, I believe it's true! But I don't want to make any mistakes, and I'm not going to grasp at the first opportunity for happiness that comes my way, thinking that it's the last one I'll have for the rest of my life."

"Ah!" Cordelia Thornberg smiled knowingly as she drew the young woman closer to her and kissed her on the cheek. "You're using that wonderful brain of yours. Good girl! That's what you must always do, so that, when the time comes, you can decide wisely what your future is to be."

Thirty-Two

Thus it was that Carla Bouchard, on the threshold of womanhood, experienced her very first romance. Though at twenty she was still naive about the ways of men, her instincts guided her to discern that Thomas Lockwood was vastly different from any men she had met in Texas, or, for that matter, even in her classes at the Academy of Fine Arts: He was sensitive and perceptive; he did not take himself too seriously, yet he possessed a quiet dignity, a self-assurance that boded well for the future of any career he would undertake. Best of all—since she had come to believe there was really no difference between the sexes, and that a woman was not inferior to a man—he treated her as a friend and an equal.

He appealed to her with his quick wit and intelligence in matters of art, culture, politics, even history and geography. He was an excellent conversationalist, yet he never monopolized the discussion. He seemed to be eager to hear her opinions; he listened to them, and she knew that he was sincere because he often made comments on some of the points she had raised in their previous meetings. Under this sort of attention, Carla began to blossom emotionally, and she realized that it would be very easy to fall in love with Thomas Lockwood.

Cordelia Thornberg, for her part, was obviously delighted that the young Bostonian had chanced to come to the gallery at the same time that she and her beautiful ward were in attendance for the opening. Nonetheless, she was concerned that Carla was becoming much too involved with this young man too fast.

One morning, just as Carla was leaving for school, she approached the young woman and asked her to sit down for a few moments. Cordelia's face was grave as she looked into Carla's eyes. "I hope you won't take this the wrong way, my dear. You know I want you to be happy, to be fulfilled. But I simply must offer a word of advice: Do not be surprised if you find that your talent and the pursuit of your career ultimately are much more important to you than marriage and a family. Believe me, my dear, marriage is not the only road to fulfillment for a woman—why, if that were true, I should believe that I'd wasted my life—yet I obviously don't feel that at all."

"I know that, Cordelia. But Thomas—well, I have to say he's really a charming person," Carla confided. "I like the way he talks and thinks. And he and his two friends, they're not at all stuffy, even if they are from Boston."

"It's a bad habit to generalize about people or places, dear Carla," Cordelia somewhat sarcastically riposted.

"I like him very much," Carla stubbornly declared.

"Do you like him enough to move to Boston for the rest of your life, if he asked you to marry him, Carla? That's something you will have to ask yourself, if he does propose. And I have a feeling, because he's a very decent young man, he'll do exactly that one of these days."

"I just want to enjoy the summer, and I like being with

him—and I shan't do anything foolish. Don't worry, dear Cordelia,'' Carla laughingly concluded the discussion.

Carla Bouchard and Thomas Lockwood began to find more and more that they had many things in common, and they became almost inseparable. Her classes at the Academy of Fine Arts occupied her three days a week, on the average of some four to five hours a day, but the rest of the time she was free. Her enjoyment of Cordelia Thornberg led her to invite her spirited chaperone on several of her outings with Thomas. To be sure, Carla did this not only out of propriety, but also—perhaps subconsciously—because she was so infatuated with her young admirer that she did not wish to risk any possible physical intimacy. Indeed, perhaps for the first time in her life, the lovely young brunette began to be conscious of the elemental, age-old magnetism between the sexes. Reared in the Catholic faith as she had been, it was inevitable that she regarded sex as the ultimate form of sacred communication between man and woman, and amorous pleasure with the man of her choice as something best confined within the sanctity of conjugal union. As for the possibility of having a temporary affair, Carla told herself that this would be a trap that would be more a deterrent than an inspiration to her emotional and spiritual growth.

It was not that she was prudish—all of the children on Windhaven Range, growing up close to nature, had perforce seen the birthing of foals and calves. They understood, perhaps better than their parents knew, how procreation came about and the end result of it. Yet she was fastidious and sensitive and inwardly not yet certain enough of herself or her talents to believe that she could unerringly judge the right or the wrong of a new relationship. For that reason alone, she knew she would not plunge into anything that seemed to point toward an illicit relationship.

Several times during the month, she, Cordelia, and Thomas—sometimes even Max and Philip, his best friends and roommates—were seen together on one of the famous swan boats in Lincoln Park. The weather was again marvelously pleasant—not too warm, and with blue, serene skies on most days—and Carla was glad to have had the company of others.

Yet despite all this participation with her chaperone, Carla found herself alone during the day with Thomas two or three times a week, going to museums or art galleries, and having lunch with him. They had long, absorbing discussions on the arts, on music, poetry, drama, and literature. She found herself engrossed by the many facets of his mind. More and more, she liked and found flattering his complete lack of condescension, his absolute candor, and his regard for her intellect as equal or even superior to his during their discussions. It was, if nothing more, an intellectual emancipation for Carla, who felt herself coming alive, becoming her own woman, in less than a year away from Windhaven Range.

By the first week of June, when her Academy of Fine Arts classes were finished except for two special summer courses, Carla found even more time to be with Thomas. Shedding more and more of her inhibitions, she went boating alone with him in Lincoln and Jackson parks, enjoying the scenic beauty of Wooded Island in the latter, explored Hyde Park founded by Paul Cornell nearly twenty years before the Great Fire, and visited some of the magnificent new buildings that young architects were putting up all over Chicago. Particularly, they admired the work of Adolph Cudell, a native of Germany, who was responsible for Aldine Square on the South Side, where houses, screened behind a superbly uniform facade, gave the illusion of a Parisian residential quarter. He and his partner also designed a mansion for Cyrus McCormick, the father of the reaper, on Rush Street. It was a sumptuous concoction of columns, garlands, rusticated stonework, as well as crestings, all inspired by the Pavillion Richelieu of the Paris Louvre—truly a home worthy of a prince of industry.

Thomas insisted on taking Carla to the Field, Leiter & Company store on State Street, and she gasped with wonder at the elegant Parisian gowns and the Oriental rugs fabricated by special order in Persia to fit the size and shape of a contemporary house. When she reported her visit to Charles Douglas, he smiled and proudly told her that ten years earlier, Field, Leiter & Company had registered sales of three million dollars; now, it was closer to twenty-four million. "That alone is proof that Chicago is booming," he declared—and it convinced Carla that she had made no mistake in selecting the Windy City as the ideal place for personal, imaginative growth.

One afternoon, when it was not too sultry, she surprised Thomas by suggesting they visit the Union Stock Yards.

Although Thomas had protested this was no place for a lady, Carla simply laughed and said, "Have you forgotten I've lived all but the last few months of my life on a ranch?" Since the Civil War, Morris and Company had been joined by Swift, Armour, and Cudahy—the "Big Four" who shared among themselves almost all of Chicago's meat packing. One of the tour guides at the stockyards told Carla that there were some five million hogs shipped into the stockyards last year, and cattle and sheep were coming in by hugely increasing numbers with each succeeding year. Much of this was because the packers had perfected the canning of meat, and one could buy at a grocer's shop such delicacies as corned beef, roast beef, ox tongue, and potted ham. The British government alone, preparing for its Sudanese expedition against the Mahdi, was to order no fewer than 740,000 pounds of Chicago beef, and a few years later would increase that order to two-and-a-half million pounds.

One early June day was especially memorable for Carla Bouchard. A circus had come to town and set up its arena on a vacant lot two miles from the Union Stock Yards. The big tent, flags and placards and pennants, the shouts of the barkers, the hucksters peddling cotton candy, soft drinks, ice cream, and sandwiches evoked a rare new world of fantasy and illusion.

After wandering around the circus grounds for hours, Thomas bought Carla a small live green lizard on a tiny imitation-gold chain. The huckster flamboyantly described how the chameleon would change color to match the background on which its owner would place it. Since Carla was wearing a blue silk dress, Thomas promptly removed his tie pin and fastened the lizard's chain to her collar. Sure enough, within half an hour, the lizard had taken on a bluish tinge. Carla laughed delightedly, then a thoughtful expression came over her face. "What does it eat?"

"Flies, mainly." Thomas answered. "We had the same circus come to Boston—my gosh, it must have been fifteen years ago—and I remember buying one of these for myself."

"Did it live very long, Thomas?" Carla wanted to know.

"No," he ruefully admitted with a boyish grin that drew a giggle from the young beauty, "which pleased my mother. She was horrified when she found that I had brought it home. She is not exactly fond of things like lizards or snakes. And as for pests—well, any cook or scullery maid who allowed the tiniest gnat or—heaven forbid!—cockroach to wander uninvited into the kitchen was summarily discharged without a reference. At any rate, I never bought another lizard, but I remember the man who sold it to me telling me just what this man did, that it's a nice, docile pet and easy to bring up.''

"Well, I'm delighted with him—her—it, Thomas. But I wonder if there's a symbolic meaning behind it?'' Carla twitted him.

"How do you mean?''

"Well, are you perhaps trying to imply that I'm as changeable in nature as this chameleon is in color?''

"Oh, no! My gracious, I hadn't thought you might attach any metaphorical significance to it. It was just—well, an impulse. You know I think the world of you, Carla Bouchard.'' His voice grew serious, and he drew her to one side away from the entrance to the main tent, where the crowd was surging against the attempts at restraint by the ticket takers. "I feel so comfortable with you. I feel I can say anything I want, and I know you won't take offense. I don't mean anything off-key—I mean the exchange of ideas we have.''

"I do too, Thomas. I mean that very seriously.''

"Well—'' He seemed to heave a sigh of relief. "Listen, Carla, I've something very important to say to you, but not here, not now. Let's just have some cotton candy and see the sights. Perhaps Saturday, if you're willing, I'll take you to dinner at Henrici's and there I can tell you what I've wanted to for quite some time now.'' He looked into her eyes, then grinned. "Perhaps we can persuade Miss Thornberg that, for this one evening, we won't need a chaperone.''

He reached for her hand and squeezed it, and Carla blushed vividly. She could guess what he intended to tell her, and if truth be known, she was not at all averse to hearing it.

And so, that next Saturday, Carla and Thomas went alone to Henrici's. Cordelia had teased her just before Thomas arrived, saying, "I'll bet you a new dress, Carla, that he's going to declare himself tonight and propose. Have you any idea of what you'll say if he does?''

And Carla had laughed and responded, "Well, I like him very much, but there's no sense crossing a bridge until one gets to it, Cordelia.''

"Of course!'' Cordelia took Carla's hands in hers and

stared earnestly into the young woman's eyes. "I just want to reiterate that you must decide whether you want this, your first love, to be your last—and whether you're ready to settle for matrimony and forgo a career. In this day and age, emancipated though women like yourself may be, Carla, I'm not certain that most men are quite ready to give us the freedom to pursue business or artistic careers after marriage. Just remember that. But above all else, decide what would really make you happiest."

"I shan't ever forget how kind you've been to Hugo and me, dear Cordelia," Carla breathed, and there were tears in her eyes as she hugged and kissed her auburn-haired mentor.

Now, as they seated themselves at the discreetly placed table, Carla's mind was awhirl. She had tried all during the day not to be conscious of what she knew was on Thomas's mind, nor of what her own reaction would be. What she had learned through Cordelia's spontaneous coping with day-to-day problems and emergencies as they arose was not to be calculating, nor to plan in advance. She was exhilarated by the awareness that her association with this personable young man had sharpened not only her intellect, but also her perceptiveness.

No matter what took place, she vowed, she would always be grateful to him: A girl's first suitor is never forgotten, and surely Thomas Lockwood had thus far followed all the rules of propriety while at the same time delighting her with his imaginative turn of mind, his wry wit, and his cosmopolitan outlook. She had to agree with Cordelia about not making hasty generalizations, for certainly he did not fit the stereotype of the stuffy Bostonian young man, already aging and set in his ways, who would be hardly distinguishable now from what he was intended to be a generation hence.

The maître d' took Thomas's order for a Rhine wine, returning promptly with a chilled bottle. The maître d' himself poured out the wine and waited solicitously while Thomas sipped it and pronounced it excellent. The man thanked him and then snapped his fingers for their waiter, who was unobtrusive and efficient, almost to a fault. They chose an excellent chicken Marengo for their entree, and Thomas suggested that for dessert she must try their famous German strudel. It was fluffy and light, full of apples, butter, and the most marvelous flavoring. Both ate it eagerly and afterwards had a liqueur with their coffee.

While Carla sipped her coffee, Thomas leaned back and smiled contemplatively at her, and she waited, knowing that perhaps the moment had come.

"Carla, I think by now you know how fond I am of you. Oh, dash it all! It's not my nature to beat around the bush. My dear Carla, it's more than that—I'd like to marry you."

"Oh, Thomas, I'm so flattered by your proposal. The time we've spent together has been the most wonderful of my life. But I'm still young. This is the first time I've been away from home, and I'm so looking forward to my next semester at the Academy—" She hesitated. "Must I give you an answer right now?"

"No," he shook his head with a sad smile, "but I do hope that you'll consider it seriously."

"I shall indeed. You know how very much I like you, but I don't know yet whether marriage is the answer for me, Thomas. Do give me time to think about it. Marriage to us Catholics is for life, you know."

"I know. Incidentally, I don't foresee any difficulty there. My family is High Episcopalian, which is very close to your religion, and my parents are extremely tolerant in such matters. Besides, your background, your beauty, and your ability would overcome any prejudice they could possibly have—and I can assure you in advance that they wouldn't have any."

She put out a hand to touch his wrist and smiled tenderly at him. "You're obviously so fond of your parents. You respect them, and I like that very much. I feel the same way about my father and my mother—although I must confess I feel I've grown apart from them. But I love them for letting me have all this freedom to find out if I really have artistic ability."

"I'd say you do, very definitely. I'm intrigued by your paintings, Carla. And I want to assure you that if you did me the honor of becoming my wife, I'd grant you every freedom to go on with your work; I'd encourage it and be of as much help as I could. I don't think that when a woman marries it means she must put a stop to all her dreams and hopes—quite the contrary."

Again she touched his hand, and a warm glow spread through her. It would be difficult to find a man with better qualities—if, to be sure, she wished to decide her future here and now. It would be very easy to love Thomas Lockwood; he was not demanding, not at all dominating, and yet manly enough to earn her respect and admiration.

"Well, just do please think about it. I'm going back to Boston in about a month because my father wants to confer with me on whether I've made the decision to go into his business or to see if I can't start my own gallery. If I did, Carla, I'd be sure to exhibit your works."

Now she vividly blushed. Praise of her work was the swiftest way to win her undivided attention, for she had worked all these past months to perfect her technique and to translate what she felt about what she saw onto canvas.

"Well then, I don't want to keep you out too late. It's been a wonderful evening, Carla. I do hope you won't say no to me—but you have all the time you wish to make up your mind. I believe, as you do, that marriage is for life—and I'd do my utmost to make you very happy."

"I know that already, Thomas." She smiled at him as he came toward her to pull out her chair. Protectively, he guided her out of the restaurant and hailed a passing hansom cab. It was quite late now, and the city lay still and seemingly at rest. He said no more, not wishing to pressure in any way, till they reached Cordelia Thornberg's house. Then, while the driver waited as Thomas escorted her to the door, the young man suddenly put his hands on her shoulders and kissed her gently on her lips. "There, Carla darling! I'd told myself I wouldn't try that tonight, but you're so lovely, and it was such a pleasant evening, I couldn't resist it."

"There's no need to apologize. I—I wanted you to kiss me, Thomas."

Thomas put his arm around Carla's waist and kissed her again, this time lingeringly. She looked up at him and smiled, blushing faintly. She put her hand against his cheek and murmured, "It's been a wonderful evening, Thomas, truly it has. I promise I'll think very seriously about marrying you. But I must be fair and honest with myself—you wouldn't want me under any other circumstances."

"No, dear Carla. But I do want you. I'd do my very best to make you happy, but you already know that. Shall we meet again next Saturday? For dinner and a concert?"

"Yes, that sounds lovely. Goodnight, dear Thomas."

She watched him as he got back into the carriage, and

waved as it pulled away, the clop-clop-clop of the horse's hooves ringing out crisply and loudly in the still, warm night.

She sighed and went into the house, sitting down heavily on the drawing-room sofa. Hugo came into the room a moment later, an anatomy book under his arm, frowning and looking deeply preoccupied. "I heard the cab drive up, and I needed a break from studying, so I thought I'd say hello to you, Carla. I haven't seen much of you lately—guess you've been out with Tom Lockwood most of the time."

Hugo had met the young Bostonian on several occasions when Thomas had called for Carla, and he had in fact invited Hugo to accompany them on one or two occasions. But Carla's brother had been so deeply engrossed in his studies, so fascinated by the unfolding scope of medicine, that he had refused, saying that he had little time for socializing. Typically, he believed that his sister would ultimately receive a proposal from this very eligible and likable suitor and would accept it. Hugo personally approved of Thomas, though he did not care at all for the insurance business, which he understood Carla to say was the foundation for young Lockwood's social background and wealth.

Of late, Hugo was becoming interested in a young woman who was a fellow student in his anatomy class. He was impressed by her coolness and efficiency as she did her dissecting work for the instructor—who often paused beside her table and made terse but generally approving comments on the way she was proceeding. Her own absorption in medicine had caused Hugo to think favorably of her, and he found himself vying with her for scholastic honors. But he never would have admitted to himself that he was taking anything but a friendly interest in her, nor did he see any parallel between their situation and that of Carla and Thomas.

In reply to Hugo's remark about Thomas, Carla eyed her brother and casually nodded. She was in no mood to discuss the outcome of her evening with Thomas Lockwood. So she said, "Yes, Hugo, I've been out with Thomas, and I've had a lovely time. I always do when I'm with him. You know, it would do you good once in a while to get away from your books and go out with some young woman. Why, during the last week or so, you've not even joined Cordelia and me when we've dined out. Cordelia likes you very much—she thinks you're brilliant, as a matter of fact—but she does wish that you'd learn how to relax a bit.''

Hugo stiffened, flushing hotly at this implied censure. "Look, Carla, there'll be time enough to enjoy evenings out and things like that once I feel I'm close to getting my certificate as a doctor. But that's still a way off, and with so much to have to learn, I have to work hard to keep up with it. There are oral examinations almost daily, besides the papers one has to do—and then there's practice and a kind of clinic every so often. My mind's on my work.''

"I know it is. I'm only saying that since you're doing so well, surely you can afford an evening or so off every other week.''

"Oh, never mind. You don't understand. But you . . . I suppose Tom Lockwood is sweet on you?''

"Isn't that just like a man!'' Carla indignantly declared, stiffening and giving her brother an irritated look. "Besides, that's an awful way of putting it. He likes me, and I like him.''

"I'll bet he asked you to marry him, Sis.''

Since he had come home from the cattle drive last year, Hugo found it easier to communicate and had adopted the colloquial diction of the other ranch hands. At this particular moment, however, Carla—her feelings ruffled by the knowledge that Hugo did not approve of her artistic endeavors— found the term "Sis" particularly condescending and denigrating. She flared, "I don't like that word at all. And it's really none of your business whether he proposes to me or not! Now I'm going to bed, if you don't mind.''

"Of course. I'm sorry I made you angry.'' Instantly, Hugo was contrite, but Carla had already sailed past him and was on her way out of the room.

"I just don't understand women, or what gets into them,'' he mumbled, half to himself. Then, opening his book, he seated himself on the sofa and was quickly occupied in the perusal of a dissertation on the anatomy of the stomach. He had divined that there was a correlation between mental and spiritual malaise and physical distress—there could be no doubt that when someone was upset or under tension or stress, the stomach especially became a kind of weathervane for what was troubling the individual. One of his professors had used the term "psychosomatic," and it had opened up a new horizon of absorbing speculation for Lucien Edmond's gifted son.

When he felt his eyelids drooping—it was nearly midnight—he closed his book with a sigh and went slowly to his room. He hoped that Thomas Lockwood had actually proposed to Carla tonight and that she would accept him. Tom was a fine fellow, and he would make a fine husband for Carla. After all, that was what she needed to make her happy. As for her painting, she could as easily go on daubing as a wife as she could now, in his opinion.

Thirty-Three

Six weeks had passed since Thomas Winters had first been admitted to Andy Haskins's sanatorium, and in those six weeks, a pattern had emerged: a temporary improvement—sometimes for two or three days—followed by a complete relapse that lasted for as long as two weeks. The doctors were completely puzzled and could only come to the conclusion that Mr. Winters was indeed suffering from an incurable emotional ailment.

That afternoon, Jim Castle went to the elderly patient's room to check on his condition. When he softly opened the door, he stopped in surprise. Thomas Winters was sitting on the bed, eating chocolates from a candy box.

"Mr. Winters! Where did you get those? You know you're not supposed to have any chocolate."

The elderly man looked up, startled. "No! Don't take them!" he whispered hoarsely. "Roger says no one is to know!"

Jim talked softly to the agitated man and finally managed to get the candy away from him. He ran down the stairs to the staff lounge, where Drs. Torrance and Salisbury were having their afternoon coffee. "I'm sorry to bother you, Doctors, but I just found Mr. Winters eating these in his room." He thrust the box into Dr. Torrance's hands. "I don't know where they come from. I can't imagine who would have disobeyed your orders like this. I'm sorry sir—"

Calvin Torrance broke in, "It's okay, Jim. I know it

285

wasn't your fault. Still, it is most peculiar. . . ." He paused and scratched his chin. "Did Mr. Winters say where they came from?"

"No, not exactly. That is, he did say something about his son not wanting anyone to know," the amiable attendant responded.

The young doctor looked up sharply, then extracted one of the candies from the box. He broke it open and tasted it; a slightly bitter taste assailed his tongue. He suddenly slapped his thigh and exclaimed, "Of course! I never would have suspected something like this, John."

John Salisbury gave his colleague a curious look and said, "Suspected *what*, Cal?"

"We were on the right track from the beginning, but we allowed ourselves to be detoured by a seeming impossibility. I'm sorry . . . I'm not explaining this very well. Let me start at the beginning."

"Please do," Dr. Salisbury said dryly.

"Your initial diagnosis was that Thomas Winters was under the influence of an opiate, am I correct?"

"Yes, but that opinion didn't hold up to the cold harsh fact that he keeps having relapses without having a source of drugs."

"His son."

"What? That's ridiculous. Surely the young man wouldn't supply his father's opium habit," Dr. Salisbury said incredulously.

"No, I don't think he was exactly *supplying* his father's habit, John. I think the boy has been giving his father opiates completely without the old man's knowledge. In chocolate candies!"

"Why—oh, I see what you mean. My God, how diabolical! He knew his father loves chocolates, so he deliberately planted the suggestion with us that the old man shouldn't have them—and no doubt he told his father that we don't allow patients to have any. So he snuck them in to him and told his father not to let us know or they'd be taken away. The poor old fellow thought his son was merely being loving and thoughtful. Yes, I think you're absolutely right! But how can we prove that it was the young man who doctored the candy?"

"I don't know," Calvin Torrance somberly replied. "But the

sooner we do, the better. I think we should go speak with Andy immediately."

As the three men sat talking in Andy's office, there was a knock on the door. Nurse Bowles stuck her head in and then apologized for intruding.

"No, it's quite all right, Nurse," Andy assured her. "As a matter of fact, we were discussing Mr. Winters, and perhaps you have a suggestion."

"Suggestion? But how could I possibly help?" Nonetheless she took the proffered seat, and sat with her hands neatly folded in her lap.

Andy proceeded to tell her what the doctors had just concluded, and the nurse sat with a stunned look on her face.

"That poor, dear old man! How absolutely shocking! Are you sure?" she finally asked.

"No, we're not sure, Nurse Bowles," Dr. Salisbury said. "That's the unfortunate part. We have no proof."

She suddenly brightened. "Excuse me, gentlemen, for proposing this—you may think it completely absurd—but it happens that I've got a cousin in Bessemer whom I visit a few times a year. Well, I was thinking that maybe if I were to visit her now, I might be able to find out something more definite. You know how some neighbors like to talk. Well, maybe someone will be able to tell me something about young Mr. Winters and his cousin."

"That's a marvelous idea, Nurse Bowles!" Andy responded. "What do you think, doctors?"

They agreed, and Dr. Salisbury made an additional suggestion. "Perhaps you might inquire with the town's pharmacies. In all probability, if Roger Winters is drugging his father, he gets his opiate locally. Since you are, indeed, a qualified nurse, you can simply tell the pharmacist that you are caring for a patient whom you believe may be using drugs, and wish to know exactly what type. As a matter of fact, I shall give you a letter of authorization for this inquiry on hospital letterhead. What do you think, Andy . . . Andy?"

Andy was sitting at his desk fidgeting with a letter opener, turning it round and round in his hands. "What? Oh, I'm sorry. I was just thinking that from the very beginning, I have had some very grave misgivings about this case. And it looks as though my intuition is being proved right."

Roger Winters returned to the sanatorium the following Wednesday. He approached Andy Haskins and very politely said, "Well, sir, when I saw you last week, you indicated that you were about to draw up the commitment papers. I presume my father still hasn't recovered or substantially improved."

To this, Andy Haskins replied, "Mr. Winters, since we're responsible to the state for our license, it means that we're subject to their scrutiny at any time. I am not going to make any decisions that will affect the lives of decent people until I have all the facts. Your father seems periodically to respond to treatment. I have hope that this will gradually extend to longer periods of time, until—eventually—he will make a total recovery."

"Oh, yes, he's very clever, Father is." For an instant, there was a telltale look of hatred on Roger Winters's handsome face, and his upper lip curled. Then, blandly, almost propitiatingly, he went on, "Can you tell me when you and the doctors will be able to give us a definite answer—my cousin Dalton and I?"

"This isn't quite the end of the week yet. Let me have a few more days, Mr. Winters. As soon as I've come to a decision, I'll send you a wire. That will save you the time and trouble of making another visit down here for nothing."

"Well it's hardly for nothing, as you say, Mr. Haskins," Roger Winters said peevishly. "After all, I'm sure Father greatly enjoys my visits."

"I'm sure he does," Andy responded wryly.

"Very well, I shall wait to hear from you. Thank you for your consideration, Mr. Haskins." Roger Winters turned his back and strode out, in an attitude that Andy later described to Jessica as "bristling like a porcupine."

Harriet Bowles came back from Bessemer that Saturday evening and went directly to Andy Haskins's house. The genial director of the sanatorium had taken the day off and was spending it with Jessica and his children, but when he opened the door to her knock, he grinned with pleasure. "I've been hoping you'd return today, Nurse Bowles! Did you find out anything about our patient?"

"I certainly did, Mr. Haskins."

"Do come in. Jessica," he said, turning to his wife, "let's give Nurse Bowles some of your pecan pie. And how about a cup of coffee to go with it, Nurse?" he said to the stout woman, who was removing her cape.

"Oh, really, I really shouldn't—I couldn't eat a thing—and I'm overweight anyhow, Mr. Haskins," Harriet Bowles weakly tried to protest. But soon, seated at the kitchen table, with Jessica at one end and Andy at the other, she was smacking her lips over the pie and complimenting Jessica for her culinary skills.

Andy waited patiently until she had finished her coffee, and then leaned toward her. "Now, tell me what you learned, Nurse Bowles."

"A good deal, Mr. Haskins." Harriet Bowles sat back, her eyes sparkling with satisfaction. "My cousin Rose knows the Winters family pretty well, and she has a lot of neighbors who know them, too. Seems that Roger and his cousin Dalton want to marry their sweethearts. From what I understand, young Roger's father didn't particularly care for the girl his son had picked out for himself and said as much. It caused bad blood between them."

"That's very interesting, Nurse Bowles. Do please go on!" Andy gestured to Jessica to refill the woman's coffee cup.

"Oh, thank you so much, Mrs. Haskins. Well then, where was I—oh, yes: You see, Mrs. Haskins, our patient had a brother, about five years younger—Dalton's father. Well, he died about four years ago, and he left some of his estate to our patient. And, from some of the gossip of the neighbors, it seems that those two young men are not only courting their fiancées, but they're also bringing fancy girls to the house, from time to time."

"I see," Andy said, drumming his fingers on the table. "I'm beginning to think that these two young men would like nothing better than to see Thomas Winters committed so they can inherit all his money."

"It would seem that way. Incidentally, I saw the pharmacist in town, and he says that Roger has regularly purchased opiates from him."

"That seems to be all the evidence we need. You've done a lot of very commendable detective work in a very short time. Thank you again."

"It was my pleasure, Mr. Haskins. He's such a nice old

man, I'd hate to think that he was being railroaded here just because he didn't get along with his son."

"Exactly. I think the thing to do is give Mr. Winters a few more days to recuperate from the last chocolates he ate, and then have a nice long talk with him."

Andy Haskins closeted himself with old Thomas Winters most of the following Wednesday. He was startled at the change that these few extra days had wrought. "I hope we're making it comfortable for you here, Mr. Winters," he began as he sat down beside the elderly patient.

"You are to be complimented, sir, on your courteous, solicitous staff," the old man replied.

"That's kind of you to say, Mr. Winters. May I ask you a direct question?"

"I'll try to answer as best I can, sir."

"Well then—do you take opiates, Mr. Winters?"

The old man looked puzzled, then shook his head. "Absolutely not, sir. Never had any reason to take any. I hear tell that some people take 'em because they're supposed to be pleasant and powerful."

"That's true. Then you're telling me that you've never used opiates at any time?"

"No, that's right, sir," Mr. Winters shook his head and eyed Andy Haskins. "What are you driving at, sir?"

"Nurse Bowles just got back from Bessemer. You see"— Andy noticed that Thomas Winters was turning a startled face to him—"she has a cousin there. I sent her to find out what she could about your son and your nephew."

"Oh?"

"Yes, sir. She confirmed what we suspected. Your son has been buying a good deal of opiates, and since you tell me you don't use it—and yet my doctors confirm that you're almost addicted to it—this could only mean that your own son has been dosing the candies he has been bringing you, for the purpose of making it seem as if your mind is giving way."

"My God—maybe—maybe—" The old man began thinking aloud his painful thoughts. "I begin to understand! To think that my own son would want—sir, bear with me. You see, my wife died when Roger was only ten. After her death, I had a housekeeper to help me bring Roger up. My brother had a son, just the one child, and when he died four years ago, Dalton came to live with us. We have a very large house, you see."

"Please do go on, Mr. Winters," Andy Haskins gently directed.

Thomas Winters dolefully shook his head and sighed. "I may have been too strict with the lads, but I didn't know any other way. At any rate, when Roger met his fiancée, I didn't like the young woman and told him so. And another thing: Although the boys are engaged, they want to keep on amusing themselves with fancy women. Roger and I have had this out many times. He just won't change."

"I rather think he will have to from now on," Andy Haskins grimly declared. "Mr. Winters, your son and your nephew have conspired to get rid of you by putting you here for the rest of your life. That would make it possible for them to take over your house and also your money."

The old man put his right palm down on the side of the bed and forcibly rose, swaying, but maintaining his balance. His face was very pale and contorted with mingled anger and disbelief. "My God, he's the only thing I have left from my happy marriage with Penelope. I planned to give him everything, sir—everything I'd worked for all my life." He sat back on the bed, weary and sick at heart. "I'm confused. If he would inherit anyway, why would he want to get rid of me, to put me in an insane asylum?"

"My guess is that he and your nephew have debts, and their creditors are pressing them for payment. They want to get your money more quickly than by the natural order of things."

"I—I just can't bring myself to believe that Roger would behave that way," the old man stammered.

Andy sat quietly, not knowing how to respond. Finally he said, "This afternoon, I'm going to have my doctors write out a certificate that attests to your sanity."

"Th–thank God. That nurse of yours, Nurse Bowles—I'll be forever in her debt."

"Your son has misrepresented this entire business from the very first day he came here with you, sir. I think it's high time that what he did meets with suitable punishment."

"I—I haven't any desire to punish him, believe me. Maybe I went wrong as a father. Maybe I should have remarried—" The old man suddenly began to weep.

Andy Haskins put his hand on Thomas Winters's shoulder and said softly, "No, sir. You did your best. Whatever injustices your son may feel you've inflicted on him, nothing could warrant the desire to get rid of a decent man by having him cooped up in an insane asylum, where he'd be safely out of the way and could not interfere with anyone else. I want to go ahead and investigate some more. Do you have any objections? If your son is guilty, I myself would like to press charges to make certain that he tasted a year or two in prison, at the very least."

"I—I don't know. All I know is that, right now, I feel more like myself than I have in a long time—since I started objecting to that Virginia Durfeld my son wanted to marry. But oh, my God, to think that he would want to lock me away here. Do I—can I get out, sir?"

"You can. My doctors will assert that in no way are you mentally deranged or unbalanced. I think you're probably saner than most of the world," Andy Haskins whimsically offered.

Andy immediately wired Roger Winters, telling him that a decision had been reached and the young man could come to the institution as soon as possible. When Winters arrived the very next day, Andy confronted him with what they had learned and what the young man's own father had declared.

Winters turned pale, but tried to bluster his way out. "You haven't a shred of proof to that. Besides, if I had put a few drops of the drug in his chocolates, what of it? It helped him sleep; he was always so active and fidgety and—"

"And interfering with you, so that you wouldn't be able to marry the girl you wanted, or have all the money you wanted to squander," Andy broke in.

"You can't prove it!" Roger Winters's features lost their arrogant mien, and he burst into a choleric denunciation, shaking his forefinger in Andy's face. "Now see here, Mr. Haskins, I'll sue you for slander if you go on like this! There's no proof, whatsoever! I don't want any trouble with you."

"Nor I with you. But I'm going to the authorities in Bessemer, bringing our physicians and Nurse Bowles along as witnesses. Your own father would take the stand, if need be, to testify as to how he now feels and what his reactions are, now that he has learned what you tried to do to him.''

"Damn you! I hope he stays here and rots!''

"You're betraying your true colors for the very first time, Mr. Winters. He's not going to stay here. The doctors and I have signed a paper to the effect that he is healthy and sane.''

Now Roger Winters had turned full cycle; he was trembling and his hands shaking as he tried to clasp them. Finally, in a hoarse voice, he answered, "Do you—I mean—is it your intention, then, to lodge charges against me?''

"I've a good mind to, and I think the authorities would agree with me. However, I'll suggest this: You and your fine cousin are to leave the house, go where you will with your fiancés, and try to earn a decent living. Try to be respectable and honorable, for a change. Your father will then go home. He's a generous, kind old man, so *he* may forgive you. But I swear to you, Mr. Winters, that if you persist in your folly of trying to get him committed—even if you attempt to go elsewhere, like the state insane asylum in Birmingham—*I* am prepared to go into court and have a warrant sworn out against you for what you tried to do to a kind, old, decent man.''

Roger Winters took Andy Haskins's advice. He and his cousin Dalton moved out of the house the very next day and, so far as Andy was able to determine, left the state forever. When Thomas Winters was told of this, he burst into tears. After he had recovered, he said hoarsely, "I propose to put a sum of money in the bank, the sum he could have had if he'd only asked me and not tried to do what he did. If ever he comes back and asks my pardon, he shall have it—it's his birthright. But no more than that.''

Thirty-Four

On the first Wednesday in July, just as Carla Bouchard was leaving her figure class, Thomas Lockwood, looking pale and drawn, approached her and said in an unsteady, hoarse voice, "Carla, I've something very important I have to tell you. I know you're free for the afternoon, so may I take you to lunch?''

"Why—why yes, if you'd like, Thomas dear. You look so worried—what's the trouble?'' She was instantly solicitous.

"I've had some very bad news.'' He bit his lip, looked down at the floor, and then added, "I hope it won't sound as if I were trying to make you come to a decision faster than you intended to—but something happened that nobody anticipated. I'll tell you over lunch.''

"All right. I'm sorry you're upset. I've never seen you like this before,'' Carla declared, a note of anxiety in her voice.

They walked quickly to a nearby tearoom, neither of them speaking, till Thomas said, "Let's take a table at the back, shall we? I'm not terribly hungry, though, since I received a telegram this morning—but it can wait. Here comes the waitress to take our order.''

Mystified, Carla glanced nervously at him, then up at the waitress. She studied the menu haphazardly, then said, "If you have chicken salad, I'd like that very much. And some iced tea.''

"Certainly, miss. Sir, what would you like?''

"It—it really doesn't matter. Anything that's ready right now, thank you,'' Thomas distractedly answered, brushing away a straying lock of hair over his forehead. He took off his glasses and nervously cleaned them with his handkerchief, all the while not glancing at Carla, who grew more and more perturbed. Tom was usually so self-assured, so joyous and zestful. Now he seemed morose and distressed. "Please tell me what's wrong, Thomas,'' she softly pleaded.

He waited until the waitress had brought their food, and then as she tentatively forked a mouthful of chicken salad, he said softly, "I had a telegram early this morning from my mother. My father—he's dying. . . . He's had a stroke, and the doctors say that if he lives more than a few days, it will be a miracle. I have to return home at once. I only hope I can get there in time.''

"How dreadful for you! I'm so terribly sorry, truly I am, dear Thomas!'' Carla exclaimed, putting down her fork and staring at him with the utmost compassion.

"You see, I never told you that my father and I had a long talk about my coming here. He wanted me to finish my postgraduate work in Boston, and he really didn't approve of my interest in art. He thought it was simply the pursuit of a hobby, which would lead to very little, and that there were enough cultural activities in New England to keep me there. But our agreement was that, in the event he were to die, I would give up my artistic pursuits and take over his insurance firm—but I never thought—I didn't dream—He's only fifty-four.''

"How awful you must feel—I wish I could do something—"

"You can, Carla." He uttered a long sigh, leaned forward, and stared intently at her. "If my father dies, and it seems certain that he will—and I pray God he'll be spared any pain and long-drawn suffering—there will of course be a proper period of mourning. But after that, I want—I'd be the happiest man in the world, Carla, if you would join me in Boston as my wife. As I told you, please don't think that I'm trying to force anything on your part by giving you this news. God knows, I never dreamed it would happen—he was so very young and active.''

There was such torment and anguish in Thomas's voice that Carla felt tears sting her eyes. "I—I planned to tell you at the end of the week—before you had this news. I have been thinking about it, Thomas, but I don't know yet that it's the right thing for me. You see, I'm still trying to—to find myself. I love my work at the Academy. I'm painting better than I ever did before, and it's only the beginning. And besides, I'm only twenty, Thomas. . . .''

"I know, my dear, but many women are already married and having families at your age. I'm sorry—I didn't mean to allude to that. But I told you before that whatever you wanted to do, I'd stand by you. Can't you give me hope?''

"I want to think about it very carefully. I know it would be easy for me to say yes. And I *do* like you, very much indeed, Thomas dear. You know that. But whether that's enough to make a life together, I don't know. Since you've said that you don't want to influence me to make a quick decision just because of what has happened, I think you should go back as quickly as you can, to be there at your father's bedside. But I'll write you; I'll be thinking it over, and I'll be examining myself just as carefully as I can. I want you to be happy—but it's very important that I be happy, too. And I'm not sure that marriage would fulfill both of us the way both of us want—

I'm being as honest as I can be. If I didn't care for you as much as I do, I wouldn't say that."

"I—I understand. You're a very fine, sensitive, and beautiful woman. It's no wonder I'm in love with you. Well, now—" He gobbled part of his sandwich, took a long swig of the coffee, then rose, took out his wallet, and laid down the money. "I'll take your advice. If I hurry, I can get the train to Boston that leaves at two this afternoon. Here, I'll write down my address for you. And I'll be waiting for your letter."

"I promise I'll send it to you—but it may not be immediately. I don't want to rush, Thomas. You wouldn't want me to. If we marry—if any two people marry—we should be sure of each other, without any doubts."

"Of course. That's the way I'd want it."

"I'll pray for your father. It's been wonderful knowing you, Thomas. And no matter what happens between us, I'd like us to be friends as long as we're alive."

"That's fair, that's honest. I—oh, Carla!" He suddenly bent, cupped her face in his hands, and kissed her on the mouth. Then, with a doleful expression, he left the lunchroom.

When Carla returned home, Cordelia Thornberg was in the garden. Troubled by her conflicting emotions for Thomas Lockwood, the young woman went out to join her hostess, who sat in the gazebo glancing through a fashion magazine that had just arrived from New York.

"Sit down, dear. I brought a pitcher of lemonade out here and two glasses, knowing you'd be panting for something cool," Cordelia invited. "Help yourself. Oh, my, what a long face! What's wrong, dear? I didn't mean to be quite so flippant—"

"It's—it's Thomas, Cordelia. He just told me that his father's dying. He's left for Boston. And he wants me to write him my decision about his proposal of marriage."

Cordelia didn't respond immediately, but thoughtfully sipped her lemonade, staring up at the cloudless blue sky. Presently, she said, "You've thought about it a good deal, haven't you, dear?"

"All the time. I know it would be so easy to say yes now, to make up for the sorrow he's going through. I know how much he loves his father. Thomas is such a fine man; I think very highly of him.''

"That's awfully intellectual. What do you *feel*—do you love him?''

"I—think I could. I'm not sure that I do yet—not enough to decide to move to Boston and be his wife for the rest of my life, Cordelia.'' Carla gave her a long, searching look.

But Cordelia did not intend to influence her young protégée one way or another. "You're angling for my advice, but I won't give it to you. You see, if you follow someone else's advice, at the end of your life there will always be times when you will deeply regret having listened. If the decision isn't yours, you'll always wonder, 'What if I had done things a different way?' No, Carla, this is your crisis, and you must emerge from it through your own resources. That's the only way you can mature and have character enough to face all the adversities of the future.''

Carla uttered a sigh, then poured herself a glass of lemonade and began to sip it, avoiding the stealthy, yet intent look the auburn-haired woman gave her. Presently, she said, "I know you're right. I think I'll go to my room and try to work it out, Cordelia.''

"You will. If you like, Carla, I'll have Mrs. Hennepin bring dinner to your room, so that you can think without any distractions. I've a feeling you'd like to be alone.''

Mrs. Ermaline Hennepin was a new cook, a German woman in her early fifties whose children were married and who enjoyed doing part-time domestic work for congenial people, so that she might be surrounded by those whom she admired. Cordelia had met her at the house of one of her friends and engaged the woman in conversation. Learning of her interest in having different jobs, she promptly engaged her for two evenings a week during this time when Carla and Hugo Bouchard were her guests.

"Thank you, Cordelia—you always seem to know exactly what my mood is. I'm so glad I'm living with you!'' Carla burst out. Then, not trusting herself to say more, her eyes already wet with tears, she abruptly left the gazebo and went to her room.

She lay on the bed, staring up at the ceiling, her hands under her head. Then, closing her eyes, she surrendered herself to introspective thought. She reviewed the pleasant months she had spent with Thomas Lockwood, trying to remember even his most casual remarks, his attitudes, his opinions. She wanted to weigh every possible factor to make certain that her decision was not tempered by loneliness or the emotion of a first romance. Of *his* feelings, she had not the slightest doubt; but it was most important that she determine her own.

Mrs. Hennepin knocked twice before Carla, startled from her reverie, rose and opened the door. Slightly disoriented at suddenly being thrust back into reality, she stammered a few unintelligible words until at last she became aware that the good-natured German woman was standing there with her dinner tray. "Oh, I forgot—thank you so much, Mrs. Hennepin. Here, I'll take it." She looked down at the plate and saw a rich beef stew, thick with vegetables and potatoes. "Mmm, it smells and looks just wonderful—you're going to make me fat! Mrs. Hennepin. Thank you again. Would you mind closing the door? And please tell Miss Thornberg that it was very kind of her to send me supper."

She found that she was ravenously hungry, and this was just the interruption she needed to stave off further self-recriminations, ruminating over anguished thoughts of whether refusing Thomas might not be a bitter blow in the midst of his grief for his father.

After a few minutes of concentrating on nothing more than the food in front of her, Carla realized that it was kindest to let him know at once that there would be no hope for the eventuality of which he dreamed—for now she knew that she would not marry him.

She felt greatly eased by having come to this decision, but she told herself that she would finish her dinner, rest a little, and then write him.

At last she sat herself down at her desk and began a long, tenderly expressed, and sincere letter in which she sought as best she could—choosing her words with the utmost care—to convince Thomas that marriage would be a mistake for both of them:

Dear Thomas:

I have said prayers for your father's life, and I hope they will be answered. I know how much you love him, and I am sure that you have always been a great comfort to him and to your mother. You have a kindness and a goodness to your nature, Thomas, that would make any woman proud to be your wife. I shall never forget the flattering compliment you paid me by asking me to marry you.

I have thought about your proposal constantly, ever since you first asked me, and I'm afraid that I must tell you no—as kindly and as considerately as I can, so as not to hurt you, but the answer must still be no.

I know that your family stands high in Boston society, and things would be expected of me by outsiders, by strangers, by your acquaintances and friends, by your parents' friends. But I'm simply not the Boston matron type, dear Thomas, and if I could not live up to others' expectations, I would disappoint *you*—and that would hurt you because you believed in me. That is one of the reasons.

But there's another thing, perhaps more far-reaching. I know that you said several times to me that, if I became your wife, you would not stand in the way of my continuing my interest in art. But it is more than interest—I feel drawn to it, almost compelled to it. I *have* to paint, Thomas, and I have to improve. I must devote all my energies and thoughts to it.

If I can create a painting that pleases others, and from which viewers will draw inspiration and pleasure, then I will have contributed something to this world. I know that being a wife and mother is a glorious profession for any woman, and it may be that, one day, I too shall be content with that role in life. But for the foreseeable future, I cannot agree to change my life so drastically so as to conform with what would be expected of me—not only by you, but by all the others who depend on you and who are friends with you, Thomas.

Please try to understand. You surely deserve a good wife, because you are a fine, decent man. Our minds touched, and you gave me inspiration and friendship

299

that I shall always value and treasure. Forgive me if I have hurt you in any way. But I know that you would not be content with a wife who could not devote her life entirely to you and your needs. Until I find what my own capabilities are, Thomas, I'm not even sure that I can fulfill my own.

God bless and keep you and bring you the happiness you so richly deserve. I want to sign myself your friend, for as long as you want me as your friend.

Carla Bouchard

She read the letter over several times and was satisfied with it. Folding it neatly, she put it into an envelope, sealed it, and laid it on the corner of the desk.

Then, exhaling a sigh of weariness mingled with relief, she opened her bedroom door and went downstairs.

Cordelia was in the living room, chatting with Hugo. Carla caught sight of them and turned to go back to her room, but Cordelia hailed her. "Carla dear, come join us. Hugo and I were just chatting about the idea of a trip up to the Wisconsin Dells next week. He'll have a break in his studies then."

"I—I think I'd like that. Cordelia—"

"Yes, dear?"

"I've written the letter. I've told him no."

Hugo rose and turned to his sister, his face bewildered, his eyes wide and questioning. "You mean you told Tom Lockwood you aren't going to marry him? But why, Carla? If ever I saw two people who got along well together and who had so much in common, it was the two of you. Why, his family's socially prominent and well thought of in a city of great historical tradition and culture—you'd have a life of happiness, ease, and luxury."

"Marriage just isn't important to me now, Hugo. You just don't understand that, do you?"

"No, I don't! I'm going to be a doctor so I can cure the sick, help people achieve happiness in life by having good health to start with. But you—you're a woman—beautiful and young and talented, true, but you're hardly embarking on all-consuming career like medicine. Your place is to make a man happy. And you could make Tom Lockwood very happy."

"And what about *my* happiness?" Carla hissed.

"What about it? Wouldn't you be happy? I thought you loved him."

"I do, in a way, yes, Hugo. But not enough to say that I'll be content just to be his wife for the rest of my life—live in Boston and be a matron taking part in society functions—No, Hugo. Even though he said he'd want me to go on with my painting, that wouldn't be the life I think I'm intended for."

"I never heard such nonsense in all my life!"

"Good for you, Carla!" Cordelia exclaimed.

Hugo whirled and turned on her. "Cordelia, this is really between Carla and myself. I think that Mother and Father would be outraged at such *outré* behavior. A man is expected to have a career, but a woman's career is ultimately and ideally wifehood and motherhood."

"That's so much twaddle!" Carla stormily countered. "You're just like most men—selfish and self-centered. You think that because you do a woman a favor and marry her and give her children, that's her whole life!"

Again Hugo turned to Cordelia. "I hope you didn't have anything to do with her decision, Cordelia, because I think she's made a great mistake."

"I don't think so, Hugo," Cordelia quietly responded, "but that's beside the point. The main thing is, it's her life, and I swear to you that I didn't influence her decision in the least."

"No, she didn't, Hugo," again Carla hotly broke in. "Ever since Thomas first asked me to marry him, I've thought and thought about it. When I learned that his father is dying, I felt terribly sorry for him. But if I had let that influence me, sway me into marrying him, and then discovered that I'm made a mistake, it would have been horrid for both of us. I must take the time to pursue my career, Hugo. I suppose you can't understand that—"

"No, frankly, I can't."

"Well then, I'm not going to try to convert you. I'll say only that if Mother, Father, and you don't accept and understand me, so be it! It hurts me that you don't understand that I must follow my feelings. But I fully intend to follow them, no matter what you or anybody else may tell me. Haven't you read Shakespeare's *Hamlet*, Hugo?"

"Of course, I have. What about it?" he said sulkily.

"As Polonius said to his son Laertes, 'To thine own self be

true; thou canst not then be false to any man.' And I'm going to do just that! And now, I'll thank you to stop meddling and just let me live my life the way I see fit." She stormed out of the room and went back upstairs.

Hugo looked over at Cordelia. "I won't say another word on the subject. I just think she's making a terrible mistake, that's all. And I'll say good night to you, Cordelia."

"I'm sorry you feel that way, Hugo," Cordelia said consolingly. "But perhaps next week, when all three of us go on that trip, we can go back to the nice, easygoing relationship we've enjoyed."

Hugo turned at the door. "On second thought, Cordelia, I think I'll use the week to study some of the notes that I've taken during recent lectures. There'll be time enough for a vacation after I've got my certificate from Rush."

He gave Cordelia a curt nod and then walked out of the living room.

Thirty-Five

Carla Bouchard was too proud to seek reconciliation with Hugo, for she felt that he must make the first overture. He had deeply wounded her by seeming indifferent to her serious artistic pursuit. This latest reaction of his seemed like the last straw, coming so hot on the heels of his poor reaction to her best work. The painting she had so proudly shown him, in which she had sought to fuse Monet's technique with her own touches of romantic expressionism, appeared to her to be the finest and most imaginative work she had ever achieved. Hugo, though, had received it so blandly and disparagingly that she had been crushed—and if she had candidly excoriated him for his ignorance of art, it would have been too much like the act of an unhappy child to whom one says no for the first time.

But his smug, *bourgeois* attitude, as she called it—copying Cordelia, who frequently used that expression to denote conventionality and sanctimonious behavior—riled her. She felt that her brother's own concentration on his medical career had made him impervious to all else. They had been such good companions in Texas—living the outdoor life, yet sharing thoughts and cultural ideas in a friendship that had nothing of sibling rivalry about it. Here in Chicago, however, things had vastly changed: Hugo Bouchard had become a virtual stranger to his own sister.

For his part, Hugo realized that he had deeply offended his sister, but he also was too proud to acknowledge his error. He believed that in due time, her displeasure with him would pass, and they would fall readily enough—without any calculation—back into the familiar pattern of friendship they had always enjoyed.

That was how things stood toward the end of July, as the Chicago weather grew humid and threatening, with occasional thunderstorms peppering the late afternoon skies. Fortunately, Lake Michigan, with its favorable wind currents, tempered this heat with a pleasant early evening coolness that made the otherwise oppressive weather bearable. Carla had a good deal of time on her hands, now that her relationship with Thomas Lockwood was over and he was back in Boston for good. To offset this loss, Carla sought consolation in Cordelia Thornberg's always inspiring and refreshing company.

For her part, Cordelia was only too happy to deepen the friendship between herself and the sensitive young brunette. Perhaps she saw herself in Carla at that age—capable of being hurt, yet with courage to meet and overcome adversity, regulating herself by what she learned from experiences and thereby developing a tougher fiber, a more resilient character, which would certainly stand her in good stead in the future. Cordelia remembered how she had been at first crushed by her fiancé's death, yet she had rebounded, and she never felt that there was a void in her life. She had an incomparable enthusiasm for living, an ability to take pleasure from the simplest things, yet seeking always the most imaginative and unusual.

She spoke briefly of this about a day after Carla had received Thomas's note announcing the death of his father and telling her that he would always remember her with the greatest affection, and that he wished her all the happiness she sought. He had added a postscript to that letter, mentioning that he was going to outdoor band concerts with a young woman, the daughter of his mother's closest friend, who had just graduated from Wellesley College. Carla was actually relieved to get this news, feeling that what sorrow he necessarily felt at her rejection of him could easily be assuaged now that he was back home with important responsibilities thrust upon his shoulders and with an attentive, intelligent young woman ready to be his companion.

Yet she had kept the chameleon he had bought her at the circus, and even Mrs. Hennepin good-naturedly helped her catch flies for the tiny green lizard. As she stroked its head with the tip of her little finger, she was sure it knew her and was fond of her. It represented a link to the first romance of her life, and she was determined to keep it as long as possible.

Cordelia had said to Carla, with tacit good sense, "It's all for the best, my dear—and I'm very proud of the way that you stood on your own two feet and made your own decision. This way, no matter what happens to you in later life, you can never reproach yourself for having denied your impulse toward creative work. Even if your talent never comes to fruition, at least you have taken the most important step of all—toward self-esteem, self-discipline, and dedication. For you, marriage can always come later—if at all. Falling very deeply in love *after* you have matured will enable you to balance your life with what your husband-to-be will offer. That's the only way it should be for a person of your background and acumen."

This praise had emboldened Carla to devote even more time to her painting and to resolve to take additional classes in the fall semester at the Chicago Academy of Fine Arts. She knew herself to be at the crossroads now, with talent that was recognizable and applauded by her instructors, yet not fully developed enough so that she could express the uniqueness of her own style, of communicating a message or feeling in her paintings. But she knew that one day she would be able to tell herself that she had either succeeded or fallen short of her own high standards. This was why she could understand Cordelia Thornberg all the better and was drawn even more closely to her handsome hostess.

A week after Carla had received the letter from Thomas Lockwood, Cordelia invited her talented guest to a society ball at the sumptuous brownstone mansion of Cyrus Hall McCormick, at 675 Rush Street. Carla was awed when she entered the foyer of this garishly furnished palacelike house, and still more so when she and Cordelia went into the munificently furnished dining room. Cordelia whispered to her, "This room, like all the interiors of the house, is the work of a very fashionable New York decorating firm, L. Marcott and Company." There were tapestries and oils on the walls, one of the most magnificent teakwood sideboards Carla had ever seen in all her life, lamps and bric-a-brac, statuettes, and exotic, expensive clocks on marble pedestals. The upholstered furniture, the scrollwork of the chairs and the tables were the fabrication of a world-renowned furniture maker.

When they had first arrived, Nettie Fowler McCormick, a handsome, regal woman of forty-five, wearing a green, brocaded evening gown, a diamond tiara, and a pearl necklace, approached Cordelia and effervescently greeted her. "Dear Cordy! And I see you've your protégée in tow."

"I have, Nettie dear. How kind of you to invite us both—Carla, this is Mrs. Cyrus McCormick. Mr. McCormick, as you probably know, is one of the great leaders of industry in our country. The machinery his company manufactures helps farmers to produce our daily bread and all the fruits and vegetables we enjoy on our tables."

"That's why Cyrus is such a glutton—for work," his sprightly wife declared with a smile at her small joke. Then, taking Carla's hand between both of hers, she murmured, "You're very lovely, my dear! And you're lucky to have Cordy as your hostess and mentor. She's told me something about you already, you know—that you paint, for one thing, and that you're considered quite talented. Also, that you belong to that new Impressionist school."

"Oh, Mrs. McCormick, I'm just a beginner, a rank amateur," Carla began to protest, prettily blushing.

"There's no need for modesty. Cordy has already given me a full dossier on you—both on your ability and your loveliness—and I should think that before much longer, you'll have all the eligible young swains of this city at your feet, collectively or metaphorically or any other way you want to put it. I look forward to chatting with you over dinner. It will be served in about fifteen minutes." Touching Carla's shoulder with her exquisite ivory fan, Nettie McCormick passed on to other guests, whom she greeted effusively.

Carla stood open mouthed in virtual awe as she looked around the room. "I'll admit it's a very impressive room and a stunning house, and there's a tremendous fortune behind it all, Carla,'' Cordelia whispered, ''but, if you ask me, it's somewhat overdone. Not for anything in the world would I hurt dear Nettie's feelings, though. I suppose, if you're a captain of industry, like Armour or Gustavus Swift or Cyrus McCormick or Potter Palmer, you like to be ostentatious and show off what you've done, so that the rest of us mere mortals can stare in disbelief.'' She grinned a mischievous smile, then declared, ''Now, I would never recommend being *too* blasé, but you must learn to take everything in stride, Carla. You're still enchantingly naive, but I detect signs of a growing sophistication. If you stay long enough with me, eventually nothing will faze you, but at the same time, I promise you you'll never lose your enthusiasm for each new day and what it will bring. And that's the best of all possible worlds. Oh, here comes Mr. Leiter—of Field, Leiter & Company you know.'' Raising her voice, she moved forward, and the middle-aged State Street merchant beamed at her, bowed, and kissed her hand. Carla was again flustered at the recognition this woman received from the very elite of Chicago's society.

When she sat down to dinner beside her chaperone, she was again spellbound by the rich chinaware, the silverware, the elegantly monogrammed fine lace tablecloth and napkins. The wine goblets, specially made for Cyrus McCormick in Belgium, bore his crest—the same monogram that appeared on his letterheads—signifying his renowed reaper that bundled sheaves of harvested wheat and prepared them for the grainery.

The menu was a full twelve courses, with wines to complement each course. For dessert, there was an ice cream *bombe* shaped in the form of a model of his first reaper. The guests applauded him, and McCormick grinned and bobbed his head, waving his hand deprecatingly as if to indicate that this was a mere bagatelle.

At the conclusion of the meal, there was dancing in the ballroom, and Carla thought to herself that this evening was as thrilling and colorful as one out of an Arabian Nights' fairy tale. When at last it came to an end, Nettie McCormick herself came up to Carla to bid her farewell. Looking at Cordelia and smiling, she effusively requested, ''I should like this charming girl to loan me one of her paintings. It would be a privilege for me to be able to view it privately—and I daresay if I like it, I'll purchase it outright. What with all the friends I have who will see it, you might consider it a showing in a most exclusive gallery!''

"But you've never even seen my work," Carla protested, scarcely able to believe her ears.

"Cordy never exaggerates," the dowager declared. "If she says you're talented—quite simply, you're talented. And, confidentially, it would give my reputation as a trend setter quite a boost to discover and promote an unknown artist before anyone else!''

Carla's dreams that night were filled with the fantasies of her appearing at elegant social balls, feted by her hosts and hostesses, and sought out by the most eligible young men of the city, who quarreled among themselves for the privilege of signing her dance card.

The next afternoon, there was a knock at the door, and opening it, she found a handsome young man wearing a McCormick worker's uniform. He tipped his cap to her and handed her an envelope with Nettie McCormick's name embossed on it. "I'm to wait and bring back a painting, Miss Bouchard," he smiled congenially.

Carla was speechless for a moment, and then recovered herself long enough to open the envelope and to find a note from the wealthy dowager simply saying, "I hope you won't renege, my dear!''

"But—but—" she stammered ineffectually. "I haven't even framed it, and—''

"That's quite all right, Miss Bouchard," the young man intervened. "I'm to take the picture to a shop that makes the finest frames in Chicago." He smiled and told her, "Please don't hurry—it's much too warm to rush around.''

Carla blushed, for the young messenger, in his early twenties, was eyeing her in a highly complimentary, though certainly not offensive, fashion.

As she hurried down the hallway to her bedroom for the painting, she passed Cordelia's door, and saw her reclining on a chaise longue, quite at her ease, reading a risqué French novel by Emile Zola, *L'Assomoir*. "That must be Nettie's messenger." Cordelia winked at her. "I told you you're going to enter the finest society of Chicago. This is just the beginning!''

"I just can't believe it, Cordelia! Imagine, my work hanging in Mrs. McCormick's palatial house! Oh, my goodness! Her messenger's going to take it to a shop to frame it, I just can't believe it all!" Caral babbled.

"It's such great fun to see you so happy. Sophisticated woman of the world that I intend to make you, you must always retain your charming reactions, like a little girl. You're not at all spoiled or pretentious, and that's what I like about you."

It was like a dream for Carla Bouchard, and she felt all the excitement of a creative artist who, for the first time, experiences someone else's appreciation of his or her effort.

The young messenger thanked her, then put a light tarpaulin over the painting and went back to his carriage. Carla returned to Cordelia and excitedly exclaimed, "I still can't believe it, Cordelia! Something of my own is going to be hung in that wonderful house!"

A week later, the same messenger returned to the Thornberg home. Asking to see Carla, he presented the astonished young woman with a check for one hundred and fifty dollars. The accompanying note from Nettie McCormick said that the dowager had decided to purchase the painting, and hoped that the amount of the check was satisfactory.

"This is only the beginning for you, my dear," Cordelia assured her protégée. "One of these days, you'll go to Paris, where you can meet your famous Impressionists—and I'll wager they'll appreciate your talent, too, just as Nettie McCormick does. Well, I believe we should celebrate! This evening I'm going to take you to the Palmer House for a fine dinner. Besides, I don't feel like cooking in this warm weather, since Mrs. Hennepin is on vacation this week," she confessed dryly. "Let's go out to the gazebo for now and just relax."

Thirty-Six

Two days after her meeting with Jeb Cornish at the Comique in Dodge City, Rhea Penrock had left on the Santa Fe train for Pueblo, Colorado. Before boarding the coach, she had shopped at the variety store in town and bought herself a sturdy suitcase that was spacious enough to contain at least a week's change of clothing and several simple dresses. Aside from the costumes she had worn in the Dodge City dance halls, she had not put on women's clothes in years. This preference stemmed from her belief that dresses made a woman more vulnerable—both physically and psychologically—and from the way she was treated in the Natchez bordello and the dance halls.

Gabe Penrock had been the only man who had known how to reach the core of her womanhood. Now that he was dead, she found it all the more difficult to dress—as she saw it—like a clinging, helpless female. Grimly determined to avenge him, she had thought out her plan for vengeance with the utmost care and with a practical cynicism that would have amazed even Jeb Cornish himself.

She knew nothing about Ramón Hernandez and Lucien Edmond Bouchard, except what Cornish and her young husband had told her: that the two men had come from a Texas cattle ranch; that several times they had interfered with Cornish's schemes; that many of Cornish's men had been killed in the attempts to bushwhack the herd and rob the Cañon City train; and that the first run-in the Indian agent had had with the "goddamned greaser," as he always referred to Ramón, was when he had tried to fleece him out of money and failed.

She felt that Ramón Hernandez was morally responsible for the death of her husband, even though he had not actually pulled the trigger of the gun that killed him. She did not know who actually had done the killing—and she did not care. In her eyes, Gabe's death wouldn't have happened if it hadn't been for Ramón. The plan she had concocted was to return to Leadville, to have Ramón Hernandez pointed out to her, and to try to find some kind of job with his outfit—perhaps as servant or housekeeper—or a cook. She knew that the two Texans operating the silver mine had built a house a few miles outside of Leadville, so as to be nearby and supervise their operation. It followed, from her reasoning, that they could use a cook, and that a friendly, attractive—and helpless—female would certainly appeal to these men, so far from home.

Once she succeeded in getting herself hired, she would learn all she could about Ramón and Lucien Edmond. Then she would decide upon her mode of revenge—narrow it, refine it, so that the man responsible for Gabe's death would wish that he were dead a thousand times over before that mercy was granted to him.

All of this reasoning was exactly why she had not told Jeb Cornish of the plan. She had been afraid that Cornish would order some of his men to follow her, to help her, to force her to be a foil, rather than the sole instigator of that revenge—and she did not want anyone else taking matters into his own hands and killing Ramón before he would suffer for the way he had robbed her of the only man she had ever cared for.

When Rhea Penrock arrived in Leadville in the middle of June, she was wearing a long-sleeved blue muslin dress and a sturdy cape to protect her from the cool mountain air. She had her hair coiffed into a very prim, thick bun at the back of her neck, and she wore a bonnet whose strings were tied under her determined chin. Thus, in every way she looked the part she intended to play—a girl traduced by her lover, who found herself alone, destitute, and homeless in a rough mining town, and was willing to do anything honest to earn her daily bread.

Staying in character, she had demurely approached two deputy sheriffs and inquired where a decent woman might stay. They directed her to Ma Donnelly's boardinghouse two blocks southeast of Main Street, and after thanking them politely, she made her way to these lodgings.

Rhea had brought along five hundred dollars to stake her on this vengeance quest, and she had carefully sewn some of the larger bills into hidden pockets inside her dresses. She was uncomfortable in all this feminine frippery, but she knew how necessary it was. To wear the riding breeches and shirts of a cowhand, the garb she enjoyed most of all—and in which Gabe had liked her best—would stamp her too readily as an eccentric. From what little Jeb Cornish had been able to tell her about Ramón and Lucien Edmond, she gathered that they were both the Bible-spouting kind, do-gooders, and that sort always looked down its nose at women who didn't fit the usual mold. Also, since her language was at times coarse and mannish in its directness, she had, all during the train journey to Pueblo, silently practiced little speeches that she would make in her attempt to find work with the Bouchard outfit. She did this diligently, persisting until she was sure they would sound natural and convincing. Even so, the prospect of playing so dangerous a game as a spy in the enemy camp— for such it really was—titillated her and presented a challenge that she welcomed, because it would demand the most of her wits and cunning. She had no doubts as to her success: She had only to remember how she had written finis to her mother's murderer.

It was easy to learn where the Bouchard mine was located, for the news had spread all over Leadville that two strangers from Texas and an old sourdough prospector had come out of nowhere, found a mine in a cave, and struck it rich. There was grudging admiration for these newcomers to Leadville: The word had spread throughout town that the two Texas partners, one of them Mexican, had cut the daily working hours to nine and were now paying wages of $5.25 a day. Rhea listened carefully to all this gossip, glad for the opportunity to learn more about her enemies before actually confronting them. Also, she devoted much thought to the choice of a name, telling herself that, once she assumed it, she must answer quickly to it, lest suspicion be aroused. Although it was unlikely that anyone connected with the Windhaven enterprise would know the name "Rhea" in connection with Gabe or any other of Cornish's men, she felt it wise not to take any chances. For her last name, she would simply resume her maiden name—Galloway. Finally, she concocted a credible background for herself that would explain why she should have come to Leadville in the first place.

Mid morning the following day, she packed her suitcase, and preparing to set her plan in motion, she left the boardinghouse. A jobless miner who owned a small buckboard and an aging mare was easily persuaded to drive her out to within half a mile of the Bouchard operation. Quitting the buggy, she hauled down her suitcase and walked slowly toward the mine. She carefully observed the smelter, the refining plant, and the house where all of the Windhaven men had their living quarters.

. The previous night, in the silence of her cramped little room at the boardinghouse, she had carefully rehearsed again what she was going to say and how she was going to act. It mustn't be too glib, too pat. She knew that if she were asked how she had come to hear of the Bouchard mine, she could explain that easily enough: Everyone in town was talking about the mine and how someone had almost blown it up. Apparently, from all that she had heard, there was a friendlier feeling toward the newcomers now than at the time of the general strike.

Santiago Dornado came out the door of the house just as Rhea was passing. He took off his sombrero and amicably called to her, *"Holá, señorita, qué pasa?"*

"Is this the Bouchard mine, mister?" she asked in her softest voice. She knew how her dominant, aggressive tone had infuriated Jeb Cornish, thwarted him, and she sensed that it might well antagonize others—or again, be misinterpreted as a direct solicitation for her favors. It was vital that no one who met her at this mine should feel for a moment that she had ever been a girl who had worked in a Natchez cathouse, and whose mother had come from there.

"Sí, está es, señorita," Santiago replied with a smile. "But surely you have not come here to apply for work?"

"But I have, mister. You see, I'm broke. I haven't got any money left."

"¡Pobrecita!" Santiago sympathetically responded. "I do not know that we need any help here, señorita, but I will gladly ask on your behalf of Señor Hernandez, who is one of the *patrones.*"

"That's very nice of you, mister."

Santiago grinned, replacing his sombrero with a flourish. *"Me llamo* Santiago Dornado, and I am at your service, lovely señorita."

"That's very sweet of you, Mr. Dorando. I was hoping I could get a job here maybe as a cook. I really have to earn some money to stay alive. You see, I had a friend, and he

312

told me to come here and we were going to be married—but when I got here, he'd taken up with another girl—well, that's how it is."

"I'm very sorry to hear that. He must be a fool to say no to such a *mujer linda*," the vaquero gallantly declared. "I will go see Señor Hernandez. I'm sure he will talk to you."

Rhea nodded her head and gave the vaquero a grateful smile. She steeled herself to remain humble and deferential in the presence of the man through whose doing her husband had died. She must convince him of her story.

Ramón emerged with Santiago, after the vaquero had explained what their lovely visitor had asked. Ramón faced her now, noticing that she was attractive and modestly dressed. He courteously asked, "How may I help you, Señorita—?"

"My name is Rita Galloway, Mr. Hernandez—your nice worker here told me your name—"

"That is correct, I am Ramón Hernandez, one of the owners of this mine. Santiago tells me that you are looking for work."

"Yes, sir." Rhea's eyes fell, and she uttered a weary sigh. "I come from a town in Mississippi, not far from Natchez, Mr. Hernandez. I had a fellow back there—well, he was ambitious and decided to strike for silver here in Leadville."

"I see."

"Well, two months ago he sent me off a wire saying I should come here, and we would be married. Trouble was, when I got here a couple of weeks ago, I found out that he was sparking another girl. He said it was all off, that he wanted to marry this other girl, and that I could do what I darned well pleased. Now I'm alone and without a penny to my name, Mr. Hernandez. That's the long and short of it."

"That's a pity. I take it you're not interested in working in a dance hall, or saloon?"

"Oh, no! My mother brought me up to be a good, decent girl, Mr. Hernandez. I'd rather die before I'd do a thing like that." Rhea spoke with eloquence and lifted her eyes to fix him with an entreating look.

"I know there's lots of unemployment in Leadville, Miss Galloway, but I don't know exactly what you could do for us."

"Couldn't you use a cook? I'm a very good one, Mr. Hernandez. And I'd work real cheap, just to have a roof over

313

my head and something to eat. You wouldn't have to pay me much, and I'd earn it, believe me, I really would!'' Rhea uttered these words in a sorrowful tone of voice and again gave him an entreating look, then modestly lowered her eyes and entwined her fingers as she awaited his decision.

"Well now, that might not be such a bad idea,'' Ramón said after a moment's thought. "We've all been taking turns doing the cooking—if you can call it that,'' he smiled. "Most of the time, it's beans, bacon, flapjacks—what you might expect a bunch of men to come up with. It's hardly the type of food I care to eat day after day, I must confess. I much prefer what my wife sets before my children and me.''

"Then I could really be of help to you. Again, all I'd want would be a place to sleep and three square meals, and whatever money over that you think my work would be worth to you. Why don't you give me a trial? Maybe I could cook the meal tonight for your men, and then you could tell me if you thought you'd want to keep me on.''

Ramón thoughtfully stroked his chin. "I suppose I wouldn't have anything to lose that way. All right then, Miss Galloway. Buy in town what you think you'll need to feed fifteen men. Try Halsey's grocery store—my men and I have found good values there, and the man isn't a gouger. Incidentally, we usually eat around six o'clock.''

"You don't know how grateful I am, Mr. Hernandez. I'd just about given up hope. Everyone else has either laughed at me or—or made improper suggestions.''

"I see.'' Ramón pursed his lips. "Well, as I said, let's give it a try. My men would appreciate a home-cooked meal—and so would I.''

"I'll have an evening meal for you that'll make you asking for seconds, I promise I will. All I want to do is earn a few dollars so I can get back to Mississippi one of these days. Only my poor old father's left alive—my mother died three years ago. He figures I'm happily married by now; I haven't had the heart to tell him the truth—well, I shouldn't bother you with my troubles.''

"I hope we can be of use to each other, Señorita Galloway.'' Ramón took out his wallet and handed Rhea Penrock several greenbacks. "I'll leave it to your choice entirely. There's money enough there to hire a driver to bring the supplies out here. Incidentally, there's only an old stove in

314

the kitchen, not much else. We more or less threw things together quickly to be close to the mine, you see, figuring we'd build more comfortable accommodations when our families came. But since we've been here, we've changed our minds about settling down. I'm afraid you would have to make do with a small room in the attic.''

"God bless you, Mr. Hernandez! I won't mind that one bit. And I'll be back—I wouldn't let a man like you down, not after what you've done for me. I'm so grateful. I'll show you tonight. Your men—are they Mexican, too?''

"Some of them. But they all like tortillas, enchiladas, *carne asada*, chili—do you cook any of those things?''

"I can make a pretty fair chili—at least, my father thought so. He got a taste for it when he went to New Orleans once and had a bowl of it in some fancy place. And I can make stew—''

"Very well, Señorita Galloway. You buy what you think best, and then, after dinner tonight, I'll tell you if we have a job for you as our cook.''

"You won't regret it, Mr. Hernandez, I swear you won't. And like I said, I don't want very much. If I can just save a few dollars to get back home—''

"We'll talk about that after we've sampled your cooking, Señorita Galloway,'' Ramón said kindly with a genial smile.

Leaving her suitcase on the porch of the house, Rhea turned and began to walk back along the trail that led to town. Ramón was about to offer her transportation back in the wagon they used to transport the bullion, but then thought better of it. If she was planning to flimflam him, he didn't want to make things too easy for her. But to tell the truth, he hoped she was honest. He missed Mara's cooking, and he was damn tired of the eternal beans and bacon. So was everyone else, for that matter.

Rhea Penrock returned some three hours later, and Santiago Dornado excitedly called to Ramón Hernandez, ''*Patrón, patrón*, the *mujer linda* has come back to us—and the buckboard is full of food! She has told the truth!''

Ramón and Lucien Edmond came out to see, and exchanged a surprised look, for Ramón's brother-in-law, after having heard the story of this abandoned young woman's visit, had cynically prophesied that Ramón would see no more of his greenbacks. "Diego, Manuel, help the señorita bring the food into the house," Ramón ordered, and Lucien Edmond walked out to the buckboard and handed Rhea down.

Once inside the house, Rhea observed the sparse furnishings in the rooms and smiled to herself. All these men living together in this claptrap house were bound to enjoy a woman's touch—and she'd be that woman. She'd be a real housekeeper, darned if she wouldn't! She'd already learned something very important about that son-of-a-bitching greaser who'd had her man killed—he had a family back in Texas. Her clever, warped mind began to conjecture ideas of making her vengeance even crueler, more shattering to him. It would be easy enough to kill him, to put a knife into his ribs some night when he was asleep and then skedaddle back to Dodge City. But now, she had a new thought to work on, worrying it almost the way a terrier would gnaw a bone to get all the scraps of meat off it. She'd make him suffer, she'd make him wish he'd never been born. And, if she could do what she was beginning to think she could, he'd never know why.

She had baked buttermilk biscuits to go along with a rabbit stew that she had cooked with vegetables and a dollop of whiskey. She'd also paid two dollars for a box of blackberries, and with them made several delicious cobblers. Coffee was dear, but Ramón Hernandez had given her enough money to pay for a real feast, and that was exactly what she gave the hungry Windhaven men. Her face flushed, but smiling valiantly, she served them herself.

When the meal was over, Walter Catlin turned to Rhea and said, "Thank you for going to all this trouble, Miss Galloway. I'm sure all the men agree with me that for the first time in months, you've helped us forget about how much we miss our homes—at least a little bit." He smiled awkwardly, then told her, "I hope you won't mind my saying something personal to you, but we've all heard your unfortunate story. We've all got a sadness in our backgrounds that's hurt us very deeply—I rambled around this whole darn country, practically, for more years than I care to think about, trying to erase my pain—" He stopped for a moment, not quite sure of his next words. "I guess what I'm trying to say is although you may think of yourself as being alone and lost, you're among friends here."

Robert Markey broke in, "That's true, Miss Galloway. And you won't find any better people to work for in the whole of these United States than Mr. Bouchard and Mr. Hernandez. Take my word for it. You're darn lucky to have found them so early in your life." He briefly outlined his own story to her and finished by emphatically nodding his head and declaring, "Yep, best darn bunch of people in the whole darn world!"

Rhea looked down at her lap. She hoped that she gave the impression of shy gratitude; in fact, she was forcing herself to keep from bursting out in laughter. She thought to herself that these men who were being so kind to her were going to make it damned easy to carry out her plan. *It will be like taking candy from babies,* her inner voice told her. *They've fallen for my story hook, line, and sinker.* She raised her head, setting her features into a worried look, and reminded her listeners, "You're all being so very kind to me, but after all, I haven't been offered the job yet."

Ramón rose and, lifting his coffee cup, toasted her: "Señorita Galloway, I, too, know we haven't had a meal like this since we left Texas. You've proved that you can cook, and I'd be happy to hire you, if you really want to work for us."

"You don't know how much, Mr. Hernandez." Rhea lowered her eyes and acted humbly grateful as she took a dishcloth and wiped her sweaty forehead. The stove had been very hot, and it had made her forget the unseasonably cool weather—unseasonable, at least so far as Dodge City was concerned. She didn't want to stay here very long, and her next step was to figure how she would get the greaser to take her back with him to Texas, when he had a mind to go back to his family. His family . . . that was where she could really pay him back.

All she had to do was close her eyes and she could see tall, slim, black-haired Gabe. She could hear his sly jokes about what he planned to do with her at night, and she felt herself melting inside, the way she always had whenever he touched or looked at her. Damn that lousy greaser, anyhow—coming along and robbing her of the only man she'd ever cared for. Things could have been so different if she and Gabe could have gone on living together. Maybe she'd even have got him to leave that fat fool Cornish's gang and start out for himself in a new territory where there wasn't a price on his head—

where the two of them could have peace and quiet and lots of loving together!

"Then it's settled, Señorita Galloway," Ramón smiled at her. "As I said, there's a spare room in the attic, and you will have complete privacy there. Don't worry, no one will dare to touch you, or offend you—I give you my word of honor."

"I'm not worried about that at all, Mr. Hernandez. Fact is, I was sort of worried about my safety all the time I was living in my boardinghouse—"

"We'll get a few pieces of furniture for you tomorrow. I'm afraid for tonight you'll have to make do with just the bed. I'll have one of the men take up your suitcase, Señorita Galloway. And thank you again. It was really *muy bueno*." Ramón smiled at her again, rubbing his stomach in the universal sign of satiety and approval.

Rhea did not bother to undress, for she was dog tired. She flung herself down on the hard bed in the small room and fell asleep almost instantly. Soon she was dreaming: Ramón Hernandez was on his knees, clasping his hands, tears running down his face, begging her for mercy. And she heard herself laugh and say to him, "Not a chance, you dirty Mex son of a bitch. You did my man in, and now I'm going to pay you back—in a way you'll never forget!"

The next day, Lucien Edmond sent one of the vaqueros into town to purchase a chest of drawers, a dressing table and mirror, and a washstand and bowl. Ramón had suggested that the vaqueros also buy a few niceties, such as a bottle of perfume, if there was any available, and some extra wool blankets, so that Rhea would not be cold in the nights when, even in summer, the high mountain air seemed frigid to anyone who had come from Texas—or Mississippi.

By mid-July, Rhea was a fixture in the frame house next to the mine. The vaqueros worked with enthusiasm, for they had never been better fed—not even when Maybelle Belcher and Felicidad were cooking for them back on the range near Carrizo Springs. Lucien Edmond and Ramón, breakfasting by themselves on this second Saturday in July, glanced up and smiled gratefully as Rhea came in with the coffee pot to fill their cups. "Thank you, Miss Galloway." Lucien Edmond graciously told her. "I'd like to say on behalf of all of the men how grateful we are to you. You've made our stay here a lot more tolerable, that's for sure.''

"Bless you, Mr. Bouchard. I can't thank *you* enough for giving me this chance." Rhea pretended to brush a tear from her eye. As she did so, she covertly eyed Ramón Hernandez, and her lips tightened for an instant. One of these days, that smile of his was going to be wiped off his face—and there'd be tears running down it, just the way she'd seen them in her dream.

Thirty-Seven

Feeling the alienation between himself and his sister, Hugo Bouchard had plunged himself even more deeply into his studies. But touched by his loneliness in becoming a stranger to Carla, he became even more aware of the attractive young woman who pursued her studies alongside him at Rush Medical College. Her name was Cecily Franklin, and she was one of the first women to be admitted to Rush. She was a virtual revelation to him, for he had always believed that women were the weaker sex and were squeamish at the sight of blood. Yet when they had undertaken dissections, she had acted with a coolness and poise that astonished him and indeed outdid his own.

She was nineteen, five feet four inches in height, and her heart-shaped face framed expressive dark-brown eyes. Her light brown hair was worn in a severe bun, giving her the illusion of being older than she was—a defense mechanism she used against the preponderance of males in her classes, who scoffed at her and looked down at her, believing that she was there only to find a man.

Because of this, most of Hugo's classmates had approached Cecily Franklin during the first year, but she had swiftly rebuffed them. She had made it clear that she was seeking no liaison and that she regarded it as an insult to be expected to be awed by them and humbled simply because they were males. During that first semester, Hugo had covertly watched her on numerous occasions and at times had bidden her a cordial "Good morning, Miss Franklin," or, "Good afternoon, Miss Franklin." But she had been cold to him, believing that he was like all the others and that his only interest in her was sexual.

Now, however, Hugo and Cecily were drawn closer together because of an incident that had taken place in the anatomy classroom. Working with several cadavers, each student had to make detailed anatomical drawings of the central nervous system, indicating the spinal nerves, the spinal cord, and the various lobes of the brain. Cecily had at once set to work and, in a single afternoon, she had completed her illustrations. She had carefully rolled up the drawings and placed them in the drawer of her table. The next day, the instructor came by and asked the students to show him their work. Cecily opened her drawer, took out the drawings, and uttered a cry of anger. "Who did this? This is vicious and unfair!"

"What's the matter, Miss Franklin?" The bearded, middle-aged doctor walked over to the table and stood beside her. He looked at her illustrations laid out on the table and saw that two of them, which should have been details of the spinal region, were nothing but cartoon stick figures. Hugo Bouchard blanched and opened his drawer guardedly, but his own drawings were as he had left them.

"Dr. Elston, I swear I finished this work yesterday—I purposely stayed two extra hours so that I could. And now you can see for yourself that my work has been mutilated. Someone did this just because I'm a woman!" Cecily declared angrily.

"It's true, Dr. Elston," Hugo spoke up. "I saw her working, and she did a wonderful job. Better than I did."

"Well now, since you're on that subject, Bouchard, let's see your work," Dr. Elston chuckled dryly as he walked over to Hugo. "Hmm, not too bad at all. You're making a good deal of headway here during your second term. You have the makings of being a fine doctor—maybe even a fine surgeon. And you say that Miss Franklin's work was better than yours?"

"I'd swear it on a stack of Bibles, Dr. Elston!" Hugo stoutly averred.

Cecily Franklin sent him a look of the deepest gratitude. Then, glancing around, she encountered the mocking faces of some of the male students who were near her. She straightened with a snort of disgust and anger, her cheeks coloring.

"I'll be very candid with you, Miss Franklin." Dr. Elston at last turned to her. He too had caught the hostile glances and the derisive sneers of the other students. "You're the only woman in this class, and there's bound to be condescension. It's an unfortunate tradition, but from the dawn of time, the male has always fancied himself superior to the female."

"Well it's not true, and it's unfair. I want to be judged on my merits, Dr. Elston, and I don't expect to be given any favors or special concessions."

"Don't worry, Miss Franklin," was his cool answer, "you won't be. When it comes time for final exams and then the oral discussions all the faculty have with you students, either you'll make it or you won't—and it will have nothing at all to do with your being a woman or a man, believe me." Then, in a kindlier tone, he went on, "Miss Franklin, I'm going to give you the laboratory here for the rest of the afternoon, and allow no one else except myself or another member of the faculty to enter. Will that give you time enough to redo your work?"

"Yes, it will. I'm grateful to you, Dr. Elston. I want very much to be a doctor."

"I know that. Perhaps if you tell the other students why, it may go a long way toward informing your colleagues what your motives really are, Miss Franklin," he said persuasively.

Cecily straightened, her dainty, firm chin tightening as she tried to maintain a stoic and impassive face. "My father was a doctor in New Hampshire, a general practitioner. One evening he went to deliver a child from a woman who had a drunken, abusive husband. The husband came home, not knowing that his wife was about to give birth, and he believed my father was her lover—and killed him, before he could defend himself."

There was a horrified murmur among the other students, and they stared at the proud young woman. She drew a deep breath, and then went on, "If I get my certificate, as I told you when I applied here, Dr. Elston, I plan to go to Wyoming. It's desolate country out there, but it's beautiful and wide open and in desperate need of medical care. I'll go to live with my aunt in a town north of Cheyenne, and there I can be of use to cowhands, cattlemen, and their families. And if I'm half as good a doctor as my father was, I'll be grateful to God."

"Thank you for telling us all this, Miss Franklin." Dr. Elston turned and regarded the other students, who had left off working and were staring openmouthed at the attractive young woman. Then he snapped, "All right, that's enough gawking. I won't press this matter any further, but whoever did this to Miss Franklin ought to be drummed out of Rush. He's not the kind of student we're looking for. Take heed, gentlemen—there's no room for jealousy or envy or treachery in the medical profession. Now, go on about your work."

At the end of class, Cecily Franklin decided to take a break before returning to finish her sabotaged work. She put away her materials in the drawer, not without an indignant glance all around her just to let her antagonistic male class-mates know that she did not intend to be trifled with again, and then turned and walked out of the laboratory room. Hugo Bouchard had gone out ahead of her, but had stopped in the hallway to talk with one of the other students.

Seeing him, Cecily paused, tightening her hold on the stack of medical books she was about to return to the library. She waited for the two young men to end their conversation, and then, somewhat nervously, declared, "Mr. Bouchard, I—I want to thank you for the way you spoke up to Dr. Elston on behalf of my work. It was very decent of you."

"It was the only thing I could do, Miss Franklin. That was a rotten trick someone played on you, and whoever did that doesn't deserve to be a doctor," he hotly averred.

Cecily looked at him and smiled. Her brown eyes were warm now as she whimsically remarked, "I wouldn't go so far as to say that—but it was rather rotten. I wouldn't think of playing a practical joke like that, not in a serious profession like this. Thank you again, Mr. Bouchard."

"Er—Miss Franklin, you—you said you plan to go out to Wyoming Territory when you get your certificate at Rush?" Hugo was a little ill at ease, for being in Cecily Franklin's presence out of class made him intensely aware of how physically attractive she was, quite apart from the intelligence and poise she had already exhibited in the classrooms.

"Yes, that's right. My aunt lives in Rawlins, Mr. Bouchard.

She's the only relative I've got left, because my mother died when I was an infant.''

"You know, I'm from Texas, Miss Franklin, and last year I went on a cattle drive from my father's ranch to deliver a herd to a Mr. Grantham from Cheyenne," Hugo proffered.

Her face brightened. "Why, that's very interesting! I wonder if my aunt knows of Mr. Grantham—Cheyenne is only about a hundred fifty miles from Rawlins. I didn't know your father raised cattle, Mr. Bouchard.''

"Yes, he does." He suddenly felt tongue-tied, and he searched for something else to say, so as not to let the conversation end. "My sister Carla is here with me—she's at the Chicago Academy of Fine Arts. She paints.''

"That's wonderful! I'm sure she must be very gifted. I've heard some wonderful things about the Academy—just as I did about Rush, which is why I came out here.''

"I—if you wouldn't think me too presumptuous, Miss Franklin, I'd like to take you to dinner some evening, if you're free." Hugo's face self-consciously reddened.

"I'd like that very much. We can trade memories of Wyoming. I was out there when I was a little girl when my father took me to visit Aunt Margaret." Her face grew somber. "Aunt Margaret's husband, my Uncle Harold, was killed in a stupid war between cattlemen and sheep ranchers.''

"I know how that can happen," he said sympathetically. "My father had some trouble with a man who was raising sheep not far from him, and the man purposely tried to get on his land.''

"But there's so much land everywhere in this country," Cecily protested, "so why should people kill one another just because one raises sheep and one raises cattle?''

"The theory is, Miss Franklin, that the sheep eat the grass down to the roots and leave nothing for the cattle, at least that's what I've been told," Hugo tried to explain.

"That's idiotic!" she shouted, then she smiled again. "You must think me terribly rude. Here I am yelling at you after you stood up for me in class. And also, you're very nice—you haven't been offensive to me like so many other fellows in class. They think that I'm just holding my breath waiting for them to go sparking with me.''

"I can't say as I'd blame them for that exactly, Miss Franklin." Now Hugo's face was redder than ever. "You're very lovely, and I can understand why they'd be attracted to you—I am myself."

Cecily Franklin tilted back her head and laughed energetically, then put out her hand and exclaimed, "Mr. Bouchard, I like you. You're nice, candid, and honest. I'd love to go to dinner with you. How about tonight? Could you call for me over at my boardinghouse? It's on Chicago Avenue, near Clark Street. It's the red-brick house, two stories—you can't miss it."

"Would seven o'clock be all right?"

"That would be fine. And now I'd really better get these books to the library—and then go back to the laboratory. Thank you again, Mr. Bouchard."

"Thank *you*, Miss Franklin," he breathed, as she gave him a pleasant nod and then walked away.

Hugo took Cecily to Henrici's for dinner, though she protested against the extravagance. "I must tell you, Mr. Bouchard," she said, looking him straight in his eyes with her own wide, direct, dark brown eyes, "I'm not the sort of person who's comfortable with elegance. I come from a very humble background; my father was sometimes paid with chickens, or a pig, or even loaves of home-baked bread."

"But, Miss Franklin," Hugo was horrified to have got off to such a poor start, "I'm not trying to overwhelm you. It's not all that expensive; I just wanted to take you to a place where we could have good food and service, and I could have a chance to talk to you about what doctoring means to you. It means a great deal to me."

She gave him a quizzical look as the waiter came with menus and informed them of the specials of the evening. "We'll order in a few minutes," Hugo told him.

After the man had left, Cecily leaned forward across the table and earnestly declared, "You know why I want to be a physician—but what's your reason?"

Hugo was flattered by her interest, and after giving himself a moment to collect his thoughts, he began, "I suppose I could have gone on for the rest of my life at my father's ranch. He's rich, but I was never aware of it—I mean, it was a simple, outdoor life. It's a big ranch practically in the middle of nowhere—the nearest large city is San Antonio, about a hundred twenty miles away. Well, last year I told my father I wanted to earn my keep, and I wanted to go on the drive with him, undergo all the same hardships that any of his vaqueros did.''

"Vaqueros?" she eyed him curiously.

"That's the Spanish word for cowboys or riders on a ranch, Miss Franklin.''

Cecily gave a little laugh and leaned back, more at her ease now. She gave Hugo a warm smile as she murmured, "I think it would be less strained if you called me by my first name, and I'll call you by yours, if you've no objection.''

"I should be delighted, Cecily. I think it's a beautiful name.''

"Now, Hugo, you mustn't get carried away,'' she teased him with a flash of humor that absolutely enchanted him, for till now she had shown only the prim, poised, and self-controlled attitude of a young woman who was dedicated to her work and would brook no interruption or ridicule on the subject.

He smiled back at her, more at ease himself. "Anyway, when you drive a herd of cattle to market, it takes months— riding all day, rounding up the strays, and if there's bad weather and the cattle stampede, sometimes it takes as much as a week to get them all back. Well, on this drive we were ambushed by bandits who wanted to kill us and take the herd—''

"How dreadful! Were you hurt?'' He detected a note of anxiety in her voice, and now her eyes had a softer look as they fixed on his face.

"No, fortunately. But my best friend was killed—that was very hard for me—and another man was severely injured. Then we had a stampede when we were driving the cattle over a mountain pass, and another man was hurt—gored by a bull. Well, you see, I helped save the lives of both of those men by utilizing needle and thread to make sutures. I—'' He looked down, embarrassed. "Everyone said they would have died if not for me. It was a wonderful feeling, Cecily. That's why I decided that I was cut out for a life in medicine. When a relative of ours, just in passing, told Mother about Rush— and the Chicago Academy of Fine Arts for Carla—I knew that I wanted to come here and study.''

"You *are* sincere and dedicated, Hugo. I've noticed how hard you work, and how you're not distracted—yet you seem

325

to get along so well with some of those louts who have been bothering me," she said almost reproachfully.

"I learned to do that on the trail with all the men. You have to get along with everyone when you're all thrown so closely together."

He took a sip of his water, then smiled at Cecily. "I guess I had inspiration from another source, too—a Dr. Ben Wilson in Wichita. His wife—she was my great-aunt—died over ten years ago, and he came to our ranch to bring their children to her mother. Then he went out to Indian Territory to help the Creeks—they were the Indians from the old South, where my great-great-grandfather originally settled when he came here from France almost a hundred years ago."

"My goodness, Hugo," she breathed, listening to him intently, "you do have a complicated background!"

He grinned and said, "I guess I do. Anyway, Ben Wilson met an Indian woman with a baby girl—she'd escaped the massacre of the tribe who'd kidnapped her, and had taken refuge in the Creek village. Well, Ben married her. Now they're settled in Wichita with all of their children, and he's a wonderful doctor. I thought of him all the time when I was on the drive. I write to him frequently, and he gives me all sorts of encouragement. If only you could meet him—then you'd understand why I want to be a doctor more than anything else in the world."

"I think we'd better order; our waiter is looking at us and wondering if we're going to just sit here all night, Hugo," Cecily whispered, a smile on her lips and in her voice.

Picking up his menu, Hugo added, "Incidentally, Cecily, Ben Wilson's wife, Elone, is a firm believer in women's rights. Kansas, you know, has several times defeated a referendum to allow women's suffrage."

"Now there's a woman I'd really like to meet." Cecily's eyes sparkled. "I believe in women's rights, too. If they existed, my work wouldn't have been destroyed—and you know it, Hugo Bouchard."

He could only nod, taken aback by the vehemence of her indignation. Seeing his tense features, she softened her tone and smiled. "I'm not by nature a virago, Hugo. I'm very conscious that I'm a woman, and one day, after I've fulfilled my vow to be a doctor, I fully intend to marry and have children. That's definitely part of a woman's life—but it's certainly not the only part. Though if you'd listen to most men, that's the only part they'd grant to a woman. By the way, that's one of the main reasons I propose to go out to Wyoming Territory. They don't have many doctors out there to begin with, and so the prejudice against a woman will be a good deal less than back East. Besides, Wyoming has already granted women the right to vote in equality with the male. That alone would decide me to go out there, even if I didn't have my darling aunt. Oh—here comes our waiter. I think we'd best give the menu a quick perusal and order the first thing that strikes us. I don't think the poor man has much patience left for us! Let's save any special conversation for coffee and dessert, shall we, Hugo, dear?''

"By all means." He was enchanted at her having insinuated the endearment into her words to him. And later, when he began to eat his dinner, he could not help glancing shyly at her from time to time, realizing that she was not only superbly vital and intelligent, but also extremely desirable as a woman.

During the last week of July, Hugo Bouchard received a wire from his mother, Maxine, telling him that Ben Wilson had written them and was planning to visit Chicago during the first week of August. Elone, his lovely Indian wife, now in her thirtieth year, was eager to visit the Windy City to attend a conference on women's rights. She and the Quaker doctor would leave young Bartholomew, Jacob, Amy, and Dorothy with Tabitha Hartmann, the widow of the former pastor of their Quaker church. The older children—Thomas, Sybella, and Tisinqua, Elone's daughter by her Kiowa captor—would accompany the Wilsons. Maxine added that she had sent a similar wire to Charles and Laurette Douglas, for Ben wanted very much to see the Chicago merchant, whom he had met at Windhaven Range.

At class the next morning, Hugo sought out Cecily Franklin to tell her this exciting news. "I want you to meet Dr. Wilson, Cecily," he urged, his face aglow. "I think when you do, you'll understand why he's becoming famous all over Kansas. And since they're coming for a conference on women's rights, I thought for sure you'd want to attend it and at the same time meet the Wilsons."

"I'd love to, Hugo, dear! Thank you so much for asking

me! He's had such marvelous experiences, hasn't he?'' she exclaimed.

"Yes, he has," Hugo responded. "He's sure had his share of excitement—and hardship."

"I can appreciate what he must have gone through in a town like Wichita—I've read about all the shootings that went on there, what with outlaws, and cowboys coming into town after a drive," Cecily proffered. "Let me know when I will meet this famous Dr. Wilson of yours. There's so much I want to ask him about practicing under difficulties—how to overcome hostility, and what sort of illness he's mostly had to deal with. I suspect Wyoming isn't going to be any picnic, but that's all the more reason I know I have to go there."

"Just as soon as they come to town, I'll ask if we can all have dinner together," Hugo promised.

Thirty-Eight

Greatly to Hugo Bouchard's delight, Laurette Douglas had come over to the Thornberg house that same evening and told him that the Douglases had invited the Wilsons and their children to stay at their large house during their visit to Chicago. "They'll be here early next week, a day or two before that conference," Laurette told Hugo. "Charles and I plan to have several dinners in their honor, and we'll invite people who are interested in meeting them."

"Well *I'm* certainly most anxious to be one of those guests, Laurette," Hugo declared with a grin.

"Of course you will, my dear boy. I'll be inviting Carla and Cordelia, too, for one evening, but I know they'll be at gallery openings next week, and I have it in mind that you should enjoy at least one dinner with the Wilsons all to yourself—I know you and the doctor will have so much to talk about. Perhaps you'd like to bring one of your friends from school—I'm sure it will be fascinating to hear about doctoring on the frontier!"

When the Wilsons arrived, the older Douglas children—the twins, Arthur and Kenneth, almost fifteen, Howard, eleven and a half, and Fleur, now seven and a half—were fascinated by Tisinqua, Sybella, and Thomas. Laurette had told her children that she would greatly appreciate their playing host to the Wilson children, taking them around town, making sure they enjoyed all the sights and particularly some of the treats like ice cream and candy, that were none too plentiful in Wichita.

Hugo was burning with eagerness to see Ben Wilson, but restrained himself until the day after the Wilsons had arrived in Chicago, knowing that they would want to rest after the arduous train journey. He was rather tired himself, for oppressive weather had clung like a pall to the Windy City, and not even the breeze off Lake Michigan seemed to relieve it in the evening. Fortunately, his classes at Rush Medical College were suspended until the second week of September.

"Cecily, this is Dr. Ben Wilson," Hugo Bouchard eagerly told the attractive young woman as he gestured toward the forty-six-year-old Quaker doctor. They were all seated in the spacious Douglas living room, across the street from Cordelia's house. "Uncle Ben, this is Cecily Franklin. She's a fellow student of mine at Rush Medical College."

"It's a great pleasure to meet you, Miss Franklin." Ben smiled at her and offered his hand, which Cecily warmly shook. Turning to smile at Elone, he declared, "I would venture to say that here we have a prime example of the movement toward the emancipation of women." He faced Cecily again and said, "Elone and I are here to attend a conference espousing the right of women to vote and to hold positions on the basis of merit."

"I'm a firm believer in the liberation of women, too, Dr. Wilson," Cecily spoke up. "Indeed, I would like very much to go with you and Mrs. Wilson to the conference—that is, if I'm not being rude in inviting myself."

"Not at all. Elone and I would be delighted to have you!" the Quaker doctor graciously responded.

"As you know," Elone said in her lovely, soft voice, "in the East, there have already been many notable examples of women graduating from academically high-ranked institutions. Like Boston University, Cornell, Swarthmore, and St. Lawrence University. It appears this movement is spreading here

329

to the Midwest. But medical schools are still rather opposed to women, aren't they?''

"Unfortunately, yes, Mrs. Wilson," Cecily said with a frown. "It hasn't been easy—to say the least—for me at Rush, either."

Howard, bursting with curiosity, suddenly interrupted. "Dr. Wilson, is it really true that you lived with all those Injuns on reservations? Weren't you scared of them?''

"Bless you, no, Howard," the Quaker doctor chuckled, with a fond look at Elone beside him. "I hope you haven't heard too many stories of how Indians want to hurt people like me, because it's really not true."

"But I read a Buffalo Bill book all about how Injuns scalp people they shoot with arrows and spears and stuff," Howard persisted, despite Laurette's putting her finger to her lips and shaking her head, while Charles scowled and shook his head also.

"You see, Howard," Ben Wilson patiently explained, "the Indians were here first on the land, long before any white men came. Then, when white men came to this country, Indians naturally tried to protect their land. If you had land and someone tried to take it away from you, wouldn't you try to fight for it?''

"Sure I would!" Howard was belligerently positive.

"Well, you see, that's why, at the beginning, there were fights between the Indians and the white settlers," Ben concluded.

"Are they allowed to leave the reservations, Dr. Wilson?" the boy continued, ignoring his mother's sign to stop hogging the conversation.

"Yes, they are, Howard," Ben told the boy. "But you see, there the government looks after them somewhat—gives them food and clothing, even sends doctors. It's true they're a long way from their original homes, but at least they can be together—although they can barely go on with their way of life."

"Gee, I saw photographs of—what are those things called? Wigwams?'' The boy stared avidly at Ben, pretending not to see the annoyed frowns of his mother and father.

"That's right, wigwams—or tepees. They're made of animal hides like buffalo, or sometimes even bark. But they're warm and comfortable, even in winter."

330

At this point, Cecily Franklin decided to take matters into her own hands. "Dr. Wilson, what would you say is the principal illness among the Indians that you lived with?"

"Miss Franklin, it's more than an illness of the body—I'd say it's a despair of the soul and of the mind caused by their isolation, their bitter loneliness, their feeling of rejection, of being castoffs from general society. Then, too, the whites have been carriers of many diseases that Indians have no natural immunization to—such as croup, whooping cough, pneumonia, influenza. These ills strike them very hard because their strength is weakened; in many instances, you see, they don't get the nutrition they used to enjoy on their own lands. Whereas once they hunted and fished and they had an active life, now they're often given inferior flour, sometimes even spoiled meat, and worn, tattered blankets and clothes."

"What did your treatment consist of, Dr. Wilson?" Cecily asked.

"Mostly, my work was constant examination of the very old—the men and women who were the elders in the tribe—as well as the children, to make sure that they received sufficient diet so their bodies could develop. It was the old story of the ounce of prevention being worth the pound of cure."

"I understand that. You really are to be admired for your humanitarian efforts, Dr. Wilson." Turning to Elone, Cecily said, "Hugo mentioned that you met on the reservation."

"To my joy, yes." Elone looked adoringly at her husband. "My daughter, Tisinqua, and I were very ill, and it was this good man who saved us both."

"Gee!" Kenneth and Arthur Douglas simultaneously chorused. "We want to hear lots more about the Injuns, Dr. Wilson!" Arthur added.

"And you shall, you shall." Ben turned to his hostess. "Laurette, we're all very grateful to you and Charles for putting us up in your beautiful home and giving us the pleasure of your company."

"There's a method in my madness, Ben," Laurette bantered, "because I had a feeling that when they met your children, our offspring would be kept so busy asking them all about life outdoors with the Indians that Charles and I wouldn't have to belabor our brains finding something to keep them out of mischief! We're truly delighted to have you. But now,

331

children, we adults want to have our coffee and chat a bit, so will you be darlings and excuse yourselves?''

"Oh, Mother!" Howard made a long face, but nonetheless grudgingly rose from the table. Not forgetting his manners, he inclined slightly toward Elone and the Quaker doctor and mumbled, "It was awful nice meeting you, and good night. See you tomorrow—" and then, as he reached the doorway, he flashed, "—I sure got lots more questions to ask about Injuns!"

Kenneth and Arthur, trying to look like adults, said their formal good-nights and rolled their eyes ceilingward, as if to deplore their younger brother's uncouth behavior. The Wilson children kissed their parents good-night, then followed the Douglas children up the stairs. When they had gone up to their rooms, the Wilsons and the Douglases, as well as Hugo and Cecily, burst into gales of merry laughter.

As they enjoyed their coffee, Elone began to talk about the importance of better vocational and educational opportunities for women. She had learned so much through discussions with Ben, through exposure to women's movements of the day and also her own wide reading, that anyone who had known her only in the days that she first arrived in Wichita from the Creek reservation might have been startled at the transformation in her. "Miss Franklin," she said with a smile, "I am sure you know about Elizabeth Blackwell, who waged such a struggle to become a doctor. But have you also heard of Mary Gobe Nichols? She was a remarkable woman who gave lectures on anatomy to young women as long ago as 1838. Then there was Pauline Wright Davis. Just the other day I was reading the most fascinating story about her. It seems that in her day it was unthinkable that females should be exposed to unclad human forms, so she tried to use mannequins in her physiology lectures—only to find that many of the female students were so shocked that they either fled from the hall or fainted dead away!"

Cecily laughed gently, recalling her own unflinching response to cadavers in anatomy class. "That is indeed extraordinary," she replied. "I am certainly glad we have made some advances since Miss Davis's day."

Elone nodded in agreement and continued. "I've also read recently about Harriot K. Hunt, who was so determined to be a doctor that when Harvard Medical School denied her admission, she practiced in any case—without a license. Of course, she was not foolish or insensitive, and she did nothing that endangered anyone. She practiced what I think today you would call physiotherapy."

"I seem to recall having heard that, Mrs. Wilson." Cecily leaned forward, her lovely face showing her absorption in the subject.

Hugo glanced admiringly at her, trying not to be too obvious in displaying his growing affection for her.

"You mentioned Elizabeth Blackwell," Cecily went on. "I've heard of her, but to tell you the truth, I don't know very much about her. Perhaps you could tell me, Mrs. Wilson."

"Well, when Elizabeth Blackwell decided to become a doctor back in the forties, it made her as much of a social outcast as—well, as being an Indian is, all too often. And just as I have had to learn everything on my own—with my dear husband's help, of course—and acceptance has been slow in coming, so Dr. Blackwell had to wage a great struggle to win her goal. Do you know, she actually had to apply to twenty-nine medical schools before she was finally accepted."

"Oh, yes," Cecily chimed in eagerly," I do remember now. The faculty did not want to admit her, and in order to conceal that fact, they put it to the students, stipulating that the students' vote must be unanimous if Miss Blackwell was to be admitted."

"That's right," Elone replied, "and the professors were unpleasantly surprised when the vote was unanimous in Miss Blackwell's favor. They *had* to let her in after that. She graduated at the head of her class and went on to study in Paris. Unfortunately, she contracted a disease and lost an eye, which ended her dream of becoming a surgeon."

"She became a friend of Florence Nightingale's, didn't she?" Cecily asked.

"Yes," Elone answered. "From what I've read, it was because of this friendship that when the Civil War broke out, Dr. Blackwell—who had returned to this country by then— championed the new profession of nursing—and those valiant women were a godsend to the wounded."

"She was quite a woman! I only hope I will have her courage. I expect to be severely tested when I go out to practice in Wyoming Territory," Cecily mused. "But do tell me about the conference."

333

"One of the things I am interested in, and which I hope to learn about at this conference," Elone answered, "is the matter of trade unions to help women secure better wages, and to hold their jobs without oppression from men." She smiled at Cecily and said, "Perhaps you think it peculiar that someone like me—a woman with no formal education, but happily married to a doctor and living out in the middle of Kansas—should have an interest in the whole notion of workers' unions. But I firmly believe that anyone who cares about the rights of others has to get involved and fight for those rights."

"I'm in full agreement with you, Mrs. Wilson!" Cecily excitedly exclaimed. "But I don't really think that you'll ever see a union for women doctors. I think each individual physician has to be prepared to be accepted on his own merits alone—and that's as true for women as it is for men. When I become a doctor, I shall have to try to convince people by my work. If they see me cure patients, then they'll know that I'm well grounded in my profession, and they'll come to accept me. That and a little prayer is about the best I can really do, Mrs. Wilson."

"Yes, and prayer is a wonderful thing. Ben and I know it well." Elone exchanged a loving look with her husband.

"Has there been any attempt to get Congress to agree to women's suffrage?" Hugo Bouchard was following the conversation with close interest.

"Yes, indeed," Elone brightly spoke up. "Two years ago, Senator Sargent of California, a close friend of Susan B. Anthony's, introduced a women's suffrage measure. It states that 'The right of citizens of the United States to vote shall not be denied or abridged by the United States, or by any state, on account of sex.' And Elizabeth Cady Stanton, another wonderful worker in this field, brought some of the finest women speakers to the Senate Committee on Privileges and Elections. Unfortunately, the measure was ignored. But I predict it will be renewed again and again until it passes—and I only pray that I may live long enough to see it become the law of our land."

"Amen to that." Cecily emphatically nodded her head in agreement.

At last, it was time for Cecily to return home, and Hugo went out to the street to find a hansom cab. As Cecily was saying her good-byes to the Wilsons, Elone took her hand and squeezed it. She murmured, "Hugo is very fond of you, it is plain to see. We heard what he did for the men on the cattle drive last year—he will make a very good doctor. He will need someone like you to stand beside him and inspire him, and how much better it will be because you intend to be a doctor yourself."

"Oh, my goodness!" Cecily was flustered and blushed violently. "We—I mean—we've only really just begun to go out together! But I do like him a lot. And, yes, he *will* make a wonderful doctor. Well, good night—I'm very pleased that you invited me to come along with you tomorrow to the conference."

After Cecily Franklin had gone out to join Hugo in the ride back to her boardinghouse, Ben turned to his wife. "How wonderful it would be if they did marry and set up a clinic out in the far West, where there are almost no doctors at all! There, she would have a chance to prove the equality of women—especially with a fellow like Hugo Bouchard to work with her and to be valiant in her defense."

"As you have always been in mine, my dearest one," Elone tenderly whispered back.

Thirty-Nine

During the first two days of the conference on women's suffrage, Hugo Bouchard escorted Cecily Franklin to the meetings, which were held in a huge tent erected on the grounds of Lincoln Park. Hugo was impressed by the lucidity and logic of the women speakers, one of whom was the celebrated Susan B. Anthony. She pointed out that some strides were being made toward limited women's suffrage, as some states extended to women the right to vote on the issues of schools, taxes, and bonds. Kentucky had led the way in 1838 by extending so-called "school suffrage": Widows with children in school were permitted to vote on school issues. Kansas likewise extended school suffrage to women in 1861, and in 1875 Michigan and Minnesota had followed suit.

"What we must have, if this goal of ours is to be accomplished," Susan B. Anthony defiantly declared to her absorbed audience, "is a sufficient show of interest at the voting booth. I am ashamed and appalled to have to tell you that in those instances where we have won the right to vote, only a very small number of women have exercised their new right. I realize that we frequently encounter ridicule, even threats of reprisal, when we enter the polling places. Earlier this year, for example, those valiant ladies who turned out for the school board elections in New York State met with male election officials who puffed smoke in the women's faces, then threw stones at them."

As cries of "For shame!" rose from her listeners, she held up a hand for silence and fiercely vowed, "But, if enough women all over the United States demand the vote, demand it of their congressmen, their duly elected local, state, and national officials, then we shall have it. We must and we will have it, if all of you are as adamant as my colleagues and I are on this matter. It is time that women, whom God made from Adam's rib, are admitted to equality before the bar of justice, the ballot box, the home, the office, and the factory!"

During a recess in the proceedings, Elone Wilson conferred with a number of the women seated around her. She spoke eloquently and gently, pointing out what she had been able to do in Wichita, and of the odds that faced her and her women associates from the very beginning. "One must sometimes turn the other cheek, as it says in the Bible, but," she suddenly smiled, "at last we have found that we are no longer being slapped, either by word, or by act. We are respected because we have not shirked our work—we have not given up our role as mothers and good wives, as comforts to our husbands. We hope to work side by side with our men, toward a happier future for all of us, and especially for our children."

When the conference was over and they left the tent, Cecily turned to Hugo, tucked her arm around his, and murmured, "How do you honestly feel about this, Hugo?"

"I never did think that a man was superior to a woman. Only maybe physically—in strength, in things like driving cattle, for instance."

"Pooh!" The lovely brunette boasted, "I'll bet I could drive cattle, if I'd a mind to!"

"I'm sure you could, Cecily—but I'm glad you won't. And I'm very glad that you're going to be a doctor. You know, Cecily, I—I've never had a girl—a woman friend—before in all my life—" He stopped, feeling very awkward. He cleared his throat, then declared, "I don't want you to think that I'm like the other fellows at Rush, trying to get you—well, you know—"

"Are you trying to say that you're falling in love with me, Hugo?" she matter-of-factly asked him. She turned to face him, put her hands on his shoulders, and stared steadfastly into his eyes.

They had by now reached a more secluded section of the park, and so in answer to her blunt question, Hugo on impulse did what he had wanted to do ever since the day he had first seen Cecily working in the laboratory: He put his arms around her and he kissed her very gently on the lips.

"Oh, my!" she breathed, and she returned the kiss with such emphatic vigor that he was thrilled beyond words—and left speechless, his face crimson.

"Hugo, I think I have the same feeling for you, but we're not going to do anything about it until after we have our certificates as doctors. Then we'll discuss what and where and how, if it's meant to happen," she told him.

Hugo was in a state of rhapsodic euphoria by the time he and Cecily reached her boardinghouse. They exchanged a quick but thrillingly satisfying kiss in the lobby, and then he went back to Cordelia's house.

Cordelia and Carla were seated in the gazebo, and Carla was finishing another watercolor as Cordelia gaily chatted. Another of her important socialite friends had asked to buy one of "that Bouchard girl's marvelous watercolors," having seen the one that Nettie McCormick had commandeered for herself.

"Well, Hugo! How was the conference?" Cordelia called out to the young man, as he came out of the back of the house and headed toward them.

"It was just wonderful!"

"I'll wager you took Miss Franklin with you," Cordelia hazarded. "Ah! I can tell from the way you're blushing that you did. I can also guess that you're head over heels with that young lady. I was very impressed with her that one evening she came over to study with you. Actually, I'd like the

337

chance to know her better—so why don't you invite her over for dinner on Monday? I'll make my delicious *coq au vin*, and it will give us all a chance to be at our ease.''

"I'm sure she'd be happy to come. She liked you very much, Cordelia," Hugo responded.

Carla was eyeing him a little disdainfully. She had not yet forgiven him his tactless commentaries on her artistic pursuit. Nonetheless, seeing him so radiantly happy, and having heard Cordelia's pronouncement, she could not help wishing him well. "Hugo, I was also very impressed with her. I do hope she likes you as much as you like her—you know I wish you well."

"That's very kind of you, Carla. I—listen, what I said about your paintings and your career was stupid. I was rude and I hurt your feelings—and I want to apologize right now."

Carla unbent at this sincere apology. She came to Hugo and held out her hand. "Friends again?"

"You bet! And I guess maybe I can understand now why you didn't want to go to Boston for good, Carla."

"Oh, Hugo!" Carla threw her arms around her brother and hugged him.

"I'm so happy to see you two young people have made up your differences," Cordelia said. "Now let's resolve to enjoy the rest of the summer together and see what it has in store for us!" Cordelia exclaimed as she came over to her guests and hugged them both tightly.

A week after the women's suffrage conference, Cecily had told Hugo that she was going to Wyoming to visit her aunt and would be back by mid-September, in time to resume her classes at Rush. "I'm anxious to see her, and besides, I want to look over the place where I'll be working as a doctor when I finally graduate, Hugo," she had explained.

On the day of her departure, he carried her bags to the train. Setting them down on the platform, he turned and faced her, awkward and ill at ease now that the moment of parting was at hand. "I—I miss you already. Do please write!"

"Of course I will. And you can write me in care of General Delivery in Rollins. I'll be missing you, too, dear Hugo," she whispered softly, and then suddenly leaned forward and kissed him on the mouth. "There! Now you'll have something to remember me by."

"As if I could forget! Cecily—" he began.

"No, don't say anything. I promise I'll write, but I'll be honest and tell you that I'm going to be very busy. I'm going to spend a great deal of time seeing what sort of people I'll have to deal with, once I go there to practice. And you, Hugo, you should spend as much time as you can with Dr. Wilson and his wife. You said they're going to stay and vacation before they have to go back to Wichita?"

"Yes, and I like their children very much. Don't worry, I'll keep busy, Cecily."

"All aboard!" the conductor bawled.

"I'll take your suitcases onto the train." Hugo hurried up the steps and carried the bags down the aisle to Cecily's compartment. Then he made his way back up the aisle to the platform, Cecily following, and just as the train slowly began to move, he hugged her hard and kissed her, then leaped down, stumbled, but regained his balance.

"You silly, you! But you're sweet!" she called to him, and blew him a kiss.

Hugo stood there transfixed with the look on his face of a man who had just been granted a glimpse of paradise.

Out of his allowance, Hugo bought Tisinqua, Sybella, and Thomas rollerskates. The Douglas children already owned their own pairs—purchased, of course, from their father's department store.

Elone and Laurette visited State Street and window-shopped, and when Laurette proudly led her through Charles's thriving department store, Elone was almost awestruck at the variety of goods displayed under one roof. As a gift, Laurette bought Elone a purse with her initials embroidered in silver thread. In return, when they got home, Elone took from one of her bags a wampum belt, exquisitely made of colored beads, that one of the Creek women had made for her when she and Ben had lived on the reservation. "This is for good luck for you, Laurette," she explained. "The pictographs say that you have a man and children who love you, and that you will live a long life."

"How sweet of you, Elone, dear! I'll treasure it all my life," Laurette exclaimed, as she fondly hugged the Indian woman.

* * *

339

In the evening, after the children had gone to bed, Hugo and Ben sat up till well past midnight as Lucien Edmond's sturdy blond son listened, engrossed, to the Quaker doctor's stories of some of the dire emergencies to which he had been called in Wichita and the surrounding area.

"Tell me, Ben, haven't you ever felt you wanted to specialize in one particular field? Like surgery, or diseases of the blood, or maybe research to try to cure consumption and dyphtheria?"

"No, I always wanted to be a general practitioner, Hugo. That's what most communities need in the way of medical care. Where your friend Cecily plans to practice, there are barely enough physicians to help the growing settler population. You know, much of what I learned came from applying general principles to crises and emergencies. Like bullet wounds, for example, because Wichita was a godless town at first, when the cattle drives were at their height. Of course, I send for all the books and journals I can, and I'm always studying. A doctor is never too old to learn. Perhaps one day, maybe when you're my age, some of these maladies, like the consumption you mentioned, we'll have a cure for, God willing."

One morning during this halcyon month of August, Laurette had taken all the children shopping to buy the Wilson children bathing attire. While they chose their suits, Tisinqua, Sybella, and Thomas told her that they had never before swum in a lake, though they had often bathed in the creeks and some of the smaller river tributaries back in Kansas.

Kenneth, Arthur, and Howard, despite their mother's pleas to the contrary, kept plying the Wilson children with questions about gunfights, rustling, and cattle drives. Howard was the most persistent, wanting to know how many gunfights they had been in. Thomas solemnly answered, "We have never been in a gunfight because it is forbidden in our Quaker faith to carry weapons and to resort to violence, Howard. Father has told me that sometimes men who are angry with each other shoot at each other to settle their arguments, but now there is not so much of that. We have a marshal and a sheriff and deputies, and there are more and more people who come to Wichita to settle down and raise families and live quietly—and they don't need guns."

340

"Shucks," Howard made a face. "I'd sure like to have me a gunbelt and holsters on each side. I'd practice hitting tin cans till I was real good!"

Sybella, who was nearing twelve and already a little woman, was fascinated by the displays of dresses and fabrics in the State Street store, and she was particularly delighted with the blue bathing dress Laurette suggested for her.

That hot afternoon, the Wilson and Douglas children, accompanied by the Quaker doctor and Hugo, strolled to the beach at Twenty-second Street to swim. The water was still extremely cool, despite the stiflingly hot temperature. Kenneth and Arthur, quite proud of their knowledge, explained to the Wilson children that it was the wind over the lake and the water currents that made it colder than one would think it should be, so late in the summer.

They went into the water. Kenneth and Arthur, as well as Howard, were already excellent swimmers. From very early ages, their parents had let them wade about, gradually instilling a confidence in their own ability to keep afloat. Thomas, Sybella, and Tisinqua, for all that they had paddled about in the creek and the smaller river streams, were only tyros by comparison.

"Don't go out too far, children," Ben Wilson called, as he and Hugo stood on the sandy beach, watching the twins indulge in brotherly horseplay by scooping up handfuls of wet sand and hurling them at each other. Then the Quaker doctor and his nephew turned and strolled up the beach, as Hugo engaged his mentor in further discussion of doctoring along the frontier.

Sybella meanwhile had waded in only up to her chest, and was happily paddling to and fro when she disappeared from view in a sudden drop-off. Tisinqua, who was nearby, noticed almost at once that she was missing, and cried out, "Father! Sybella went under! I'm scared—oh, Father, I can't see her!"

Hugo immediately rushed into the water, hurling himself forward. With powerful strokes, he reached the point where Sybella had disappeared, and dove down. Here the bottom dipped without warning by at least a dozen feet. He brushed by her form, by now inert—for the child had lost consciousness. Frantically, he encircled Sybella's waist with his left arm and lifted her to the surface of the water, turning her so that she was on her back with her face toward the air. "It—it's all right," he whispered, terrified at the girl's pallor and lack of movement. "I'll get you ashore. . . . The bottom just dropped out, didn't it. . . . You'll be fine. . . . Oh, God, please let her be all right!"

He carried Sybella ashore in his arms and laid her out gently on the beach. Then, without a moment's hesitation, he turned her over and began pressing down firmly on her back with both hands, then releasing the pressure, in an even rhythm. It was a method his instructor had discussed the previous semester, when one of the students had asked how one might resuscitate someone who had apparently drowned.

Ben had come up hurriedly to the girl's side and was now kneeling down beside her with Hugo. "Dear God, Hugo, let's hope what you're doing is going to work. . . . Oh, if I'd only been watching more closely—"

At this moment, Sybella gagged and coughed, spitting out the water from her lungs and then wanly opening her eyes. Her face was contorted with anxiety and distress as she looked up at Ben. "Oh, Papa—Papa—"

"There, now, darling!" Ben cradled her with an arm around her shoulders. "You're fine now. Hugo saw to that."

"Thank you, H-Hugo. You—you saved my life—I never would have come up—" Sybella stammered.

"God bless you," Ben murmured, as his eyes met Hugo's. "Sybella means so much to me—she's a living reminder of my dear Fleurette, you see." Then, recovering himself, he said, "We mustn't tell Elone! She would be terrified if she knew what almost happened." He sighed. "We are all in God's hands, and He has been good to us. Hugo, He obviously directed your footsteps to the road that will enable you to save many a life. I think what happened just now is prophetic."

Forty

Coincidentally, while Ben and Elone Wilson were in Chicago attending the conference on women's suffrage, Judith Marquard and Geraldine Bouchard in New Orleans met twice for lunch to discuss the rights of women and other minorities.

Several months earlier, Lopasuta had invited Judith and her blind husband, Bernard, to dinner, and the two couples had become fast friends. Judith welcomed this warm communicative relationship. She had come to feel less like a subordinate and more like a participant in Lopasuta's defense work. It engaged her in causes in which she was deeply interested—for there were a number of cases involving a woman's vulnerability to an unscrupulous man. There were thousands of cases all through the United States where honest, decent, law-abiding females were being ruthlessly exploited by male employers, sexually harassed, made to feel obligated for the mere privilege of earning their daily bread at starvation wages.

After having had lunch on this Thursday afternoon in August, Judith and Geraldine were discussing the bill restricting Chinese immigration. "Last year, President Hayes vetoed that bill as a violation of the 1868 Burlingame Treaty," Geraldine commented, "but, judging from all the newspaper reports in the far West and Northwest, there seem to be many states that want just such a restriction. It's dreadful! I received a letter from Maxine Bouchard some time ago, and she relayed some news from her husband, Lucien Edmond—he and Ramón Hernandez are up in Leadville, Colorado, working their fabulous silver mine. Anyway, Lucien Edmond told her that two Chinese who had come to town had been literally torn to pieces by an angry mob. It's barbarous—inhuman— to think that, in this day and age, we should have such dreadful prejudices!"

"I've read," Judith volunteered, "that there's just as much hatred shown the Irish, the Poles, and German and Russian Jews in various parts of the country—immigrant Jews who fled Russia and the pogroms of the Czar are living in ghettos in New York. And blacks still don't have total recognition in all the states of this supposedly emancipated union." She sighed. "I guess it's a long educational process, Geraldine. I don't know if you or I will live to see it, though I surely hope so. I admire the way Lopasuta fights for minorities."

"Why shouldn't he?" Geraldine countered. "He belongs to one himself, and the Indian probably has had the worst deal of all in this country. He's not even considered a citizen in most states, and many people consider him even lower than black." She suddenly laughed and exclaimed, "My gracious—there I go, getting on the soapbox again! I'll tell you what, Judith, Lopasuta is in court all afternoon, so he's not going to keep track of your being at the office. Let's sneak in a little bit of window-shopping. It's such a lovely day!"

"Well, since you're my employer's wife, and you authorize my going along with you, I'll say yes this once," Judith smiled in reply. Then, her face sobering, she added, "I understand why you feel the way you do about the Chinese, Geraldine. It's because of Mei Luong, isn't it?"

"Yes. I love her; she's almost like a sister to me. She's so good with the children, so unselfish and thoughtful of others. Poor thing, she's barely had the chance to know what love is—but at least she does now. Tell me," Geraldine asked with a giggle, "does Eugene DuBois sit around the office with a mooning, dreamy expression as often as Mei Luong does at home?"

"Oh, yes!" Judith laughed. "Sometimes when I'm going to the courthouse with him to check official records on deeds or whatever, I'll be talking to him—asking him a question perhaps—and then realize he hasn't heard a word I said!"

Geraldine sighed. "I wish there was something I could do for Mei Luong and others like her. I've been thinking about starting a grass-roots movement on behalf of the Chinese, and I wonder if you'd want to be one of my charter members, Judith?"

"You can put me down for sure! If the only Chinese I'd ever met was Mei Luong, I'd vote yes to allow them to become citizens," Judith stoutly avowed.

After Eugene DuBois had agreed to Lopasuta's proposal that he come to read law with him, the earnest young man worked diligently to prepare himself for a future in which he hoped many doors would be opened to him—doors that were now closed because of the tinge of black blood in his veins.

He had gone to work in Lopasuta's office exactly a week after his client had agreed to settle out of court and pay Eugene the money due him for carpentry work. Judith Marquard had found Eugene a sympathetic, hardworking individual, who went out of his way to run errands for her and to relieve her of a good deal of the details that had become her responsibility since last November. One of the duties that Eugene took onto his shoulders was a daily trip to the stock exchange, just before its closing, to bring back the latest quotations for Leland Kenniston's factor, René Laurent.

For at least an hour, either early in the morning—if Lopasuta did not have a court case, or was not otherwise engaged in Leland's business affairs—or late in the afternoon, Lopasuta and Eugene shut themselves up in Lopasuta's library. Lopasuta had lent Eugene many of his law books, which contained the fundamentals of the law, particularly as regarded business contracts. The Creole took these home and assiduously studied them, and Lopasuta was delighted to find him asking questions that showed his new pupil had a feeling for the law and would certainly be able, within six or seven months, to qualify to take the bar examination for the State of Louisiana.

Lopasuta and Geraldine were also delighted that Eugene had so obviously fallen deeply in love with Mei Luong. They saw to it that the young Creole was a frequent guest at their house for dinner, which Mei Luong herself often prepared. After dinner, the Comanche lawyer and his beautiful, compassionate wife tactfully absented themselves from the salon to give the two young people a chance to do their courting.

During one such evening recently, Eugene finally found the courage to tell Mei Luong of his love for her. She in turn shyly admitted that she was extremely fond of him. Self-effacing as always, she then turned away and, looking at the wall, said in a low voice, "But I do not understand how such a fine man as you could love me. You know my background— that I came from a poor family and that—"

"I don't care at all," he interrupted. "I don't want to marry your family, Mei Luong—I want to marry you. If you'll have me."

Her eyes filled with tears, but she kept her face turned away from him as she continued. "But I would not come to you without experience of men. I know that even in our country, a man who prepares for marriage expects that when he takes a woman to be his wife, he will be the first to take her. But you know I was already married. Realizing this, do you think I would be a good wife for you, Eugene DuBois?''

Now there were tears in his eyes as he moved toward her, sat down behind her, put his hands on her shoulders, and murmured, ''Please look at me, Mei Luong. Please.''

Slowly, very slowly, she turned, and there were tears running down her cheeks, and her lips were trembling.

''I love you. I don't care what you came from, what you were, or whether you were married or not. To me, you are the dearest, sweetest, loveliest young woman I have ever known. You are kind and good. You make a man proud to know you because you show him respect. You make him want to be better than he is, and that is what I need most of all. I have no family; I have no one who cares for me, either. Look—you are Chinese, and for thousands of years your people had the greatest culture in all the world. Beside you, I am a poor, ignorant savage.''

''Oh, no, you must not say that!'' she protested, and impulsively put her soft palm over his mouth.

He kissed it tenderly and murmured, ''Mei Luong, you would honor me, you would give me great joy, you would make me the happiest man in all the world, if you would become my wife. I want to have children by you. I want to live all my life with you. And I want to hold you in my arms and make you happy and know that you are loved.''

She could not control her tears as she bent her head and clung to him, weeping with such joy as she had not believed she could ever know. He wept too, and in this commingling of tears there was a sweet communion. Neither race nor difference in background or history lay between them. They loved, and that was enough for them—and it would last a lifetime because it was true and honest, tender and exalted.

At last, he tilted up her chin and smiled into her eyes, then he gave her his handkerchief, so that she could blow her nose and dry her tears. She took a deep breath and confessed, ''I think I loved you almost from the first moment I saw you. I dared not dream that anyone so handsome and important as you would notice a poor Chinese girl—''

''I will not let you say that of yourself ever again, Mei

Luong. You are rich in so many things. Why, you speak English better than many of the white people for whom I've worked and who pride themselves on their families and their backgrounds."

"But surely in this city, there must be many girls who are more beautiful than I, who will bring you a dowry—I am poor; I have only what Mr. and Mrs. Bouchard pay me—"

"Will you *please* stop talking like that! I'm not marrying you for a dowry. If you bring only yourself to me, I will have all the riches in the world, Mei Luong. I will tell you something—when Mr. Bouchard invited me to dinner and I saw you for the first time, I knew that I must accept his offer to work for him, to better myself, so that I would be worthy of you. And I promise you, Mei Luong, that if you become my wife, I will try to improve myself every day of my life, so that you will never be ashamed of me as your husband."

"Oh, my dear one, never say that! You do me too much honor—"

"The honor that we have for each other is part of our love. Dear Mei Luong, will you marry me?"

"Oh, yes—whenever you wish! But I must ask Mr. Bouchard how it is done. You must have heard that my people are not welcome in many states of your country."

"I will ask him myself, but we have never had that problem here. New Orleans is a very different city from most others. It is what we call a melting pot, Mei Luong—it has people from Haiti, Jamaica, the Caribbean, even Africa. They are respected and honored; they have done great things, and their names are part of the history of New Orleans. Here, we do not look down upon your people—we are wise enough to know the Chinese were highly civilized when most peoples of the world were practically still living in caves! Never again apologize to me that you are what you are, for it is because you are what you are that I love you, and only you, Mei Luong."

She could not hold back her feelings, and she flung her arms around him and kissed him passionately. He was awed by the reciprocity of her love, by her exotic and delicate beauty, and by the wistful and tender promise of such ecstasy and joy as he did not believe he could ever know.

* * *

The next morning, when he reported for work, Lopasuta, smiled and encouragingly asked, "Well now, Eugene, how goes it with your courting?"

"She—she said she'll marry me, Mr. Bouchard! I'm the happiest man in the world! But first," he frowned with anxiety, "we need to know if there are any legal difficulties to prevent our marriage."

"I don't think there can be any problems, but I'll certainly check. Incidentally, you are Catholic, are you not?"

"Yes, of course. But we have already discussed this, and Mei Luong would abide by my religion. We all believe in one God, Mr. Bouchard, and it does not matter what we call Him, so long as we obey His laws."

"I think even the most hidebound priest would say that your theology is sound, Eugene," Lopasuta said with a smile. "I'll tell you what—tomorrow I'll talk to Judge Ehlers. I've defended several cases before him, and he seems a kind, forthright man. I'll ask his opinion of what he believes might be any obstacles to stand between you and Mei Luong. My personal guess is that there are none."

Lopasuta Bouchard had visited the judge in chambers, and the day after that meeting he told the affable young Creole, "I've very good news for you. Just as I suspected, there's nothing in our statute books that would prevent you from marrying Mei Luong. But Geraldine has come up with a wonderful idea, and it also seems most appropriate. You know, of course, Eugene, that the late Luke Bouchard adopted me as his son after he heard from Sangrodo that I was ambitious to learn and to help my people, to be their spokesman in a world dominated by the whites. Well, since he adopted *me* and I became a citizen, Geraldine said to me, 'Why don't I adopt Mei Luong as my sister? That way, nobody can ever question her rights.' "

"God bless you both, Mr. Bouchard. The luckiest day of my life was when Aurelio sent me to see you to help me out against George Carrolier. I was given a new life, and a woman I shall cherish till my last breath."

"I'm very happy for you and for Mei Luong, too. We both love her." He laughed and continued, "Geraldine said that since Mei Luong was already like a sister to her, they may as well make it legally so. By the way, do you know the Jesuit

348

Church on Baronne Street? There's a young priest there who's very liberal in his views, and I'm sure he'd like to meet you both."

That Saturday morning, Mei Luong and Eugene DuBois went to the church, one of the oldest in all New Orleans. Mei Luong told Father Deladier of her desire to convert to Catholicism, and that she would raise her future children in that faith. After speaking with the young couple for over two hours, the priest made the sign of the cross and said, "You are good people; you have God in your hearts, and I will be happy to marry you and give you our Lord's blessing. I will read the banns tomorrow, and in three weeks you may come before me to enter the holy state of matrimony."

Meanwhile, Lopasuta had filed the petition for adoption, and a week before the wedding, he, Geraldine, and Mei Luong appeared before the friendly judge, who formally granted the petition. And when they had returned to the house on Greenley Street and were enjoying tea in the parlor, Lopasuta turned to Mei Luong: "Well, my dear, you are now Geraldine's sister and come to think of it, I'm now your brother-in-law. You've gotten *two* new relatives in one day—no! Make that *five*: two nephews and one niece, too!"

Mei Luong laughed delightedly, then a perplexed look came into her eyes. "What is my name now?" she asked diffidently.

Lopasuta and Geraldine smiled at her puzzlement, and Lopasuta said, "Well, in this country, Mei Luong, since a woman takes her husband's name when they are married, Geraldine is now legally a Bouchard—so that makes your legal name Bouchard, too. If Geraldine had adopted you before she and I were married, your name would have been Mei Luong Murcur. However, all of this is really quite moot, because in one more week, you will have yet *another* new name, won't you? You will be Mei Luong DuBois."

Mei Luong giggled, then blushed as she weighed the full significance of his words. She looked down at her lap and shyly asked, "Will you still want me to work for you?"

"If you wish," Lopasuta gently replied, "but I think once you are married, you will want to spend most of your time in your new home, with your husband. But," he winked at his lovely wife, "I think you can convince Geraldine to let you help care for the children a few days each week."

"Oh, my, Mrs. Bouchard! I hadn't thought—what will you do—I mean, you will need a new nurse—"

"Mei Luong, the last thing in the world I want you to be doing now is worrying about me," Geraldine declared. "I can find another nurse, I'm sure—although your shoes will be very hard to fill."

The young Chinese woman looked down at her feet, then up at Geraldine. "I do not understand. Why do my shoes need to be filled—and with what, other than my feet?"

Geraldine and Lopasuta laughed with delight, and it was only by sheer dint of will that Geraldine could stop laughing long enough to apologize and to assure Mei Luong that they were not laughing at her. After she composed herself, Geraldine managed to explain the colloquial expression as best she could, and Mei Luong soon was laughing along with them.

Suddenly, Mei Luong's usual shy reserve seemed to slip from her shoulders, and she looked unquaveringly at Geraldine and Lopasuta, then asked, "Since we are now all relatives, I wonder if you would grant me the honor of addressing you by your given names."

Geraldine exclaimed gleefully, "Good for you, Mei Luong! That's the spirit! And you're absolutely right. You can hardly call your sister and brother-in-law 'Mr. and Mrs. Bouchard,' can you?"

Lopasuta interrupted, "Incidentally, Mei Luong, I think you will be pleased to know that I think Eugene will be ready to take his examination for the Louisiana bar around Christmas. He's progressing very well—and I'm very proud of him. It is my hope that next year, when he's a full-fledged lawyer, he and I may open our own separate legal office, working together. That way we could devote even more attention to defending those who need our help and still continue to work for Mr. Kenniston. In any event, you'll have money enough so that you can have children, and give them all the comforts that they should have."

Mei Luong was overcome with joy. She took Lopasuta's hand and brought it to her lips and kissed it. "You are the kindest of men. Lu Choy was very fortunate to have known you. Her child grows stronger and more of a man each day, and he will one day know and honor his heritage—that he came from a girl who fished from a sampan and who loved you very deeply. And he will not be ashamed of it, as I was not ashamed but proud to serve you.''

Lopasuta kissed Mei Luong's forehead and murmured, "In you is the spirit of Lu Choy. If it had not been for her, I could not have survived those terrible hours of loneliness, thinking that Geraldine was lost to me forever. And if I had not found you to take care of Luke, I would have been lost. Mei Luong, you will always be to me the reincarnation of Lu Choy, and you will always remind me of her courage and sincerity and devotion. It is fate that brought us all together, and it is fate that has decreed you shall have happiness, after your years of sorrow—as a small reward for all that you have done for Geraldine and me. I respect and honor you, my sister-in-law.''

And then, very gravely, as if she were a princess, he took the hand of the young Chinese woman, brought it to his lips, and kissed it.

On the morning of the wedding ceremony, a messenger came to the Bouchard house with a telegram from Leland Kenniston, addressed to Eugene DuBois. After expressing his pleasure over Eugene's having joined the Kenniston firm, Leland advised him that, if he would call at the Brunton & Alliance Bank of New Orleans, he would find a bank draft in the amount of two hundred dollars as a wedding present for him and Mei Luong.

When Mei Luong and Eugene entered the church to take their marriage vows, with Lopasuta and Geraldine following them, they were radiant. Lopasuta was to be best man, while Geraldine would serve as matron of honor. Judith and Bernard Marquard attended, as did René Laurent.

The ceremony in the old Jesuit church was simple and yet memorably beautiful. Mei Luong had taken instructions from Father Deladier, wishing to please Eugene by accepting his faith. She was not concerned for her immortal soul; in her simple, practical outlook on life, there was but one Deity, who ruled the heavens, the earth, and the seas, to whom one prayed. As a child, her parents had burned offerings to Lord Buddha, whose gentle philosophy was not unlike that of the Nazarene.

She smiled to herself, feeling that it was hard to believe she wasn't merely dreaming and that the adoring, idealistic love this handsome Creole professed for her—she who had been the lowest of the low in her own land—was real. She felt that, at last, she had come to a home and a guardian and champion for whom she could toil with unabated delight for the rest of her days. Standing before the altar, tears misting in her eyes, she clung to Eugene's hand and stole adoring looks at him throughout the ceremony.

She had come to this strange city to start a new life, and now that she was Mrs. DuBois, yet another new life was beginning.

That night, as she bathed and prepared herself for their union, Mei Luong said a secret little prayer to an ancient deity, still cherished by some Chinese—the Moon Goddess, the protector of women, who looked down with smiling eyes through cloudless skies upon nights of love.

She trembled when Eugene came to her, but not in fear. Her eyes encompassed him, took his measure, and rejoiced in being his mate. When the ceremonial gown was gently dropped from her slim, lovely body, when she felt his reverent kisses and his gentle, yearning touches upon her flesh, she sighed, feeling the ecstasy of rebirth, acceptance, and fulfillment.

Forty-One

After the terrible Galveston hurricane three years earlier, Arabella Hunter and her daughter, Joy, had moved closer to the center of the city, away from the waterfront, and now lived in a one-story brick house with a flourishing garden in the back. Care of the garden was entrusted to Joy: Now halfway through her eleventh year, the girl displayed a strong sense of responsibility, added to which were a precocity, wit, imagination, and sunny disposition that kept Arabella from realizing that she was approaching the milestone of sixty years.

While Arabella and Joy frequently visited the elder Hunter children—Melinda and Andrew—and their families, they were happiest when alone together. Neither Melinda nor Andrew had ever been quite so close to Arabella as Joy—appropriately named indeed, and in these twilight years not only a child to be reckoned with, but a constant source of maternal gratification and companionship.

As a young woman on Windhaven Plantation, when Arabella had been capricious and headstrong by nature, she had secretly dreaded the eventual coming of middle and later years, the inevitable time when all the laughter and coquetry and teasing would be done with. But now, it seemed to her that each new day brought greater zest than when she was in her teens and twenties. Most of this she attributed to her attentive, devoted younger daughter.

Joy had progressed remarkably in school, and her teachers invariably sent Arabella letters of glowing praise over Joy's interest in class and the quality of her homework and her oral recitations. Joy was particularly fond of history and of fiction, and whenever they had an hour or two in the evening with no socializing, she would always ask her mother to tell her a story. In turn, during the last several months she had amazed and delighted her mother by making up excellent stories of her own, then anxiously asking her, "Mama, do you think it would make a really good story, if I were to write it all out?"

These summer days of 1880 were, indeed, among the happiest Arabella Hunter had ever known. She had long ago reconciled herself to the fact that the world was not hers to conquer—particularly the world of men. (When she looked back, she could reflect that James Hunter had been a remarkably indulgent and tolerant husband who had put up with her foibles and given her almost free rein, though with the wisdom to know exactly when to draw up the reins and pull her up short.)

Now she looked forward to evenings at the opera or the theater—either with her daughter or her companion of late, Dr. Samuel Parmenter. Joy thoroughly enjoyed these evenings out, and the next day she would discuss what she had heard and seen with appreciative pleasure.

Arabella also spent part of each week as a volunteer nurse at the Galveston General Hospital—where she had met Samuel Parmenter, the hospital's administrator—and two days at the Douglas Department Store. This, too, kept her mind alert, and she wanted that, so that she could keep up with Joy. Indeed, as she had written to Maxine Bouchard this summer,

"I remember how shocked Melinda was when she discovered that, at my advanced age, I was going to have a baby. I rather fancy that at that moment she considered me an outrageous creature—but I pray that she may have a child late in life, a child born in love, who will make her forget the wrinkles and the gray hair and all the telltale signs of age."

On the second Friday in July, Arabella had accepted an invitation from Samuel Parmenter to have dinner with him at the best restaurant in Galveston and, of course, to bring Joy. He had extended the invitation early in the afternoon, as she was finishing her volunteer shift as a nurse, and he had said with a mischievous twinkle in his eyes, "I've something rather important to say to you, and I'd feel safer saying it with Joy there to hear me."

"Why, Dr. Parmenter, whatever do you mean?" She gave him an archly flirtatious look, but this time, she told herself, it was not just the capricious show of coquetry that had once been part of her nature; she knew it meant more.

The fact was that Arabella Hunter had thought that at the age of fifty-six there were no more surprises in store for her. But the widowed Arabella found herself, greatly to her surprise, in love with her attentive companion. It was a curious feeling to look inward upon herself, and to examine her feelings at this stage of her life. She had not considered remarrying, for she had mourned James deeply, and it had been Joy who had almost solely helped her assuage that grief. When she started working at the hospital during the yellow fever epidemic of April 1878, Arabella had at first been merely grateful to Dr. Parmenter for making her feel useful again by taking part in a world she had first sought to shun when James had been taken from her.

Learning that he had been a childless widower for the past seven years and that his administrative work at the hospital had been his own way of trying to remain impervious to his bereavement, she had felt an enormous compassion and admiration for this tall, gray-haired doctor, so soft-spoken and reserved. To her surprise, he had asked her to have dinner with him and be his guest to hear Gounod's *Faust*. She had discovered that he was remarkably well-read, with a droll sense of humor, and that he was also a model of courtesy and gallantry, the kind that she had believed vanished with the

Civil War. She had reciprocated the invitation and invited Dr. Parmenter to her house for dinner. And Joy had taken to him at once, mainly because he had treated her like an adult.

Soon, the doctor and Arabella had a close platonic relationship. But of late, their feelings for each other had been growing into something more. Arabella thought of all this as she dressed for this evening's outing, with more than usual care.

Finishing up his meal, Dr. Samuel Parmenter beckoned to the waitress to bring Arabella and himself coffee, "And half a cup for the young lady, if you please, miss." Turning to Arabella, he added, "As a doctor, I think I may safely prescribe half a cup for Joy."

"Oh, thank you, Dr. Parmenter!" Joy exclaimed with a radiant smile. "Mama doesn't let me drink coffee too often; she says it will keep me awake at night."

"Well, young lady, since I've a notion that you may be up later than usual this evening because of the announcement I propose to make in a few moments, I do not see the harm. Have I your permission, dear Arabella?"

"Oh, Samuel, of course you do! I know it will be a treat for her!" Arabella laughed.

"Oh, and, miss," he turned to the waitress who was returning with the coffee pot, "would you bring each of us a small pony of your excellent *framboise*?" He explained to Joy and Arabella, "It's a French raspberry cordial, and I think a sip or two will be most beneficial to round off so elegant a meal."

"Oh, my!" Joy exclaimed, hopefully looking at her mother for approval.

"I do declare, Samuel, you're behaving very mysteriously tonight; it's most uncharacteristic," Arabella teased him.

When the cordial was brought, Samuel handed one of the round glass goblets to Joy and cautioned, "Sip it very slowly— just a little at a time, my dear." To Arabella, as he lifted his own goblet, he said, "This drink gives me the courage to make this declaration—and Joy, I want you to listen very attentively."

"Samuel, you're keeping me in just dreadful suspense, you know!" Arabella shook her head and made a helpless gesture.

He set down the goblet, and—his face serious—he took a

355

deep breath and averred in a soft voice: "Arabella, I love you, and I would feel greatly honored and privileged if you would consent to marry me."

"Mama, that's wonderful!" Joy burst out. Then seeing that her mother was staring at Samuel almost openmouthed and was not noticing her at the moment, the girl surreptitiously picked up the goblet and took another sip of the raspberry cordial.

"I hadn't thought of remarrying, Samuel—my gracious, I never dreamed you were going to say anything like this! Certainly not in front of Joy!" Arabella exclaimed, blushing like a schoolgirl.

"I'll tell you very frankly, Arabella, while I have come to love you very dearly, I happen to love Joy almost as much. The two of you would make such an irresistibly wonderful family that you would make me young again."

"Mama, you know how much I like Dr. Parmenter; I think you ought to marry him! We would all be so happy together." Joy ingeniously observed.

Arabella turned to stare at her daughter, then burst into merry laughter. "You certainly know how to overcome my resistance, don't you, Samuel? Yes, you know perfectly well that I truly love you—and since you've declared your undying affection for my favorite daughter, I have no arguments left to say no to you!"

"Oh, Mama, I'm so happy for both of us!" was Joy's irrepressible commentary. Getting up from her chair, she went over to Samuel, put her arms around him, and hugged him and kissed him on the cheek.

"Darling girl, you and your mother have made me the happiest man in creation," he chuckled, but the mistiness in his eyes bespoke a far more intense emotion.

Then, as he held Joy close to him, he turned to Arabella and said, "I promise you that you'll never regret it, my darling. I'll make you both very happy."

"Samuel, you've really left me just about speechless! But I will say that, in turn, I promise you that I'll make you a very good wife. We get along so famously, we like so many of the same things—and Joy will share them all with us. Yes, Samuel, I'll marry you whenever you wish."

"Well, then, how about in two or three weeks?" he proposed. "Then we can have a honeymoon as the perfect excuse for getting away from the terrible heat that devastates Galveston in August."

Joy, who had gone back to her seat, clapped her hands and exuberantly declared, "I want to come along, too, Mama!"

"Well, I never, young lady!" Arabella pretended righteous indignation. "You and I will have to have a little chat when we get home tonight. As a rule, a honeymoon is for a husband and a wife, and not for a tag-along daughter."

"Mama!" Joy said in a reproachful tone.

Arabella laughed again, reached out, and hugged her daughter. "I was only teasing."

"I think it will be delightful to have you with us, Joy." Samuel raised his cordial. "I toast the both of you—my wife-to-be, my daughter-to-be. God is very good to me in my declining years."

"Samuel Parmenter, I don't believe for a second that *you* believe you're old!" Arabella chided. "I've never known anyone so full of vitality and knowledge and good common sense." Then, in a soft, low voice meant only for his ears, she murmured, "I love you so much, Samuel."

The day before the wedding, Maxine Bouchard sent a telegram from Carrizo Springs, wishing Arabella and Samuel long years of happiness. Arabella, who had written to the Kennistons to tell them of the impending nuptials, also received a reply from Laure, inviting Arabella, Samuel, and Joy to visit her and Leland at their new house in New York City.

"What would you think of a honeymoon in New York, dearest Samuel?" she asked, and he enthusiastically agreed.

"Do you know, Bella, I've never been there, and I think it would be wonderful. Especially for Joy. We'll take her to Coney Island, sail on a river cruise down the Hudson, and see a thousand sights New York has to offer. And what a relief to be able to miss the very worst of Galveston's summer heat! Incidentally, I've six weeks' sabbatical leave due me, and I've gone on record that I intend to take it."

So Arabella immediately wired Laure Kenniston and accepted her invitation, notifying her that she, Samuel, and Joy would arrive in New York about the sixth of August. She declared that she looked forward to meeting Laure's new husband, of whom she had heard so much.

357

Arabella Hunter and Dr. Samuel Parmenter stood before the bespectacled priest in the cathedral—which had been rebuilt since the terrible hurricane—that stood near her former home. Wearing a dress of pale mauve silk, Arabella carried a spray of white orchids. Slightly behind her stood lovely little Joy, the maid of honor, with a bouquet of yellow roses that matched her dress. She continuously eyed both her mother and her new stepfather, a radiant smile playing on her lips.

It was a small wedding. Though the Galveston newspapers had made much of it, Arabella and Samuel had agreed on inviting only immediate family and closest friends. "There's no need to make a spectacle or have a Roman holiday, my darling Bella," he had told her. His calling her by that diminutive—by which James Hunter had addressed her in their most intimate moments—gave Arabella the wonderful feeling that, somehow, the solidity of her life was being continued, almost without interruption. Indeed, before the marriage, she had gone to the small chapel to the side of the rectory to pray, and there she had talked to James: "My dear one, I hope that you've watched over us since you left us. I'm only sorry that you couldn't be with me to share the delight of Joy's growing up day by day and becoming more of a treasure, always bringing something new and stimulating to this aging woman—yes, I am that, James darling—to keep me young and eager to cope. I know you'd approve of Samuel, and pray for us both, dear James. Look down upon us and watch your daughter, born of love, become a talented young woman who will live up to her name in every possible way."

Her older children—Melinda and Andrew—and their families were there as were her friends Max Steinfeldt, the manager of the Houston branch of the Douglas Department Store, and his wife, Alice. Dr. Parmenter had invited the prim head nurse, Susan Enderby. Displaying exactly the playful sense of humor that Arabella adored about him, he had whispered to his wife-to-be just before the priest began the ceremony, "When it's over, dearest Bella, toss your bouquet to Susan. She lacks nothing in the way of professional skill—and now it's my medical opinion that the perfect prescription to make her more human is a husband!"

Thus—after the priest had pronounced them man and wife and they had exchanged a long, happy kiss; and after Samuel had kissed Joy and said to her for all to hear, "Young lady, you're the loveliest maid of honor a man could ever have at his wedding, and I'm very glad you're going to be my new daughter"—Arabella turned and tossed her bouquet to the startled Susan Enderby, who turned scarlet as all eyes were on her.

That night, Joy went unbidden to her room, still carrying her bouquet of yellow roses. She closed the door, put the bouquet into a vase on the top of her dresser, got into her nightdress, and then knelt down to pray aloud:

"Dear Lord, I'm so very happy that Mama married Samuel. I like him very much; he's so smart and yet he doesn't show off—and he treats me as if I were as grown up as Mama. Oh, I know I'm not, but just the same it's wonderful to pretend I am—and, dear Lord, I promise I'm going to try to improve all the time so I will be as smart as he thinks I am. Oh—also, dear Lord, thank You for letting me go to New York with Mama and my new father. But mostly, I'm so glad You let Mama be happy again with someone who is almost as nice as my real daddy was. I know he's with You in heaven now, dear Lord, and I hope You'll tell him that I miss him a lot and think of him all the time, but that I think Samuel is going to be lots of fun to be a daughter to. Thanks again and good night. Amen."

Forty-Two

Laure could not have been more delighted with Leland's choice of the house in which they would begin their new lives. He had purchased a handsome brownstone on Twenty-first Street, on the East Side of New York City, facing Gramercy Park, which was kept private for the use of the families living on the square. There were excellent schools for both boys and girls nearby, and the beautifully groomed park provided an ideal place for children of all ages to play. It was a peaceful, quiet enclave within the bustling city growing by leaps and bounds around it.

Clarabelle Hendry had been as excited as Laure when she

led the children into the house. Leland, his eyes aglow with adoration, had given Laure his arm and conducted her on the "official sight-seeing tour of our new mansion, dear Mrs. Kenniston." He had shown remarkably good taste, too, in the furniture and decor, and the house already looked comfortably lived in. With a wry grin, he had told her, "For your information, my darling, since I know the familial loyalty of all you Bouchards, I purchased most of these fine things from the Douglas Department Store. I remember your telling me that Laurette Bouchard married the enterprising founder of New York's extremely popular new department store. And by the by, I was personally assisted by that most capable young manager, Mr. Alexander Gorth. He has a marvelous way of making a man completely at his ease, even when he has a major problem like outfitting a new house and he is praying that his beloved wife won't come and say, 'How could you pick such ugly things?' "

Laure had embraced him and then laughingly rejoined, "First of all, you're forgetting, Leland darling, that I know you pretty well by now and what your tastes are. You're such a connoisseur of food and wine, of art and music and books, the theater, opera—how could I even speculate that your taste in household furnishings wouldn't be on an equally high level? The fact is, Leland, I'm absolutely astounded, awestruck, and enchanted. And I'm very glad that I decided to leave Alabama and come here to live with you—my wonderful husband!"

He had taken her into the drawing room, drawn the door closed, taken her in his arms, and kissed her very gently and lingeringly. Laure shivered and closed her eyes as she clung to him. "It's just paradise being with you. I feel as if I've been reborn, starting life all over again," she confided.

"You don't know how happy you've made me, too, dear Laure. And because I have the greatest respect for the man who had the privilege of preceding me, I only hope that I shall never give you any cause to dwell nostalgically on days when you were happier. I know it will sometimes be difficult not to make comparisons, but each of us is new to the other—and, as you say, Laure, each of us is beginning a new life here and now."

"You're such an incurable romantic, Leland. That's one reason I'm so very much in love with you. Oh, my dear!"

she teased him as he began to kiss her again. "It's only midafternoon!" She was blushing like an adolescent on her first outing with a person of the opposite sex, and she found the sensation delicious.

Leland smiled, released her, stepped back, and made her a courtly bow. "I'm your devoted servant, madam," he declared. "Your wish is my command."

"No, my darling, just devoted. Never my servant," was Laure's soft, urgent entreaty, as she gave him a last kiss. Smoothing her full silk skirt and adjusting a wayward curl of her chignon, she rather breathlessly said, "The children will wonder what's become of us. Let's go see how they and Clarabelle are enjoying their new rooms. Oh, I think it's perfectly wonderful that you found this place so near good schools. Now I'm convinced more than ever that the future of our children will grow apace with this energetic, vital city. Alabama is too somnolent, and brilliant minds will find it difficult to flourish in such an atmosphere."

"I'm happy to hear you agreeing with my estimate of New York, Laure. Oh, there are discomforts, I warrant you. There are those who say that New York has the dirtiest streets in all the United States, and there are others who don't like the elevated trains, and of course, we have some slum areas that are disgraceful, thanks to the huge exodus of the persecuted and the poor from Europe. But, for business opportunity, for education and culture, and for challenging living, I don't think there's another city in this country that can match New York—and it will be my pleasant duty to try to prove all that to you in the long years, God grant, we have ahead of us." He smiled at her as he took her arm and led her out into the hallway.

It was indeed, as Laure almost at once discovered for herself, the difference between night and day from longtime residence in a peaceful, drowsing land to this interminably fascinating, noisy, exciting metropolis. When she went sightseeing, she saw fashionable women and their children watching a cook prepare pancakes in the window of a restaurant. Top-hatted businessmen stood in the crowd, wearing elegant waistcoats and diamond stickpins in their lapels, making gustatory comments that would have been suitable to those many social ranks and thousands of dollars beneath them. Down-

361

town, ragpickers plied the streets with their dog carts. Coffee-urn carts also passed through the slum areas of New York; these were the brainchild of one Dr. John Kenyon, who hoped thereby to convince people to stop drinking whiskey. They were offered coffee in porcelain cups and large pieces of bread and butter, and Kenyon had established missions for the drunkards of Brooklyn—places that drew large attendance but did not, alas, cut New York's by now enormous consumption of spirits.

German street musicians made leisurely strolls through the city, and when they set up near Gramercy Park one afternoon, the Bouchard children listened openmouthed, turning to one another with delight upon recognizing some of the tunes they had heard back on Windhaven Plantation. They were completely enthralled when Laure and Leland took them to Coney Island on the Atlantic Ocean. They shrieked and shouted with delight as the waves crashed over them, dressed in their bathing garments. Laure and Leland went bathing with them, then treated them to sandwiches and ice cream. Later—after dressing in their street clothes in the movable changing rooms that rolled right down onto the shore—the family enjoyed the fireworks display farther down the boardwalk at Brighton Beach.

Laure found window-shopping—that infallibly exciting free diversion available to every female residing in a city—a fascinating new pastime. The windows of R.H. Macy attracted her, as did those of Lord & Taylor and Stewart's. And after so many years of having most of their foods supplied from gardens and livestock at Windhaven Plantation, Laure found it peculiar but stimulating to shop for food for her family in stores. She quickly found an excellent greengrocer and a butcher, for Leland appreciated good food and did not stint on it. He was also emphatic in decreeing that the children should eat plenty of fruit and vegetables, no matter what the cost, for their good health. They had always enjoyed the fine produce grown on Windhaven Plantation, so this presented no parental problems for Leland and Laure, since all of the children savored their meals. Clarabelle Hendry helped Laure with both the shopping and the preparation of the meals, and she proved to be as capable a cook as she was a governess. She went out of her way to learn new recipes and even to take a quick course in French cuisine upon learning that her employer was particularly fond of such dishes as *coq au vin* and *canard à l'orange*.

New York was hot in July and August, but Laure was used to the sometimes intolerably humid atmosphere that emanated from the Alabama River in midsummer, so New York's climate presented no difficulty for her. She had never cared to wear corsets, and besides, since she had always maintained her svelte and lithe figure, she found them to be completely unnecessary. One day, as she was strolling down Broadway with Paul, Celestine, and Clarissa (John, now three, had been left at home under Clarabelle's charge), she saw a crowd gathering around a woman who lay inert on the Broadway sidewalk. The woman apparently was tightly corseted and had suffered from sunstroke. Soon a hospital wagon was drawn up to the curb by two champing horses, and the attendants carefully lifted the woman and carried her inside. Wide-eyed, Laure asked one of the spectators, "Where are they taking her—and what will they do for treatment?"

The woman she addressed, a large, heavily set, well-dressed matron in her mid-forties, shrugged and said, "Why, dear, they'll take her to St. Vincent's Hospital, where she'll be put on a cot above a large bucket filled with ice. Then the doctors will see to her temperature and pulse, and an intern will spray ice water all over her." With this, she chuckled, glanced almost indignantly up at the blazing sun high in the cloudless sky, and added, "I wouldn't mind having gone off with her to get some of the same treatment. Goodness, it's fearfully hot! Are you from New York, dear?"

"No, I've just come from Alabama."

"Then you know what heat is. Well, I'm off. Good luck to you—hope you like New York!"

"I do—very much. And thanks for the information," Laure acknowledged with a smile.

One afternoon, she and the children watched the laying of pavement, and found this novel and instructive after being used to the cobblestone streets of Lowndesboro. Here in New York, the Fisk concrete method was used, with a pavement of gravel, broken stone, coal ash, cinders, tar, rosin, and asphalt being laid in layers to a thickness of from six to nine inches and then rolled flat. And the children, remembering the buggies of their stately chateau back in Alabama, made comparisons as they watched the fine carriages, landaus, coaches, and

363

hansom cabs pass to and fro on the main thoroughfares, which were incredibly congested.

With the coming of August, Laure was able to play hostess to Arabella and Samuel Parmenter and their precocious, lovable daughter. Joy, on her very best behavior—serious and well-mannered—formally thanked Laure and Leland for having invited her and "my mama and new daddy."

"You're quite welcome, my dear," Laure responded with a warm smile. Leland chuckled and reached out to offer his hand to Joy, who shook it with a very serious face, then stepped back and glanced up at her mother and stepfather for approval.

"Well now, Joy, I want you to meet our children," Laure resumed. "This is Paul, he's almost twelve. Celestine is nine, Clarissa is seven and a half, and this is John, who is three."

"I'm pleased to know you, Joy." Paul Bouchard stepped forward and offered his hand. He had been at once attracted to Joy because of her serious and intelligent manner, which vastly differed from his rather frivolous younger sisters' behavior. They were constantly teasing him, and since his older brother, Lucien, had decided to remain in Dublin for the summer and not come home until next summer's recess, Paul had found himself the butt of many a practical joke by the playful girls.

"What a manly boy," Arabella whispered to Laure, observing how Paul and Joy shook hands like grownups. "Joy is certain to like him; he seems mentally advanced for his years, just as she is. You know, Laure, that often is a problem in school; sometimes precocious children have a hard time making friends. The rest of their classmates, who are of the run-of-the-mill type, look down on them because they're different, they're not conformists."

"That's very true, dear Bella," Laure nodded agreement. "You know, some doctors hold that when a child is born late in the mother's life, it almost always is more intelligent, more sensitive, and more precocious than the early ones. Maybe there's some truth in it. I suppose by that reckoning, John would have to be the genius of the lot. But he'll be hard put to surpass Lucien. Incidentally, in case you've wondering about my oldest son, he's doing quite well in the private school we found for him in Dublin, thanks to Leland's wonderful recommendation."

"It must be fascinating for a boy that age to be abroad." Arabella mused. "I never had a chance to go to Europe myself, nor did poor James, either. We were stuck down in the South, what with the war and all. And then, when we went to Texas, we became much too settled to think of gadding about and meeting new situations. But now—" She glanced over at her genial husband, who was animatedly engaging in conversation with Leland on the mayoralty campaign, which would be of tremendous interest in New York this fall, and murmured, "Samuel is so different in so many ways, and I've a feeling that we may do some traveling after all. He's not at all a stick-in-the-mud, even if he is the head of the biggest hospital in Galveston."

"I'm so glad for you, Bella. I know, from what happened to me when I lost Luke, that a woman who has been loved, and feels herself secure in that husbandly love for so long, is absolutely lost when he's taken from her, as your James was, too. Now both of us have our second chances—and I'm as grateful for mine as I know you are for yours."

"I certainly am, Laure!" Arabella glanced back at her husband, who turned at this moment and blew her a kiss. "See, Laure? You're only as old as you feel. And, my gracious, I feel like a young girl all over again, thanks to the way he loves me. It's such a comfort, and it certainly makes a woman know how blessed she is, when she finds a considerate man who makes her the center of his life."

She smiled conspiratorily at Laure, then commented, "My goodness, Paul and Joy seem to have hit it off splendidly!" The two youngsters had, indeed, formed an immediate attraction for each other. Paul had asked her about her hobbies, saying that he liked stamps and books and history, and Joy admitted that she was extremely interested in history, but also in contemporary politics. "You know, I like to write stories," she had already confided to this handsome, brown-haired boy who treated her with such directness and with none of the condescension that so many boys of his age showed toward girls of hers. "And I've thought that, when I grow up, I'd just love to be a writer, maybe even a newspaper reporter."

"Wow, that's fine, Joy," Paul said excitedly. "You know, I've got some copies of the New York *World*. There are stories in there by Elizabeth Cochrane—everybody knows her as Nellie Bly.''

"Oh, yes, of course, I've heard of her! One of her articles was written up in our Galveston paper back home.'' Joy beamed, happier still to have found shared ground on which she could communicate with this delightful boy. ''I'd like to see your stamp collection, if you want to show it to me sometime.''

"Maybe after supper,'' Paul proposed.

"That's fine! You're nice, I like you,'' Joy said with a naive candor that Paul, in his turn, found refreshing.

"I'll ask Mama if I can take you around New York,'' Paul went on, his eyes shining with enthusiasm. ''There's so much to see and do here! We've only been here a short time, so I've barely seen any of it. I find something new every day. Back in Alabama, where I used to live, it's mostly farming and nice, easy-going things and not much in the way of things to do. Of course, I rode horseback, and sometimes I went out in the fields with the men and took a hoe or a spade. It sure could get hot in the sun!''

"There's sure plenty of sun here; I don't feel as if I am so far away from home, really.'' Joy uttered a nervous little laugh and flushed as she saw Paul staring admiringly at her. She quickly added, ''You have ice and snow in winter, don't you?''

"Well, they say so, but of course we only got here in June, so I don't know yet. But Mama says that people ice-skate in Central Park and in some of the other parks, too. It sounds like fun, and I want to try it. Oh, Mama just made a sign to me—I guess that means we're going to have dinner. Can I sit next to you so we can go on talking? I'd like to hear all about what Texas is like!''

"I'd like that, too. I'll ask Mama.'' Joy smiled at him, then walked over to her mother, who was talking with her husband. ''Mama, excuse me, would it be all right if I sat next to Paul at dinner? He knows a lot of things I know about, and he's a nice boy, and I like him a lot.''

"Of course you may, my darling! I think he's a fine boy too, Joy, and I'm so glad you've made a new friend. The two of you can have lots of fun while you're here, before we have to go back.''

"I don't even want to think about that, Mama! I like this

366

place so much, and I like Paul,'' Joy declared, and then had the good grace to blush.

Arabella glanced at her husband and uttered a soft laugh of pleasure. "Samuel, this is such a brand-new world for all of us—I'm ever so glad that we came here for our honeymoon!''

"Likewise for me, darling. By the by, I propose to sit next to you at the table tonight, as a man should with his own beautiful new wife.''

"Samuel Parmenter, I do declare, I think I'm the luckiest woman alive—because when I think of how charming you are and you having been a widower so long, I'm just amazed that no other Galveston belle had a chance to snap you up before this—and there must have been lots of them!''

"You flatter me too much, Bella—but I'm quite happy to be flattered.'' He kissed her cheek. "Now, my dear, take my arm, and we'll go in to dinner in style.''

During the weeks that the Paramenters stayed as guests at the Kenniston house in Gramercy Park, Paul and Joy became fast friends. When the time came for them to leave, and Arabella and Samuel were saying their good-byes to Leland and Laure, Joy came up to Paul and offered her hand, saying in a solemn voice, "I do hope you'll write me.''

"Of course, I'm going to write to you, Joy, and whenever there's something interesting in the newspapers, I'll cut it out and send it to you. Especially those articles by Nellie Bly.''

"Oh, that's nice! You're very thoughtful, Paul. I want you as my friend—always.''

"I want you for mine, too, Joy.''

She nodded gravely, squeezed his hand, and then stepped back and said, "I think we ought to make a promise that each of us will always be able to count on the other for advice. And also that we'll write whenever we have something to say that we think the other would be interested in. Don't you agree?''

"Of course, I do. I promise, cross my heart and hope to die.'' Paul's right forefinger traced a cross over his heart.

"Me, too,'' Joy somewhat ungrammatically, but enthusiastically, chimed in as she emulated her new friend.

Forty-Three

With the first week of September, the oppressive heat wave that had swept the Eastern Seaboard relented, and cool, pleasant weather welcomed the children of New York City back to school. Paul Bouchard attended a school six-and-a-half blocks away, while his sisters were enrolled in another, which was three blocks in the opposite direction. Laure and Leland had spent time prior to the opening of school walking the children to the buildings where they would resume their formal education so that they might familiarize themselves and estimate how long it would take them to walk to and from school, and not be late. They could also come home for lunch, which was a highly enjoyable prospect in view of Clarabelle Hendry's culinary skills.

On this Friday of the first week of school, Paul left the building after the last class and exhaled a sigh of pleasure. The sky was blue, and fleecy clouds drifted lazily overhead. He told himself that he had almost begun to forget what Alabama looked like because there was so much to see and do here in New York City. And his teachers were wonderful— school was going to be lots of fun this semester.

It was still early in the afternoon as he set off for home. He liked everything he saw, and it was all unfamiliar enough to offer new realms of conjecture. He had made his own little world, defining the boundaries, setting the landscape: The elegant buildings, the brownstone houses with their bow windows and their elegant doors with grotesquely shaped knockers; the plots of grass and the iron fences around them; the plodding of the carriage horses along the street on the circuitous route back to his own house—all these things formed a kind of magical terrain. Paul fancied himself as ruler of a fief, like one of those vassal lords of the Middle Ages. And those people who smiled at him, those of his own age as well as the adults, were all his subjects and owed allegiance to him and paid him tribute in just such nods and smiles and gestures.

Usually he went right home to study, but since this was

Friday and the afternoon was so lovely, so pleasantly cool after the intense heat that had besieged the city through most of the summer, Paul decided to take a longer walk than usual in going home. He hummed to himself as he walked, thinking about the letter he'd received yesterday from Joy Hunter in Galveston. She had told him about how she was preparing for her own new school term, and what books she was reading. Also, she had enclosed some clippings from the Galveston paper in which she thought he would be interested. He remembered her sweet, serious face, her adult manner, the way she spoke, comparing her words with what Celestine or Clarissa had to say to him. They were forever teasing, and they called him "an old-greasy-grind" just because he liked books and school and things like that. He wished that Joy lived here, close by—although they couldn't ever be in the same class, because he attended an all-boys' school.

Today, Mr. Jacobson, the history teacher, had complimented him in front of everybody by saying that although he was a new student all the way from the South, he seemed to know a lot about history up North and had obviously done some reading during the summer. And, of course, the other children had looked at him and hated him because he was singled out for excellence. Joy would have understood how happy he felt, and she would have known, too, how one could get impatient with one's fellows just because they didn't care for the same things. If you opened a book, you lost yourself in a brand-new world of adventure and romance, and you could see the colorful clothing and the armor and the swords and the cathedrals—How strange it was that so few children in his class really enjoyed school. When the final bell rang, they all seemed to want to rush out of class, without even saying good-bye to the teacher.

He walked and walked, going farther downtown than he had intended, but it was all so marvelous. There was a greengrocer's shop, with strange things in the window that he hadn't seen before. There were huge sausagelike things hung up to dry, and bottles of wine, and newly baked loaves of bread, much darker than he himself ate. And there was some writing on the window he couldn't read at all; it looked something like Chinese hieroglyphics, though he knew it wasn't because there weren't any Chinese in there.

He found himself in the bustling, teeming streets of the

Lower East Side. There were sights and sounds and smells of this undiscovered new territory, strangely fascinating, all marvelously new. Here was another store with lots of food in it, and it was crowded, and there was a man with a beard and a strange little cap on his head who was talking to the butcher. The plump woman in front of the counter was asking for something, and the man in the skullcap was nodding and tugging at his beard. He had never seen people like this before. And the man with the skullcap was dressed all in black, and he looked very old and very wise.

Paul knew that he had wandered into totally unfamiliar surroundings, and that he was not certain how to retrace his footsteps to the brownstone house in Gramercy Park. And yet, something tugged at him, compelled him to keep walking farther and farther away from home. *If only Joy could be here!* he thought to himself. He had never seen so many people, dressed so differently, and when he heard them speak, he did not recognize the words. They were thick, guttural, quick, and sometimes shrill, coming from men and women, all shabbily dressed. He saw a plump, smiling mother with a shawl over her head, in a long dark, thick skirt that seemed much too heavy for this weather. A small boy clung to her left hand, a girl to her right, and she walked behind an elderly man who carried a thick black book under one arm, and he was saying something in a mumbling, singsong voice that Paul could not at all comprehend. He stopped now at the corner to wait for a cart to pass, and then nodded to the woman and the children as they joined him abreast and walked across the crowded street. Paul saw how the children looked up at the elderly man with eyes warm and wide and joyous. He felt himself a stranger here, and yet there was an almost magnetic, compulsive desire to follow these people, to see where they went and what they did. He could not explain it, but it pulled at him and made him keep walking after them.

He found himself in the middle of an open-air market. He looked up at the street sign, which read Hester Street. He had never heard of it. The sounds of voices grew louder, noisier, swifter, a veritable battle. Women were lifting melons, peaches, bunches of radishes, cucumbers, and kohlrabi, gesticulating to the vendors who gesticulated back and argued with them. He saw coins being passed and the women's purchases being wrapped in brown paper. And when the women left with their purchases, there were others to take their places, pushing and shoving and clamoring for attention.

There was the smell of fish, of coffee, of chickens, and of fruits and vegetables. There were barrels of potatoes, herring, and apples. He was suddenly aware that it was almost dinner time, because there was a hollowness to his stomach—and he knew now that he was lost, and that his mother and stepfather would surely be worried about him.

He turned around and saw a gray-haired woman wearing a babushka, a thick skirt, and a gray blouse poring over a display of cauliflower heads. "Please, ma'am, can you tell me where I am? I live in Gramercy Park, and I've lost my way—" he began.

The woman glanced at him, scowled, and in a deep voice replied, *"Vos iz, kind? Vos zogstu?"*

He shook his head, trying to make a sign that he did not understand her, but she impatiently turned away as a vendor came up and began to talk to her. She had picked two heads of cauliflower and now took out an old purse to extract coins. The vendor shook his head so grudgingly, with a flurry of words that Paul did not understand, that she added another coin, then triumphantly bore away her purchases.

Farther down the street along the sidewalks were rickety tables on which were piled clothes of all descriptions, from children's knee pants to bulky, ill-fitting dresses, made of the cheapest cloth. Two women stood there tugging at a garment that each of them wanted, each reluctant to yield it to her rival, while a vendor clasped his hands above his head and harangued the heavens as he tried to settle this dispute without the wisdom of Solomon. A torrent of guttural, harsh-sounding words poured from the lips of all who surrounded these tables, and Paul was nonplussed, staring uncomprehendingly, yet fascinated, rooted to the spot.

Once again, he tried to ask directions, this time of a stout man wearing a heavy vest over his collarless shirt, but the man shrugged, threw out his hands on each side of him, and marched off. He glanced back with almost indignant irritation at this well-dressed boy who had wandered out of his elite neighborhood into the very Tower of Babel—or so it seemed to Paul.

Just then, there was a tap on his shoulder, and Paul turned. He found himself looking at a boy about his age, yet a boy so totally different from himself in appearance and demeanor that he might as well have been from another world.

This boy was raggedly dressed, and Paul saw that his shirt, though clean, had been repeatedly mended and patched. His too-large trousers were held up by suspenders and showed the tops of his almost worn-out shoes. A cap perched squarely on his closely cropped head, and he was gravely regarding young Paul.

"Can you help me?" Laure's younger son almost plaintively demanded.

The boy stared at him, his dark eyes huge in his olive-complexioned face as he regarded the fashionably dressed blond Paul. At last, he asked in excellent English, "Are you lost?"

"I—I guess I am. I live in Gramercy Park."

"Oh, that's a long way from here. You'd best come home with me. It will be getting dark soon, and it's not safe to travel these streets at night. I will take you to my house, then you can find out how to get back home after you are safe with us," the boy invited.

"Leland, I'm terribly worried about Paul; he should have been home from school hours ago!" Laure went upstairs to the master bedroom, where Leland Kenniston was dressing. They had planned to go to Delmonico's tonight and then to the theater to see the great, beautiful Polish actress Helena Modjeska in *Frou-Frou.*

"It's not like him at all—he always comes directly home from school, goes to his room, and starts to study." Laure added, "I only pray that something didn't happen to him."

"Now don't worry, Laure, darling, he'll be all right. I'll tell you what, I'll go down to the precinct police station and have them look for him. I'm well known there, and the desk sergeant, Harry O'Toole, is a friend of mine—a fellow Irishman, so you know he'll look after my kith and kin." Leland tried to make light of his beautiful blond wife's frantic anxiety, although he was now just as worried as she was.

"That's so good of you, Leland. I don't know what could have happened to him or got into him to stay away without letting us know—"

"Now don't fret, sweetheart." He hugged her, and added lightly, "Modjeska will have to carry on without us. The

372

important thing is to find your son—our son. You go have a glass of sherry, and then you rest. I'll be back presently, after I've seen Sergeant O'Toole.''

Putting on his light overcoat, Leland left the brownstone house and hurriedly walked to the police station four blocks away. There, he greeted Sergeant O'Toole, a stocky, middle-aged Irishman from County Mayo, who greeted him but then, seeing Leland's anxious face, demanded, ''What's the matter, Mr. Kenniston? What can we do for you this evening?''

''It's my stepson, Paul Bouchard. He's only eleven, and he's lost. He should have been home from school hours ago.''

''Well now, we'll look for him. Patrolman Hennessey, come here a minute, that's a good lad.''

The sergeant beckoned to a black-haired patrolman in his early twenties, who respectfully touched the peak of his policeman's hat as he approached and addressed Leland Kenniston: ''Good evening, sir. What may I be doing for ye?''

''You're Irish, too,'' Leland chuckled.

''That I am, as Irish as Paddy's pig. From Dublin, nigh two years ago, sir.''

''Hennessey,'' the sergeant declared, ''this is serious business. Mr. Kenniston's little boy is lost. Should have been home from school hours ago, and not a word from him.''

Hennessey expressed his sincere concern for the well-being of Leland's stepson and then questioned the worried father as to the boy's height, weight, eyes, and hair color as well as what clothes he had worn to school that morning.

''We'll find him, Mr. Kenniston,'' the young patrolman assured the handsome businessman. ''Begorra, you'll pardon me for saying so, but aren't you a Fenian, too? I thought I saw you at one of the meetings last month down near the waterfront—''

''You did. And I am a Fenian.''

''Well now, that puts a different light on the matter. I'll work twice as hard, even if I have to put in overtime without pay—and that's my word on it, as sure as my name is Michael Hennessey,'' the patrolman energetically assured him.

''Thank you. Sergeant O'Toole knows where I am, in Gramercy Park. I'm going to go home and look after my wife now. She's terribly worried. Anything you can do to help will be greatly appreciated.''

"You have no fear, now, Mr. Kenniston. We'll handle it," Sergeant O'Toole graciously assured Laure's husband.

As soon as Leland had left, the sergeant turned to the young patrolman. "I wouldn't let that nice Mr. Kenniston know what I'm really thinkin'. There are a sight too many gangs of thugs in this city. Now maybe, seeing the boy was well dressed when he left school, he may have run afoul of some nasties—maybe they kidnapped and robbed him. Saints preserve us, I hope they didn't kill him, or leave him for dead in some dirty alley! Now then, Hennessey, you go make inquiries. Go over to Hell's Kitchen—and take Patrolmen Duwald and McPherson along with ye. I'll use this new-fangled contraption here to ring up some of the other precincts—Sergeant Thomas's down in Five Points, and Captain Delaney on the Bowery. Damn, I do hate to use this telephone!" he declared. "These young lads they've got for opey-rators are the surliest lot!" He sighed, then added, "Come back and tell me anything you learn. I'll have to get word to Mr. Kenniston—good or bad."

Forty-Four

The sun was starting to set, and Paul Bouchard watched the lamplighters coming to the lampposts. They lifted up the long, cone-shaped lighters, creating bright flares of light, which threw everything around them—the faces, the pavement, and the sidewalks—into mottled patterns of light and shadow.

Paul's young guide said, "It is too late for you to go back home now; you shall stay with us and partake of our *shabbes* supper."

"*Shabbes* . . . ?" Paul uncomprehendingly echoed.

"Yes, that is right. I am David Cohen. I am a Jew, you see, and our Sabbath day is Saturday—only, in fact, it begins tonight, at sundown. Come, we must hurry so as to be at home when the sun sets and the Sabbath begins. My father is waiting—and he will explain everything."

374

"It—it's very good of you to invite me—but you're sure I am not intruding—?"

"No, no, of course not. It is part of our tradition to welcome strangers as if they were members of the family. My family will be honored and pleased by your presence at tonight's meal."

"Well—in that case, I—I'll be glad to come. . . . I *am* lost—I don't know how to get home. . . . By the way, my name is Paul Bouchard. I started walking home from school, and it was such a lovely day out I thought I'd go walking some more and see New York—you see, my mother and my new stepfather and my sisters and my brother and I moved here from Alabama in June, and I don't know my way around yet."

"Do not worry. It is easy to get lost, but you will be safe with me. Come, this way."

The two boys had by this time reached David Cohen's apartment building, a tenement on Rivington Street consisting of six stories, with a long set of steps leading up to the front door. "Here we are," David indicated. "It is up these steps, and then up the staircase all the way to the top floor. Be careful—once we are inside, there is almost no light, and some of the steps are broken."

By now, Paul's legs had begun to ache from all the walking, and the long, hazardous, groping climb up the rickety staircase to the top floor of the tenement made him utter a sigh of weariness. David turned to him and cheerily said, "We are almost there, Paul. Just a few steps more. Then you can rest and share our Sabbath meal." Pausing and putting his arm around Paul's shoulders, he added, "Now you will meet my father and my mother and my sister, Rachel."

The landing was obscured by darkness, but David went to the last door on the right, knocked, and called in a clear voice, "It is David," and then turned the knob and entered, murmuring to Paul, "Come in, come in!"

As he followed his newfound friend into the interior of the apartment, Paul looked around in wonder. The room in which they were standing—obviously the family parlor—was dilapidated beyond anything he had ever seen. Paint was peeling from the walls, and in places the plaster was worn and chipped away. In a few spots, the lath beneath the plaster was visible. Nevertheless, the walls and floor looked as if they had been scrubbed as clean as human hands could make them, and altogether the room gave an impression of neatness and order in a valiant attempt to overcome its shabbiness.

Almost at once, Paul's eyes were drawn to the center of the room, where there was a large table covered by an old, faded, yet clean cloth. In the center of the table—which was carefully laid for a meal for four—were two elaborately wrought candlesticks, whose candles were as yet unlighted, and at one end of the table Paul could see in the dim light a man sitting quietly; he, like his son, was wearing a small round cap of soft cloth.

"David," the man spoke now, his voice stern but not unkind. "What has kept you, my boy? The sun soon sets, and the Sabbath begins."

David lowered his eyes. "I am sorry, Father, but I met a friend—he was lost, and I asked him to join us. His name is Paul Bouchard."

"Be welcome, Paul Bouchard." The man rose with a kindly gesture toward the boy, looking him over carefully. "You are not of our faith, I assume?"

"N–no, sir," Paul stammered shyly. "I hope I am no bother to you—"

"Not at all. You are more than welcome. At the Sabbath supper, the stranger is blessed. David, be quick and find a *yarmulke* for our young friend." He smiled again at Paul, then pointed to his cap. "All male members of our household wear the *yarmulke,* and as our guest, you will do likewise. Ah—here is my wife, Miriam, and our daughter, Rachel."

At this moment, a small, pleasant-featured woman entered the room, carrying a large tureen. She was followed by a young girl of about ten, black haired, with large dark brown eyes; she was carrying a smaller dish, also covered. Both she and her mother, Paul noticed, wore kerchiefs.

"Mother, Rachel, look—I have brought an *oyrech auf shabbes,*" David said. "This is Paul Bouchard. He lives in Gramercy Park, and he walked from school all the way here to see what New York is like."

"Oh, that is a long way," the woman exclaimed, in a heavily accented English. "And it does not look to me as if you are used to such long walks," she added, with a glance at Paul's well-made, if slightly wrinkled suit.

"No, Mrs. Cohen, I'm not," Paul replied sheepishly, "but

376

I'm glad to be here—it's awfully kind of you to have me."

"It is our pleasure. Be welcome," Mrs. Cohen replied, then turned to her daughter. "Rachel, run and set a place for our weary young traveler, and bring Elijah's cup and put it by his plate. She turned to Paul and said, "Elijah is the symbol in our faith of the wanderer, whom we wish to make welcome— and we welcome you. David, show him where he may wash his hands."

David disappeared into the room from which his mother and sister had come—obviously the kitchen—and almost immediately returned, holding a bar of soap and a towel. He beckoned to Paul and led him out onto the landing, where the boys made their way to a narrow door at the other end of the hallway. Turning the knob and pushing open the door, David pointed to a small wash basin that was within—for this was the single washroom and water closet that served the entire floor.

"If we are lucky, the water will be running; it was turned off earlier this week," David explained.

The taps yielded water, after a delay and an ominous banging in the pipes, and David then handed his friend the soap he had brought.

"This is kosher soap," he said. "It contains no animal fats. We always use it, and you will find that it does the job very well."

Paul took the soap and scrubbed his hands vigorously, wiping them on the clean towel that David proffered to him.

When David had also washed, he turned to Paul: "Come, let us return and take our place at the Sabbath table."

When they reentered the Cohens' tiny parlor, a fifth place had been laid at the table and a chair drawn up to it. Paul noticed that at his place there were two wine glasses; at each of the others was a single glass. Red wine filled every glass.

The two elder Cohens and Rachel were already seated, and the father pointed to the place with two glasses. "Sit here, my young friend, at the place with the cup of Elijah."

As David hesitantly seated himself, the mother spoke up. "We are honored to have you. David will sit beside you, also Rachel."

The young girl smiled brightly at Paul. "May you have a happy *shabbes*," she said warmly.

Paul looked around at the family, then at the room, in

wonder at his new surroundings. Suddenly, his eyes fell on an object beside the door that he had not noticed before: a small rectangular container that was on the right side of the door frame.

The father observed Paul's curiosity and gently volunteered, "We call that a *mezuzah*, Paul Bouchard, and it serves us as a reminder of God's presence everywhere. Inside it is a tightly rolled parchment on which are printed verses from Deuteronomy. The first sentence is the watchword of all Israel: 'Hear, O Israel, the Lord our God, the Lord is one.' This we call the *sh'ma*, and it is the most important prayer in our liturgy. Its presence in the *mezuzah* reminds us that here, in our homes, we must practice the godliness and the decent way of living that our forefathers learned from Moses, who went up to the top of the mountain and was given the Ten Commandments."

"Th–thank you for telling me, Mr. C–Cohen."

"You are quite welcome."

Miriam Cohen now spoke up. "I hope you are not too hungry, Paul, and do not mind waiting a few minutes," she said with a compassionate little smile. "We must first say the prayers."

"I—I don't mind waiting—th–thank you." Paul was flustered both by so much attention and feeling himself so out of place. But the smiles from the two children, as well as from the parents, reassured him somewhat.

The mother now rose. "First," she said, "we bless the candles." Turning to Paul, she added, "Do not worry if you do not understand the words we speak. With these prayers, we offer praise to Him who has sanctified our lives through His Commandments and has enabled us to celebrate this Sabbath."

Paul looked on in wonder as Miriam Cohen reverently took up a taper, which she lighted with a match, then used the taper to light each candle. As she did so, she spoke words in a language that the boy had never heard; for all its strangeness, the sound of the prayer had a power that overwhelmed him.

When all the candles were lighted, the mother sat down and her husband rose. Turning to Paul, the elder Cohen said, "Now we recite the *kiddush* over the wine. For it is written, 'Wine gladdens the heart of man.' This is our way of giving thanks to Him who provides the *shabbes* feast and who has brought you here first as a stranger, and then as our friend and welcome guest.''

The father's voice rose as he chanted the words of the *kiddush*. Then all of the Cohens reached for the glasses filled with wine, and sipped, and the father nodded to Paul to do likewise.

"And now," the elder Cohen resumed, when they had set down their glasses, "we bless the *challah*." And without further explanation, he took a loaf of bread, whose dough appeared to Paul to have been braided before baking; the father broke off several pieces of the bread, distributing them to each person at the table. Again he chanted a few words in the language Paul could not understand, then he sat down.

David's mother now rose again and lifted the cover from the tureen in front of her, allowing a delicious aroma to escape from its steaming contents.

"This is matzo-ball chicken soup," she explained to Paul. "It has carrots and homemade noodles, and I hope you like it."

"I'm sure I will, ma'am," David rejoined enthusiastically.

The soup was followed by several dishes, none of which Paul had ever tasted before, though the ingredients—which Mrs. Cohen explained to him—were not wholly strange: There was gefilte fish, followed by chicken, which had been cooked with the soup and then removed and was now served with potatoes. With it came homemade applesauce, further portions of the *challah*, and hot tea with lemon. For dessert there were delicious little honey cakes, which Paul particularly liked, and he eagerly accepted the offer of a second serving. What Paul did not realize was that this meal was the most important one of the entire week for the Cohens and not just in a religious sense. The Sabbath dinner was as elaborate and satisfying as it was because all of their other dinners were meager ones. The Cohens subsisted on scant fare six nights a week so that on this one night they could enjoy their traditional *shabbes* meal.

When Paul finally put down his knife and fork, the meal finished, the elder Cohen beamed at him. "There now, do you not feel better?"

"Much better, sir. It was all so good—I hope you didn't mind my taking second helpings—"

"Of course not. This is why we offered. In our view, a

379

good meal, in good company, is often the best answer to life's travail. This is true particularly if the occasion is a holy one, as in the *shabbes* meal. You see, this meal in a sense liberates us, declares that each of us—including strangers among us—is equal before God and has equal rights. It is a time of great peace and tranquility."

Then David's mother leaned toward Paul and said gently, "I hope you did not find our food and our customs too strange, Paul. You have not known any Jews before?"

Paul shook his head. "No, I haven't. Where I lived in Alabama, near Montgomery, I didn't know of any. Of course, in school I've read something of your history—"

"We never forget our history," the father spoke up, with a smile. "Tonight, you have had but the briefest introduction to it."

"Were you born here?" Paul could not help asking.

"Oh, no. I was a diamond merchant in Kiev, which is in Russia, you see, young man. I was known as Jacob Cohen, the rich diamond merchant. My father before me was also a diamond merchant, also well-to-do. It was he who saw to my education, and that of my brothers, also; we even had lessons in English, which, as you observe, I speak more easily than does my good wife. But all that ended. . . . The Czar sent his Cossacks in pogroms throughout the land of Russia, and I knew that my family and I must escape quickly, or we might die. One morning I went to my shop to take some jewels—jewels that would enable us to continue to live well in another country—and I found that it had been completely looted. I hastened back to our house and gathered almost everything we owned—except these silver candlesticks here and a few other items—to raise the money for passage in steerage on a ship. It was so dirty and foul below that my wife, the children, and I stayed on deck throughout the entire journey, even in the worst weather. We came to this free country two years ago."

Paul looked around. "But it seems—it's so small here—and there are four of you—"

"Yes, but the rents are very high in New York, young man," Jacob emphatically nodded. "Our landlord gets twenty dollars a month for this place, even though it does not have much heat in the winter, and it is very hot in the summer. All of us have to work. I sell old clothes now, and there are times

380

when I work fifteen hours a day. I put away what few pennies I can save, after the needs of my family are taken care of, so that one day we may leave this ghetto. In some ways, we have exchanged one ghetto for another. Not us personally—in Kiev we lived very well—but many other Jews who were poor and were therefore persecuted even more by the Cossacks than we were. But we knew that America was the promised land, and we remembered the words of our ancestors—which were handed down from Moses—that we would be delivered up from bondage, unto the promised land. At least there are no Cossacks here," he added with a chuckle.

"But life must be awfully hard for all of you, in these little rooms," Paul protested.

"Boychik," Miriam Cohen spoke up, with a gentle smile, "we are grateful for what we have. We are better off than many of our countrymen in this very city, living in this very building. There are some who live with ten people in rooms identical to these. There is a man, Chaim Persitz, who was a fine tailor in Moscow, catering to the nobility. Now, he sews garments together and makes fifty cents for sixteen hours of hard work—and he is quickly losing his eyesight. Rachel, when she is not in school, works a few hours in the shop of my husband's cousin, who is rich by comparison—he came here five years ago. And David, during his free hours away from school—and of course all during the summer—runs errands for one of the kosher butchers in the open-air market. We manage. It is true that things are dear. We pay fifteen cents a day for bread, and two quarts of milk a day cost eight cents. A pound of meat for dinner, when there is money to spare, is twelve cents. We use a pound of butter a week—another twenty cents—and if we wish to treat ourselves to coffee, or even potatoes and pickles, this too costs money. Yet, we are free. Free to express our idea, free to bring up our children in the holy ways of love for all mankind, free to practice our religion without the dread that, one night, there will be a fist at the door, and the Cossacks with their sabers will come in and do harm to the female children and kill the old men and the women. No, young man, we count our blessings, and we give thanks for them."

"You must all be very brave—" Paul began, and then put his hand over his mouth, fearful that he had offended his gracious hosts. But Miriam gave him a fond smile and then turned to her husband to say, "Everyone is brave, knowing that he will be given the strength to survive when he most needs it. At least in this country there is opportunity. We hope we shall not always be here—but if we are, we do not suffer. If those who see us for the first time as you do, young man, think we are sad because of our poverty, it is not completely true. We have hope for the future, and we have our dear children. This, too, is the meaning of the *shabbes,* which we were honored to share with you tonight as our guest. And now, you are no longer a stranger to us, young man, and you know something of what we believe in and what gives us this strength and this bravery, as you put it."

"Yes—yes, I do." Unconsciously, Paul yawned, then clapped his hand over his mouth and looked abashed, aware of his bad manners.

"You have walked a great deal, my son tells me," the father gently interposed, "and you are probably not used to wine. It is not too strong, but it makes you sleepy after all your exercise. Besides, we all must soon go to bed. We have to get up very early tomorrow to go to *shul*—the synagogue. We give thanks for our life here. It is hard, but our children are fed, they have clothes to wear, and they are being educated."

"I—I *am* awfully tired, I guess, Mr. Cohen," Paul agreed.

"All we can offer you is a place in the kitchen. We can prepare a bedroll from knitted shawls that we brought from the old country—they are among the few things we could save. If you place them under your back and your head, the floor will not seem so hard," Mrs. Cohen prompted.

"Thank you, you've been awfully kind to me, and I won't forget you. When I get home, I'm going to tell Mr. Kenniston— he's my new stepfather—how nice you were to me, and how David found me when I was lost and brought me here," Paul declared.

"You are quite welcome, and you owe us nothing. It was our pleasure to have you as our honored guest, young man." Jacob Cohen came to put an arm around Paul's shoulders. "I am afraid, though, that you are used to more than we can offer. But the improvised bed won't be too bad. Nor will you be lonely. David and Rachel sleep there, too."

"It must be awful to be so shut up like this with so many people," Paul naively observed.

382

"Well, young man, when one is not rich like Mr. Astor or Mr. Vanderbilt, then one does what one can. Goethe, the great German poet, has said—I will translate it for you—'What you can do without, do without.' Well, we have learned that long ago. And perhaps, if this good man Mr. Grace is elected mayor this November, we shall be able to do better. He believes in fair wages for the working man. I must confess, so do I," he said, with an amused little chuckle and grin.

"Well then, Mr. and Mrs. Cohen, th–thank you again for your hospitality. If you don't mind, I think I will go to sleep; my legs feel awfully tired," Paul Bouchard admitted.

"Sleep, *boychick*," Miriam Cohen tenderly murmured, "a sweet, innocent sleep with no bad dreams. And, in the morning, David will help you find your way home."

"You're very kind—all of you. I'm so glad I met David," Paul said, and yawned again, turning scarlet with mortification as he put his hand over his mouth and sheepishly followed his newly found friend into the kitchen. David took the shawls into one corner of the kitchen, patting them down and making a kind of pallet of them, then gestured to it. Paul understood. With a mumbled "Good night," he flung himself down and was soon fast asleep.

Forty-Five

Undoubtedly, it was the least comfortable bed in which young Paul Bouchard had slept in all his life, yet David Cohen had to prod repeatedly and urgently whisper to get a response from his new friend. "Wake up, Paul, wake up! It is time for you to go back home; I am going to take you, so please wake up! I have got to go to *shul*. Please!"

Blinking his eyes, Paul suddenly sat up, remembering where he was, "Oh, gosh! I—I really did sleep, didn't I?"

"Yes, you did. I must go to the synagogue, but first I will see you safely on your way back home. Mother, Father, and Rachel have already gone, but they said it would be all right for me to walk you part of the way back. I am sorry I cannot offer you some breakfast, but we do not eat until sundown tonight.''

Paul slowly rose to his feet, yawning and stretching. He looked around the kitchen and was appalled to see that, despite its cleanliness, even by daylight it was dingy. An old stove sat in one corner—so black from years of use that no amount of scrubbing could alter it—and nearby stood a table, its glazed top cracked in a dozen places. Several rickety chairs and an old cupboard comprised the rest of the furnishings. There was a tiny window, speckled with dirt from the outside—ingrained dirt, which even many cleansings had failed to dispel. But through it, he could see that the sun was bright outside, and there below, on the streets and on the sidewalks, were throngs of people going to pray in their synagogues, a veritable hodgepodge of humanity in one of the most crowded sections of all New York. As far as the eye could see, there were six-storied, dun-colored tenement buildings jammed side by side, all of them covered with the ugly iron lattice of fire escapes. It was a cheerless landscape, with neither trees nor grass to brighten it, as dull and hopeless as the lives of the thousands of sweatshop workers living here. They had flocked overseas in steerage and landed at Castle Garden, there to wait their turns to be admitted to this land of promise, this country of freedom and the rebirth of opportunity.

Paul Bouchard was thoughtful enough not to prolong his dressing, and he hurriedly pulled on his clothes and shoes. David was anxious to join his fellow Orthodox Jews in their service, Paul well realized, and he did not wish to put his friend to any more trouble than necessary. Also, he was drawn to this highly articulate, well-educated boy his own age, who spoke English so well and who seemed to care so much for his mother, father, and sister.

But now a new thought assailed him: What would his mother say, and his stepfather, Leland? They probably had been awake all night worrying about him, thinking that he was lost forever! That was awful, and if he got a thrashing from his new father, he couldn't very well object, because he had done wrong in not coming straight home from school. Then, gratefully, he remembered David's saying that he would take him part of the way back. Perhaps David would agree to go home with him, and if he acted as a witness,

384

Leland would know that he was telling the truth and perhaps would let him off with a verbal scolding.

He wasn't afraid of a whipping, but he liked Leland so much that he didn't want to disappoint him and make him unhappy. And he hoped he hadn't caused any trouble between Leland and his mother.

"I'm ready," he announced. "Would you do me a favor, please, David?"

"If I can, of course I will, Paul."

"I've just been thinking about how worried my parents must be, not having heard from me all night long. I wonder if you would go home with me and tell them what happened. Please, David? So they'll know that I'm not fibbing when I tell them I went for a walk and got lost?"

"You were not fibbing at all!" David laughed jovially. "I never saw anybody more lost than you were on Hester Street." He chuckled and said, "I never saw anything funnier than when you tried to ask old Mrs. Rabinowitz to give you directions back home. It was all I could do to keep from laughing. She speaks only Yiddish and Russian, and if it were not for her son having a good job, she would starve to death. Why, he makes seven dollars a week! And they have one big room, and their kitchen has its own bathtub! It is luxurious compared with what we have." He drew himself up proudly. "But, just as my father said last night, Paul, one day we will move out of this place into something nicer. Then Mother will have more room, and maybe she will sew and make more money at home than she does going to the shop."

"I hope so. It's awfully crowded—and so dark," Paul remarked.

"Yes. But, when you work all day and almost into the night, it does not really matter what you have, so long as you can lie down and go to sleep so you can wake up and be ready for the job in the morning," young David philosophically remarked.

They walked quickly, and Paul was once again struck by the fact that every few blocks, it was as if they had wandered into a different theater—with new stage sets and a whole new cast of characters. David took several short cuts and only half an hour later they arrived at the brownstone house. Paul turned to his new friend. "Please, David, be sure to come in with me and help me out."

"Well, I guess I can be late to *shul* this one time," the Jewish boy announced with a grin.

Paul and his new friend had hardly climbed the steps, when the door was suddenly flung open. Laure hurried out, her eyes filled with tears, and she hugged Paul to her, exclaiming, "Oh, my darling, I was so worried! Where did you go? What happened to you? We had all sorts of fears about you, not knowing if you were even alive—Leland was just beside himself! He went to the police station several times during the night, just to find out if they'd had any news about you."

"Mama, this is—this is David Cohen. He's my friend," Paul blurted. "I'm awfully sorry I made you and Leland worry about me—I didn't mean to, honest I didn't. It was so nice out after school that I just walked and walked and walked. Then I got lost, and I didn't know where I was, and David, he heard me ask people how to get back, and he said it was too late. So he took me to his place, and I had dinner with him and his sister and mother and father. And I slept in the kitchen, and now I'm back. Isn't that right, David?"

The Jewish boy nodded. "Yes, what he says is true, ma'am. It would not have been right to let him walk all the way back home late at night, because the area just above our neighborhood can be very dangerous—especially at night."

"I'm terribly grateful to you. It was kind of your parents to take my son in and to feed him and to give him a place to sleep. Come in, both of you. Paul, go and see Leland—he's in the kitchen having breakfast now. Bring your friend in— would you like some breakfast, perhaps, David?"

"No, I thank you, ma'am. I do not eat breakfast or lunch on the Sabbath, but *Paul* is probably hungry," David politely replied as he grinned at his new friend.

Hearing the sound of boys' voices, Leland Kenniston emerged from the kitchen, where Clarabelle Hendry had been serving him a hasty and belated breakfast. He uttered a cry of relief as he went to Paul and hugged the boy, greatly to Paul's embarrassment. "Thank God you're back safely, Paul! Your mother and I were so terribly worried about you."

"It's all right, Leland, darling," Laure spoke up. She reiterated all that Paul had told her about his adventurous day. "We are in this boy's debt," she concluded.

"That was very thoughtful of you, young man—what's your name?" Leland inquired.

"David Cohen, sir, and now, if you do not mind, I must be getting back."

"David, I would like to show you my gratitude in taking such good care of my boy," Leland offered. "If Paul had stayed overnight at a hotel and had dinner, he'd have had to pay for it. So I'd like to give you five dollars for you and your family."

"Oh, no, sir, I could not take that," David protested. "It would not be right. You see, Paul was our guest. It would not be right to take pay for that."

"I see." Leland eyed his honey-haired wife, who was looking at the frail Jewish boy, dressed in his tattered clothes with compassion. "May I ask what your father does, what kind of work he does?"

"He sells old clothes, sir."

"That can't be very profitable." Leland paused and looked at Laure again. "Won't you take this five dollars, then, as a present for yourself? You came all this way to bring my son safely home to me. You know, if Paul hadn't come home, I'd have offered a reward. You can look at it that way, if you like."

"No, sir," David shook his head. "I do not mean to be rude, sir; it is just that my father and mother would never let me take money for that. They would make me return it to you, honest they would. Besides," he suddenly grinned impishly, "we are not permitted to handle money on the Sabbath. We are Orthodox Jews, you see."

"You're a remarkable young man," Leland Kenniston pronounced. "And you must have a remarkable father and mother, too I'd like to meet them."

"They are both in *shul* now, with my sister, Rachel. I should be, too."

"Perhaps this evening you'd all be at home? I'd like to come visit you and meet them, if you don't mind."

"That is very kind of you, sir. But really, they would tell you the same thing. They would never take any money for making your son our guest and welcome at *shabbes*," David Cohen earnestly avowed.

"Well, young man, you see we're very grateful for all you've done for Paul, and we'd like to tell your family personally. So this evening, we'll pay you a visit. Please tell your parents they mustn't go to any fuss to receive us. We'll come after dinner—around eight o'clock—just to have a little talk with your mother and father, and your sister, too, David.''

"That is very nice of you, sir. Thank you. Paul knows where we live. Well, I guess I had better be getting back now. Good-bye, Paul. See you again, maybe.''

"I'd like that a lot, David!'' Paul blurted out.

Laure saw David out, then came up behind Paul, put her hands on his shoulders, and bent to kiss his cheek. "Paul, it's all right. We're not angry, though we were really worried. David's a fine boy. You were very lucky that he took you in.'' She turned to Leland. "Just think, he went through some of the worst areas of New York! Someone might have hurt him or kidnapped him, or something—it was very fortunate David realized that Paul was lost and took him in for the night. We really must do something for him, Leland.''

"I intend to, my dearest.'' Leland turned to his stepson. "Now why don't you go up to your room and take a bath and then rest, Paul? You've had quite an outing, and I think you've learned a great deal.''

"Yes, I have, sir.'' He looked down at his lap. "I'm awfully sorry, sir.''

"Paul, you don't owe me an apology. This is a new life for all of us here in New York City, and we're going to learn a great deal about one another as time goes on. But I feel toward you as I would toward a son of my own flesh and blood, and that's the truth. Now you go take your bath and rest. This evening, after dinner, you can show us where the Cohens live.''

"Oh, yes, they were so nice to me—Father!'' Paul could no longer suppress the surge of affection he felt for this strong, handsome man, who had not scolded him or spanked him, though he had been certain that he deserved either one or both for his thoughtless escapade.

After dinner, Leland, Laure, and Paul drove down to Rivington Street in their new carriage, which the affable Irish importer-exporter handled with practiced skill. Laure brought with her a basket of fruits and cheeses that she had packed for the Cohen family.

As they approached the Cohens' block, Leland studied the

crowded, dirty streets and shook his head. "I realize now that, in some ways, there is even more poverty in this booming city than in my own native land, Laure, dear. And I'm grateful to you, Paul, for opening my eyes. Perhaps I wanted to overlook it, remembering my own impoverished boyhood and the oppression of the poor tenant farmers by the absentee English landlords. But here there are sweatshops run by wealthy men who don't give a fig for human life, who don't care if a child's lungs or heart or eyesight are destroyed by long hours at pitiful wages. That boy, David Cohen, touched me deeply. I'm going to do something for him and his family."

"I know you're kind and generous, Leland, but you mustn't reproach yourself. You can't possibly solve all the problems of the world," Laure murmured.

"I know, Laure. And yet, I remembered the words of the great English poet John Donne, to the effect that all men are brothers, and that one should 'never send to know for whom the bell tolls; It tolls for thee.' But for the grace of God—and a little luck along the way, Laure—we might have been as badly off as the Cohen family, cramped into two dirty rooms at an extortionate rental, with neither privacy nor comforts, all of them forced to work long hours to survive. The irony is that they came here for freedom—well, freedom is hardly what I would call their existence. Yes, I'm very glad that Paul decided to go for his long walk yesterday. If Mr. Cohen is anything like his son, he is a fine man with background and learning. If I can, I'm certainly going to help him."

Half a block from the tenement building where the Cohens lived, there was a tethering post to which Leland attached the reins. Then, seeing a earnest-looking fellow of about seventeen leaning against the brick wall, he beckoned to him. "How'd you like to earn two dollars, my good lad?"

"Two dollars!" The young man's dark eyes widened. "Is it honest work, sir?"

"It is, indeed. My family and I are going to pay a visit to a friend. We shan't be long, perhaps half an hour, or maybe a hour at most. If you'll look after the carriage and the horse and see that no one rides away with them, you'll have the two dollars."

The young man nodded and walked over to the carriage,

389

took hold of the reins, and began to stroke the horse's head, crooning to it.

"You've a way with animals, I see, young man. Good! We'll try not to keep you waiting too long. Come along, Laure, Paul," Leland urged.

He carried the basket as Paul gestured toward the building to which David Cohen had brought him last night. "It's very dark, and the stairs aren't very good," Paul volunteered.

"We'll manage. Careful now, Laure, darling. Slowly, one step at a time. Whew! One can tell what all the people in this building had for supper tonight—all the smells, crowding in. It's pretty obvious from the peeling paint and plaster that the landlord doesn't care about doing one iota more than he has to." Leland Kenniston made a face, then shook his head. "Well, if Mr. Grace is elected mayor and beats Tammany Hall out of their gouging once and for all, then maybe we'll be able to tear down slums like this and build fine, bright new buildings where people can live at decent rentals and hold their heads high. And that'll mean work, construction work, for lots of people."

They reached the top of the landing, and Paul went ahead and knocked on the door.

Jacob Cohen opened it, then uttered a cry. "*Boychick!* It's good to see you! Oh, do come in, please! David told us that you were coming with your parents, but I thought perhaps this was just said out of propriety—do come in. Sit down on that couch over there."

"Thank you, Mr. Cohen," Leland said. "I hope we aren't disturbing you."

"Oh, no, it was good of you to come. This is my wife, Miriam, and here is my daughter, Rachel. David you know already, of course."

"Indeed we do, Mr. Cohen. I am Leland Kenniston, and this is my wife, Laure." Leland shook Mr. Cohen's hand, then smiled. "This basket is for all of you, Mrs. Cohen. I hope you'll enjoy the things we've brought."

"Sir, it is good of you." Jacob Cohen stiffened, and his smile faded. "But we do not seek charity. We did not take in your son last night with the hope of any reward—"

"But it's not a reward. Please don't be offended. My son tells me that in Russia you were a diamond merchant."

"Yes, in Kiev. As I told him, there were pogroms against

Jews, and so we came here in search of freedom. I sell old clothes now, but we are free. To me, that means much more than rich foods, fine clothes, or even a mansion in which to live—'' A melancholy smile appeared on his face as he added, ''though, if we are blessed, I may one day be able to offer my family all those things. They have earned it for their hard work, their love, and their loyalty.''

At Miriam Cohen's insistence, Leland, Laure, and Paul seated themselves at the table, where David's mother served refreshments, consisting of honey cakes, tea, and one of the cheeses that Laure had brought. Leland put many more questions to the Cohens—and David's father in particular—about their lives in Russia and their journey to America. At last, putting down his tea cup, he turned to the elder Cohen with an earnest expression on his face: ''Mr. Cohen, I have an importing and exporting business with branches in New York, New Orleans, San Francisco, and Hong Kong. I have been planning to expand my importing business to include jewelry. Your background leads me to think that you could be of great value to me, with your knowledge of fine stones.''

''Is this really true?'',Jacob Cohen incredulously asked, glancing at his wife.

''It is very true. I assure you that I mean what I say,'' Leland Kenniston pleasantly replied.

''I cannot believe it, Mr. Kenniston. You would want me to work for you?''

''In the trade you know best. You would qualify more than any other man I know in New York. I would be willing to start you at one hundred fifty dollars a month. If all goes well, there will be bonuses and salary raises.''

''Can I believe my ears? Miriam!'' Jacob excitedly exclaimed. ''This is what I have been praying for!''

''Is it not written in the Bible that when one casts one's bread upon the waters, it is returned a thousandfold?'' Miriam Cohen replied, and there were tears in her eyes as she stared gratefully at Leland and Laure. ''We took a stranger in last night, and because of this we are blessed. Oh, Mr. Kenniston, my husband will have back his pride, for he was well thought of in Kiev—until the trouble and the persecution.''

''Then it's settled. And if you won't object to some help, Mr. Cohen, I'd like to get your family moved out of this dreadful tenement. It's certainly no place for children. There's a building on Sixteenth Street, not far from where we live in Gramercy Park, that is owned by an acquaintance of mine. He recently mentioned that he has a vacant apartment there, at not much more rental, most likely, than you're paying for this place."

"It is a miracle, Miriam," Jacob Cohen murmured in a voice of rapturous wonder. Then he took his wife's hand and pressed it fervently. "Our prayers have been answered! Now, Rachel and David will have their chance to grow up healthy and strong, and ready for the lives we have wished for them."

By October, Jacob Cohen, his wife, and their children had moved to a four-room apartment in the building on Sixteenth Street. Jacob Cohen had gone to work for Leland Kenniston, appraising the jewelry that the Irishman was importing.

Laure Kenniston and Miriam Cohen soon became fast friends. Miriam told Laure much about the hundreds of families coming every month to New York City in hope of escaping the poverty and tyranny of the Old World, adding that she herself had begun to work twice a week at a settlement house in her old neighborhood, helping others who were arriving to adjust to the New World and their new way of life. "Not everyone is as fortunate as my Jacob and I," she said. "They do not have the good luck to meet friends such as Mr. Kenniston and yourself. For those people I must work to provide what help and comfort I can. Often there is not much I can do, but I must try."

Following this conversation, Laure told Leland about Miriam's work; then she was struck with an inspiration: "Leland, starting next week I would like to go with Miriam to the settlement house, and do what I can, too. It is so important to help the new immigrants and their children to adapt themselves to our ways, and when I consider how the Cohens extended themselves and sheltered Paul when he was in need, I want to help all the more."

"That is a commendable feeling, my darling," Leland replied, "and I'll be glad to contribute financially to the work of the settlement house. If it can give the opportunity to only one or two families like the Cohens, then the money will be wonderfully well spent!"

392

Forty-Six

By September of this year of 1880, Alexander Gorth no longer had even the slightest misgiving about the wisdom of his decision to leave Galveston for the unknown, terrifyingly huge metropolis of New York. If truth be told, when Charles Douglas had first proposed that the young man become manager of a big New York department store, competing with nationally renowned institutions, Alex had had a few uneasy moments.

For one thing, because of his lack of formal education, he was not certain that he could meet the challenges of sophisticated retail operation that would have as its clientele the elite of New York society. Also, Galveston had a warm, sentimental attraction for him. It had been his home for nine years; it was the city where he had gotten his start; it was there he had met and married Katie McGrew, the pretty, saucy redhead who had clerked at Gottlieb's Bakery.

Yet now, after ten months as manager of the New York retail establishment, Alex had just received a telegram from Charles Douglas expressing his great satisfaction over the continual increase in profits, which had come about through Alex's capable management. Charles informed him that there would be an additional three-hundred-dollar raise per year, effective immediately, bringing Alex's annual salary to twenty-eight hundred dollars. That telegram was the kind of accolade that convinced Katie's ambitious, earnest husband that he had succeeded even beyond his greatest expectations.

If he had had any lingering doubts over Katie's approval of this transcontinental move, these had been eliminated for all time. And it was due entirely to Harold and Lila Vanderpool.

The prominent member of the New York Stock Exchange had been extremely grateful to both Alexander and Katie when the young wife of the manager had apprehended the society matron in the act of stealing a piece of costume jewelry. Katie's discovery of Mrs. Vanderpool's kleptomania, and Alex's promise that the store would not press charges, had caused Harold Vanderpool to feel a sense of obligation for the face-saving way in which Alex and his wife had behaved throughout this distressing affair.

Harold Vanderpool had invited the young couple to dinner at his summer mansion on Long Island, built some four years ago and magnificently furnished, before he and his wife resumed residence in their Fifth Avenue town house. For the occasion, Alexander had purchased at wholesale price—a prerogative to which Alex, as junior partner and manager was entitled—an exquisite evening gown for his piquantly lovely, red-haired wife. It was a shade of electric blue, made of shimmering silk, with puffed sleeves and dainty bodice with a narrow V. Katie exclaimed loudly when he came home that evening with the dress, and she promptly tried it on. "Alex, you angel, it fits perfectly!"

"And why shouldn't it, Mrs. Gorth?" He pretended to be haughty. "After seven years, I should think your husband ought to know your dimensions. You're just as delicious— even more so—at twenty-six as you were at nineteen, if you care for my opinion."

"I rather do, you know," she giggled, and then hugged and kissed him effusively. "I'm so excited about going out to that mansion—I've read about the Vanderpool house in the society column of the *Tribune*. And now, just think, here I am, an orphan from Galveston, married to a tycoon who buys his wife evening gowns so she can go out in style to visit one of New York's most distinguished couples. You certainly have brought me a long way, my darling!"

"And we'll go farther yet," he had promised.

Harold and Lila Vanderpool were extremely gracious to their guests that evening, and the dinner, served by a butler and two maids, was an affair of some ten courses with three kinds of wine. The dinner concluded with coffee, cigars and brandy for the men, and French *framboise* for the ladies. One sip of this potent raspberry cordial, and Katie was ecstatic. "Oh, my, this is so good!"

"I'll have Harold send a case of it to your house tomorrow, my dear," Lila Vanderpool proposed, a warm smile on her face.

"Oh, dear, I didn't mean to hint that I want you to do that, Mrs. Vanderpool—"

"Please do call me Lila; all my friends do. But I want to, Katie—if I may call you that."

"I'd love it if you did!"

"Very well, then." Lila leaned forward and lowered her voice as she went on, "Needless to say, Katie, dear, I can't thank you enough for the sympathetic way you handled a very unpleasant situation."

"I've already forgotten it. We're friends now, and that's all that matters."

"You are very kind, my dear. You know, my husband thinks highly of your husband—you've every right to be proud of him. I know that many of our friends are patronizing the store already, and you'll get more customers before the year is over. Harold will see to that."

"My husband and I are most grateful for your kindness, Lila."

"Nonsense!" the older woman sniffed. "Yours was the real kindness. You have children, don't you, Katie?" the stockerbroker's wife asked with interest.

"Why, yes, Lila. Jennifer was four in January, and our son, Patrick, will be two in December. They're just darling. They're cared for by our nurse. She's an Irish girl—you know, I'm Irish too—and she's a treasure."

Lila smiled sadly. "How I envy you, Katie, dear! Harold and I always wanted children, but the Lord didn't see fit to bless us. I do want you to bring them the next time—I really love children."

"Next time, Lila, I'd be proud if you and your husband would come to *our* house for dinner. Then you can meet them."

"I'd like that very much. Now do have some more of this *framboise*, Katie."

Indeed, just ten days later, the Vanderpools visited Alexander and Katie in town, and Katie prepared a splendid dinner. It did not have many courses, but it was delicious. She had also baked some Irish soda bread with raisins, a delicacy that neither Harold nor Lila Vanderpool had ever before tasted, and they were loud in their praises. Lila had brought presents for Jennifer and Patrick, and she and Harold took the children onto their laps and delighted in playing with them, thereby making fast friends of the two little Gorths.

395

Katie stood by, her eyes glowing with maternal pride and love, and when she saw the Vanderpools off to their carriage, she impulsively declared, "Alex and I like you both so very much, and we do hope you'll visit us often."

"I mean to, dear Katie." Lila gave her an affectionate hug. "You know, my doctor tells me I'm well on the way to getting over that unfortunate habit I had—"

"Habit? What habit?" Katie interrupted with a laugh.

"No, let me finish, dear," Lila said gravely. "My doctor understands just such things. He and I had a long talk about my background as a child and young girl, and I learned what caused this compulsion in myself. But I'm not tempted any more; I don't have to catch myself when I go into a store—and it's all due to you and your nice husband. If someone else less thoughtful than you had caught me that time, I shudder to think what shame I could have brought upon Harold. In his position as a member of the Exchange, such a scandal would have destroyed him." She held out her hand, and Katie shook it warmly. "You'll be hearing from us again soon, and thank you so much on behalf of my husband and myself for an absolutely marvelous dinner. I'd love to have the recipe for your soda bread. It was just divine!"

"I'll write it down for you right now, Lila. Your husband is busy chatting with Alex, so we have time."

The Vanderpools had by now moved back to their New York town house on Fifth Avenue. When they reached their home, Harold lit a cigar and turned to Lila. "You know, my dear, I admire that young man as a born merchandiser, but aside from that, he has the gift of knowing how to get along with people from all strata of life. That's a priceless attribute, and you don't find it too often. I think he'd have been a success in anything he tried—even as a stockbroker, if he'd wanted to go into that kind of enterprise."

"I agree with you, Harold, dear. And Katie Gorth is just adorable. It's easy to see how much they are in love with each other—" She sighed wistfully. "How I wish you and I could go back to those happier days when we were both as young as they are, and I could have avoided some of the mistakes I've made."

"Hush now, Lila, dear, I've nothing to reproach you for. You're a wonderful wife. And now that you don't have that problem any more, we'll both be happier. But you know, I've been thinking a good deal about young Gorth. It's true that he doesn't belong to society, but I'd like to introduce him and his wife into our intimate circle. After all, just about everybody in the so-called Four Hundred has made his own fortune, including myself. Who's to say that young Alexander won't be in the same position some day? Maybe if I introduce him to the elite of New York, it'll give him a bit of a push. What do you think about that, Lila?"

Lila looked doubtful. "Well, I don't know, Harold," she hesitantly began. "Of course, they're young and personable—and they're certainly not boors. We wouldn't have to be ashamed of them—"

"That thought never even occurred to me, Lila," her husband said reprovingly. "Besides, you know my private opinion about some of the members of society—they're stuffy, pompous, and a good many of them are frauds. Some of them are merely cashing in on inherited famous names, but they themselves haven't lived up to them. The Gorths would be a refreshing and welcome addition to our circle, Lila."

"I understand how you feel, and I love you for your loyalty, Harold, dear. Just the same, I wouldn't want to embarrass them; they're too nice for that."

"Granted. The way I'll do it won't embarrass them. Come now, Lila, be honest, don't you think they're as gracious and sincere as anyone we've met in the city?"

"There's no doubt of it. Well—" Lila hesitated. She understood the snobbery and the insularity that had sprung up about the Four Hundred. But then she began to remember what could have happened to her if Alexander Gorth and his wife had not been so sympathetically understanding. She took a deep breath, then acquiesced. "I'll do whatever you want me to, Harold. I just don't want them embarrassed and held up to ridicule."

"You leave that to me, Lila, dear," he said jovially. "For one thing, I'm going to have Mrs. Astor invite them to a ball as my friends."

"Harold, you can't be serious!" Lila gasped.

"But I am, never more so, my dear. And next, I'll see to it that the Gorths are invited to the house of Alva Vanderbilt."

"Now you're really joking! Why, those two women are staging a bitter war to see who will be the social leader of New York," his wife incredulously responded.

397

"I know that," he chuckled again. "It amuses me. As for Ward McAllister, everyone has been pestering him to learn just who is on this exclusive list of the Four Hundred. From what I understand, he isn't going to give it out for another year or so. But that's not important. You and I are sure to be on the list, and even if we weren't, our invitations from the Astors and the Vanderbilts are quite sufficient evidence that the name of Vanderpool is highly regarded in this city."

"As well it should be! Why, it isn't every man on the Stock Exchange who can make a million dollars in two years, the way you did, darling."

"I had a little luck. Inwardly, it amuses me to have all this fawning and scraping and envy and admiration." He stood up and stretched. "Well now, I'm going to bed because I want to get to the office early tomorrow. But in the next week or so, I'm going to wangle Katie and Alexander Gorth an invitation to a gathering with the high muckety-mucks of New York."

During the first week of October, Harold Vanderpool kept his word. He and Lila had been invited by Mrs. William Astor to her mansion on Fifth Avenue and Thirty-fourth Street, its splendid rooms banked with masses of flowers. With them came Alexander and Katie Gorth, he in a fine black formal suit of tails of the most elegant linen, with a white cravat and white gloves—the *de rigueur* dress at such soirees, Harold had pointed out. Katie was resplendent in a pointed-bodiced gown of dark brown velvet, and a soft fur muff. The Vanderpools and the Gorths went through a wide hall, proceeding to the first of three connecting drawing rooms. There the fabulous Mrs. Astor received them, standing before the life-size portrait of herself that she had commissioned from Carolus Duran.

"My dear Mrs. Astor, you've outdone yourself." Harold Vanderpool inclined his head toward her, then continued, "An invitation from you is almost equal to a call from the gods to enter the Elysian Fields."

The tall, commanding woman, of formidable dignity, permitted herself a faint smile. She was magnificently gowned by Worth, the leading French fashion designer of the day. Exquisite antique lace was draped about her shoulders and edged her huge puffed sleeves. The long train and panniers were of rich, dark velvet, and the satin skirt was embroidered with pearls and silver. Diamonds glittered on her fingers, and her black pompadour was crowned by a diamond tiara and embellished by diamond stars. In addition, she wore a triple necklace of diamonds, a sunburst, and a jeweled stomacher; chains of diamonds fell from her corsage.

It was all Katie Gorth could do to keep from standing openmouthed when she was at last presented to this goddess of New York society, scintillating as if she were made entirely of precious stones. "This is Mrs. Alexander Gorth, Mrs. Astor," Lila Vanderpool made the introduction. "We've become inseparable friends."

"Really? How nice!" The patrician goddess unbent a little as she contemplated Katie, scrutinizing her from her head to toe with one of those quick, shrewdly appraising glances for which she was famous. "You're young and very beautiful, and you have many years in which to enjoy those prerogatives. You and I will have a little chat sometime during the evening."

"It's a great honor to meet you, Mrs. Astor," Katie managed. Lila led her away through two more crowded drawing rooms into the spacious ballroom that also housed the Astor art collection. Lander's society orchestra was playing in the musicians' gallery. The walls were hung with famous paintings, though it must be admitted that much of their fame depended upon the selective choice of the patroness who hung them.

About an hour later, after all the introductions had been made and the glasses of sherry and champagne had been served, dinner, catered by Pinard, was served in the huge dining room from an immense table. It was covered with flowers, and terrapin and fowl reposed on the most expensive, gleaming silver.

As if this were not enough, a week later, Mrs. Astor herself sent, by way of Lila Vanderpool, an invitation for Katie and her husband to attend her weekly dinner parties. "This," Harold Vanderpool told Alexander Gorth, "puts you 'in,' to use the vernacular. Only the topmost ranks of the hierarchy are convoked at Mrs. Astor's weeklies."

"I can't believe it; it's like an Arabian Nights fairy tale." Alex shook his head, bemused.

"Enjoy it. It's little enough I can do for you to thank you for the courtesy and tact you showed toward me. Besides which," Harold asserted, "we're good friends, and I like you more than most of these pampered, obscenely wealthy socialities, who probably never did an honest day's work in their lives."

Katie could not believe her eyes when she was seated at the Astor dinner table. It was illuminated by golden candelabra, decorated with golden *épergnes* and hundreds of *gloire de Paris* roses. All guests were seated at eight o'clock, and the dinner usually took three hours, till at last Mrs. Astor, by means of a slight bow to the lady facing her, signaled that the gentlemen were to be allowed to enjoy their Madeira and coffee with the finest Havana cigars.

Because Harold Vanderpool enjoyed the arts and was not snobbishly insular or pretentiously ambitious—even though he was accepted by such an empress of elite New York society as Mrs. William Astor—he saw to it that Alexander and Katie Gorth became patrons of the ten-year-old Metropolitan Museum of Art, one of whose vice-presidents was none other than the great poet, William Cullen Bryant. On the committee was the already world-renowned landscape architect Frederick Law Olmsted, who, assisted by Calvert Vaux, had designed New York's magnificent Central Park. Unbeknownst to both the Gorths, Harold Vanderpool also sent in a subscription in their names to benefit the National Academy of Design, located in a pseudo-Venetian palace on the corner of Fourth Avenue and Twenty-third Street. The Academy featured the work of such avant-garde artists as John La Farge, Homer D. Martin, and George Inness, as well as the sculpture of Augustus Saint-Gaudens. They also featured the paintings of new stars on the horizon like Albert P. Ryder and William M. Chase. To be seen at these exhibitions was to achieve social recognition.

Thus it was that, out of the happenstance incident of Katie Gorth's seeing a socialite in the act of stealing a piece of costume jewelry, these young people, both orphans of no background, found themselves accepted by the elite of New York society.

What amused Alexander most was how quickly his saucy, red-haired wife blossomed from a small-town, socially awkward creature into a sophisticated, charming woman. Indeed, as he confessed to her this October, after they had attended an exhibition of the National Academy, "You are making me keep on my toes, Katie, and that's good for any man. I want you to be always one step ahead of me, so I'll be so busy catching up that I'll never have time to even so much as look at another woman."

"Oh, you may look, Alexander—but don't ever do any touching," was Katie's swift reply.

Forty-Seven

By the middle of August, Lucien Edmond had been looking forward to leaving Leadville. Though he could look with satisfaction upon the developing mining operation in Leadville, which had begun to pay handsome dividends, he nevertheless was thoroughly weary of the dreary mining community, with its muddy streets, exorbitant prices, and perennially cool weather. Most of the men, too, were glad that their families had never uprooted themselves and joined them, for they would have hated the stark poverty of so much of this rough-hewn clapboard city and its apparent lack of prospects for steady, long-term growth in the future.

Lucien Edmond and Ramón had already heard that the big mine owners were beginning to feel the pinch of expenses—not only for labor, but also for the constantly increasing cost of further excavations and smelting. There was also some talk that some of the largest silver lodes were beginning to run out and that the assays showed a marked decline in the proportion of silver to lead.

Additional wagon loads of bullion had been driven to Denver & South Park railhead by the vaqueros—well armed, and leaving in the dead of night—and the partners had celebrated the news that the total deposit at the Denver bank had now reached the sum of $387,550—a windfall that assuredly more than compensated for the hardships the Bouchard crew had encountered during their sojourn in Leadville. "Indeed," Lucien Edmond cheerfully said one evening as he poured himself a glass of port, following the dinner that Rhea Penrock had set before him and the other men, "there's enough money for us to approach one of the main railroad lines and

401

offer to help finance a feeder line down to our ranch, so we can ship our cattle without interminably long and dangerous drives."

"Yes," Ramón spoke up, "and with the people of Kansas insisting on even stricter laws to keep any Texas cattlemen from crossing their land with Texas-bred cattle, a feeder line would be a godsend to us."

"There remains," Lucien Edmond had thoughtfully pursued, "a decision as to how long all of us should stay here, and when some of us should be getting home to our families. Letters and telegrams are all very well, but I, for one, miss Maxine and the children, just as I know that all of the rest of you miss your wives and your children."

"That's for certain," Joe Duvray grinned, as he held out his glass to be filled by Rhea, who demurely presided at the table and saw to it that all of her employers were well fed.

"Me," old Frank Scolby spoke up with a cackle of merriment, "I'd jist as soon stay on here. An ol' grubstakin' prospector like me is only happy when he's around a mine he's got an interest in."

Lucien Edmond chuckled. Then, his face sobering, he added, "All the same, let's talk about who should stay and for how long, and who should leave fairly soon. Of course, some of that will depend on the strength of the vein. If it holds out, whoever stays could be here through the winter, a rather grim prospect, considering the isolation and the cold."

"I'll be glad to stay here and supervise another few months, Lucien Edmond," his handsome Mexican brother-in-law volunteered. "I don't mind telling you that it's a weight off my mind, not having to move Mara and the children up here with me. They wouldn't like it at all."

"Well then," Lucien Edmond declared, "I, for one, plan to go back to Texas by the end of next month. Joe, there's no need for you to stay on here, since Ramón will be able to work with John Darwent. Four of the vaqueros want to go back, but two others have expressed a desire to remain on, and even bring their wives. That's very encouraging. Walter and Timmy, I think you should go back too, because I'm sure that neither Connie nor Conchita would want to come up here and settle in Leadville."

"That's true enough, Mr. Bouchard," Walter Catlin declared, shaking his head. "It's rough country. It's fine for men, it's a good outdoor life, and it keeps you on your toes, but it's no place for a wife and kids.''

"Will you have enough people on hand to take care of the mine, Lucien Edmond?'' Timmy Belcher wanted to know.

"More than enough. Ramón will be here initially, of course, but I'm sure that by the time he leaves, John Darwent will be more than able to handle matters. Incidentally, he told me yesterday that we ought to continue to excavate to the end of the year, at least. In his opinion, this next yield could be tremendously rich. Mr. Scolby will stay, and he's certainly going to watch out for all of our interests. But I think I'm just going to pick two of the vaqueros to go back with me and leave four here for the meantime. Those four will be responsible for moving the occasional loads of silver on to Denver until the railroad is finished. And when I go back next month, I'll take one of the loads with me to the San Antonio bank.''

"That's an excellent idea," Ramón concurred.

Robert Markey had told Lucien Edmond that he preferred to remain in Leadville to aid Ramón on the operation of the mine, and Lucien Edmond had readily agreed. Now Ramón turned to Robert and told the former farmer that, from this day on, he would receive one hundred dollars a month and room and board—plus a five-hundred-dollar bonus for his heroic and timely defense of the mine on that fateful day of May 26.

"Now it is we who are in your debt, Robert," Ramón said, as he shook hands with the man whom he had once saved from lynching. "And one of these days, when we go back to Windhaven Range, you'll have a good nest egg to put away, so you can start all over again. As your friend, not your *patrón*, I say to you, you should think of finding a girl whom you can love, and with whom you can have children. I am sure that your wife would have wanted that.''

All the while, Rhea had been moving here and there to see that the men had all the coffee, port, and whiskey they wanted. Hearing Ramón's plans, her heart had begun to beat faster. She must get back to Windhaven Range—she must! She paused a moment and looked at Lucien Edmond.

Intercepting this gaze, he smiled at her, then said, "Miss Galloway—Rita—I wonder if you would like the chance to go back with us and work as a cook at Windhaven Range. You see, Santiago Dornado will be staying on here, and he'd

403

very much like his bride to join him. However, she's been the assistant cook on the ranch, so that would leave us short-handed down there—unless you took her place. Of course, you'd have to cook for a great many more men than you're doing now, because we have a good thirty vaqueros on the ranch. But down there we have a much bigger kitchen and a far better stove. And we'll increase your wages, too.''

''My gracious, you must be reading my mind, Mr. Bouchard,'' Rhea gleefully exclaimed. ''You know, a gal like me from Mississippi can't possibly go for this chilly climate up here the year around. My guy, Eddie, he told me it was going to be cold, but he never told me it would be this cold so long, even in summer. I'd just love to go back to Texas with you. That's my sort of temperature and people and such, if you know what I mean.''

''Well then, it's settled. You'll go back with us at the beginning of September,'' Lucien Edmond declared.

Rhea said nothing. She merely bowed her head and smiled. *At last!* she told herself. *At last!*

A week before he planned on returning to Windhaven Range, Lucien Edmond paid a call on Sister Martha at her soup kitchen in the parish house of the Catholic church. He was hoping to persuade her that she and the other nuns should return with him, and be content to take up their old duties at the school in the Windhaven chapel.

When he had entered the church, Sister Martha had declared effusively, ''Why, Mr. Bouchard! What a pleasant surprise! We've both been so terribly busy that we seldom get a chance to see one another. Please, do sit down.''

He doffed his Stetson, and took the chair that she offered him. He hesitated for a moment, then baldly stated the reason he was there. ''Sister Martha, I know you're going to argue with me—''

She interrupted him with a twinkle in her eye as well as her voice. ''If you know in advance that I am going to be argumentative, my son, perhaps you should come some other time!''

He laughed with her, then became serious once again. ''I have decided to return to the ranch, and a number of the men and I will be going in a week's time. While it is true that some of the others—Ramón Hernández among them—will be

404

staying on for a while, probably until winter, I would feel a good deal better about your safety if you would come back with us next week."

"But what makes you think that I wish to return, Mr. Bouchard?" the elderly nun asked.

"Surely you can't want to stay on here, Sister Martha, if the rest of us won't be here." Lucien Edmond was somewhat taken aback by her determination.

"Mr. Bouchard," she declared gently, "I have come to think of you and, indeed, all of your men as my family. And I would truly miss you. However, I would be false to my calling if I were to allow my personal feelings to interfere with my spiritual duties."

She looked down at her hands folded on her lap, then quietly continued. "One of these days, my son, when I feel that we have done all that we can do here, Sisters Concepcíon, Luz, Margarita, and I will return to Windhaven Range. I realize now that some of our proposed plans were a bit misplaced," she said with a wry smile, "seeing as how the existing school is quite sufficient for the few children in Leadville. But the miners are so grateful for the food we have for them, and I cannot in all good conscience close up our facility."

"I understand," Lucien Edmond told her softly. "And I admire your dedication tremendously. Still," he smiled, "I do hope that by the time the vaqueros leave for good once the mine has been played out, you, too, will be ready to leave for home."

"Home." Sister Martha said the word so softly that Lucien Edmond wasn't quite sure at first what she had said.

He took her hands in his and looked into her eyes. "Yes, Windhaven Range will always be your home."

It was early October now, and the country was stirred by the prospect of the oncoming Presidential election. In the opinion of most political experts, the popular vote between Garfield and Hancock would be extremely close, and everything would depend on the electoral college vote. Most conceded that James Garfield and his running mate, Chester A. Arthur, would have the edge there, though it was too early to tell.

There was more talk of the Chinese Exclusion Treaty,

which was to be signed next month with China at Peking, giving the United States the power to "regulate, limit, or suspend" the coming of Chinese laborers into the country. In New Orleans, Lopasuta and Geraldine Bouchard were most unhappy at this legislative turn of events, for such a treaty, if passed by both the House and the Senate, would prevent people like Mei Luong from contributing their innate honesty and concientious labor to the growth of the nation. Lopasuta sadly said to Geraldine, "I fear the worst from this treaty. So long as there is an exclusion that is fixed upon any certain race or people, the fire of bigotry will have fuel added to it—and there is already too much in this land."

In New York, the mayoralty campaign was being hotly waged, but it was conceded that William R. Grace would head the list when the final count was in next month. Throughout America, there seemed to be a mood of expectancy, and the voters believed that the colorless, do-nothing administration of Rutherford B. Hayes—which at one time had been looked upon as a salvation from the corrupt influences of the Grant administration—would be exchanged for a brighter, more vigorous regime, no matter who should win.

Rhea Penrock had accompanied Lucien Edmond Bouchard—along with Joe Duvray, Walter Catlin, Timmy Belcher, Felipe Sanchez, and Narciso Duarte—back to Windhaven Range, arriving there the middle of September.

In just over a month, Rhea established herself at Windhaven Range as an excellent cook, showing so much capability in preparing meals for all of the vaqueros that Felicidad was able to devote more time to her beloved Lucas and their children. Rhea seemed to thrive on the work, and her pleasant disposition, her constant attempts to please, and her experimentations in the kitchen to produce tastier meals had won enthusiastic acceptance.

The vaqueros built Rhea a two-room cottage, shaded by a huge cottonwood tree, and when one of the men went to San Antonio for supplies, he brought back curtains and even some dress materials. In her spare time, Rhea worked on her rudimentary sewing skills, and in very short order she was ingratiating herself with the wives of the vaqueros by making clothes for some of their children. Maxine Bouchard and Mara Hernandez thought highly of her, for, on several occasions, she had volunteered to take care of their children whenever either of them wanted to go into the town of Carrizo Springs, or when Mara wanted to spend an evening visiting with Lucien Edmond and Maxine without having her children in tow.

Rhea quickly learned all she could about the family of Ramón Hernandez, the man who, in her mind, had been responsible for Gabe's unjust death. She took pains to make Ramón's children like her, going out of her way to win over the more reserved boys, Luke, almost thirteen, Jaime, going on eleven, and Edward, who had had his eighth birthday in August.

Dolores, who had turned nine in July, was also very fond of Rhea, but it was three-and-a-half-year-old Mara who seemed to be fondest of her. The very first time Mara had introduced Rhea to her namesake, who was nicknamed Gatita—Spanish for kitten—Rhea had taken the child in her arms and kissed her on the forehead, saying, "What a little beauty you are, just like your mother!" Gatita had giggled with delight and flung her arms around Rhea's neck, kissing her on the cheek.

Mara had delightedly replied, "You certainly have a way with children! You're so young, too—you've never been married?"

"Oh, no, ma'am. I had a fella, but as I told your husband up in Leadville, I came all the way from the South to meet him because we were going to get married, but then I found he'd picked somebody else and left me high and dry."

"What a pity—he was a fool! Never mind, Rita, one of these days you'll find someone who'll appreciate you."

"Thank you, Mrs. Hernandez; you're very kind."

Margaret Duvray was equally fond of Rhea. Now that Carrizo Springs, a few miles away from Windhaven Range, was developing with the addition of new settlers, she and Mara often enjoyed spending an afternoon there with other wives. Some had come from back East or the Midwest, and one recent arrival had moved from San Francisco because her husband, who had formerly worked for a steamship company, had had a sudden urge to become a farmer, and also wanted to be close to his relatives who lived in San Antonio. For the women of Windhaven, this association with other women of their own comparative age proved to be a stimulating opportunity to exchange fresh viewpoints—a contrast to the pleasant but sometimes monotonous and insular life on the ranch.

Curiously, despite her sordid background, Rhea genuinely got along well with all the children. Perhaps, it was because she saw all these children in a setting where there was neither poverty, nor malice, nor violence. as opposed to her own tragically shadowed life. She found herself wistfully thinking how much she would have enjoyed having a child by Gabe—a dream that had been shattered. This realization hardened her resolve and she became even more vindictively directed toward her now obsessive goal: to achieve personal vengeance against Ramón Hernandez. The plan that she had conceived a week or two before she had been asked to come back with Lucien Edmond Bouchard to Texas was crystallizing in her mind, in to a plan of action. Although at the outset she had intended to lure Ramón away from the others, kill him, and make her escape, she had dismissed this idea entirely after learning of his family.

It was on Gatita, the child to whom she seemed to show the most favor of those on the ranch, that her plan focused. If she were to kidnap this child, take her far from Windhaven Range, and bring her up in an atmosphere of penury and degradation similar to what she herself had encountered as a child, it would be a perfect vengeance. Ramón would never know what happened to his cherished daughter, and the girl herself, being so young, would soon completely forget her origin and past. What she would remember would be only that which would occur under Rhea's own carefully planned supervision. And all that while, Ramón would be driven nearly mad by the anxiety of not knowing where his Gatita was, what had happened to her, and he would be compelled to make frantic and futile quests to find her. Nothing could be more delicious than the prolonged anguish and suffering he would endure!

At night, she often lay awake in her cottage, exulting, savoring the careful details of how she would bring this about. She would imagine to herself Ramón's agony when he came back from Leadville and learned what had happened. Conversely, with each new day, she outwardly showed more tenderness and affection toward all of the children than she had ever shown before, together with a humility that bespoke her gratitude for this chance to be among people who loved and were loved. They, in turn, suspecting nothing, taking her at her word and having already judged her actions as demonstrative of that word, believed that her affection was a kind of compensation for the love she had been denied when her supposed fiancé had made her come to Leadville, only to forsake her for another woman.

Mara Hernandez, indeed, trusted Rhea Penrock so much that often she would read Ramón's letters to her, to acquaint the diligent, hardworking young cook with what was taking place at the mine in Leadville. One evening, she read to Rhea a paragraph Ramón had written, conveying his best wishes to "Señorita Galloway" and expressing his thanks for the way she was helping out, becoming so valuable and reliable a part of the Windhaven Range community. Lowering her eyes and adopting her attitude of self-deprecating modesty, Rhea had replied, "Mrs. Hernandz, I'm only doing the best I can, to thank your husband for the chance he gave me. It's sort of embarrassing to have you read what he says about me because I've never been so happy, and I've never earned so much money. But bless you anyway for telling me."

Then, on the twelfth of October, two telegrams came from Leadville, one addressed to Mara and the other to Lucien Edmond. In essence, both of them read that Ramón planned to leave Leadville around the end of the month and expected to be back during the second week of November.

The day after the receipt of these telegrams, Maxine and Mara came into the kitchen as Rhea was preparing the noon-time meal for the vaqueros, and Maxine hesitantly began, "Rita, dear, I wonder if you could possibly do us an awfully big favor?"

"Of course, I'd be glad to, Mrs. Bouchard. What did you want me to do?"

"Well, Mara and I would like to go to San Antonio for some new dress material."

"Yes," Mara eagerly added, "I want to make some new clothes for myself—after all these months I want to look my best when my husband returns—and also get new shoes for the children. The point is, I wonder if you can look after my children. We'd like to leave tomorrow morning, and we ought to be back in about five days. Luke, Jaime, Dolores, and Edward will be in school for most of the day, so you'll really just have Gatita to watch over until dinner time."

"I wouldn't mind at all, Mrs. Hernandez," Rhea eagerly proffered. It took an effort for her to stifle the inclination to

409

burst out laughing. Here was the perfect opportunity for the kidnapping being offered by the child's own mother. It couldn't have been better! She could take the child before Ramón came home, and both Mara and Maxine—the two people most likely to be a hindrance to her plan—would be completely out of the way.

Some weeks ago, in preparation for when the right opportunity would present itself, she had set another phase of her plan in motion. She had intimated to both Mara and Maxine that she knew how to ride horses, that she had ridden them back in Mississippi when she had been a little girl. Maxine had expressed some hesitation, but at last had asked one of the vaqueros to saddle a gentle mare for the young cook. Rhea had mounted it, taking pains not to show Maxine that she was really an accomplished horsewoman, and had ridden around the corral until Maxine was convinced that she knew well enough how to handle a horse. Then she had proposed to Mara that she be allowed to take Gatita for a ride once in a while, "because I really think she would enjoy riding with me to see all the lovely sights and get used to horses."

"That sounds very reasonable," Mara had responded.

So Rhea had mounted the mare and had Mara hand her daughter up. The little girl clapped her hands and squealed with joy as Rhea, holding her tightly to her bosom with her right arm, took over the reins with the left and went for a short, placid ride around the compound.

Later that day, Mara and Maxine compared notes and pronounced Rhea's latest contribution a most helpful one. "You know, Mrs. Hernandez," Rhea spoke up, "I think it's never too early for a child to learn new skills. I bet if she and I could go riding every morning, when the weather's nice, why, she'd take to a horse the way a duck does to water."

"Well, it can't do any harm. Just do be careful, please," Mara solicitously asked.

"Mrs. Hernandez, I'll take care of your daughter as if she were my own flesh and blood," Rhea promised, and once again it was all she could do to keep from bursting into mocking laughter. She thought to herself how ironic it was that she should assure the woman that she would look after the little girl as if she were her very own, for that was exactly what she planned to do. With one difference: If she had had a child by Gabe Penrock, she would have tried to bring it up

410

with every advantage, exactly the kind that Gatita had right now. But, because she had been fated to be the instrument by which Rhea would avenge her husband's death, the child would be destined toward a life whose rigors and debasement not even her own father could envision.

Forty-Eight

The morning Mara Hernandez and Maxine Bouchard planned to depart for San Antonio was sunny and pleasantly cool. Rhea Penrock, who had risen particularly early, met with Mara in the Bouchard hacienda and made a great show of concern in getting all the particulars in order. She asked Mara if there were any special foods she should prepare for the children, what time they should be put to bed, and so on.

Mara was impressed by Rhea's diligence and devotion. She hugged the younger woman as she was leaving and asked, "Is there anything I can get you in San Antonio?"

"Well, now that you mention it, Mrs. Hernandez," Rhea slowly seemed to deliberate as she frowned and looked up at the ceiling, "I could use a new comb and maybe a hand mirror."

"Of course, dear. I'll be glad to get you the finest comb and mirror I can find," Mara warmly declared. Looking over her shoulder she called, "Maxine! We'd best get out to the wagon before our driver thinks that we've changed our minds." Turning to Rhea, she added, "We'll try to get back as quickly as we can, Rita, dear. The older children will be off to school in about half an hour and out of your hair." Looking down at her younger daughter, who sat on the floor playing with one of her dolls, she said to Rhea, "You will take good care of Gatita, won't you?"

"Of course I will! I love her so very much." She looked out the window. "The weather's so pleasant out, I thought I might take her on a picnic with me."

"That's a lovely idea! I'm sure she'd enjoy that. Well, we'll see you in a few days. And thank you again so very much for looking after the children. I really hope it won't be

411

too taxing for you, with all the cooking you're doing for the vaqueros. But I'm very grateful, Rita."

Maxine added, as she came into the room, "My husband says that starting next month he's going to give you more money for your work; you certainly deserve it."

"I'm so grateful, I haven't even thought of the money, Mrs. Bouchard." Rhea's eyes lowered, and she adopted her calculated attitude of grateful humility. "You've given me such a chance here, and it's so nice to be with these lovely children and people like you. Why, I'm just happy being here. Please tell Mr. Bouchard how pleased I am that he appreciates me so much."

"We all do."

"Come, Maxine, we mustn't keep poor Jorge waiting," Mara urged.

"Right you are, Mara," Maxine said, as she picked up her daughter Ruth. Noticing Rhea's quizzical expression, Maxine said with a laugh, "My husband will have his hands full enough with our older children without this little devil getting under his feet for five days!"

"I'll see you off, Mrs. Bouchard, Mrs. Hernandez," Rhea proposed.

She walked out of the ranch house with them and watched them climb into the wagon. As Jorge Valdez raised his carriage whip and flicked it with a sharp crack over the heads of the two sturdy geldings, Rhea called, "Please don't spend too much money on the comb and the mirror; I'll be satisfied with anything you bring me. Have a wonderful time shopping!"

Rhea waved to the departing wagon and then went back toward the Hernandez house, holding Gatita by the hand. The four older children came out, carrying their books under their arms, heading for the school, where the nuns would continue their lessons in geography, history, reading, and spelling. She waved good-bye to them and called to Jaime, "Tell me how well all of you did in school, and whoever gets the best grade will have a special treat for dinner—I promise!"

"Thank you, Rita!" the boy, sturdy and handsome and black haired, called out.

Rhea's heart was beating so loudly she was afraid everyone else could hear it. She forced herself to maintain a smiling face as she walked into the Hernandez house. The time had come; the hour of vengeance was at hand.

412

She knelt down to Gatita's level and brushed the little girl's hair with her hand. "Gatita, dear," she crooned, "how would you like to go for a horseback ride with me and have a picnic?"

The child clapped her hands at the idea, for she adored riding around the ranch with Rhea and, indeed, loved the attractive young woman who was so kind and sweet to her. "Oh, yes! Nice picnic!" she shouted, again clapping her hands with joy.

"Then come along, honey. We'll go find a place in the shade by the stream and eat the lunch I've made for us," Rhea purred. Trustingly, the little girl held out her hand, and Rhea took it.

All was in readiness. Last night, long after she had finished her work in the kitchen and everyone on the ranch was asleep, Rhea had crept out to the barn to put dried beef and canteens of water into her saddlebags.

One thing remained to be done. Before leaving the house, Rhea drew a small envelope from her bodice and put it on the mantle, sliding it under a cut-glass vase filled with wildflowers. It would eventually be found, but not too soon, she knew. The time she would gain before it was discovered would be in her favor. She smiled to herself as she thought of what she had written in the note. If they believed it, just as they had believed all the other things she had told them from the very start back in Leadville, no one would ever find her and the little girl. That deception would be the culmination of what she had planned so cunningly, so lengthily, and even Gabe would be proud of the way she was preparing to avenge him.

There was no one around; Lucien Edmond had ridden out with the vaqueros to make an inspection of the yearlings. Rhea had seen him ride off, chuckling and making jokes with the men who accompanied him. He had seen her too, when she was saying her good-byes to his wife, Maxine, and to Mara Hernandez. He had waved to her, and she waved back.

She reached the barn, drew open the door, then took the child by her hand and led her over by the corral fence. She went to the stall, saddled her mare, then led the animal out.

"Up we go—that's a girl!" Rhea lifted the girl into the saddle, then in one fluid movement, she hoisted herself up behind Gatita, her right arm encircling the little girl's waist,

413

and then reached for the reins of her mare. She clucked her tongue and kicked her heels against the mare's belly, and rode off toward the northeast. As she rode at a leisurely gait, she talked gently to the child.

After a few hundred yards, she halted, turning back for a last look. It was somnolent, peaceful, and she saw far to the southwest the cattle grazing in the fields. There was no one at the hacienda. The sun was high in the sky now; she felt the warmth . . . and then she remembered Leadville. Her lips tightened, her eyes narrowed, and with a soft little laugh she turned the horse around and, kicking her heels against its belly, urged it forward at a faster gait.

Forty-Nine

A little after three o'clock that same afternoon, Luke, Jaime, Dolores, and Edward came home from school and eagerly went into their house. All four of them flung down their school-books on the living room table, and then Luke, the oldest, proposed, "Let's go out to the barn. Jaime, you and I could hitch up that old cart to Mary and we can all go for rides."

"That'd be fun!" Dolores giggled. "I don't know, though, if we should—I wonder where Rita is."

"Maybe she went out riding with Gatita; she does that a lot," Luke said.

"I think we should ask Rita first," Dolores cautiously suggested. "Anyhow, I don't know if Mother would want us to hitch up the cart, even if Mary is a nice old mare."

"Don't be such a spoilsport. We won't go far. It's too nice an afternoon to stay in the house—come on," Luke decreed.

Since he was the oldest, the other three children obediently followed him out to the barn. Mary, a piebald mare, fourteen years old, nickered softly as she saw Luke coming, and was easily led out of her stall toward an old cart just outside the barn.

For the next two hours, Luke and Jaime took turns driving the cart, with Dolores and Edward giving directions to them.

Finally, as the sun began to set, Dolores called out plaintively, "Let's go inside! I'm hungry, and I want my supper!"

"I'm hungry, too," Jaime grumbled. "Luke, go in and ask Rita if she can make us supper right away."

"Good idea." Luke bobbed his head in agreement and climbed down from the driver's seat on the cart, while Jaime led the gentle, aging mare back to the barn and her stall. Dolores and Edward, having scrambled out of the cart at the thought of food, ran toward the Hernandez house just behind Luke.

Luke opened the door and went in, calling out, "Rita? Rita, where are you?"

But there was no answer. Then he said half-aloud to himself, "Oh, sure, I know. She's with Gatita." So he walked up the stairs to the little girl's room, again calling out Rhea's assumed name. Reaching the door, he knocked on it. Still there was no response.

He walked down the hallway, calling out their names. Nothing. Luke frowned with concern, thinking it strange that they should still be out so late. The sun was already setting. Hurrying back downstairs to the parlor, he told Jaime, Edward, and Dolores, "They're not here! Maybe they're still out riding—but it's awfully late. We'd better go tell Uncle Lucien Edmond!"

"We sure better," Jaime assented, worry creasing his forehead. "She's never been out this late with Gatita before. She should be back in time to fix our supper, don't you think?"

"If nothing else," Luke showed his practical nature, "Uncle Lucien Edmond will give us something to eat. Now come on, let's go find him!" The four children hurried over to the main ranch house and scrambled up the steps. Once again, asserting his prerogative as a spokesman by virtue of his age, Luke turned to face them. "Now don't be in a rush, and don't be too frightened! You'll only worry Uncle Lucien Edmond. You leave it to me; I'll tell him."

"All right, then," Dolores sulked, "but do please hurry— I'm so hungry I could eat a whole jackrabbit raw!"

"Bet you wouldn't," Edward teased her.

"Bet you I would!" Dolores flared up.

Lucien Edmond was in the living room, seated at the spinet, where he was trying—with great concentration—to play the music before him. He had always been content to sit back and enjoy Maxine's musical skill; however, last year, when he had injured his leg and had to endure a long period of inactivity, Lucien Edmond had started practicing with some deliberation. Now, he was so completely absorbed in a piece which was more advanced than his abilities as yet, that he was totally unaware of his nephews and niece entering the room from behind him.

Luke made a gesture to the three other children not to make a sound. He thrust his hands in his pockets, stoically waiting for his uncle to notice them. After a moment, Lucien Edmond, reaching a particularly difficult passage, shrugged and gave up; he turned and at last saw the children, letting out a gasp. "Oh, you startled me! What's the matter? You all look so worried—"

"Uncle Lucien Edmond, Gatita and Rita are nowhere around," Luke explained. "We were out playing with the cart and the old mare for a long time after school, then when we got hungry, we went back to the house. We looked all through the house, but couldn't find either of them."

"Now, Luke, there's no need for alarm. I'm sure they just went off for a ride together, as usual. Rita's very devoted to your sister, and she'd never let anything happen to her." Lucien Edmond tried to appease the frightened boy. "I tell you what, I'll go with you, and we'll see if they've gotten back while you were all here. Chances are they have. But, if they aren't home yet, we'll go to the kitchen and ask Rosita to prepare you all something to eat."

"That's fine, thank you, Uncle Lucien Edmond," Luke nodded. Then, turning to his brothers and sister, he ordered, "You heard Uncle Lucien Edmond, so let's go back to the house. Don't sniffle, Dolores. There's no reason for that."

Lucien Edmond left the house, the children following at his heels. He systematically examined every room, but found nothing. "You know, Luke," he addressed the oldest of the Hernandez children, "it's possible that maybe Rita's horse was frightened off by a snake or something, or maybe it shied and they were thrown. I'll go look for them as soon as I get a bite to eat. Listen, you all go back to my house, and Luke, you go into the kitchen and ask Rosita if she'd mind preparing dinner for all of you. I don't want very much myself; a small piece of steak and some vegetables and coffee will do fine. Go ahead—I'll be along in a minute."

"All right, Uncle Lucien Edmond." Luke gestured to Edward, Jaime, and Dolores, who followed their brother back to the big ranch house.

When he was finally alone, Lucien Edmond shook his head, obviously worried. As he started to walk past the fireplace his eyes caught sight of the envelope placed under the flower vase on the mantle. Out of curiosity, he lifted up the vase and slid the envelope out, pulling out the folded piece of paper. Then, turning his back to the fireplace, he unfolded the note. He uttered a stifled, incredulous gasp. "Oh, no! Oh, my God!"

The curt note was addressed to Mara Hernandez, and read as follows:

I have taken your daughter. We are going to Mexico— and you'll never find her again. Ever.

Rita

"This is absolute madness! Why in the world would she do such a thing?" Lucien Edmond helplessly mused aloud.

He found himself in a dreadful quandary. His first impulse was to saddle his horse and ride to San Antonio, to find Mara and Maxine. But he was hesitant, not altogether certain that he should be so quick to impart to them the dreadful news. The hope—vain though he suspected it to be—flashed through his mind that perhaps Rita would repent of her actions and return to Windhaven Range with the child, beseeching Lucien Edmond's forgiveness for whatever fiendish motive had driven her to abduct the girl. . . . Even if she did not return, might not some neighbor or passerby or even some law officer see the pair riding away and report to Windhaven Range their location? The knowledge that almost no one would be able to recognize either Rita or Gatita did not prevent Lucien Edmond from entertaining this possibility. Perhaps even now a rider was speeding toward the ranch with good news. Then, too, there were the other children to consider; they must not be left alone. . . . No, much as he wished to take action at once—to do something, anything, to relieve the horrible anguish he felt—Lucien Edmond knew that he should stay where he was, and await the return of his wife and sister. And the waiting was the hardest part of all.

417

Lucien Edmond did not tell the Hernandez children the true contents of that terrifying note. Instead, keeping as composed an expression and as steady a tone to his voice as he could, he explained to his niece and nephews that their sister had come down with a touch of fever while the children were at school, and Rita had not wanted to leave the child alone while going for a doctor. He said Rita had left a note saying that she was taking Gatita to the doctor in Carrizo Springs, and she would probably not bring the child back until Gatita had fully recovered. He was able to do this convincingly, and all four children expressed relief at knowing their little sister was not lost and expressed the hope that she would soon be better and back with them.

Why he had told them this tale Lucien Edmond wasn't really sure. Obviously the children would learn the truth as soon as he told their mother. He sighed. His daughters—Edwina, Diane, and Gloria—came into the room to say that dinner was ready. He sighed again, and lifted himself up from the chair he was slumped in.

He agonized throughout dinner, but forced himself to be cheerful and to talk of games and school and vacations and all the things that are dear to children's hearts. All the while, looming into his mind, was the fact that Rita Galloway had been able to get many hours'. head start. He decided that he must wire Ramón immediately; his brother-in-law must be told that his youngest child had been stolen—and by a trusted servant, too. Lucien Edmond would have one of the vaqueros ride to Carrizo Springs first thing in the morning, and send the wire to Ramón.

It was torture for him during the next day to go about the business of the ranch. That afternoon, having finished all the chores he could find to occupy himself and feeling at loose ends, he walked over to the schoolhouse to accompany his daughters home after class. Catayuna was just emerging from the building and, knowing her courage and staunch spirit, he revealed to her alone the shattering story.

Catayuna was deeply saddened by the news that Lucien Edmond imparted. She advised, "You must tell the Comanches at the stronghold of this. My son, Kitante, as chief of the People, will surely send out searching parties. You know well that Comanche scouts are tireless and always find their quarry, Señor Bouchard.''

"Thank God you thought of that, Catayuna! I've been so distraught worrying as to what to do—'' He paused, then continued, ''Although I should go to Kitante myself and tell him all that I know, I am reluctant to leave until Maxine and Mara arrive; I must tell them the dreadful news myself.'' His face was drawn with tension, and his eyes were swollen, for he had slept very badly.

"Let the vaquero who is your best rider go for you, Señor Bouchard, and let him ride the fastest horse you have in the stable. Do you have an knowledge as to where in Mexico this woman might have gone with the child?''

Lucien Edmond shook his head. ''No, she just said Mexico and that we'd never find her.''

"There are only two trails one would take from here, Señor Bouchard,'' Catayuna spoke thoughtfully and slowly. ''One would be through Nuevo Laredo, and the other would be through Piedras Negras. Taking any other direction would force this woman to pass through land that has very little water—no creeks, no rivers—so she would have had to stop at villages along the way to use their wells. And, if she did that, the villagers would be curious about a single woman and a small child riding out in that wilderness.''

"You have given me hope, Catayuna. I thank you deeply.''

And so, late that afternoon, the day after Lucien Edmond had found Rhea Penrock's note, Tomas Aburcio, a vaquero who had broken many of the wild mustangs used by the men as trail ponies and who was considered the finest rider on Windhaven Range, saddled his spirited gelding and rode south. Following Catayuna's careful directions, he galloped toward the village that had become the new stronghold of the Comanches—they who had once ruled the Southwest and yet now had taken up the ways of peace and intermarried with the Mexicans.

Three days later, Mara and Maxine returned to the ranch. Standing wearily on the porch of his house, Lucien Edmond watched with sagging spirits as their wagon came slowly over the crest of a low hill, and he steeled himself for their reunion.

As the wagon pulled up, Maxine was the first to alight.

"Lucien Edmond, how nice of you to be here to welcome us back home," she exclaimed, as he strode forward to greet her. "I would have expected you to be out on the range. I must tell you, we had a lovely time—even Ruth enjoyed the ride!"

Shaking his head, as if to ward off pain, Lucien Edmond bent down to pick up his youngest daughter, who had jumped down from her seat. He hugged her, and then set her down and turned to help Mara descend. "Well, now, Mara," he asked, "did you find the dress materials and things you wanted?"

"Oh, yes, Lucien Edmond. We had such wonderful luck—I can't wait to show you what we found. I hope you won't be angry that we bought so much—we get to town so seldom. . . . After supper, I'll show you everything—"

A look on Lucien Edmond's face made her stop suddenly. Her brother bit his lip, shifted from foot to foot, and then, in a hoarse voice, said, "Mara, I would rather die than have to give you this news, and I wish there were an easier way of breaking it—"

Mara put a hand to her bosom and recoiled with a stifled cry. "What are you trying to say, Lucien Edmond? Has something happened to Ramón?"

"No. Ramón is fine. It's Gatita. Rita rode off some days ago with her. She left a note saying that she's taking Gatita to Mexico—God knows where—and we'll never see her again."

"Oh—oh, no! Oh, my God!" Mara was swaying on her feet, and her brother put his arm around her to keep her from falling. "Why? Why, Lucien Edmond? Tell me why!"

Lucien Edmond could not supply the answer. He could only explain to his distraught sister the facts as he knew them, concluding with his finding the note—and not having had the courage to tell her other children the truth. "I wanted to wait until you were back to tell them," he confessed to Mara, "because I was afraid that they would have been even more frightened and upset, with both you *and* Ramón away."

"Oh, dear God—but why—why would she do this terrible thing? Why, Lucien Edmond? Tell me why," Mara repeated. Her eyes were huge with disbelief in her pale face, and her lips trembled uncontrollably.

He could only shake his head hopelessly and look down at the ground.

Maxine put her arms around her sister-in-law, as Mara's grief became too much for her to bear and she began to sob unceasingly. Maxine tried to comfort her, and Lucien Edmond did what little he could to soothe her. But both of them knew that there was nothing that they could say that would possibly ease Mara's pain and hopelessness.

"Mara," Lucien Edmond said gently, "I've already sent off a wire to Ramón, and he's sure to come back here quickly. Catayuna made the excellent suggestion that I send a rider to Kitante in the stronghold across the border. She said that he will send out scouting parties. Mara, at least they cannot have gone far—a lone woman and a small child. Come into the house; lie down and rest. Later, we will all go to the chapel and pray for Gatita's safe return."

When Ramón Hernandez received Lucien Edmond's telegram, he uttered so blasphemous an oath, crying out in such a strangled tone, that Robert Markey and John Darwent turned and ran to him, frightened by his sudden outburst. His face contorted, livid with fury, he showed them the telegram and swore. "That woman—I trusted her—I took her in and gave her charity—and this is how she repays me—"

"We'll go back with you, Ramón," Robert urged. "We can help you find your child."

"No, no." Ramón controlled himself with a supreme effort. "I appreciate your concern, but this mine must run smoothly." He uttered a bitter, terse laugh. "Perhaps all this silver will help to offer a reward for anyone who finds my daughter—" He choked. "That sweet child; God knows to what barren, desolate part of Mexico that treacherous woman took her! I never thought I could kill a woman—but I very nearly could do it now, if I had my hands on her! How could Lucien Edmond and I have been so blind—be taken by her sweetness and gratitude and her humble way? But, that's of no consequence now—" He straightened, dug his fingernails into his palm, and in a cold, harsh voice his ears hardly recognized, said, "There's plenty of manpower at the ranch, *amigos*. They will help me find that woman and Gatita, never fear. I've got to! And, when I do—" His voice choked up again, and his words trailed off.

Fifty

Ramón had made excellent connections by train and coach on the way back from Leadville to Windhaven Range, but each minute of that journey seemed endless. Desperately he prayed to *El Señor Dios* for His help in finding his stolen child, and he counted the hours until he would be at Windhaven Range, ready to mount up and ride off in search of his beloved daughter.

As he rode along, a virtual prisoner of the vehicles that conveyed him homeward, unable to alter or hasten their progress, he had ample opportunity to reflect on all his dealings with Rita Galloway. His first impulsive outbursts of rage had by now spent themselves, and he turned his feverish mind to a consideration of his own possible mistakes. He could not escape the conclusion that he had somehow misjudged the woman. Had his preoccupation with the mining venture so blinded him that he had failed to notice some early sign of Rita's weakness of character? Had she given some signal, or let fall some words, in all those weeks in the little house in Leadville, that he should have perceived? Try as he might, he could recall nothing: She had been the image of goodness itself. But had she been perhaps *too* good, too solicitous about the men's welfare—and should that in itself have been a source of suspicion? He ground his fist into his palm in frustration, berating himself: Why had he been so beguiled by the wealth coming out of the ground in Leadville, and why had he imagined that he was doing so much for his family simply by laying up this store of the world's riches? Was this not the sin of avarice, and had it not caused him to lose something far dearer to him than all the silver or gold on earth?

He reached the ranch late one morning, his mood somber, his face hard and obdurate, his eyes dark and narrowed with agony and hate. Only briefly did he console his beautiful wife, Mara, who had been close to hysteria all these days during his journey. After her initial breakdown, Maxine had appealed to Mara on behalf of their other children, saying, "Dear Mara, Edward and Jaime, Luke and Dolores need you—now more than ever. To neglect them to mourn for Gatita—and she will be found, I know she will, we're praying so hard for it—to neglect them would be cruel."

And so Mara had rallied herself, although her spirit was perilously flagging. She had embraced and tearfully kissed Maxine and had gone to explain to her older children the truth about their sister's absence. She told them that Gatita would soon be back, and then they would be happy once again.

Not three hours after his return, Ramón met Lucien Edmond out at the corral. Twenty vaqueros, carrying enough provisions in their saddlebags to see them through several days—or until they should reach the next village—awaited their orders. Lucien Edmond briefly outlined what Catayuna had told him. "Because of this," he said, "I think we should each take separate routes. I've talked to many of the vaqueros, and they agree with her that only two ways south into Mexico would have been feasible for Rita to follow. Each of us will take ten vaqueros. I'll take the route through Nuevo Laredo. You take the other toward Piedras Negras. We'll make inquiries of anyone we meet along the way: men who have been on the trail, the parish priests, the local authorities—anyone at all."

"It is all we can do," Ramón said in a low, despairing voice.

"Don't worry, Ramón." Lucien Edmond put a hand on his brother-in-law's shoulder. "We'll find them, or Kitante's braves will. We won't give up; we won't come back till we find her—I promise you that."

It was at the end of the fourth week of October that Lucien Edmond and his vaqueros stopped for provisions in the town of Mier, some seventy-two miles southeast of Nuevo Laredo. The *jefe* of the town, a man in his early fifties with an enormous mustache, saluted the tall *gringo* and said, "We are honored to have you visit our little village, señor. It is not often that we see *norteamericanos* south of Nuevo Laredo."

"But you do see them, *jefe*?" Lucien Edmond hazarded.

"*Pero sí*. There was a *mujer*—I am sure that she was a *norteamericana*—about a week ago."

Lucien Edmond tried to contain his rising excitement. "Tell

423

me, señor," he asked, "this *norteamericana*—could you describe her? Was she fair or dark, was she young or old, fat or thin? You see, señor, I am looking for a young *mujer;* she is thin and dark haired. It is *muy importante* that I find her."

"Well, señor," the *jefe* said with a broad grin, "perhaps you are in luck. I saw the face of the *mujer* only from a distance, so I cannot in truth say that she was young, but the *norteamericana* that passed through my village otherwise was like the person you are seeking."

"Jefe," Lucien Edmond declared, "please think very carefully. Did the woman you saw have a small child with her?"

The Mexican stroked his chin in thoughtfulness. After a moment, he finally answered, "Señor, in truth I cannot be certain. She rode into town toward sunset in a buckboard; there were bundles on the seat next to her and in the back—whether any of those bundles was a child asleep, I cannot say. All I can say is, it is *posible. Sí,* it is quite possible."

"That's wonderful news!" In his eagerness, Lucien Edmond took hold of the man's arm. "Tell me, *jefe,* do you know where this woman went?"

"Pero sí," the man repeated with a smile. "She said that she was going to the village of Burgas. There are many *indios* there, the Toboso. They are friendly now—although it was not always that way, señor."

"I thank you for this information, *jefe.* If this woman is who I seek, I will give a large reward, *dinero,* for the poor of your village."

"That would not exclude me, señor," the mayor chuckled. "We do only a bit of farming here, and it is not very good. Many of our young men go off to Mexico City, to join the *federales.* At least they get three good meals a day, plus *dinero.* Go with God, señor, and I hope you find the woman you seek."

"The child, even more than the woman, *señor jefe. Vaya con Dios,"* Lucien Edmond told him, then mounted up and whistled for his vaqueros to follow.

It was a day's journey to the village of Burgas, a squalid place of about thirty huts. As Lucien Edmond and his men rode up to the sturdiest and the largest *jacal* of the lot, a woman emerged. She was tall, with angular features, and gray liberally streaked her dark brown hair.

"Good day to you, señora," Lucien Edmond courteously

inclined his head. "I wonder if you can help me," he said in Spanish. "I am looking for a *norteamericana*, who I was told came to this village recently."

"That must be me," the woman said in English. "My name is Penelope Edison. I am a missionary with the Baptist Church of Baltimore; I'm here to work with these Indians who are living in the most abject poverty—as you can see for yourself from these huts." She scrutinized Lucien Edmond's face. "You are troubled by something, sir."

He smiled. "You are very perceptive. You see, Miss Edison, we are on the trail of a dark-haired woman who worked for me—and who stole off to Mexico with the three-year-old daughter of my brother-in-law."

"How dreadful! What a cruel thing for anyone to do! Ah, I see now—you were looking for this woman, and you were told by the *jefe* that I had come through his village, and you thought that perhaps I might be the woman you seek?"

"That's it exactly, Miss Edison. Thank you for being so understanding—and good luck in your mission." He wearily mounted into the saddle, turned to wave to his vaqueros and commanded, "*¡Adelante!*"

Penelope Edison waved to him as he rode off, and called, "Good luck in *your* mission, too, sir!"

The days turned into weeks, and still Ramón and his vaqueros had heard nothing, seen nothing of Rhea Penrock and the kidnapped child. As they rode southward for hour upon weary hour, Ramón's mind was in a turmoil; he pondered again and again what it might have been that had driven Rita Galloway—whom he had trusted—to do this evil thing. What possible motive could she have harbored—what hatred and insane anger? And why had she singled out *his* family to receive this special cruelty? Looking around him, Ramón found no answer or consolation in the landscape through which he and his companions were riding—only scenery of such desolation that he began to fear that his little daughter could not survive a trek through such country.

For three weeks they rode, stopping at every village south of Piedras Negras for nearly a hundred miles. They then radiated out for a mile or so along their route in the hope that they might have overlooked a small farm, or a scattered group of huts that comprised an obscure, forgotten hamlet. In every

425

saloon, in every hotel, in every church, to every mayor of every town into which they rode, they posed the same question—and the answer was always much the same: "No, señor, we have not seen any such persons as you describe. But now that you have told us about it, we shall watch for her."

At last one of the vaqueros rode up to Ramón as they passed out of one village heading for the next. *"Patrón,"* he called, "forgive me for asking this, but I am curious about one thing. We have stopped to inquire of every *jefe* and every village priest as to your daughter's whereabouts; why have we not approached the federal authorities? It is true some of them are corrupt and care nothing for what happens in their districts. And you have told me how your father was whipped to death by a cruel *federalista* in the days when Miguel de Miramón was *el presidente,* and how your sister took her life rather than endure servitude to this same man. But, *señor patrón,* that was many years ago; the times have changed. Miramón and his supporters are gone, *gracias a Dios.* Should we not at least try our fortune now with the *federales* whose sworn duty it is to enforce the laws and bring justice to the people?"

Ramón bristled, though the suggestion was hardly unexpected; in fact, he had given much thought to the idea himself. Still, it was a terrible decision to make. He had never forgotten or forgiven what had happened to his father and sister, events that had caused him to hate and mistrust Mexican officialdom. Yet he knew that in the end, he would do what he must to bring his Gatita back to him.

"You are right, Jorge," he sighed. "I cannot let old wounds stand in the way at a time like this. Twenty years is a long time, as you say, and I can at least hope that the *federales* of today are not as corrupt as Miguel de Miramón's officials."

When they next reached a sizable town, one with a detachment of federal troops, Ramón—after a moment's hesitation—dismounted and strode into the troop's headquarters.

The captain on duty asked how he could be of service, and Ramón—still with some reluctance—unburdened himself of his story. "I cannot believe it, señor," the officer declared. "Do you mean to tell me that this woman had no grievance against you? You did nothing to her?"

Ramón felt his anger rising, and worked hard to control it. "*Capitán,* I assure you I did nothing to the young woman. I wasn't even home when she—stole my daughter. I was still up in Leadville, Colorado—the place where Rita Galloway first came to me for work out of nowhere—I swear to you!"

"Forgive me, señor," the captain gently declared. "It is just so hard to believe that this young woman would do something so cruel, so sinful, against someone who has done nothing but kindness toward her." He shook his head slowly. "Truly she will have much to answer for in the eyes of God."

Ramón sighed, then looked the officer straight in the eyes. "Tell me, *Capitán,* what do you think the chances are of finding this woman and my daughter?"

The captain looked down at his desk for a few moments before replying, "Senór, I wish I could give you assurances that we will find them—but in all honesty, I cannot. Mexico is a very large country, and a dark-haired woman with a dark-haired child . . . well, they are not exactly conspicuous." He rose and held out his hand to Ramón. "But I *will* assure you that I will alert every garrison between the border and Mexico City to be on the lookout for them. We will do whatever we can, I promise."

At last, by the end of November, Ramón and his ten men rode dispiritedly back to the border, there to meet Lucien Edmond and his vaqueros at the agreed upon rendezvous in Nuevo Laredo.

Upon seeing his brother-in-law, Ramón hoarsely blurted out, "Nothing at all, Lucien Edmond." Ramón then burst into tears and covered his face with his hands. "It is as if they had never lived. Every hour that I was in the saddle, all I could think of was what poor little Gatita was feeling, whether she was cold or hungry or . . . or thirsty. That accursed woman must be a witch, with the luck of the devil himself to have come so far without being noticed by anyone. They seem to have vanished into the thin air! Oh, God, what have I done that my beautiful Mara should be punished like this and the little girl who bears her name has been taken from us forever?"

He buried his face in his hands and again burst into agonized weeping, and Lucien Edmond could only put his arm around his shoulders and murmur useless words—words that

427

did not comfort in the slightest but that showed his deep concern and passion.

Presently, Ramón straightened and looked at Lucien Edmond. His haggard face was wet with tears, and droplets glistened on his beard, for he had not shaved during these past weeks. "But I won't give up. I'll go by myself if necessary, and if I wear out every horse between Windhaven Range and Mexico City, I'll find them!"

"Of course, you will," Lucien Edmond gently murmured. "Take courage. Kitante's scouts are looking through areas we can't possibly know about. One of these days—very soon, I'm sure—his couriers will come with the news that they've found your child."

It was the last Thursday in November, 1880. James Garfield and Chester A. Arthur had been elected as President and Vice-President by an electoral vote of 214 to 155 for Hancock and English—though the popular vote showed only a difference of some ten thousand votes, with Garfield receiving 4,454,416 to Hancock's 4,444,952. The infamous Chinese Exclusion Treaty was signed with China at Peking, and henceforth there would be a regulation, or a limitation, or even a suspension of the coming of Chinese laborers into the United States. It was expected that the Senate would agree to the treaty some time the following spring.

A bright, sunny cloudless sky heralded this Thanksgiving Day in Alabama. As Andy Haskins and his family reached the door of their church, a tall, white-haired man, frail, but with a proud bearing, halted him. Firmly planting his feet on either side of his walking stick, the old man declared, "Mr. Haskins, sir, I just want you to know I came to church specially to pray to God to bless you for what you've done for me."

Andy smiled warmly at the man. "Mr. Winters, how good it is to see you looking so well!" He reached out and shook Thomas Winters's hand, then declared, "I only did what is right, Mr. Winters."

"Don't you try to weasel out of the good deed you did, the kind, thoughtful way you looked after me, Mr. Haskins," the old man fiercely interrupted. "You know well enough what my son and nephew wanted to do to me. And they might have

428

done it, sure enough, if there'd been someone else at the head of the sanatorium.''

"It's good of you to say that.''

The old man cleared his throat and swallowed several times to hide his emotions. ''Thanks to you, sir, I can come to church, I can go where I please, I can even talk out against the damned Democrats—no offense meant.''

"And none taken, because I've always been a Republican, Mr. Winters.'' Andy chuckled, as he put a hand on the old man's shoulder. "You look fine, just fine.''

"Well, I'll tell you, sir. I hired a new housekeeper and— well, dammit, I may be almost sixty-eight, but do you know, that woman—Harriet Milgrass—she's the sort who'd make an old man like me a wonderful wife.''

Andy laughed and nodded. "That's the spirit, Mr. Winters. There's no reason in the world why you shouldn't marry, if you want her. You've had a period of hell, and now you're entitled to happiness for whatever time you've got left—and I sincerely hope it will be a long time.''

The old man turned, and holding himself proudly erect, his head high, he walked into the church, clutching his walking stick tightly. Andy Haskins watched him go up the three short steps, then turned to Jessica and said, "That makes me feel mighty humble and mighty proud. I'm glad I could help that fine man.''

"God will bless you for it, Andy. I'm so happy you took the job—I can't begin to tell you. Now let's go in and give our own thanks.''

On this same Thanksgiving morning, just after he had conducted the service at his church, Dr. Ben Wilson bade good-bye to his wife and children. He was setting out for Dodge City, called there to attend to the wife of a wealthy saloonkeeper. The man had, in desperation, wired Ben in Wichita, hoping that the Quaker doctor could save his wife from a tumor that the local physician had diagnosed as terminal.

Yesterday morning, Ben had received a letter from Hugo Bouchard. Hugo had written that he hoped to marry Cecily Franklin and go out with her to Wyoming, there to establish a clinic for patients.

The Quaker doctor mused aloud, his homely face lighted by a radiant smile, "What a fine young man; may God bless

429

him and Cecily, for together they will do great good in so isolated a place. What a wonderful challenge it will be for Hugo—and he will be up to it, I'm sure. How flattered I am that he looks upon me as his inspiration."

Arriving at last in Dodge City, with his black bag of surgical tools tied securely to his saddle, he halted his horse in front of the address given by the saloonkeeper, dismounted, and tethered his horse to the hitching post. He looked up at the cloudy, gray sky and adjusted his greatcoat more tightly, for the November winds were sharp and cold.

He uttered a sigh of happiness. It was a good feeling to know that his own reputation as a doctor had spread throughout Kansas. He would not otherwise have had this telegram from Jason Tibbets, the rich saloonkeeper who had said in his wire, "If you can cure her, Dr. Wilson, I'll turn over my saloon to you and go back to farming—I pledge it. I love my Nan, and I don't want her to die. Come as quickly as you can; I'll pay all your expenses. Please hurry."

He looked a last time up at the sky before he went into the house; he told himself that he would pray to have more skill than he had ever had before, so that he could save this woman whom a simple saloonkeeper loved so much that he would send a wire like that.

He felt his eyes watering with tears. It was the sharp wind, of course. Reaching to unhitch his medical bag from the saddle, he saw a buckboard driving down the street. At the reins of the roan mare was a young black-haired woman, bundled in a greatcoat, and beside her sat a girl of perhaps three, wearing a bonnet and a heavy wool coat. The woman's right arm was casually draped around the girl's shoulders, and the child was looking up at the woman and smiling, talking with great animation.

He watched the buckboard go down the street and disappear from sight. The black-haired woman and child reminded him of his own dear Elone and Tisinqua. He smiled at the thought of his wife. The saloonkeeper obviously loved his wife as much as he, Ben Wilson, loved Elone. It was good to know that there was still love in the world. With a smile wreathing his face, he strode up to the front door and, with a resolute grip on the knocker, rapped sharply.

*   *   *

It was December 18, 1880, the one hundred eighteenth anniversary of the birth of Lucien Bouchard, the founder of the Bouchard dynasty. On this morning, Lucien Edmond went alone to the chapel to pay tribute in prayer to his great-grandfather, and to pray also that the cause of the despair that had descended on Windhaven Range might be dispelled through the return of Gatita Hernandez.

As Lucien Edmond knelt in the cool, dim church, tears of anguish ran down his cheeks. No matter how hard he tried, no matter how much Maxine and Mara had tried to convince him otherwise, he could not escape feeling responsible; it was he and he alone who had offered Rita Galloway the opportunity to return to the ranch, thereby enabling her to bear away the child.

"Great-grandfather," he said aloud, "your courage and fortitude have always guided me as they guided my father. I only pray that God will grant me the same wisdom and strength that He saw fit to give you, so that I may somehow rectify the terrible wrong that has been done. I am not a vengeful man. Yet I am imbued with a righteous fury for the evil that has been done—a terrible sin against an innocent young child and her grieving family."

He rose to his feet, wiped the tears from his care-worn face, and gazed at the gleaming brass crucifix above the altar. Crossing himself, he murmured, "Lord, I have not been one to ask Your help lightly, and it is not for myself that I ask Your help now. But I am pleading with You to invoke the prophesy of Isaiah: 'Behold the day of the Lord cometh, cruel both with wrath and fierce anger, to lay the land desolate; and He shall destroy the sinners thereof out of it.' "